Wild Rose Pass

by

Karen Hulene Bartell

Trans-Pecos Series

Wild Rose Pass

Cover Art by *The Wild Rose Press, Inc.*

The Wild Rose Press, Inc.
PO Box 708
Adams Basin, NY 14410-0708
Visit us at www.thewildrosepress.com

Publishing History
First Cactus Rose Edition, 2020
Print ISBN 978-1-5092-3083-9
Digital ISBN 978-1-5092-3084-6

Trans-Pecos Series
Published in the United States of America

Reining his horse between catclaw and prickly-pear cactus, Ben Williams squinted at the late summer sun's low angle. Though still midafternoon, shadows lengthened in the mountains. He clicked his tongue, urging his mare up the incline. "Show a little enthusiasm, Althea. If we're not in Fort Davis by sunset, we'll be bedding down with scorpions and rattlesnakes."

As his detachment's horses clambered up Wild Rose Pass, the only gap through west Texas' rugged Davis Mountains, Ben kept alert for loose rocks or hidden roots, anything that might trip his mount. A thick layer of fallen leaves created a pastiche of color shrouding the trail from view. He glanced up at the lithe cottonwood trees lining the route, their limbs dancing in the breeze. More amber and persimmon leaves loosened, fell, and settled near the Indian pictographs on their tree trunks. When he saw the red- and yellow-ochre drawings, he smiled, recalling the canyon's name—Painted Comanche Camp.

"How far to Fort Davis, lieutenant?" called McCurry, one of his recruits.

"Three hours." *If we keep a steady pace*.

Without warning, the soldier's horse whinnied. Spooking, it reared on its hind legs, threw its rider, and galloped off.

As he sat up, the man groaned, caught his breath, and stared into the eyes of a coiled rattler, poised to strike. "What the…?"

Flicking its tongue, hissing, tail rattling, the pit viper was inches from the man's face.

A sheen of sweat appeared above the man's lip. "Lieutenant—"

Praise for *WILD ROSE PASS*

"When Ben Williams, a mustang—an enlisted man promoted to lieutenant on the battlefield—transfers to 1880 Fort Davis, Texas, Cadence McShane's world is turned upside down. The captain's headstrong daughter Cadence was raised in the sheltered shadow of the fort. As their two worlds collide, Cadence and Ben grapple with Apache raids, Tejano refugees, Buffalo soldiers, jilted suitors, land grabs, arson, bigotry, discrimination, and burgeoning love in the Old West. Couldn't put it down!"

~Dianne Mueller, MSLIS

Dedication

To Peter Bartell, with all my love.
With admiration for the Texan women
who've invented their own destinies

Acknowledgments

My deep appreciation to Olga Harwell and the family of José Maria Bill for sharing his story.

The African-American contribution to the settling and safeguarding of the American West deserves recognition. I'd particularly like to acknowledge the courage and contributions of the 24th and 25th Infantry Regiments—the Buffalo Soldiers of the 1870s and 1880s. In keeping with the historical accuracy of the era, I've sometimes used the term 'Negro' when referring to these soldiers but primarily 'colored,' as in the 'United States Colored Troops (USCT),' when referring to the troops.

The American West of the late nineteenth century was a crossroads of cultures: Native American, European, and Asian. I'd like to give tribute to the Indians of every nation who struggled to provide for their families while surviving in a harsh environment and a rapidly changing world. Again, in keeping with the historical accuracy of the era, I've used the term 'Indian' most often, but it in no way is meant to offend.

I'd like to acknowledge Emily Dickinson, Clement Clarke Moore, and Anthony Trollope, whose works I've referenced. Emily Dickinson's poem "Some Keep the Sabbath Going to Church" was published in 1864 under the title "My Sabbath." "'Twas the Night Before Christmas," also known as "The Night Before Christmas" and "A Visit from St. Nicholas," is a poem originally published anonymously in 1823, then later attributed to Clement Clarke Moore in 1837.

Chapter 1
Catclaw and Cactus

Reining his horse between catclaw and prickly-pear cactus, Ben Williams squinted at the late summer sun's low angle. Though still midafternoon, shadows lengthened in the mountains. He clicked his tongue, urging his mare up the incline. "Show a little enthusiasm, Althea. If we're not in Fort Davis by sunset, we'll be bedding down with scorpions and rattlesnakes."

As his detachment's horses clambered up Wild Rose Pass, the only gap through west Texas' rugged Davis Mountains, Ben kept alert for loose rocks or hidden roots, anything that might trip his mount. A thick layer of fallen leaves created a pastiche of color shrouding the trail from view. He glanced up at the lithe cottonwood trees lining the route, their limbs dancing in the breeze. More amber and persimmon leaves loosened, fell, and settled near the Indian pictographs on their tree trunks. When he saw the red- and yellow-ochre drawings, he smiled, recalling the canyon's name—Painted Comanche Camp.

"How far to Fort Davis, lieutenant?" called McCurry, one of his recruits.

"Three hours." *If we keep a steady pace*.

Without warning, the soldier's horse whinnied. Spooking, it reared on its hind legs, threw its rider, and galloped off.

As he sat up, the man groaned, caught his breath, and stared into the eyes of a coiled rattler, poised to strike. "What the…?"

Flicking its tongue, hissing, tail rattling, the pit viper was inches from the man's face.

A sheen of sweat appeared above the man's lip. "Lieutenant—"

"Don't move. That's an order." Gripping his saddle horn with a sweaty palm, Ben eased down from his horse.

"I'll get 'im, sir." Unsnapping his holster, Dawson reached for his Colt .45.

"As you were, soldier." *Don't need twitchy fingers shooting McCurry by mistake.* Scouting the area, Ben spotted a forked branch on a nearby live oak and snapped it off. Faster than the snake could strike, Ben pinned its head to the ground with the cleft stick. Then before it wriggled away, he grasped the rattler just behind its jaws with his free hand and tossed it out of range.

Dawson stared, slack-jawed. "Why didn't you kill the varmint, sir?"

Ben shrugged. "No need, soldier."

McCurry paled. "But it could've attacked me."

"That snake let you off with a warning. It's only fair to return the favor." Ben helped the man to his feet. "Now round up your horse, and steer clear of sidewinders. If you find one on the trail, you might find more nearby—could be a nest."

McCurry gulped, his Adam's apple bobbing as he turned to pick his way through the piled leaves. Grumbling, his voice faded in the distance. "Why didn't he just shoot the danged thing?"

****

As the sun's fingers lost their grip, slipping behind the mountains, Ben led the cavalrymen inside the fort. Tucked in a canyon with steep volcanic rock walls flanking it on three sides, the garrison provided shelter from the winter's blue northers. However, from a military tactical perspective, the fort offered little defense against Apache attacks launched from the surrounding vertical cliffs. The elongated barracks and most of the structures clustered at the south end of the parade grounds. Several larger houses were huddled at the north end.

He swept his gaze across the fort's crew of buffalo soldiers, officers, dependents, and civilians. Washerwomen hung laundry near their thatched, wattle-and-daub huts along "suds row" as they watched the infantry drill on the parade grounds. The officers and their families socialized on their front porches during the evening Retreat Parade as the Tenth Infantry band regaled the garrison with spirited march tunes.

Ben noticed a chestnut-haired young lady on the veranda glance toward him and then, seemingly absorbed in her companion's story, turn back to the officer. Her laughter floated on the twilight's breeze. As he rode through the entry, Ben returned the Negro sentry's salute. "Where can I find the commanding officer?"

The guard pointed to a short, trim figure standing beside the woman. "That's Captain McShane."

"Obliged." Ben turned toward his retinue. "Follow me." Then he guided his mare toward the porch, the hairs on the back of his neck prickling as he sensed the young woman's gaze. Riding closer, he noticed the freckles on her buttermilk complexion and her upswept, auburn hair. He stared at her starched, gold-and-green tartan dress, comparing it to his dusty, wrinkled uniform.

Though her amused eyes twinkled, her demeanor was condescending. *Look but don't touch.* Outclassed, he squared his shoulders and sat taller in the saddle. Then he turned to the graying captain with a crisp salute. "Second Lieutenant Ben Williams reporting for duty, sir, with Privates Dawson and McCurry." Though seated on his horse, he still had to look up at the imposing figure on the building's high porch. He counted the steps—seven. Not a porch, it was a podium, a stage.

"Welcome to Fort Davis," said Captain McShane, his back ramrod straight. "I've heard excellent reports about your reconnoitering skills at Fort Clark."

"Thank you, sir." Ben straightened his spine.

The captain indicated the woman seated beside him. "Allow me to present my daughter, Cadence McShane."

Ben tipped his hat, his throat dry. "Miss McShane."

His backbone rigid, the captain gestured toward the officer seated beside her. "This is First Lieutenant James West."

"Sir." Ben nodded to the mustachioed man as his eyes grazed the woman's.

"We can use another good man." West nodded. "Too many Apache attacks on travelers along the San Antonio-El Paso Road."

"If I understood the commander at Fort Clark," said Captain McShane, "Williams knows Indians. He

4

was raised by Comanches."

Uncurling her spine, the lady stared at the newcomer. "Is that true, lieutenant?"

"Yes, ma'am." Ben nodded, mesmerized by her copper-flecked, amber eyes that trapped and radiated the sun's ebbing light. As she sat in a rocker on the raised veranda, her eyes were nearly level with his. Gazing into them, he was reminded of a hungry wolf.

"Fort Clark's commander also spoke highly of your hunting skills." Captain McShane puffed on a cigar. "After you get settled, maybe you could organize a wild turkey hunt for the officers."

Ben's shoulders drooped. *When will I be accepted as an officer instead of a scout?* "Yes—"

"Hunting's good in the area," said West, rising, "though as the situation is now, we can't go more than three or four miles from the fort."

Chafing at the interruption, Ben stifled his sigh. "Why's that, sir?"

"Too many Apache raiding parties," said West. "The remnants of Victorio's renegades would like nothing better than to ambush a lone hunter. Private Willis found a good lake for bass fishing, not five miles from here, but unless a large detail is assigned, the men are easy pickings."

"No skirmishes if they're outnumbered. They just make quiet retreats." Familiar with the Apaches' tactics, Ben nodded. "They prefer guerrilla warfare, ambushes, and sorties."

"With your skills, you'll be a welcome addition to Fort Davis." Then waving a hand, the captain signaled to a passing soldier. "Corporal, escort Lieutenant Williams to the unmarried officers' quarters. Then show these men to the barracks."

"Yes, sir." The corporal came to attention as he saluted.

Dismissed. Though his skills were welcomed, Ben reckoned, *I'm not...socially.* Saluting, he sat tall in the saddle. "Thank you, sir." Again the outsider looking in, Ben watched the captain and his group settle in for the evening. Then ignoring the familiar pang of exclusion, he tipped his hat with a courtly flourish. "Ma'am." Looking for validation as a fellow human being, he watched her response. *Just because they see me as a savage, do I have to act like one?*

Chapter 2
Painted Comanche Camp

Cadence McShane watched Ben's retreating figure, a dark silhouette against the waning sunset's ruddy blush. While he had talked to them, she couldn't help but notice his chin-length, dark, wavy hair, warm brown eyes, or how his uniform hugged his lean, muscular body. Neither had the tantalizing chest hairs peeking from beneath his shirt's neckline escaped her. *What would running my fingertips over his chest be like?*

"Cady. Cadydid."

As his raised voice drew her attention, she spun her head toward him. "Yes, Father?"

"You were a million miles away."

"I was just watching the sunset." Covering her fib, she glanced at the sky's last glimmer of light. The evening's crimson and gold colors morphed into plum and amethyst. Elongated shadows stretched across the parade grounds.

"Tell your mother to set another place at the table. I've asked Lieutenant West to stay for dinner after we make the rounds."

Echoing his words, the bugle sounded retreat as the post officially observed the day's end.

She glanced toward the unmarried officers' quarters. *I wonder what Lieutenant Williams is doing tonight?*

****

The following afternoon, Cadence sat on the front veranda, sipping tea with two officers' wives. She wore a straw hat, perched at a jaunty angle, that waved with the breeze. Both shielding her eyes from the sun and concealing her as she peeked from beneath its broad brim, the hat let her watch unnoticed as Ben mounted his horse while she chatted with the ladies.

A sudden gust of wind swept down from the mountains, blowing sand into a dust devil. It captured several dried leaves, swirling them round and round as they spiraled higher into the air. As another gust lifted aloft her bonnet, she shrieked, helpless as the wind carried it to the ground and rolled it along its rim toward the tiny cyclone.

Ben dug his heels into his horse's sides, steering it toward the dust twister at a gallop. Veering at the last moment, he reached with his left hand and grabbed the hat just before it lifted skyward. Then slowing his mare to a walk, he kept his gaze on the young lady as he rode up to the high porch. "I believe this hat is yours, ma'am."

Standing, she smiled, never taking her gaze off his. "Thank you, lieutenant."

"You're welcome, ma'am."

As he reined away his horse from the veranda, she inhaled, catching the masculine scents of sun-warmed leather and horses. Warmth crept to her cheeks. "Cadence," she said. Her voice stilled his hand on the reins.

His smile faltering, he touched his fingers to his hat. "Pleased to be of service, ma'am—"

8

"Cadence," she corrected him. Noting her companions' raised brows and exchanged glances, she gestured toward him, her palm up. "Mrs. Sarah McIntyre and Mrs. Flossie Purdue, permit me to introduce Lieutenant Williams."

"Ma'am." He tipped his hat to each. "Pleased to meet you, ma'am."

Seeing him start away with an informal salute, she gave a polite bow. "Thank you again for fetching my hat…Ben."

"My pleasure, ma'am—"

"Cadence." Though she meant to establish an informal friendship, she hoped for more.

"Cadence." Maintaining eye contact, he grinned as he pulled the reins to one side, turning his horse. "Ladies." With a courteous nod to the women, he rode off.

Cadence watched him canter away. *How wonderful to be so free.* Sighing, she glanced back in time to see the lieutenant's petite, fair-skinned wife pouring tea. "Thank you, Sarah, just half a cup."

"A handsome man, but once you're spoken for, is flirting prudent?" Flossie arched her brow.

Cadence resisted the urge to argue. Instead, she shrugged her shoulders. "Whatever do you mean?"

"It's common knowledge you're pledged." Sarah narrowed her gaze.

"Not to my knowledge." Cadence lifted her bare left hand.

Flossie exchanged a sidelong glance with Sarah. Stirring her tea, she gazed at Cadence. "But you have been seeing a lot of James, haven't you?"

"Do you mean Lieutenant West?" Knowing full

well what she meant, Cadence gave her a wide-eyed smile.

"Of course, I mean Lieutenant West." Her spoon clinking against the cup as she stirred her tea, Flossie pursed her lips, accentuating her left cheek's dimple. "What other James is stationed at this post?"

Pretending not to notice the tone, Cadence smiled. "The quartermaster—"

"I meant the James who's under sixty"—Flossie rolled her eyes—"the one who's been calling on you these past weeks."

"I've heard it on the highest authority," said Sarah. "He has a glowing career ahead. As I understand it…"

Following her train of thought, Cadence stifled a frustrated sigh while her gaze tracked Ben leaving the fort's broad exit, its double gates swung wide open. *How I'd love to canter alongside him.*

But strict military protocol prohibited her from riding unchaperoned with officers or even fraternizing with enlisted men. Though other women resided at the fort, social order prevented her from associating with the enlisted men's wives or the hired laundresses. Officers' wives provided her only social outlet.

She glanced at Sarah and Flossie. Beside her mother, these women were her sole companions, but both were married with half-grown children. *If not for tea and gossip, we'd have nothing to talk about.*

Raised within the same social structure and well versed with their traditions, she sensed their thoughts. These women expected her to marry a dashing, young officer from West Point, someone like James. They considered marrying into the fold her destiny—and privilege—but Cadence questioned its wisdom.

Where's the adventure? Where's the challenge? Is James even the right one? If only someone else…

"Cadence…?" Sarah tapped her foot. "Cadence."

"I'm sorry." As Sarah's raised voice penetrated her thoughts, she emerged from her reverie to notice the woman's thinly veiled scowl. "What was it you'd asked?"

"I said"—Sarah drew in a breath, her lips pressed into a thin line—"you and James make such an attractive couple. When are you two setting the date?"

Cadence sipped her tea before she smiled. "I don't think we are—"

"Only because he hasn't asked you yet…" Flossie's words hung in the air.

As if I have no say in the matter. Annoyed as much at the woman's knowing smile as at the conversation's personal turn, Cadence arched a brow. "Whatever do you mean?"

"A little birdie told me…" Flossie paused. "James is planning to propose at the Harvest Ball." Her smile bright, her eyes gleaming, Flossie leaned forward. "Aren't you thrilled?"

Blinking and shrugging, Cadence asked herself the same question.

****

Waiting for dinner to end, Cadence fidgeted, glanced at the clock on the mantel, and stifled a weary sigh.

As he finished his last forkful of applesauce cake and downed his coffee, James turned toward his hostess. "Mrs. McShane, without exception, that trout dinner was the finest I've ever eaten."

"Cady made dinner herself." The woman beamed

at her only child.

"A beauty and a good cook, what a heady combination." Sitting across from Cadence, James eyed her.

Mrs. McShane exchanged a sidelong glance with her husband.

The words are flattering, those of a beau courting his girl, but his tone sounds like a lieutenant bucking for a promotion. Irritated as much with her parents' sly exchange as James' appraising stare, she shrugged before looking away. "I didn't catch the trout. Lieutenant Williams did."

"I've heard he's quite the fisherman," said Captain McShane from his chair at the head of the table.

"Really?" Glancing at Cadence, James tweaked the ends of his dark handlebar mustache before turning back to the captain. "Then instead of a turkey hunt, why don't we have him organize a fishing party?"

"An excellent idea." Nodding, the captain smiled. "It'd be a diversion for the officers."

"And the ladies." Cadence lifted her chin at a defiant tilt.

"Oh, heavens, not me." Shuddering, Mrs. McShane held up her dainty hands. "And I doubt Sarah or Flossie would be interested in handling wriggling worms or slimy fish, either."

Cadence agreed. "But wriggles or slime wouldn't bother me. I'd like to go fishing," she blurted out, recalling how she had envied Ben's freedom as he rode from camp.

"You always were a tomboy." The captain chuckled.

"I'd hoped she'd have outgrown it by now." Her

mother sighed.

"A good cook who's as beautiful as she is adventurous." James' eyes twinkled as he smiled from across the table. "I find the boldness refreshing."

Adventurous…refreshing…Have I misjudged him? Tilting her head, Cadence peered at him. *Is he flattering me or ingratiating himself to my father? Is his goal to be my husband or the captain's son-in-law?*

Three days later, Cadence, her father, Ben, and Lieutenants James West, Tom McIntyre, and Michael Purdue went on a fishing expedition to Limpia Creek.

Ben acted as the guide, sitting in the wagon driver's seat with Private Smith, a Negro cavalryman.

Smith moonlighted as the captain's striker, an orderly, who earned additional pay for his extra-duty work—whatever odd jobs the captain required.

A vibrant indigo sky outlined the Davis Mountains' craggy peaks. Seeing the dusty magenta blossoms of the cenizos in full bloom, Cadence inhaled their spicy-sweet fragrance as she took in the day's splendor. Though the sun blazed overhead, the ride was comfortable, with a light wind tousling her upswept, chestnut hair.

Sitting across from her, Tom ran his fingers over his blond hair, smoothing it. "I didn't know trout were so close to the fort."

Ben turned to address him. "Traveling from Fort Clark, I saw what looked like a good fishing hole, and that's just what it turned out to be." Then he stopped the wagon beneath an aged cottonwood growing alongside the creek.

As James helped her from the wagon, Cadence noticed Ben was not with the other officers ambling toward the stream. Instead, he unharnessed the horses, a menial task usually assigned to enlisted men. She frowned. "Why's Lieutenant Williams unbridling the horses?"

James gave him a passing glance. "He's a mustang, an enlisted man who was brevetted during the war."

Cadence did a doubletake. "He's not a West Point graduate?"

"He's not an elementary school graduate." James snickered.

"I've never met an officer who wasn't academy trained." She turned to stare at the tall stranger. *How fascinating. What stories could he tell?*

Cadence dangled a line from a bamboo pole, using a cork for a bobber, while the officers fly casted.

When Ben finally joined the group, he dropped his line at a location several yards upstream from the others and, within minutes, caught the first trout.

"Good show," called Tom.

She watched the other officers congratulate Ben on his first catch. However, when he caught a second, then a third trout without anyone else getting so much as a nibble, she saw their smiles turn to grumbles.

Cadence pulled her line from the water and joined him. "What's your secret?"

His eyes crinkled at the corners. "Tree roots," he murmured.

"What do you mean?" She cocked her head to one side.

He gestured toward the water's edge with his chin.

A maze of tree roots tangled beneath the waterline. The sun's rays penetrated the creek's translucent water, highlighting the outlines of trout hiding among the roots.

"They're shy." His eyes twinkled.

"Why are you whispering?"

"Don't want to scare the fish."

How could I forget? With an understanding nod, she pitched her voice low. "I haven't fished in a while. Mind if I join you?"

"I'd like that."

Though his smile beckoned, his upraised palm stopped her.

"But step back."

"Why?" His contradictory actions were confusing, and she wrinkled her brow.

"See how the sun's casting shadows?"

"Sorry, I've been out East too long." Stepping back, she stifled a sigh, recalling how fish scatter if they see shadows. Standing just inches from Ben as she dropped her line in the water, she studied him in her peripheral vision: his amazing height, aquiline nose, five o'clock shadow, and full lips. *How would they feel*—A fish nibbled her bait, pulling on her line, and she flinched.

"Easy," Ben whispered. "Don't jerk the rod."

Concentrating, she held her breath as she gripped her bamboo pole with both hands. This time, the bobber went under a moment before she felt the bite.

"Steady," he murmured.

The cork bobbed in response to the fish's nibbles, but she kept firm hands on the pole, waiting. Waiting.

Then the bobber disappeared beneath the water as the fish took the bait and ran. Instinctively, she yanked the pole up and back, hooking the trout as she lifted it from the water.

"You caught a beaut." Ben swept up the fish in the net.

"I did, didn't I?" Beaming, she looked from him to the trout and back. One arm holding the pole, she had an impulsive urge to reach out with the other in a victory hug. Then a hair's breadth from his broad shoulders, she stopped with a self-conscious laugh. "Thank you for your help." As an afterthought, she connected with his gaze. "Ben."

"My pleasure, ma'am."

Captain McShane approached with a red-faced, white-lipped James following close behind. The captain looked at the fish and then nodded. "That trout must be fourteen, fifteen-inches long. Good show, Cadydid."

At her father's approval, she struggled to keep a straight face. Though the fish was the largest she had ever caught, she shrugged. "Beginner's luck." Then turning her head, she shared a private smile with Ben.

"If you'd like to hand me that line, ma'am, I'll just add your catch to the stringer." Palm extended, he reached for her fish pole.

"Thanks again." As she handed him the pole, she swallowed a smile.

After removing the fish and baiting her hook, Ben returned her bamboo pole. "Ma'am." His back was toward the captain and James.

Though his tone was cordial but aloof, only Cadence saw his eyes crease at the corners in a conspiratorial grin. She couldn't resist returning a smile.

Captain McShane shifted his gaze between the bristling lieutenant West and his daughter. "Cady, maybe you can teach James your technique."

"Excellent idea, captain." James offered her his arm. "Let's try our luck in another spot...over here, shall we?" Their fish poles in hand, he led her several feet upstream.

Dragging her feet, she peeked back over her shoulder. *What other hidden talents does Ben possess?*

Chapter 3
Limpia Creek

Standing at an oblique angle to them, Ben watched with sideways glances as James taught Cadence to fly fish.

James stood behind her, holding her wrist, while she held his fishing rod. As she drew back her arm, he helped her fling her wrist, cracking the rod like a whip. Then just as fast, she pulled it away and repeated, the flicking lure resembling an insect landing on the water.

Though he could not hear them, Ben studied the pair. The lieutenant held her body close each time she leaned back to cast. Decoding, Ben nodded. *West thinks she's his.*

Just then, Cadence turned toward him.

The question is, does she? He stiffened, speculating what she would do next. When she favored him with a beguiling smile, Ben grinned back as he caught his breath.

"Lieutenant Williams." Captain McShane motioned with a wave. "Maybe you'd care to let McIntyre and me in on your fishing technique."

"Be happy to, sir." Ben was glad for any camaraderie with the fort's captain and officers, especially through fishing or hunting, which came naturally. Tired of being the stranger and the outsider looking in, he cheerfully shared several angling tips with them, and soon their string was full of trout.

"Private Smith," called the captain.

"I believe he's too far away to hear, sir." Ben peered through the trees but could not see the striker. "Can I be of help?"

"Thank you, lieutenant. Tell him to clean the trout for lunch."

"Yes, sir." Taking the stringer of fish, he found the colored soldier by the campfire, watching a wrought-iron cauldron of potatoes and ears of fresh corn boil.

Instead of coming to attention, Private Smith stayed crouched over the fire as he gave a casual salute.

Giving him a sharp look, Ben saw the man purse his lips, as if he had something to say but thought better of it. "Something on your mind, soldier?"

"Permission to speak, sir?" The man poked a stick into the fire, agitating the flames.

Ben was wary. He walked a fine line between earning respect as an officer and recognizing his men's views, but he nodded.

"Sir, you was an enlisted man. Me 'n the others admire you, but…"

"Go on."

"You different from them West Point officers. I be watching 'em while you showed Miz McShane how to fish." He shook his head. "They's a clannish breed, 'specially with their womenfolk. B'sides…" Smith scratched his chin.

Ben cocked his head to one side. "Go on."

"Painted dolls ain't got no business at no fo'ts."

"Painted dolls?" As he waited for an explanation, Ben arched an eyebrow.

"Officers' womenfolk. They be nothin' but

trouble." Smith spat into the fire, and the flames hissed. "Best to steer clear of 'em."

In the distance, Ben saw Cadence laughing and joking with the lieutenant more than fishing. "Seems to me a woman could make a man's life more tolerable on the frontier."

"You mean mo' miz'ble." Smith grimaced.

"Time to speak freely is over, soldier." His tone a no-nonsense command, Ben handed him the stringer of fish. "Clean these for lunch."

"Yes, sir." Responding to the tone, Smith stood as he saluted and then took the stringer.

Ben returned to the stream and resumed fishing.

Tom McIntyre ambled toward him. As Tom cast his rod, he gestured with his chin toward Cadence and James. "They make a fine-looking couple, don't you think?"

"I've seen better"—Ben shrugged—"seen worse."

"The talk around the fort is they're about to get engaged." Tom chuckled. "At least, that's what my wife tells me."

Ben's head spun toward him.

"You didn't know?" Tom's eyebrows shot up.

Recovering his composure, Ben recalled her private smiles and conversations. "Their personal life is none of my business, but I didn't get the impression they were planning a wedding."

"According to my wife, Sarah, James plans to propose marriage at the Harvest Ball."

"When's the dance?" Ben tried for a casual tone.

"In less than two months." Tom glanced up from fishing. "You going?"

At the thought of attending a ball, Ben shuddered.

"You need to make an appearance." Tom's eyes twinkled. "The unmarried ladies and their mothers expect all the single officers and eligible bachelors to attend."

I don't appreciate being exhibited like a prized bull at a county fair. Ben rolled his eyes.

"What's the matter?"

"I don't know how to dance." Ben scoffed. "At least, not ballroom dancing, though I can hold my own in a war dance."

"Then it's true?" As he studied him, Tom held back his head. "You were raised by Comanches?" Tom's eyes sparkled. "Why'd you leave?"

"A woman."

"You don't say." Tom hooted. "That's a story I'd like to hear sometime."

Private Smith banged a ladle against an empty cast-iron pan. "Come 'n git it."

After putting away their gear and washing their hands in the stream, the group found Private Smith had laid out blankets to sit on, along with china and silverware. Bowls of steaming potatoes, corn on the cob, sweet butter, coleslaw, and dill pickles were set out, but the heady aroma of sourdough bread freshly baked in a Dutch oven filled the air.

His appetite whetted, Ben inhaled deeply.

Then Smith brought over a platter of sizzling fried trout. "These here is the fi'st fillets. 'nother batch comin' right up."

"Thank you, private." The captain removed his hat. "Let's bow our heads."

During grace, Ben surveyed Cadence and James through sidelong glances, gauging their relationship.

"Amen," said Cadence, opening her eyes in time to catch Ben watching her. From a startled, silent gasp, her lips curled into a warm smile.

West offered his hand to help her sit on the blankets.

"Thank you, James." Accepting his help, she turned toward him.

Cadence, the captain, and West helped themselves to the first batch of trout, while Ben cut into the crusty sourdough bread, still steaming, and Tom and Michael served themselves vegetables.

"Maybe Ben will regale us with the story of how he escaped the Comanches," said the captain between mouthfuls.

Ben shook his head with a reluctant laugh. "Not much to tell." He buttered his bread and bit into its warm, yeasty interior.

"Do tell us." Cadence smiled. "Please?"

He did a doubletake. Her smile seemed encouraging as if she were coaxing him. His mouth suddenly went dry, and he swallowed hard. Then yielding, he took a deep breath. "I barely remember my parents. Except for a few early memories, I lived my entire childhood with the Comanches."

"What do you recall of your family?" Her eyes dancing, she tilted her head.

A topic he rarely discussed, Ben debated whether to share the intimate details, but her reassuring smile and apparent interest convinced him to continue. "My earliest memory is watching the Comanches kill my father and brother."

"Oh." Her eyelids flew open. "I'm so sorry—"

"It's all right, ma'am." His gaze connecting with

hers, Ben shook his head. "The massacre happened so long ago, sometimes it seems more like a bad dream than a memory."

"Would you mind sharing your story?" She stared into his eyes.

"If it wouldn't bore you folks…" *Her gaze seems sympathetic.*

Everyone but James urged him on.

After Private Smith delivered the second batch of hot trout, he stood off to the side, listening.

"You seem to have our undivided attention, Williams." Glancing at the picnickers' faces, the captain chuckled. "Please proceed."

"All right." To keep emotional distance, Ben spoke with disinterest as if repeating a story he had once heard. "A roving band of Comanches raided my parents' farm, burning the crops and torching the log cabin my pa had built with his own hands. Then using that same ax he'd used to cut the logs, they swung it into his back, breaking his spine and killing him."

A gasp escaped Cadence's lips.

"Sorry, ma'am, I don't usually speak of such violence"—he winced—"especially in front of a woman."

"Please don't stop on my account." Her smile shaky, Cadence focused on him.

"I never saw what happened to my mother, but as my brother ran away, they shot an arrow in his back."

Cadence gasped.

"One Comanche slung me over his horse and rode back to camp, carrying me in front of him. At first, camp life was bad." Ben spoke in a slow monotone, pushing through each word as it conjured painful

23

memories. "The man beat me so often another Comanche took pity. He and his wife had three daughters but no son, so he traded me *mula ensillada*, for a mule and a saddle, and raised me as his own son."

"Were you happy there?" Michael sat on the group's fringe.

"Enough." Ben considered his words while he helped himself to a grilled trout fillet. As its smoky, wood-fired aroma filled his nostrils, he swallowed, his mouth watering.

"Then why did you leave?" Michael searched his face.

"A woman." Tom's eyes twinkled.

Cadence caught Ben's eye and arched her brow.

"I had a combination of reasons." Since she seemed to question whether Tom spoke the truth, Ben gave her a tactful grin. "According to the ongoing terms of the Guadalupe Hidalgo Treaty, Apaches and Comanches had to return all captured Mexicans from the States."

"You're Mexican?" The captain's voice and eyebrows shot up.

"I don't know." As Ben shrugged, he spread his hands. "I was captured at such an early age, I can't remember, but my Comanche father said I was born near the west Texas-Mexico border."

"Did he say on which side?" The captain studied him with narrowed eyes.

"Borders meant nothing to him." Ben shook his head. "He didn't recall."

"But he treated you well?" Staring beyond him, Cadence spoke barely above a whisper.

"Like a father." Ben had the odd sensation she was

looking into the past, seeing him as the boy, but not the man before her. "He raised me as his own."

"Then again I ask, why did you leave?" Michael watched him.

"I've already told you"—Tom's eyes sparkled—"a woman."

Straightening her spine, Cadence whipped her head toward Ben.

"In a roundabout way, a woman was the cause." He spoke to her questioning gaze. "Marriage in the Comanche *campamiento* is straightforward. If a young man sees a woman he wants to marry, he simply asks her father for her."

Cadence looked at the captain and then at Ben. "You mean, like in our culture, where the man asks for the woman's hand in marriage?"

Swallowing a smile at her lack of experience, Ben shook his head. "Betrothal is more direct. When a man asks for another's daughter, the father hands her over."

Cadence's mouth and eyelids flew open.

"As you'd guess, divorce is common." Ben scanned the group for their reactions.

"So, what happened?" His jaw clenching, Michael gave an impatient snort. "Why did you leave?"

"One day, my best friend and I noticed a pretty girl. He said he'd ask for her. Teasing him, I told him no, I'd ask for her. I meant it as a joke, but what started in jest fanned into a feud. Even after they married, my friend was suspicious and jealous of me. As *la Indiada* said, we had bad blood between us." He drew a deep breath, inhaling the memories like smoke from a distant fire.

"I knew what I had to do—leave the camp before

his resentment turned to bloodshed. I told my family and the tribe's *capitán* about the quarrel. He offered me my choice of young women to change my mind, but I knew my friend would never let go his bitterness. His grudge had become a sickness." Ben pursed his lips, still wounded and resentful about losing not only his friend, but his adoptive family and clan.

"So, what did you do?" asked Michael.

Ben lifted his shoulders then dropped them. "I left." He gulped down his trout between queries, resigned to the interrogation. *The questions are bound to come. Might as well get them over with.*

"Where did you go? How did you live?" Cadence asked, wide-eyed.

"Since I didn't know which side of the Rio Grande I'd been captured on, I decided against being repatriated to Mexico, and an American Anglo family took me in. They helped me with my English and taught me how to read and write."

"How did you become an officer? Your background's so"—head back, James looked down his nose—"different. You're the only officer here who isn't a West Point graduate."

Different...the only. Taking in James' narrowed, skeptical eyes, Ben stared him down before stifling a weary sigh. "I started as a packer and guide here at Fort Davis—"

"Here?" Captain McShane's brow creased. "Why wasn't I informed of your tour at Fort Davis?"

"My duties are all listed in my records, sir." Ben struggled to maintain a courteous tone. "Though so much has happened since the War to Preserve the Union, the earlier personnel records might be buried in quartermaster reports." He paused to wolf down his potatoes.

"When the war broke out and I enlisted, I was assigned to the USCT, the Colored Troops. As you know, those regiments are made up of colored men— but some Indians, too. I rose through the ranks, and during combat, I received the title of brevet lieutenant. Then after the war ended, my commanding officer recommended I apply for an officer's commission to the buffalo soldiers." As he finished, he homed in on Cadence, waiting for her reaction now that she knew about his upbringing, as well as his lack of family and education.

She stared down in her plate.

He paused, watching her. She seemed deep in thought, but when she looked up, respect flickered in her amber eyes like a candle flame. As his gaze locked onto hers, the connection was like a homecoming or a broken chain rejoined. *Does she sense it, too?*

The next day, the Butterfield Overland Mail coach rolled into Fort Davis. Leading a patrol of ten cavalrymen, Ben accompanied the stagecoach along the Fifth Division Route to Fort Quitman. The next refuge along the Rio Grande, the garrison was located near the New Mexico Territory border, one-hundred-twenty miles from Fort Davis. With the horses walking four miles an hour, the trek took almost two weeks roundtrip.

Thirteen days later, when Ben reported to the captain, Cadence and her family were just finishing dinner.

"Stay for dessert," said her mother, Mrs. McShane. "Tell us about your patrol."

He studied the woman, an older, graying version of her daughter, but whose tired blue eyes lacked the same lively sparkle. *Still, she must have been a beauty in her day*. "In that case, let me get the canned peaches I brought back from Fort Quitman's commissary."

Their cook, Jenny, brushed away a wisp of gray hair with the back of her hand. Then she set another place, transferred the peaches to a bowl, and brought them to the table with a platter of steaming gingerbread squares.

Dusty and perspiring from his long ride, Ben gave Cadence a hesitant smile before sitting across from her. Then his smile broadened as he realized Lieutenant West was absent. *No competition for once*.

"Help yourself, lieutenant." Mrs. McShane gestured toward the peaches.

"Thank you, ma'am." Her warm smile was encouraging, and he mustered the nerve to lift a piece of gingerbread with metal tongs. After successfully delivering the crumbly dessert to his plate, he stifled a relieved sigh, turned the tongs toward the captain, and held the platter.

"How did the patrol go?" The captain removed two gingerbread squares before taking the platter and tongs from Ben and handing them to his daughter. "Have any trouble finding water?"

"No, sir, not on the trip out." Ben shook his head as he ladled peaches over his steaming gingerbread, their sweet and pungent aromas mingling as he inhaled. "Our first water stop was at Barrel Springs Station, about four-and-a-half hours from here, where we camped for the night. Eighteen miles later, after traveling over rolling country, we camped at Deadman's Hole, or *El*

Muerto Spring, and filled our water barrels, knowing the next night we'd have to make a dry camp." *Maybe these details would be better left for the written report.* He glanced at the ladies, but they appeared mildly attentive, as if accustomed to hearing such verbal accounts at the table.

"Thirty-three miles from Deadman's Hole, we found water at Van Horn, but barely enough for our horses. Nineteen miles from there, we stopped at Eagle Spring, where we camped for the night and refilled our water barrels. Then thirty-one dry miles later, we arrived at Fort Quitman, where we spent the night."

"How about the return trip?" asked the captain.

Has he heard of the Indian raid? Ben gave him a sharp look. Then he looked at Cadence and her mother before continuing. "Heading back, we came across a wagon train that had been attacked and burned at Eagle Spring."

"Apaches." The captain nodded.

Recalling the scalped men's swollen bodies lying face up, exposed to the sun, Ben grimaced. So much of their hair had littered the ground, the scene looked like spring shedding at the stables. Intending to spare them the specifics, Ben stole a glance at the women. "Maybe I should—"

"Go on." The captain rolled his hand in front of his chest. "My family's aware of the dangers of frontier life."

"Yes, sir." Despite the directive, Ben played down the gruesome details, reserving the particulars for his written report. "We dug the graves, buried their bodies, and made crude crosses from deadwood." Squinting to cover his revulsion at the memories, he glanced at

Helen and Cadence. "We found no women or children."

"Captured as slaves." Jaw set, the captain gave a quick nod.

Swallowing the bile in his throat, Ben bobbed his head in a curt nod. "The Apaches' trail was cold, but we tracked them as far as the Rio Grande, where they split up and escaped into Mexico." He drew a breath between his teeth to quell his tight stomach.

No one spoke for several minutes.

Then Cadence peeked at Ben. "What strength of character must be required to survive, let alone overcome such obstacles. Though traumatizing for an adult, how does a small child deal with being torn from home and brutalized?"

"Many don't survive. Those children that aren't strong—whose *spirits* aren't strong—weaken and die." As his gaze met hers, Ben saw her lips lift in what appeared a sympathetic smile.

Though caught off guard, she did not look away. Instead, her eyelids fluttered.

While Jenny cleared away the dessert dishes, the bugle sounded retreat as the post observed sundown.

"Shall we have our coffee on the veranda and watch the sunset?" asked Mrs. McShane.

Ben held the door as they strolled outside.

Stars glimmered in the brisk September evening as the rising harvest moon reflected the sun's last embers.

"Full moon tonight." Leaning against the railing, Cadence peered at the sky, her face outlined against the moonlight.

His gaze traced the gentle curves of her cheeks as they met her lips in a rosebud smile. *How would it feel to kiss those pouting lips?*

"Lieutenant." The captain puffed on a cigar. "Today, I received a report of three army horses and forty-one mules stolen from Barilla Springs."

"Apaches?"

"Mescalero." The captain nodded. "In the morning, take all the available Tenth Cavalrymen to recapture those mules and horses. Punish the Indians but take no risks that would endanger the safety of this command."

"Yes, sir." Having looked forward to a reprieve from sleeping on the hard ground, he stifled a weary sigh. *Guess one night on a straw mattress is better than none.*

"Use your best judgment regarding the troops and livestock."

"Yes, sir." Though passive defense irked him, Ben accepted the logic behind it. The fort lacked the trained personnel, horses, and funding to pursue the renegades. Just as at Fort Clark, resources at Fort Davis were overextended because of erratic federal policies and a central lack of tactical strategy. Washington's authority was divided between the Department of the Interior, which managed the Indian reservations, and the War Department, which fought the Indians.

"You may not know this, Williams, but recently, the Tenth Cavalry cooperated with the District of the Pecos to station troops at strategic crossroads and springs in the arid Chihuahuan Desert. Initial reports confirm the subposts are effective in intercepting the Apaches, but they strain the forts' inadequate resources. Soldiers are spread too thin to take aggressive action against the Indians." The captain harrumphed. "That will be all."

"Yes, sir." Reacting to the captain's dismissive

tone, Ben drained his coffee and turned to Helen. "Thank you for dessert, ma'am. That gingerbread was a real treat."

"As were the canned peaches."

Noting her cordial smile, Ben looked at the family comfortably gathered on the veranda, and the old yearning, the urge to belong, gnawed at his marrow. But the captain's ramrod back indicated his presence was no longer required or even welcome. "I'd best take my leave." He gave Helen a polite bow. "Ma'am, thank you again."

Then as he turned toward Cadence, a tenderness welled up in him. *How fragile she looks in the starlight, as delicate as translucent porcelain.*

Without warning, he was tongue-tied. Everything he wanted was on this veranda: a home, family…wife. So close, he could touch them, yet they were beyond his reach. Socially, he was as restrained as if tethered to the railing downstairs with his horse.

He yearned to fit in and belong to a family. He wanted the companionship and lifestyle, but his lot in life had always been the same. From his earliest days in the Comanche camp to this moment, he had always been the outsider looking in.

Straightening his spine, he stood to his full height, all six-foot-three inches, his backbone as rigid as his discipline. "Good evening, Miss McShane." Self-contained, he spoke with precise diction, his tone revealing none of the emotions sweeping through him.

"Cadence," she corrected, chuckling in the evening shadows.

Her warmth surrounded him like an embrace, eroding his self-control. "Cadence," he repeated, awed, cast in her spell.

"Good evening, lieutenant."

"Good evening, sir." The captain's clipped, curt tone woke Ben from his reverie, and he turned toward his superior with a crisp salute. Then he walked down the seven steps from the front porch, leaving behind the rarified air of home and hearth for his cramped bunk in a spare room. *Will I ever be home?*

****

Following orders, the next morning Ben led thirty-four men to recover the stolen mules and horses. After riding northwest for sixteen miles, they encountered a wide trail running east to west, where he picked up the shod mules' hoofprints. Skirting the White Sand Hills as he tracked them, he discovered a deserted Apache campground.

After fifty huts, he stopped counting, estimating the camp housed several hundred people when occupied, and he made a mental note to destroy the camp on their return. From the fresh tracks and warm ashes in the fire pits, he figured the Apaches had less than a day's lead. After ordering his men to rest their horses for two hours while they ate dinner, he tracked the Mescaleros through the night.

In the gloom before daybreak, with barely enough light to use his field glasses, Ben spotted the Apaches a half mile below in a narrow ravine. Though a lone scout guarded the mules, nearby were several wikiups—pyramid-shaped shelters made of brush and poles lashed together. He proceeded with caution, not knowing how many more Apaches slept inside.

Ben divided the patrol into two groups. The sergeant led half the men around the back side, while he led the other half into camp, riding without cover the last five-hundred feet.

The Indian scout spotted them and let out a war whoop as he jumped on his pony.

Joining him, three Mescalero Apaches dashed from the wikiups and rode off, firing at the soldiers as they escaped.

His right arm upraised, Ben halted his men. "Our orders were to recapture the mules, not pursue the renegades." He posted sentries while they wolfed down breakfast in case the Apaches joined with others and attempted a raid. "Assemble a detail," he told his sergeant. "Burn these wikiups behind you and set fire to the renegades' campsite on our way back. Then rendezvous with our troop. Let that damage be a warning. Without hideouts, maybe they'll stop looting and stay on their reservation." Then he instructed his men to herd the mules back to Fort Davis.

Ben wanted as many miles as possible between them and the Apaches since retaliation was a constant threat. Aware of his responsibility for the soldiers' safety and his orders to "take no risks," he stationed spotters along the flanks and rear of the cavalrymen to keep watch as they rode. Then he posted sentinels while they ate a cold dinner of hardtack and salt pork.

Alert at every bird call, he was wary of every shadow moving in the moonlight, and he remembered his Comanche father's advice. While the mouse keeps still, the coyote keeps watch. No sleep for thirty-six hours, Ben ordered the detachment to press on to the fort, riding them through the night. *But can the men and horses keep up the pace?*

Chapter 4
Rodriguez Family

Cadence stood outside the single officers' quarters, saying goodbye to James. The Butterfield Overland Mail coach had rolled into the fort, and since he was officer of the day, her father had ordered him and a patrol of ten men to accompany the coach to Fort Quitman.

Almost two weeks would pass before she saw him again, and she found the situation embarrassing to say goodbye so publicly on the front steps. She clenched her jaw. *The lack of privacy is exasperating.*

"Excuse me, sir." A soldier approached, leading a small group of Mexicans.

"Yes, private?" Returning his salute, James stiffened.

"Near as I can figure, sir, these folks are looking for shelter. They've been burned out by Apaches and need a place to stay."

The group spoke rapid Spanish, talking over each other.

"Enough." James rolled his eyes as he held up his arms for silence. He turned to the soldier. "Do you speak Spanish?"

"A few words, sir, but not enough to understand the details."

James swept his gaze over the dusty lot: three men,

a young girl, and an elderly woman. "I'm riding out in a few minutes. Let these people refill their water bags. Then escort them out."

"Yes, sir." After saluting, the private motioned to the group to follow. "Vamoose."

The people exchanged anxious glances. Tears glistened in the old woman's cataracted eyes as she held out knotty, calloused hands to Cadence. "*Por favor, senorita. Ayúdanos.*"

Despite not understanding Spanish, Cadence heard the desperation as the hoarse, parched voice strained to communicate. Staring into the woman's weatherworn face, she saw the lines of despair radiate from her cloudy eyes, each wrinkle a mute testament to the struggles and perseverance.

Though an army brat familiar with being uprooted and accustomed to following her father's assignments from fort to fort, Cadence had no experience being homeless or destitute. Putting herself in the woman's shoes—escaping with nothing but the clothes on her back—she could not imagine surviving outside the system. *The forts might be a cage...but they're also a refuge.* "Can't we do something to help?" As her concern for the woman swelled to include the group, Cadence turned to James. "Let them camp here for the night? Give them some provisions?"

"Let one in, and they'll all come begging." Shaking his head, he let out a sigh. Then he mounted his horse. "Besides, I don't have time for this interruption. I'm under orders to leave immediately. I'll see you when I return."

Following orders was essential to fort life. Fourth generation of military families, she'd had duty drilled in. With a curt nod, she shielded her eyes from the sun with one hand, while with the other, she waved goodbye. But when he cantered past the Mexican group without a second glance, his disregard toward the refugees galled her.

Without warning, Ben's story flashed through her mind. He did not know on which side of the Rio Grande he had been born. *These Mexicans might be his relatives. Any one of them could have been Ben.* "Private," she called to the soldier.

"Yes, ma'am?" Stopping, he turned toward her.

"Bring those people to our quarters. I'm sure Jenny can spare something from the kitchen." She led the way.

"Yes, ma'am." Again, the soldier motioned to the group to follow him. "Vamoose."

Cadence noticed while James and his men escorted the Butterfield Overland Mail coach out of the fort, Ben led in his patrol. As they rode closer, the cloud of dust behind them proved to be the recovered mules. Getting an idea, she waved to Ben, catching his eye.

He issued orders to his men and then rode toward her. "Ma'am." After tipping his hat, he glanced at the group. "What's going on?"

"This soldier believes Apaches burned out these people, and they need a place to stay, but I don't speak Spanish. I thought maybe a sack of beans and some cornmeal might tide them over."

Nodding, Ben turned toward the refugees and spoke in Spanish.

Ben's fluid use of the language impressed Cadence.

"*¡Gracias a Dios!*" At his words, the woman

crossed herself while looking heavenward. Then her words spilled over each other as she explained their plight.

Ben turned back to Cadence, translating. "You're right that Apaches burned their ranch. Escaping on muleback, they've lost everything but their lives."

Cadence gasped. Hearing her suspicions confirmed was far worse than imagining it. "Can they stay at the fort?"

He chewed his lip. "I know somewhere better. Can you round up whatever food and household items you can spare?"

As he peered in her eyes, she was unsure if he was appealing to her conscience or challenging her. "Of course." She glanced at the forlorn group before turning back. "Whatever I can do to help."

"Good."

She caught the glint of respect shining in his eyes.

Then he resumed his no-nonsense tone. "I'll meet you back here in an hour."

With a curt nod, she hiked her skirts and raced up the stairs to the front door. Hand at the handle, she paused on the veranda, watching him direct the Mexicans to a shady spot beneath a gray oak tree.

Then issuing orders, Ben passed his horse's reins to the private as he started toward the trading post.

Cadence could not help comparing his actions to James'. Where James showed no compassion, Ben sprang into action, even though he was coming in from a long ride in the saddle.

Calling her mother and Jenny as she gathered supplies, Cadence thought—*Those people could have been,* could be, *his family. Is that why he's sympathetic?*

****

An hour later, Cadence, her mother, and the assembled officers' wives watched Ben and the captain's striker pull up in the fort's ambulance with the refugees' mules tied to the rear.

"Everyone contributed." Cadence gestured toward the other women. Then with a proud jerk of her chin, she beamed, pleased she had mustered their donations.

"Thank you, ladies." When Ben saw the stack of food and household supplies, his eyes opened wide. "You've enough food here to feed the Rodriguez family for weeks." Turning toward the refugees, he pointed to the food and addressed them in Spanish.

Their tired faces brightened into smiles as they each spoke his or her thanks in a chorus of "*Gracias.*"

The elderly lady approached Cadence and reached for her hand. Speaking in Spanish, she turned toward Ben to translate.

"Lupe Rodriguez wants you to know how much they appreciate this food," he said. "They realize supplies are limited, and you're sharing from your own provisions."

"*Gracias.*" Her opaque eyes aglow, Lupe pressed Cadence's hand against her face.

"How do you say, 'You're welcome'?" Wishing she could express herself, Cadence glanced at Ben.

"*De nada.*" The corners of his lips lifted in a smile.

Cadence pressed the woman's calloused hand between hers as she repeated the words. What accent lacked, she offset with enthusiasm.

Wearing a wide smile, the woman clasped her hands and held them in a tight grip.

Ben told the men and Private Smith to load the food in the back of the ambulance. After instructing Lupe and the girl to get inside, he turned back to Cadence and the other women.

"Thank you again. I'll settle this family near the fishing hole on the Limpia—should be back in an hour or two."

"I'm going with you," Cadence said a beat too quickly.

Eyebrows arched, Sarah and Flossie exchanged sharp looks with her mother.

When will I learn to think before I speak? Cadence recognized their expressions. Her actions were unbecoming to a young lady.

"I'll be back in an hour or two," she said as if the words compensated for her rash decision. Then sharing an impish grin with Ben as he helped her into the ambulance, she sat in the front seat, facing Lupe and the girl.

Ben ordered Private Smith to drive and told the men in Spanish to climb aboard.

Two sat in the third seat, and the third man sat up front with Private Smith.

"Don't worry, ma'am," Ben told Helen. "Your daughter's safe with me." With a slight bow to the ladies, he thanked them again. Then he climbed in next to Cadence. As they began the bumpy ride to the creek, he acted as translator, so she could communicate with Lupe and the girl. "This young lady is Mariana." He pointed to the slim wisp of a child with large dark eyes and long black hair.

The Tejano girl stared at Cadence's auburn hair, craning her neck to peer at her curls. Reaching out, she rustled the fabric of the store-bought clothing between her fingers. Then eyeing a handmade lace kerchief held in place with a cameo, she wanted to know how old Cadence was, and was she married?

"Twenty-two." Cadence smiled and shook her head. "Not yet."

"The Apaches stole our horses," Lupe explained via Ben. "If we hadn't hidden the mules in the back pasture, we couldn't have escaped to the fort."

"I can't imagine your ordeal." Shaking her head, Cadence grimaced.

"The walls were adobe." Lupe hugged Mariana. "We can rebuild."

"Are you her...grandmother?" As Cadence studied the two, she heard the forced bravado in the woman's tone.

"My son, Juan, is her father," said Lupe at Ben's translation. "The other two men are my younger sons."

Cadence wanted to ask about the girl's mother, but she hesitated to bring up what might be a delicate subject. As the pause lengthened, the silence grew awkward.

"Mariana's mother died last summer, giving birth." Her tone soft, Lupe broke the lull in conversation.

Mariana pressed her head into the crook of Lupe's arm.

How could the child deal with the loss of her home so soon after losing her mother? Cadence bit her lip as she glanced at Ben, guessing the trauma he experienced as a child. Without thinking, she unfastened the cameo. Then she took off the lace kerchief, arranged it around the girl's neck, and pinned it in place with the cameo. "There," she said, sitting back, admiring Mariana. "It looks much better on you than it ever did on me."

The girl's dark eyes brightened. Putting up her hands to touch the brooch, she turned toward her grandmother.

"*Bonita*," said the old woman. "*Muy bonito. ¿Qué estás diciendo?*"

"*Gracias.*" The girl blushed.

"*De nada.*" Chuckling, Cadence glanced at Ben. "Some things don't change from language to language or culture to culture."

"Most things." Raising his eyebrow, he smiled.

"You communicate with people in English and Spanish, so you must understand both cultures." Cadence studied him as if seeing him for the first time.

"An exchange is often all it takes." He nodded. "If groups can't share their thoughts through words, their actions can be misinterpreted. Communication makes all the difference."

"What about when you lived with the Comanches?" She glanced at Lupe and Mariana, concerned whether *Comanches* was the same in Spanish as in English. "What did you think then?"

"I learned to speak their language and understand their thoughts. They treated their families well, but anyone not of the tribe was considered an enemy."

She watched him. "Dog eat dog?"

"Survival of the fittest." He shrugged.

"Yet, they accepted you."

"Accepted?" Ben stiffened at her choice of words. "No, I was never accepted. When I was first captured, I was treated like a slave. Had I been a man, they would have killed me. Had I been a woman, they would have…" Pursing his lips, he caught his breath.

"Because *Elan* sympathized with me, he adopted me, and I was raised a Comanche. Without his and his family's kindness, I would've been sold into slavery or killed."

A shudder rocked Cadence. Hearing of his harsh childhood, she swallowed to rid the bitter taste in her mouth. "His family treated you well?"

"Very well." His face relaxing, he nodded. "But to many in the tribe, I was always an outsider."

His nod seemed to emphasize his adoptive family's compassion. "*Elan* was your Comanche father?" Cadence digested his words as she studied him. His features softened as if he recalled a fond memory.

Then wearing an unfocused gaze, he nodded.

"What was your Comanche name?"

"*Ezhno*."

"What does that mean?"

"Solitary. I was always alone." He ducked his head. "Always the *blanco*, I was the outcast."

"Sometimes, I feel that way at the fort." Seeing his eyes take on a faraway expression, Cadence began to identify with him.

"You?" He scoffed. "If you're not surrounded with admiring officers or doting parents, you're drinking tea at ladies' socials."

"I suppose that's the way I appear." She leveled her gaze. "The truth is, I have no one to talk to or confide in. My parents aren't my friends. They're…well, they're my parents. My only two other companions at the fort are both married women with children. I have nothing in common with them except…" Stifling a sigh, she winced, having divulged more than she had meant.

"Except what?" He grinned. "I can keep a secret."

"Except tea and gossip," she finished, surprised she could be so relaxed with him. She studied his face, debating whether to trust him. "Believe it or not, I understand feeling left out or being excess baggage."

"Huh." He arched an eyebrow. "I never would have thought that of you."

She met his gaze. "Isn't it interesting what a difference communication makes?"

The striker stopped the wagon beneath the aged cottonwood trees lining the creek's shore.

Like tiny, gilded baseball gloves, a stand of late-blooming Desert Gold Poppies caught the morning sunbeams in their wide-open petals. Cadence breathed in the flowers' slightly sweet, citrusy scent. Though on a mission of mercy, she welcomed the reprieve from the fort's confines.

"This canvas will become a tent once it's assembled and the support poles are in place." Ben took a large bundle from the ambulance. "Private, help this man." Switching to Spanish, he instructed the other two men to unload the supplies.

"Where'd you get that tent?" Ben's resourcefulness surprised Cadence.

"I bought it." He turned toward the refugees, telling them in Spanish, and then translating for her. "This site has fresh water, and fishing's good." He handed the Rodriguez family a package of fishhooks and fishing line. "Best of all, you're just two miles from the fort, so you'll be safe from Apaches until you can return to your ranch."

"Here are a few blankets, a cast-iron pot, and several cups and bowls." Cadence offered Lupe the items, while Ben translated. "You'll also find sacks of beans, cornmeal, and flour, even a small bag of ground coffee." She gave the woman a warm smile, glad she could help.

As they prepared to leave, the Rodriguez family thanked them repeatedly.

"*Quédate un poco más.*" Mariana dashed from her grandmother's side and threw her arms around Cadence's small waist. Hugging and tugging at her, the girl had tears in her eyes.

"What's she saying?" Blinking back sudden tears as she hugged the girl, Cadence turned to Ben.

"She wants you to stay longer." He smiled at the exchange, but then his smile faded. "It's late. We should head back to the fort."

"Why?" Cadence gave him a mischievous grin. "Do you think tongues will wag?"

"Without a doubt." Wearing a lopsided smile, he helped her in the ambulance.

Cadence waved goodbye until the family and stream were out of sight. Then sitting across from Ben in the back seat, she glanced over his shoulder. The striker driving the rig was too far away to overhear them.

She took a deep breath, less restricted by social confines than since she had galloped across the Chihuahuan desert alongside her father. With no prying eyes and no eavesdropping ears, she was no longer bridled or shackled—but emancipated. Her breathing quickened.

"What?"

"I was just thinking how free I feel away from the fort. What a liberating sensation." Though his eyes danced with interest, his chuckle sounded uncertain, as if he were unsure how to react.

"Why?"

"I think…" Studying him, she inhaled again, feeling content, like after eating a satisfying meal. "You're the one person at the fort who doesn't judge me."

"I'm in no position to judge." He gave a short laugh.

"Why do you say that?" She leaned toward him.

"I wasn't raised with Anglo customs." He shrugged. "I can tell right from wrong, but I don't know enough about parlor manners to criticize anyone."

"You know right from wrong better than most." She compared his reaction to the family in need as opposed to James' curt response.

Color crept into his cheeks as he shrugged and glanced at a grove of trees in the distance.

No display of bravado. No brash façade. Cadence found his humility appealing. With his back toward her, she studied him, admiring how his broad shoulders filled his uniform.

When he looked back, he caught her staring.

She glanced down.

"Do you like pecans?"

"Love 'em." She squinted at his *non-sequitur*. "Why?"

"You're in luck." Raising his voice, he called to the striker. "Private, head for that stand of trees to the right."

Within minutes, the soldier halted the carriage beneath the shady canopy.

"What a windfall." Glancing from the empty,

brown husks on the trees' branches to the ripened nuts scattered on the ground, she grinned.

"Nature's bounty." Jumping down, he helped her from the wagon, and they collected pecans.

"What can we carry them in?" When her hands were full, Cadence looked about. Then answering her own question, she caught up her skirt like an apron, creating a container for the nuts.

"Great idea." Then he leaned over to gather the nuts and drop them in her skirt's pouch.

"We have enough pecans to make a dozen pies." His eyes twinkled in the dappled sunlight. After ten minutes, her skirt sagged from the weight.

"Have to admit, I am partial to pecan pie." He grinned.

"Oh, you are, are you?" Playing coy, she swallowed a smile.

"In fact, I'd go so far as to say, I love pecan pie."

"Seeing how you're not only *fond* of pecans, but you *found* them, sharing them is only fair." As he towered above her, she peered through her lashes. "Come to Sunday supper."

"I'd like that."

As his eyes peered into the distance as if looking inward, she turned to hoist herself into the wagon. But the situation presented a dilemma since her hands were full holding her pecan-packed skirt.

"Allow me." Ben gave a polite bow before whisking her into his arms and onto the wagon.

Startled, she let out a delighted squeal, which led to a giggling fit. She laughed so hard, she covered her face with her hands, letting go of her skirt and scattering the pecans across the wagon's floor. That chaos brought on another round of laughter, lasting until she wiped the tears from her eyes.

"What's so funny?" He studied her.

"Nothing. Absolutely nothing." Still chuckling and with her shoulders shaking from suppressed laughter, she caught her breath. He watched, wearing a perplexed smile. "I just don't remember when I've had a better time." Then mesmerized by his nearness, she gazed into his eyes. "This day's been so much fun…"

His head inched closer as she leaned toward him, closing her eyes.

" 'Scuse me, sir." The striker cleared his throat. "Shouldn't we be headin' back to the fo't?"

As reality invaded their private world, she snapped open her eyes. Self-conscious yet intoxicated with Ben's nearness, Cadence shared a mischievous smile.

"Yes, soldier." His grin hardened into a tight-jawed grimace. "It's high time we returned."

Music to her ears, Cadence listened to the bass tenor of his no-nonsense voice.

With the crack of the striker's whip, the carriage lurched forward.

As if the soldier's prompt jolted Ben's sense of propriety, Ben moved to the seat across from her. Though she missed his nearness, she enjoyed his new role of guide as he pointed out the ocotillo, buckhorn cholla, agave, and fishhook barrel cactus.

Then he found an empty water pail and collected the scattered pecans from the wagon's floor.

By the time they returned to the fort, the late summer sun had begun its retreat behind the mountains, and the shadows were long. Despite the day's excitement, as Cadence watched the first stars appear, she worried. *What will my father say?*

****

Cadence gladly accepted Ben's hand as she stepped from the ambulance.

Like the setting sun, the ember of the captain's cigar tip glowed an angry red each time he inhaled. Standing stiffly at attention on the front veranda with his wife, the captain puffed his cigar as he watched Ben and Cadence from his lofty perch.

"That'll be all, private. Dismissed."

Cadence winced at her father's brusque tone.

"Yes, sir." Smith saluted before driving off.

"Lieutenant Williams." Almost as red as his cigar's ember, Captain McShane's eyes glinted in the sun as he turned his glare on Ben. "What's the meaning of commandeering the fort's ambulance and our striker, while stealing off with our daughter?"

"Sir, when I learned of the refugee family's predicament, I thought it best to settle them in a temporary camp near the fort until they can return home." Coming to attention, Ben saluted.

"And after Ben—Lieutenant Williams—discovered a grove of pecan trees, we couldn't resist gathering these." Cadence held up the pail, interceding for him. She did not want the memory of her afternoon escape marred by her father's over-protectiveness.

"I see." He cleared his throat. Then he glanced at his wife before peering hard at Ben. "I'll expect a full report on my desk tomorrow morning, lieutenant."

"Yes, sir."

The low pitch of Ben's no-nonsense voice stirred her.

"And, uh"—the captain inhaled his cigar—

"excellent work on recapturing those mules."

"Thank you, sir."

"That will be all, lieutenant." Captain McShane harrumphed.

"Good evening, captain." He bowed to Helen. "Good evening, ma'am." Turning toward Cadence, Ben smiled as his eyes twinkled. "Thank you for your help today with the Rodriguez family."

"My pleasure." Then, she turned toward her parents. "I promised the lieutenant a reward for discovering the pecans, and I've invited him to Sunday supper."

"Cadence…" He drew out her name, his voice rising on the last syllable.

She grimaced at his stern tone.

"Your mother and—"

Helen cleared her throat.

He peeped at his wife in a sidelong glance.

Cadence recognized their signals. Her mother's arched brow, lowered chin, and alert gaze implied *I'll handle this matter*.

"We'll expect you after church." Helen turned to Ben with a smile.

"Thank you, ma'am. I look forward to it."

Me, too. Cadence caught his eye, her heart skipping a beat. *What will Sunday bring?*

****

Sunday morning, Cadence woke thinking of Ben like a catchy tune she could not get out of her mind. The pecan pie cooling on the kitchen's windowsill and even the breakfast coffee reminded her of him and their ride to the Rodriguez camp. While she dressed for church, her thoughts kept returning to him, and when she glanced at the mirror, she caught herself grinning.

Cadence searched the faces outside the chapel's entrance. The moment she spotted Ben, she smiled, her pulse quickening, and she spoke before she thought. "Sit with us." She pretended not to notice her father's raised brow.

As usual, the captain's family sat in the front pew. The junior officers and their families occupied the next two rows, and the enlisted men sat behind them.

Following the captain's lead, Ben whisked off his hat.

Cadence stole a sidelong glance. After a moment of arching his neck, straightening his shoulders, and loosening his collar, he adopted a posture of frozen stoicism. She ignored the surprised stares of the officers' wives as they scrutinized him beside her. When the congregation sang the opening song, she shared her hymnal with him, even pointing to the words, but he remained silent and detached.

The readings were from Luke, about the man who left ninety-nine sheep to rescue the lost one, the woman who cleaned her house until she found the tenth coin, and the prodigal son, who wasted his inheritance, and then returned to his father penniless but penitent.

"How many of you didn't want to come to church today?" The gaunt, balding chaplain smiled as he rose to preach.

The people murmured and chuckled.

Cadence heard Ben draw a deep breath, apparently in tacit agreement.

"I'm reminded of the boy who didn't want to wake up for church." The chaplain surveyed his congregation. "His mother called and called, but he pulled the covers over his head and wouldn't get out of bed. Still, his mother persisted until the boy said, 'Give me one good reason to go to church.'

" 'Better yet,' she said, 'I'll give you three. First…' " He punched the air with his index finger. " 'I'm your mother, and I say so.' " He brought up a second finger. " 'Second, you're forty years old, and you should know better. And third…' " He lifted the third finger. " 'You're the chaplain.' "

Through a sideways glance, Cadence watched Ben's stiff jaw relax, and she leaned back in the pew.

"Today's reading was about loss." As the chaplain raised both arms, the sleeves of his robe slid to his elbows. "Loss and hope. This past week, several settlers' homes were destroyed by fire, and their livestock was stolen. Two men lost their lives defending their property against Apaches. That's loss." He rested both hands on the podium and surveyed his congregation.

As a hush fell over the group, Cadence glanced at their subdued expressions.

"You'll notice in the parable, the shepherd left ninety-nine percent of his sheep to find the flock's lost one percent. The woman searched her house until she found the tenth coin—ten percent of her savings. And last, the prodigal son wasted his inheritance—fifty percent of his father's holdings—yet when he returned, his father rejoiced."

He held up an index finger. "One percent." He splayed the fingers of both hands. "Ten percent." Then he spread his right arm before him to encompass the assembly's right half. "Fifty percent. The parable shows the items' increase of importance: livestock, wealth, and family."

"What if you've lost something valuable? Do you search for it?" His snicker was a wicked laugh. "Of course, you do. The human approach is to look for something lost based on its monetary worth, but worldly value is not the divine gauge." He rested both hands on the podium and leaned forward. "Trust me, my friends. There'll be more rejoicing in heaven over one sinner repenting than over ninety-nine upright people, who don't need to repent."

"But…" He pointed his index finger toward heaven and paused as he surveyed his congregants. "Another hidden message is often overlooked." As he lowered his hand, he shook his index finger. "This parable is *not* just about loss." Again he paused before cupping his hand around his mouth. "No, my friends. It's also about hope. The shepherd *hoped*"—he banged his hand on the podium, rattling the papers—"he'd find his lost sheep."

"The woman *hoped*"—he slammed his other hand on the podium—"she'd discover the misplaced coin."

"The prodigal son *hoped*"—he whacked the podium a third time—"his father would allow him back into the family. Hope enables the present by embracing the future. My friends, spend this day searching, not for what you've lost, but for what you need—hope."

Hope. With an oblique glance at Ben, Cadence asked herself, *What do I hope?*

****

The McShane family discussed the sermon over a wild-turkey midday meal, starting with the creamy turkey giblet soup, still steaming in Mother's Chelsea porcelain tureen.

Though caught up in the conversation, Cadence

inhaled the savory, sage aromas as she helped herself to the oven-browned turkey with wild rice stuffing.

"I always took the older son's side." Pausing between mouthfuls, the captain leaned back in his chair. "He was within his rights not wanting to celebrate the return of his ne'er-do-well brother." He glanced at his daughter and Ben. "Besides, the chaplain was wrong. The younger son did not get fifty percent of his inheritance. As the younger brother, he was entitled to one-third, and the older brother was entitled to two-thirds."

"But the point *was,* one of the father's two sons left and then returned." Accustomed to their Sunday-supper debates, Cadence leaned across the table to make her case. "Half the family was restored to the father. The *Father.* The parable was about the lost son's homecoming—not the inheritance percentages. It highlighted the lost soul returning to the fold."

"What do you think, lieutenant?" Helen's words broke into the melee. Sitting across from her husband, she turned toward their guest.

Cadence recognized her mother's subtle mediation in her soft drawl. Yielding to the mild rebuke, she leaned back in her chair.

Her head tilted, Helen gazed at Ben. "Was the parable about inheritance percentages or renewed families?"

"Families, ma'am. To me, family is more important than anything else." He shrugged. "A person can always earn money. Livestock and goods can be replaced—"

"At the right price."

Cadence stiffened at her father's fractious tone and

spun her head to see his expression.

"I hear the price of—"

"Samuel, we were listening to the lieutenant's opinion." Her smile in place, Helen turned toward Ben. "Please continue."

"Thank you, ma'am." He acknowledged her with a nod. "To my way of thinking, neither wealth nor position measures up to family."

Position isn't paramount? Isn't he bucking for a promotion? Cadence compared him to James.

"Why, lieutenant?" Helen's eyes flickered.

"Because, ma'am, without family, what does a person have?"

"Well said." Helen's face warmed into a smile. Then straightening, she glanced at the faces around the table. "Who'd like pecan pie?"

"I sure would, ma'am." Ben grinned. "I don't often get home cooking."

"That you have the first piece is only fair, lieutenant." Helen cut into the dessert and handed him a generous slice. "I understand your sharp eyes spotted the pecan trees."

As her mother passed Ben the plate, Cadence inhaled the pie's sweet, nutty fragrance.

"Pecans might be good by themselves, ma'am,"— he accepted the pastry with a nod—"but it's the baker who brings out their flavor."

"You're absolutely right." Cadence got an idea as she glanced at Ben. "It's the baker."

"Thank you, dear." Helen smiled as she handed her daughter the next slice.

"No, I didn't mean it that way." Then embarrassed her words had come out wrong, Cadence lifted her hand to her chest. "What I meant was, of course, you're a wonderful cook, Mother"—she forced a quick smile as she accepted the dessert—"but baking makes the difference. The Rodriguez family has supplies but no oven. They can cook over an open fire but not bake."

"What are you getting at?" Head tilting, Helen studied her daughter.

"Wouldn't surprising them with fresh bread tomorrow be wonderful?" Grinning, Cadence looked from her mother to Ben and back.

"An excellent idea." Helen nodded. "Maybe Sarah and Flossie would each bake an extra loaf, too. I'll speak to them this afternoon."

"Thank you, Mother." Cadence smiled at her new-found ally and then turned toward her father. "Could you spare Lieutenant Williams tomorrow morning to escort me to the refugees' camp?"

Hesitating, he snorted.

"Samuel?" Helen caught her husband's eye. "What do you say?"

After Ben left, the McShanes sat around the fireplace with Helen embroidering and Samuel reading.

Cadence rose to stoke the embers and add firewood.

"I don't approve of you seeing Lieutenant Williams."

"Why not?" Stove poker still in hand, she spun around to see her father's expression.

"The subject isn't open for debate." Frowning, he took his gaze from his journal.

"Then give me one good reason."

"I'll give you two." The captain raised his eyebrow. "He's not a commissioned officer—"

"Battlefield promotion." Cadence coolly met her father's eyes.

"A brevet officer in name alone." He shook his head. "No increase in pay or grade."

"During the war, perhaps, but not now." Turning toward the fire, she added a log and stoked the coals with such energy, they ignited into flame. After she replaced the poker, she crossed toward him. "You heard Ben say his commanding officer recommended he apply for an officer's commission to the buffalo soldiers. He has the same pay and grade as any second lieutenant."

"A field promotion is not West Point."

"It made Ben a commissioned officer." She tossed her chin at his patronizing smile. "That advancement cancels out your objection, doesn't it?"

"Perhaps I'm not expressing myself well." The captain glanced at his wife, but her gaze was focused on her embroidery. "Lieutenant Williams was raised as a Comanche, not as an officer or a gentleman." He sneered. "He's not like us."

"In case you weren't aware, Ben sprang to action when James turned away the Rodriguez family." Cadence stiffened at her father's snobbery. "Is that what you mean by him not being like us?"

His eyelids half open, he raised his brow. "I'm sure James was preoccupied—"

"Yes, he was." Her father's bored expression irked her. "His sole concern was to follow orders, not help people in desperate need."

"There you have it." The captain waved her off. "A good officer's priority is to his duty."

"James hadn't even begun his orders." Cadence

wrinkled her nose. "He'd been off duty at the fort, while I understand Ben and his men went without sleep to recapture the stolen mules from the Apaches. Coming in from that patrol, he must have been exhausted. Ben not only distinguished himself by going above and beyond duty, he put others' needs before his own." She stared down her father. "If that action doesn't show priority of duty—and good breeding—I don't know what does."

"Interesting choice of words—breeding." Setting his journal on the floor, he rose from his chair and regarded his daughter as he stepped toward her.

Have I gone too far? Swallowing, she instinctively took a step back. As captain, he was not used to anyone questioning his word or opinion—except her mother and, on occasion, herself.

"Cadydid…" He broke off with a sigh.

When he used her pet name, he was either delighted or disappointed with her, nothing in between. Opening her eyes wide, she watched his next move.

"Some people call Lieutenant Williams a half breed." He frowned.

"Ben isn't a Comanche, not half or any part. They just raised him." Straightening her backbone, she squared her shoulders. *How can my father be so condescending?*

"Take care your conduct isn't misconstrued as unseemly. All your mother and I've ever wanted for you is a secure future, where you'd be well-provided for…and happy." He rested his hands on her shoulders as he smiled. "I have it on the highest authority…"

Hearing Sarah's words echoed, Cadence drew a deep breath. Despite her father's gentle touch, affectionate tone, and smile, she steeled herself against what was to come.

"James is planning to propose at the Harvest Ball. He's already spoken to me, and I've given my blessing—"

"Of course, you have." Leaning away, Cadence stifled a frustrated sigh. "He's the son you've always wanted. You've treated him like the heir apparent for months."

"He's the perfect officer, a rising star in the Army Cavalry, and graduated at the top of his class in West Point." Her father dropped his hands from her shoulders. "He has family connections on both your mother's and my sides...he's one of us. Believe me, family ties are important to a solid marriage." He bent his head closer. "Uppermost, he'll be a good provider and a solid, dependable husband."

But he's heartless. As her father's whispered words registered, Cadence blinked, processing her thoughts.

"Don't you want a good match?" Her father stared.

"I used to think so." Shrugging, she sighed.

"Used to...?" His elbows spread wide, he placed his hands on his hips. "And what, may I ask, has changed your opinion?"

"Samuel." Her mother set aside her embroidery.

Grateful for her soft-spoken support, Cadence glanced at her. "All the men I've known might just as well be gingerbread men. They're all made from the same cookie cutter." She straightened her shoulders.

"Are you telling me—"

"Samuel, listen to the girl." Glancing at her husband, Helen lifted a petite hand. Then she turned toward Cadence. "What are you looking for, dear?"

"Until recently"—she flashed her mother an appreciative smile—"I never questioned the values Father mentioned. You've raised me to respect those traditions." She spread her hands. "James will propose, and everyone…" Panicking at the idea, she looked pointedly at her father. "*Everyone* expects me to accept, no matter how I—"

"And accept you will." Barking an order, her father pulled himself to his full height.

Cadence flinched at her father's harsh tone and edict.

"Samuel, let the girl finish." Cocking her head, she glanced at her daughter. "What qualities do you want in a husband?"

"I've never expressed these feelings." Despite her mother's soft drawl and gentle coaxing, Cadence was uncomfortable sharing her emotions, and she strained to put her thoughts into words. "I know everyone expects me to marry James—as if my life's been predetermined—but where's the challenge?"

Shaking an index finger, her father spun toward her. "I'll tell you—"

"Samuel, I'll thank you *not* to interrupt our daughter again."

His eyes opening wide, he harrumphed, sat in his chair, and lit a cigar.

"If I marry James"—she glanced at her father—"*who's one of us*, I'll belong to the same circles and be related to the same people." Cadence crossed toward her mother and knelt beside her. "I'll know just what to expect. Life will hold no surprises or challenges. Nothing will be new."

"What's wrong with stability, young lady?" Sitting

erect, he held his cigar in the crook of his fingers.

"Samuel…"

"The question is fair, Mother." Cadence turned toward her father. "I want new experiences, not a repetition of what I've always done. I want to *live* life, not sit idly, drinking tea and watching life pass me by."

"Live life…" Leaning toward her, Helen cocked her head to the side as she raised her chin. "You mean gamble. If you refuse James' proposal, you'd take a chance. You'd risk never meeting another man of his caliber. You could end up marrying a brute or a ne'er-do-well. Worse things can happen than knowing what to expect in marriage."

"I'm not sure James is the right one." *He's just been the only one—until now.* "Or maybe I'm not ready for marriage." Thinking aloud, she appealed to her mother. "Or maybe…"

"Go on, dear." Helen inclined her head, listening.

"I'm not even sure I want a husband—"

He propped his hands on the arms of his chair, preparing to stand. "You're not sure—"

"Samuel!"

Cadence glanced at her father, whose face was beet red, and he looked apoplectic as he sat back in his chair. She turned toward her mother.

"If you didn't marry, dear, how would you support yourself?"

Focusing her eyes on the future, Cadence lifted her head, surprised at the unconventional question. Many women earned money by sewing or knitting and in the East, women worked in factories.

"Have you given any thought to your livelihood?" After a beat, her mother leaned forward. "Have you?"

"No, but since you raise the question…" She met her mother's gaze before looking inward. "I could be a seamstress and make ladies' riding outfits." Then she smiled, recalling a gratifying week at her father's previous post, when she substituted for an ill teacher. She recalled the look of satisfaction on the students' faces as they absorbed fresh concepts and ideas, but one boy stood out from the rest.

He could not comprehend the words as he read, and the teacher described him as slow. Cadence learned his immigrant parents spoke only German at home, and English was his second language. By teaching him how to use the sentence's context to guess at words' meanings, she helped him understand the words, and he quickly caught up with the other children. "I know what I'd do. I'd teach school."

"When I'm cold and buried in the ground." The captain snorted. "No self-respecting father allows his daughter to work."

"Why not?" Cadence tossed her chin.

"Because providing for his wife and family is a man's responsibility." He puffed his cigar. "Enough of this balderdash. When James proposes, you're graciously accepting. End of matter."

Seething with resentment, she glared at her father. *Is it?*

****

The next day, Cadence woke to a thunderstorm, but by the time she met Ben in front of the house, the rain stopped, and a rainbow arched over the foothills. After each packed two loaves of fresh bread in their saddle bags, she mounted her horse from the steps, swung a leg over the saddle, and sat astride.

His jaw slack, he stared wide-eyed.

Unable to ignore his shocked expression, she struggled with her poise as she glanced at her handmade outfit. This was the first time she mustered the nerve to wear her convertible riding skirt in public. What appeared to be a skirt at first glance was flared pants that allowed her legs mobility. Modesty panels covered the front and back slits when she stood but also covered her ankles when she rode astride.

"When I was out East, I rode side saddle like a proper lady, but riding aside on these trails is dangerous." Squaring her shoulders, she lifted her chin. "Why risk breaking my neck when I can sit more comfortably and safely in the saddle?"

"I reckon you're using your head." He tipped up his hat's brim with a knuckle.

"In case you have any lingering doubts, let me prove the skirt's practicality." Noting a gleam of respect in his eyes, she winked. "Race you to the trading post." Then clicking her teeth, she pressed her knees into her horse's sides and took off at a gallop, leaving Ben behind, still mounting. Glancing over her shoulder, she had the lead.

A quarter mile later, when they pulled up at the store, her horse beat his by a neck. "I win." Grinning, she turned toward him as she affectionately patted her horse's withers. "Now, what do you think of my riding"—rather than risk sounding arrogant and saying *skills*, she chose—"skirt?"

Chapter 5
Freedom Can Get Mighty Lonesome

"You beat me...even if you hadn't had a head start." Ben looked at her flashing eyes challenging him. *What a feisty woman.*

Throwing back her head, she burst out laughing.

Her sheer joy attracting his attention, he saw how the bloom in her cheeks offset her rosy lips. Then he noticed Sarah and Flossie peering from the trading post's porch.

The building's two-story, rough frame structure boasted a wide-plank porch with an overhanging tin roof supported by four, wood-beam columns.

Heads together, whispering as they sat on the portico's varnished, wooden bench, the two women stared down their noses.

"Good morning, ladies." He tipped his hat.

Their conversation ceasing, they glanced at each other before rising.

"Good morning, lieutenant." Sarah arched an eyebrow. "Cadence." She gave a terse nod.

"How are you, Sarah? Flossie." Cadence nodded and smiled. "What a beautiful day for a ride."

"A ride, perhaps"—Flossie's eyes narrowed—"not a steeplechase." Noses in the air, the women turned their backs and strode inside.

"I'll hear about this race tonight." Muttering,

Cadence reined her horse to the side and started away at a slow walk.

"Hear about what?" Suspecting she meant gossip, he glanced at the ladies' retreating figures before catching up.

"Conduct unbecoming for a young lady. Nothing goes unnoticed at a fort. Living on a post is like living in a cage. Whether because of clothes, saddles, or society, I'm always confined." She examined her gloves and riding skirt, and then sighed. "The pins of patience."

"The pins of patience…?" He squinted, unsure he heard right.

"Flossie has a favorite saying. 'Women ought every morning to put on the slippers of humility, the shift of decorum, the corset of charity, the garters of steadfastness, and the pins of patience.' "

Though she wore an irritated frown, Ben smiled at Cadence's singsong voice.

"I'm never free." She spun toward him. "You're so lucky to come and go as you wish. You have no idea…"

"Freedom can get mighty lonely." He gave a wry laugh.

"How do you mean?"

"You call living here a cage. I call it belonging, whether to a fort, tribe, clan, or family." He gave her a half-smile. "What you call free, I call friendless."

He rode along in thoughtful silence for several minutes, listening to the sound of the horses' hooves on the caliche trail.

"Are you lonely at Fort Davis?"

Her voice broke into his thoughts. "I've been alone

everywhere I've lived, except possibly at my parents' cabin." Though the sun shimmered overhead, a passing cloud cast its shadow. His wide shoulders sagging, he slumped.

"How old were you when the Comanches captured you?"

"About three." He shrugged. "I barely recall a time when I wasn't the outsider."

"The enlisted men like you." She glanced toward him.

"How would you know how the men feel?" He studied her face.

"I overheard Tom telling my father."

"Tom's a good man and an independent thinker. He's the one officer here I consider a friend." As Ben inhaled, a deep sense of belonging filled him. Then he recalled Sarah's behavior from a few minutes before. *Too bad his wife's not more like him.*

"Then you're not so isolated, after all, are you?"

"Maybe not." He connected with her gaze. As she peered through her eyelashes, and her face warmed into a coquettish smile, he lost his train of thought.

"Tom said the enlisted men not only like you. They respect you."

"Because I rose through the ranks, they consider me one of their own." Palm up, he lifted his hand loosely. "When I enlisted for the War to Preserve the Union, I was assigned to the USCT."

"Why to the Colored Troops?" She watched him.

"In the USCT, Indians fought alongside the colored. Since I was raised a Comanche, the Army classified me as an Indian." He sniffed at the irony. "Half the men at this fort are transferred from USCT regiments."

"The buffalo soldiers." She nodded.

As his horse picked its way through the hardscrabble, Althea nibbled at a woolly tuft of black grama grass.

"You know why they're called buffalo soldiers, don't you?"

"Colonel Pierson said it's what the Apaches call the colored soldiers."

"Some say that's the reason." Shrugging, Ben tilted his head. "Others say the Cheyenne gave them that name when a war party shot out the horse from under a colored cavalryman."

"I haven't heard that story." Her ears perking, she sat taller in the saddle. "What happened?"

"When they attacked him, he took cover behind railroad tracks, defending himself with just a pistol and seventeen rounds of ammunition. Though they shot him in the shoulder and wounded him eleven times with a lance, he survived. The Cheyenne said he not only fought like a cornered buffalo, he looked like one, too, with his thick, curly hair."

"So is *buffalo soldier* a term of respect or a racial slur?" She arched a brow.

"Depends on the point of view." He frowned. "The buffalo's a fierce animal, so from an Indian's standpoint, I'd say the title is high praise. But some colored soldiers take it as an insult."

She gave him a quick nod.

Again, he rode along the hardpan trail, listening to the whistled song of the black-headed grosbeak as the wind blew through the sage.

"What are those flowers?"

Her words interrupted his reverie. "What?"

She pointed to a stand of giant, yellow wildflowers. "Maximillian sunflowers. Deer and livestock love them."

On cue, Cadence's horse leaned over and grabbed a mouthful while walking past. She chuckled at the yellow blossoms dangling from the horse's mouth as it munched.

She takes life in stride. Ben enjoyed her casual ways. She didn't make him feel self-conscious. With her, he was relaxed. *Like Tom, she thinks for herself and makes up her own mind.*

"What?" The corners of her mouth curled.

As a quizzical smile played at the corners of her lips, her tawny eyes flickered in the sunlight like rustling autumn leaves. Caught off guard, as well as caught staring, he considered admitting his thoughts. *If I put her to the test, would she accept me for who I am?* "You have a leaf in your hair." Covering his fib, he made a passing swipe at the left of his head.

"Did I get it?" She brushed her swept-up, auburn hair with a hand.

"Yeah." Lifting her arm accentuated the rise of her breasts, and he caught his breath, wanting to say more—much more…

"*Hola.*" Ducking through the branches, Mariana approached them, beaming and chattering in Spanish.

"*Hola.*" Cadence grinned back.

As he translated, Ben smiled at their rapport. Cadence seemed to enjoy the girl's company, even if she could not understand her, and Mariana obviously was glad to see them, while she walked alongside, escorting them to the camp.

Lupe greeted them with open arms. Speaking in rapid Spanish, she invited them for lunch and sent Mariana to fetch the tablecloth. Then when Cadence brought out the fresh bread, Lupe hugged her before hungrily inhaling the loaf's yeasty, fresh aroma, while Mariana laid the cloth on the ground, picnic style.

Within minutes Lupe set out a feast of roast venison with a fruity yet piquant barbecue sauce and fresh bread.

"What's in this sauce?" Cadence licked her lips. "It's delicious."

"*Ciruelas silvestres*." Pointing to a pail, Lupe motioned to Mariana. "*Por favor traiga eso*."

"Wild plums." Ben translated as Lupe shared her recipe. "She mashes wild plums to a pulp and then adds brown sugar and *chiltepin*—hot, wild peppers."

Mariana brought over a pail of what looked like frosted cherries.

"These are plums?" Wide-eyed, Cadence turned toward him. "What's the cloudy blush on them?"

"Natural yeast." He smiled. "When Lupe bakes sourdough bread, she doesn't need to buy yeast from a commissary."

"So resourceful." Wearing a half smile, Cadence shook her head.

Cadence is her own woman. Comparing her to the other ladies at the fort, Ben could not imagine Sarah or Flossie sitting on the ground or enjoying this simple meal, let alone being impressed by Lupe's ingenuity.

After lunch, he got an idea on the ride back to the fort. "Would you like to pick wild plums yourself?"

"Absolutely." Her honey-brown eyes glimmered in the sunny afternoon's glare.

"A stand of plum trees is just a mile or so north of here." He grinned at her enthusiasm, again comparing her to the other women at the fort.

The arid vista stretched to the volcanic mountains on the horizon. Along the unmarked trail, he pointed out a javelina lurking behind a creosote brush, and a daring roadrunner sprinted across their path to catch a striped lizard. Fifteen minutes later, he reined his horse toward a grove of trees beneath a craggy rock outcrop.

"These are plums? This looks like a Christmas tree decorated with frosted purple and red ornaments." Her eyes sparkling in the sun like amber flames, Cadence chuckled. Then reining her horse beneath the branches, she reached up and picked a plum.

"Careful of the pits."

"Eeuw." Taking a cautious nibble, she scrunched her face. "*Eeuw*. That plum tastes awful. Did I get a green one?"

"The skin's bitter. Don't bite into it." Holding the plum to his lips, he demonstrated. "Instead, slurp out the fruit, leaving behind the pit and skin."

"Delicious." She tested one his way, and her face relaxed into a smile until she glanced at the remaining skin and pit. "Not much fruit, but what's here is tasty." Then she looked around the area. "What a gorgeous glen."

The trees provided a shady canopy from the late afternoon sun. A small sierra rose overhead with a cleft between its boulders, forming a snug, inviting ravine. A spring bubbled from the rocks, watering the alpine meadow of blue blossoms beneath.

"What are those feathery, bottle brushes called?" Cadence pointed to the fuchsia flowers.

"Blazing stars."

"And the bushy plant?"

"Mealy blue sage." Glancing at the flowering plant, he smiled at a fond memory. "These were my Comanche mother's favorite flowers."

"They're such a vivid blue." She turned toward him. "Was she the one who taught you to recognize the different plants and trees?"

Taking a deep breath, he nodded. "When I was small, she'd take me to gather wild fruits, berries, and nuts. She was a medicine woman who knew when and where to pick every grass, herb, root, and flower, as well as how to prepare them for food or remedies."

"Did she use the blazing stars for anything?" She pointed to the spiky flowers.

"Yes, she made a poultice of the roots to treat snakebite."

"She sounds like a talented woman." Cadence smiled and then sat up in her saddle, turning to gaze at the area in all directions. "This place is lovely and so peaceful—almost like a chapel."

"I feel the same way." Warmed by her interest, he nodded. "God's handiwork is my church."

"Is that why you seemed uncomfortable in the chapel yesterday?" As she faced him, she met his gaze.

"Was I obvious?" His cheeks warmed.

She nodded.

"Sitting in the front row, I was on display like a prized hog at a county fair." Wary, he debated whether to speak freely. "For me, church isn't a weekly event. In fact, yesterday was only the third time I'd ever been inside a church. The other two occasions happened years ago, when the Anglo family took me in—once at my baptism and once the Easter I spent with them."

She canted her head and blinked. "Then why did you go to church Sunday?"

"I reckoned the best way to time your mother's supper invitation for 'after church' was to attend the service and go from there to your quarters."

"I thought you seemed stiff." She nodded slowly.

As she seemed to mull over his actions, Ben swallowed, ill at ease. "I wasn't sure how to behave, and sitting in the front row, I was exposed—my every move scrutinized."

Slouching in his saddle, he felt inadequate without any formal schooling—especially compared to someone educated out East. *I'm a fish out of water*.

"Is that why you didn't sing along with the hymns?"

He let out an uneasy sigh. "I can't read music, and I didn't recognize the tunes. The times you shared the hymnal, I just stared at the pages." He hesitated. "Plus, I couldn't stop thinking about the sermon."

"Why?" She leaned toward him.

While he studied her, he rubbed his chin, deliberating. *Should I let down my guard?* Then his Comanche father's words came to mind—*Men keep their own counsel*—

"Why couldn't you stop thinking about the sermon?"

She broke into his reverie as he debated. *Will she accept me or ridicule me?* "I try not to dwell on my past." Her expressive eyes seemed receptive and encouraging, but he was leery of criticism, and he peered into her eyes one last time before testing her. "In fact, my childhood is something I've never discussed before…with anyone."

"How did the sermon connect to your past?" Her gaze met his.

Her warm smile was sympathetic, and her tilted head invited more information. Bolstered, he ignored his misgivings. "The parable reminded me of what I've lost: my parents, brother, home, and culture…no, *cultures*. Besides my Anglo heritage, after I left the Comanche camp, I left behind the way of life I'd learned there, too. Once again, I belonged in neither world—not Anglo. Not Indian."

For the first time he could remember, he wanted to share his whys and wherefores with another person, but then he recalled his Comanche father's words—*Men don't whine*.

"So, the parable spoke to you?"

Her nod encouraged him to continue—despite his father's advice. "Yesterday in church, I felt like a rabbit in a foxhole." Searching her face, he saw empathy, not condemnation, and his wall of reserve crumbled. "I've never looked for God inside a building. I've always found Him in the outdoors."

"I can see why." She surveyed the scenery, gazing from the flowers and bubbling spring, up the boulder walls, to the top of the mountain. After a pause, she turned back. "Have you read Emily Dickinson's poetry?"

"Nope." His hackles stood on end. Already self-conscious about his lack of education, he popped the P, pronouncing the word in two syllables. Like ice water thrown at him, her question was a rude awakening, emphasizing their social distance.

"Emily Dickinson wrote a poem called "Some

Keep the Sabbath Going to Church," and the words remind me of this place and what you've just told me." Her eyes focusing inward, Cadence recited.

" 'Some keep the Sabbath going to Church—
I keep it, staying at Home—
With a Bobolink for a Chorister—
And an Orchard, for a Dome.

'Some keep the Sabbath in Surplice—
I, just wear my Wings—
And instead of tolling the Bell, for Church,
Our little Sexton—sings.

'God preaches, a noted Clergyman—
And the sermon is never long,
So instead of getting to Heaven, at last—
I'm going, all along.' "

When she started, he was too irritated to focus. Reminded how his schooling did not measure up—*he* did not measure up—he fumed as his deep-rooted sense of inferiority surfaced. Not until she continued from memory did he begin listening. By then, her rosy lips distracted him as his mind wandered, imagining how they would taste in a kiss. But at the poem's end, as the words sank in, he slipped into a deeper connection. No pledges were exchanged. No promises were made, but a bond formed.

What in tarnation just happened? After she finished, he stared, too moved to speak. Searching for words, he took a deep breath. "That poem describes how I feel in nature. God surrounds me. I don't need to go anywhere to find Him. He comes to me and embraces me."

"Did you learn this belief from the Comanches?" Her lips parted slightly as she tilted her head.

Her soft, breathless voice seemed to contain wonder, and her interest reassured him. "No, I think I recalled my mother's earliest teachings about faith." Reflecting, he glanced at the towering rocks above and then across the rolling meadow's blue pastiche of flowers. "Because of my earliest memories, I've looked for God in nature."

"That's understandable with such a magnificent place to worship." Turning in her saddle toward the panoramic view, she sighed. Then she peeked into his face. "Do the Comanches have a religion?"

"Yes, though not what you'd call an organized religion. The Comanches believe in spirits, both good and bad. When they meet for counsel, they smoke a peace pipe and take the first puff for the Great Spirit."

"Their incense."

"Could be." He recalled the fragrant aroma of incense from the Easter Sunday his Anglo family had taken him to church. Then he glanced at the uplifted and fractured rock formations surrounding them, and he returned to the moment. "The Comanches believe the spirits can take the shapes of mountains, rivers, animals, dead people, and little people."

"Little people?" Flinching, she raised an eyebrow.

"Pixies—dangerous elves that shoot arrows with deadly aim." He picked his words, never having described their ways before. "The Comanches' faith is personal. Each person has his or her own. The spirits appearing in their vision quests are important, but personal, guardian spirits."

"Like angels?" Her eyes lighting, she smiled.

"In a way." He shrugged.

"Are a heaven and a hell part of their beliefs?"

"Comanches believe in an afterlife." He watched her reaction. "Although, not everyone goes to the land of the dead beyond the setting sun."

"Their heaven?"

"Yes." He nodded. "But they don't believe in a hell."

"If they have no hell, why wouldn't everyone go to their heaven?"

Uncomfortable at sharing such personal information, he grimaced but answered. "They believe scalped people can't be reborn in the afterlife and strangled people die with their spirits locked inside them."

"What do you mean?" Her eyes narrowed.

"Comanches link breath with life. If a person's strangled, their breath—*their spirit*—can't escape their body."

"Some things sound similar but not all." Her smooth brow wrinkled. "Despite the Comanches' teachings, you said you remembered your mother's beliefs about God?"

"I think so." Gathering his thoughts, he ran his hand over the back of his neck as he glanced at the vertical, weathered cliffs. "My earliest memories are so vague. I'm not sure if I recall her teachings or God's. I've just always found Him in nature."

"*God's* teachings?" Cocking her head at an angle, she scrunched her nose.

"God's never been a concept or an idea. He's always been a quiet knowledge. He's always *been*." He paused, struggling to put his innate thoughts into words. "Sometimes, I wonder if I don't remember Him from before I was born."

She dipped her head, concealing her features.

Is she mulling over my words or laughing?

"You say Comanches believe spirits dwell in mountains?" After glancing about the ravine, she peeked at the mountaintop. Then she gazed at him.

Her whiskey-colored eyes were as placid as a still lake reflecting a sunset's golden glow, and he took a deep breath, reassured of her interest. "They can lodge in any natural formation: springs, rocky outcrops"—he scanned the volcanic peaks in the distance—"but especially in high places like mesas or cliffs."

"Being here while you describe their beliefs, I almost find them plausible."

Her hushed voice and parted lips stirred him.

"Whatever the reason, this gorge has a sacred quality—I feel like I'm in a cathedral." She scanned the steep limestone cliffs dotted with paintings.

"You're not the only one." His gaze followed hers, focusing on the rock wall's pictographs. "Did you know they called this area Painted Comanche Camp?"

"Because of these rock paintings?" She studied the artwork.

"Comanches filled sacred places with drawings of their world and their beliefs." He nodded. "If you know where to look, you can find them on canyon walls or in hidden niches of rock formations—even along Limpia Creek on the trunks of cottonwood trees."

"Really?" Her eyes danced. "Show me."

As her face lit up in an elfin grin, Ben loosened his knees' grip on Althea, and his boots momentarily slipped in his stirrups as he wavered between yielding to her request and protecting her. *We're close to the Comanche War Trail—too close.* The trail was a crisscrossed web of diverging paths, sometimes a mile wide. Good sense told him to skedaddle before the Mescaleros spotted them, but her eager gaze tempted him. Wavering, he glanced at the long shadows. *Too risky*. He shook his head. "It's late." Already regretting his decision, he repositioned himself in the saddle. "How about another day?"

On their ride back, Ben saw a cloud of dust on the horizon, and he broke into a cold sweat. "Race you to the fort." Keeping his tone light, he winked. "And I'm giving you fair warning, unlike *some* people I know. On the count of three. One…"

Her eyes flashed. Then laughing out loud, she spurred her horse and took off at a full gallop.

Chuckling, he caught up and kept abreast until the fort was in sight. Then glancing over his shoulder, he saw the dust cloud fade in the distance. Stifling a sigh, he slowed his pace to let the horses catch their breath.

"Give up?"

Her eyes challenged his. He swallowed a smile.

"Then why did you slow down?" Her eyes narrowed. "And why do you keep looking behind us?"

"I spotted a small party of Apaches." The danger past, he saw no need to maintain the charade.

"So, you let me think our escape was a race?" She leaned back, her whiskey-colored eyes squinting against the low afternoon sun. "And I believed you."

"The important thing is we're safe." He searched her face. "Nothing wrong with trusting. Just depends on who you put your faith in…" Then keeping her in his peripheral vision as they rode side by side, he continued scanning the horizon for Mescaleros.

"Are you going to the Harvest Ball?"

Though she spoke without looking, apparently more absorbed in the passing scenery than his answer, her question caught him off guard. "Hadn't given the matter any thought." Too uncomfortable to admit the truth, he hedged.

"You should." She spun her head toward him. "The Harvest Ball is always fun and so festive with pumpkins and hay bales."

Her voice bubbly, she spoke rapidly. Her eyes sparkled and gleamed as her face warmed into a smile.

"Then there's the dancing. Lots and lots of dancing."

"You like to dance?" He studied her.

"Love it." Her honey-brown eyes flashed. "Do you?"

Now what? Admit I've never set foot on a dance floor? As he pulled back his head, he pushed his shoulders forward. His chest muscles tensing, he took a deep breath. At the thought of interacting socially, he felt a trickle of perspiration roll down his back. *I've been less afraid going into battle. What do I say?*

****

Outside the stables the next day, Ben caught Tom as he was mounting his horse. "I've got a favor to ask."

"Shoot." Taking his foot from the stirrup, he turned toward Ben.

"Do you—"

The blacksmith's hammering interrupted.

Ben raised his voice. "Do you know how to dance?"

"I must not have heard you." Tom shielded his eyes from the sun. "Did you just ask me to dance?"

"No." Ben gave a sheepish laugh. "I'm asking if

you know how to dance, or if you could steer me toward someone who does."

"You've never learned?" Eyeing him, Tom frowned.

"Only from Comanches." Ben shrugged. "I haven't a clue how to act on a dance floor."

"Let me guess. You want to learn to dance in time for the Harvest Ball." Tom smirked. "Any particular reason?"

"Even if I had one, it'd be none of your business." His cheeks burning, Ben turned away, grumbling. "Never mind. Sorry I asked."

"Don't go off half-cocked. You took me by surprise is all. Give me a minute to think." Tom ran his hand across his face. "Come by my quarters tonight, say after seven."

Ben did a double-take. *Is he laughing up his sleeve?*

At four past seven, Tom's wife opened the door, and Ben stepped back involuntarily. "Mrs. McIntyre...I didn't expect to see you."

"I *do* live here, you know." She rolled her eyes.

"Of course." Ben forced an awkward chuckle. "Is Tom home?"

Wearing a sneer, she stood back and held the door wide. Then she led the way to the front room, where Tom was pushing back the parlor furniture as their young daughter and son stood watching, wide-eyed.

"You said you wanted to learn to dance, didn't you?" Tom grinned.

Ben gave a terse nod, unsure what he wanted now, other than to do an about-face and escape.

"Then help me roll back this carpet." Tom lifted

the rug's edge. "Grab the other end."

A few minutes later, they cleared a small dance floor in the center of the room.

"What do you have in mind?" Ben looked from face to face, unsure what to expect next.

"You'll see." Tom turned toward his son. "Got your harmonica, Travis?"

Nodding, the boy took the mouth organ from his pocket.

"Can you play 'Home on the Range'?"

"Sure, Pa." Nodding in time to the beat, the boy played the tune.

Tom took Sarah in his arms and spun her around the small area. "See how we're moving our feet?"

"Sort of." Opening his eyes wide, Ben went cold.

"One, two, three. One, two, three." Sarah called out the time to the music.

Her counting helped him feel the beat, and he studied their steps as they dipped and swayed.

When the song ended, Tom gave his lithe wife a polite bow and turned toward him, offering his wife's hand.

"Now you try."

Truth be told, she scares me. Ben dropped his jaw. With a gulp, he recalled Sarah's cool reserve in the past and her actions that morning, but under Tom's watchful eyes, he nodded.

Shoulders rigid, she returned a sneer as she held up her right hand.

When he did not make a move, she lifted a brow and beckoned him with her left hand. Then she rolled her eyes.

Is Tom blind? Doesn't he see his wife's

disapproval?

"You have to put your left arm around Sarah's back. Hold her right hand in yours."

Ben couldn't ignore her haughty smirk or the irritated lift of her brow as he absorbed the directions, but he stepped toward her. Scarcely touching her hand, he stood at arm's length as he put his left arm about her.

Sarah stiffened, and her eyes threw daggers at her husband, but she did not pull away.

"Go ahead, Travis." Tom rolled his hand. "Play 'Home on the Range' again."

The boy broke into the tune.

"One, two, three. One, two, three." Sarah called out the measure.

After several false starts, Ben stepped on Sarah's toe, making her cry out.

"Mrs. McIntyre, I'm so sorry."

Grumbling under her breath, she gave him a simper for a smile.

"Don't stop." Tom clapped his hands, reinforcing the beat. "Go on."

Ben took a deep breath as though preparing for battle. Again, he took her right hand in his, but this time with a bit more authority. He put his left arm around the small of her back and stepped in time to the music.

"That's the way." Tom turned toward his son. "Keep playing, Travis." Then he held out his left hand toward his daughter.

Ben watched the girl bashfully approach her father like a miniature lady.

Her eyes wide, Emily accepted his hand.

Ben listened to the music with one ear and Sarah's counting with the other. After several spins around the floor, he forgot about his feet and discovered he was dancing.

When Tom signaled Travis to end the music, Ben and Sarah were laughing and breathless.

"Thank you, Mrs. McIntyre. I appreciate your being such a good sport." Her face warmed into a gradual, almost begrudging smile.

"Call me Sarah." She glanced at Tom. "I think he's catching on."

"If I am, you're both the reason." Ben smiled at his teachers.

"Let's try this one more time, but let's trade partners." Tom winked at his wife as he gave his daughter's hand to Ben. "Once more, Travis," he called.

When the music started, Ben began dancing with a girl not much larger than Mariana. Afraid he might crush her feet, he held her gently as the doting parents looked on, smiling.

Several spins around the floor later, Tom held up his hands. "That's enough 'Home on the Range' for one night, Travis." He turned toward Ben. "Think you have the gist of it?"

"Thanks to you and your family, I do." Confidence restored, he nodded.

"What prompted you to learn how to dance?" Sarah eyed him.

Ben debated whether to tell the truth, anxious she might twist his words into gossip. But instead of her previous smirk, she smiled, and her eyes crinkled at the corners. "I want to learn for someone else, who likes to dance."

"I see…" She glanced at Tom, giving him a deep nod before turning back to Ben. "Then we'll need to practice again before the Harvest Ball."

"Thank you, Sarah." Ben did a double-take. Grateful for her support, Ben returned her smile with one of his own. *But even with practice, will I make a fool of myself on the dance floor?*

Chapter 6
Madrones

Two days later, Cadence ran into Ben at the stables. "Were you planning to visit Lupe and Mariana anytime soon?"

He shook his head. "Why?"

"Sarah gave me two dresses her daughter outgrew. She thought they might fit Mariana."

"Really?" His eyes opening wide, he raised his brow. "How considerate."

"Would you have time later to escort me to their camp?" She flashed her most persuasive smile.

"I'm off duty." He answered quickly.

"How about in ten minutes?"

Watching Ben approach with the saddled horses, Cadence gathered the clothes and rose from her seat on the porch's bottom step. "That was fast." She gave him a playful smile as she tucked the bundle in her saddlebags.

"Didn't want to keep you waiting." He returned her smile as he held her horse still.

She mounted from the bottom step. Perched astride her saddle, she was taller than Ben. Studying him from this new perspective, she noted his thick, dark hair, dancing eyes, finely chiseled face, and symmetrical bone structure—and she caught her breath. *He's handsome from any angle.* Then remembering her manners, she smiled. "Thank you for escorting me, especially on such short notice."

"My pleasure." He gave a nod.

Taking a different route to the creek, she rode past the community milk pen, where enlisted men's wives milked the cows, while several soldiers sat with rifles, scanning the horizon for Apaches. A mile out, a gnarled, blue-green tree growing out of what appeared to be sheer rock caught her attention. With little else around it, the bristly evergreen stood out against the chaparral backdrop. "Is that some variety of pine?"

"Piñon."

"The kind that grows pine nuts?" She blinked.

"The same." His hat dipped as he nodded. "Do you want to pick some?"

"Yes. I love pine nuts." She squinted, trying to remember what her grandmother had told her. "But don't they need to be processed some way?"

"They do." He nodded. "But they're easy to harvest. Just gather the green cones." He reined his horse toward the tree. "Let them dry for about three weeks in a sunny window. Then crush the pinecones to release the seeds."

"That's all?" Her pitch rose at his easy directions.

"You don't need a sheepskin to harvest pine nuts…just a lot of elbow grease to shell them."

Chuckling, she glanced at her saddle bags, bulging with clothes. "But where can we carry them?"

"Put them in my saddle bags. I have plenty of room."

After picking enough pinecones to fill his bags, she wiped her sticky hands on a handkerchief, but the pitch would not come off. *No matter. I'll wash them in the stream*. She remounted her horse and continued toward the camp.

"Three weeks to dry…" She thought of the church's upcoming event and her grandmother's recipe for Honey and Pine Nut Tarts. "Maybe they'll ripen in time for the bake sale auction."

A half hour later, Mariana greeted them, smiling and chattering as she led them to Lupe.

Cadence rinsed her sticky hands in the stream's sun-warmed water. The dust washed off but not the pitch. She sighed. *I'll have to wait until I get back and use Grandmother's remedy—cooking oil.* Picking up the bundle by the string only, she handed the clothes to Lupe, while Ben translated, explaining the outfits were for Mariana.

The girl's eyes flashed.

"Try them on," Cadence urged with a smile. "See if they fit."

Holding the clothes to her chest, the girl posed before dashing inside the tent.

"*¿Café y pan de maíz?*" Cups in hand, Lupe gestured toward the campfire.

"Cornbread?" She glanced at the woman. "How did you make bread without an oven?"

Lupe brought over the cast-iron skillet and demonstrated, while Ben explained. "I set the pan directly over the campfire's hot embers and place more hot coals on top its flat lid. That way, the bread bakes evenly." She removed the lid to show them and then served the slices.

When Cadence inhaled the fresh cornbread's familiar aroma, she detected an unusual nutty scent. She bit into the crumbly bread, slowly chewed it, and smiled. "This tastes like a sweet cornbread. What's that subtle flavor?"

"Mesquite meal. It makes the corn meal go further."

"Where did you get it?" She did a double-take.

Ben translated. "I ground mesquite beans on a makeshift metate of flat rocks."

"Amazing." She shook her head in wonder.

"My sons spotted a band of Mescalero Apaches when hunting." Lupe spoke in Spanish and caught Ben's gaze as she poured the coffee.

"Have they come near your camp?" He stiffened.

"No, but I don't feel safe here, anymore. The camp is beautiful but vulnerable. We want to go home and rebuild."

When Ben shared Lupe's conversation, Cadence caught her breath as her chest tightened. "When are you leaving?"

"*Mañana.*"

As worried for the Rodriguez family's safety as she was disappointed at their departure, she stifled a sigh. Even if they had to communicate through Ben, she was fond of Lupe and Mariana. *And him.* Pressing together her lips, she grimaced. She enjoyed these excuses to go horseback riding. Now, she couldn't justify her jaunts through the mountains.

Mariana ducked out of the tent, wearing one of the dresses. Beaming and chattering in Spanish, she pirouetted, letting the skirt swing around her.

"It fits you perfectly." Cadence needed no interpretation for Mariana's obvious delight.

The girl hugged her. "*Gracias.*" Then calling over her shoulder, she scurried back inside to try on the other dress.

She watched the retreating figure and sighed. *Yes, I'll miss these little adventures.*

"Is anything wrong?"

"No." Embarrassed at him catching her daydreaming, she shook her head. Then honesty prevailed. "But I'll miss Mariana and Lupe…and I'll miss…" She paused, wanting to express her thoughts but afraid to say too much. "Coming here."

"So will I." His gaze caught hers and held it a beat.

"*¿Más café?*" Lupe held the pot, ready to pour.

The woman's words interrupted her reverie, and holding out her cup, Cadence inhaled the coffee's crisp, smoky scent. "*Sí, por favor.*"

Several minutes later, Mariana emerged from the tent, wearing the other dress and a wide grin. Her dark eyes shining, she flicked her skirt's hem back and forth.

Cadence, recognizing the moves from a visiting dance troupe, clapped and cheered as the girl imitated Mexican folk dancers. The colorful Tejano culture fascinated her.

Mariana threw her arms around her and squeezed. "*Muchas gracias.*"

When the time came to say goodbye, she turned toward Ben with a sigh. "How do you say, 'Be safe'?"

"*Cuidate.*"

She repeated the word as she hugged her friends goodbye, wanting to do more. After she rode out of sight, she turned toward him. "Think my father could spare an escort for the family?"

"You could ask…" He raised his brow.

"But…"

"He isn't likely to have enough soldiers to man the

fort and subposts, escort mail coaches, construct telegraph lines, *and* spare an escort for the Rodríguezes."

The labor shortage again. She considered his words as she rode, but no solutions came to mind.

A half-mile later, she noticed a tree's twisted trunk. With its glossy green leaves, shiny red bark, and red blobs suspended from the branches, the tree stood in sharp contrast against the surrounding dusty-green vegetation. "That tree looks so out of place." Reflecting the afternoon sunlight, its bark gave off a magical, orange glow. "What kind is it?"

"Madrone. Want a closer look?" He reined his horse toward the tree.

As she rode nearer, more details came into focus. The red blobs proved to be clusters of plump berries hanging from the branches. "The berries look like cherries, but they're in clumps like bunches of grapes. Are they edible?"

"Yup, try some—but be sure they're ripe."

"Why?" Pausing mid-reach, she watched his response. "Are the green ones poisonous?"

"No, but they can upset your stomach." He shook his head. "And *overripe* ones can ferment and make you tipsy if you have too many. The red ones are the sweetest and juiciest."

She reached high overhead to pick the reddest berry she could find. Cautious, she sniffed the fruit as she fingered its slightly bumpy texture. "Smells like licorice." Then nibbling, she smiled at the berry's sweet-tart flavor and reached for another. "But it tastes something like blueberries."

"Some Indians consider the madrone sacred."

"Why?" His words caught her imagination, and she sat back in her saddle.

"They believe when their ancestors survived the great flood, they tied their canoe to a madrone tree high on a mountaintop."

"A kind of Noah's ark story." She smiled at the ironic resemblance.

"In a way. They respect the tree—revere it—and won't burn it for firewood."

"It has such a curious trunk and branches." She trailed her fingertips along the tree's peeling, paper-thin bark and spiraling boughs.

"Those are the reasons Indians think the madrone tree's a wise teacher." The corner of his lips rose in a half smile.

"What do you mean?"

"See how its branches twist?" He gestured toward the distorted boughs. "They bend and change direction, competing with nearby trees for sunlight. That struggle shows us to reach for what we want. Besides growing in new directions, the madrone teaches us to shed the old, so the new can grow." He peeled off a small tab from the tree's bark.

"Not just beautiful, the madrone holds secrets for those wise enough to see." Nodding, she looked at the tree from a new perspective. "How clever."

"Like some women."

Was that a back-handed compliment? She spun toward him to read his expression.

"Or horses." He patted his mare's neck. "I've learned many of life's lessons from Althea."

"Your horse is as clever as a woman…or a tree…?" Squinting, she peered at his face. "How so?"

"For one thing, Althea's taught me self-control. For each of my actions, she has a reaction. A sensitive mare won't put up with thoughtless behavior."

"You catch more flies with honey than vinegar." Swallowing a grin, she asked tongue-in-cheek, "What else has Althea taught you?"

He stared at the horizon. After a moment, he ran a calloused hand through his chin-length, dark, wavy hair. "Patience." He turned back. "Tolerance is the key to any good relationship. Every new step, trick, or transition takes time. First, Althea must understand what I'm asking. Then, she has to agree to participate."

"How do you know what she feels?" Concern for a horse's state of mind was not taught at her riding school. *Is he broadminded, or is he discussing more than horses?*

"I watch her closely. If her nostrils are relaxed and her ears are forward, I know she's ready. If I rush through the process and don't "listen" to her language, she balks, which only delays any progress." He caught her gaze and held it several beats.

His steady, intent stare unsettled her, and she reached over to pat the horse's muscular shoulder. "She's a smart girl."

At the same moment, Althea stepped forward.

Cadence's fingertips grazed Ben's thigh, and she caught her breath.

He bristled as his gaze locked with hers. Then he inched closer, leaning into her space.

As if magnetized, she inclined her body toward his. *How will his lips feel on mine?* Eager to learn, she closed her eyes, parted her lips, and waited…

Moments passed.

"We'd better head back."

His words sounded gruff and strangled. Opening her eyes wide, she stared horror-struck. *Did I just make a fool of myself?* Huffing, she jerked the reins. "Fine," she called over her shoulder as she wheeled around her horse, dug her knees into its sides, and took off at a canter. *The sooner I'm home, the better.*

The ride home was silent except for the horses' hoofbeats and the blood pounding at her temples.

His horse overtook hers, and he rode abreast.

She stared straight ahead, fuming while she ignored him.

Halfway back, he rode behind her, single file.

Good. Let him eat my dust. Flushing as a fiery tingling crept up her neck to her cheeks and ears, she recalled a similar incident when she was eight. After dinner, her cousin told her to close her eyes and wait. He had a surprise—a special dessert just for her. Expectancy rising as she imagined one sweet treat after another, she waited at the table two—three—five minutes before she heard muffled snickers. Opening her eyes, she spotted her cousin and his friend doubled over with laughter. Then she spied the cat's gnawed, half-eaten mouse on a plate.

As the memories burned her cheeks, she imagined Ben laughing behind her back or, worse, later bragging what a fool he made of her. Back at the fort, she refused to meet his gaze and ignored his outstretched hand while she dismounted.

"I'll send over a man with the pine nuts."

"Thank you, lieutenant." Turning toward her quarters, she called the words over her shoulder.

"Ma'am."

From the corner of her eye, she saw him tip his hat, but still seething, she strode away without another word. When she entered her house, she saw James in the parlor, sipping lemonade with her parents.

His dark hair gleaming with Macassar oil, he jumped to attention the moment he saw her. Then, pausing only to smooth his chevron mustache, he rushed to her side. "Cadence, my dear, how I've missed you."

Her pride stinging from Ben's rejection, she appreciated his attention. Her pulse quickened despite her usual ambivalence, and she smiled, recalling the rumors of his proposal. Then she stared into his eyes, searching for affection, not affectation. *Does he really care for me, or is he just bucking for a promotion as my father's son-in-law?*

"Come sit beside me."

She hesitated as she compared his crisply pressed and pleated uniform with its gleaming officer's insignia to her own clothes, crumpled and dusty from the ride. *He looks like a dandy in his regalia.* But after Ben's rebuff, she found James' attention flattering. Sweeping back her windblown hair with hands stained red from picking berries and still tacky from the pinecones' sap, she groaned internally. *If only I'd had time to change or wash.*

He took both hands in his, but the moment he touched her sticky palms, he faltered. Fingers stiffening, he let go of one hand, while with the other, his grip slipped to her wrist.

Feeling grubby, she dug her fingernails into her palms, instinctively drawing away.

"Let me feast my eyes on you." Guiding her by her

wrist, he positioned her on the settee and seated her at an oblique angle, so she faced him as he gazed at both her and her parents.

For several moments, she complied, her back twisting at an uncomfortable angle. *What am I? His adoring lapdog?* Irritated at his manipulation, she turned toward her parents, keeping him in her peripheral view.

"How did you pass the time while I was gone?" After straightening his cuffs, he side-glanced but kept his gaze on her father, not her.

His inconsistent signals put her off-balance. She considered mentioning the Rodriguez family until she recalled his inhospitable behavior. She mentally listed her recent activities: picking wild plums, collecting pine nuts, tasting madrone berries and mesquite cornbread, riding astride in her split skirt, and racing on horseback. *But he'd probably disapprove.*

"Cady's been helping the refugee family by taking them supplies."

She shot her mother a grateful smile for deftly keeping the conversational ball rolling.

"Oh?" James pulled back his head as his brow arched. "Riding unescorted?"

"An officer always accompanied me." Not caring for his overbearing tone, she shrugged like a horse shaking off a fly.

"An officer…" His eyes narrowed. "Tom?"

She shook her head, bristling at his probing question.

"Michael?"

"No." Tired of his interrogation, she stifled an irritated sigh. "I fai—"

"Which leaves Lieutenant Williams." His upper lip stiff, James sneered. "Alone?"

"I fail to see how my escorts are any of your business." She gathered her skirts to stand.

"Now, Cadydid." With her teacup poised midair, her mother curled her lips into a smile. "I'm sure James' one concern is your welfare. You must forgive an impetuous young man in matters of the heart."

Cadence groaned inwardly. *Two for two, Ben and now James. Am I the one who's disagreeable?* She sat back, chastised. "Maybe you're right, Mother." Forcing a smile and a change of attitude, she turned toward James. "How was your patrol? Did you see any Apaches?"

"No." He shook his head. Then, he caught her father's gaze. "They avoid escorted mail coaches, preferring to attack unprotected ranches instead."

"You found evidence of raids?" The older man leaned forward, his gaze intent.

"Yes, sir, we did. On the way back, we saw two burned ranches." James hesitated as he glimpsed the women and then looked at the captain. "We buried the dead."

"I see." The captain glanced at his family and snorted. "I'll read your report in the morning."

"Scalped?" Imagining the worst scenario, Cadence stated the word more than asked.

James grimaced before nodding.

"Is the area safe for settlers?" Her pulse quickening, she recalled the band she and Ben outran, and she thought of Mariana and Lupe.

"Hard to say whether one place is safer than another." He spread his hands. "War parties still roam the area."

"I should warn the Rodriguez family." Her fingers trembling, she gathered her skirts.

"Only the Apaches know where they'll strike next." He grabbed her wrist.

She pulled away from his controlling grip and perched on the settee's edge. Appalled at his rough behavior, she debated whether to go or stay. Though she resented his overbearing tactics, she had to agree with his logic.

"We're so glad you've returned safely, James." Her mother leaned toward him. "I understand…"

Disregarding the conversation, Cadence worried about Lupe and Mariana. *Should I slip away to warn them?* She glanced at James. *He wouldn't take me. Would Ben?* Then, remembering his rebuff, she felt her cheeks burn.

"Cadydid."

Her mother's voice cut through her thoughts. "Yes?"

"Aren't you feeling well? You look feverish."

"No, I'm fine." Cadence pressed her hands against her warm cheeks.

"Enough talk of Apaches and war parties."

James' thin smile was as patronizing as it was pompous. Rolling her eyes at his condescension, Cadence huffed.

"I forget ladies' delicate constitutions."

She curled her lip. "What a ridicu—"

"Which comes from being a bachelor." Her mother flashed a broad smile. "Of course, you can't fathom ladies, James. You're still unaccustomed to the company of the fair sex. The remedy for that condition is taking a wife."

The perfected product of gentility, her generation tolerates narrow-minded views of women. Her toes curling, she cringed at her mother's reaction.

But James chuckled at her banter.

Then, she saw her mother's intervention for what it was. *Sidestepping an argument, she outmaneuvers him, and he's oblivious.*

Her mother caught her gaze with a subtle lift of her brow.

With a newfound respect, Cadence recognized the discreet message as her mother kept smoothing the guest's ruffled feathers, and suddenly she understood. *What a crafty fox...* Stunned by the skillful evasion of a clash of wills, she slumped back against the settee, speechless.

Her mother gave the faintest of nods.

She returned the acknowledgment with a warm smile. Then she glimpsed James. *But do I want her to encourage this peacock?*

Chapter 7
Mescalero Apaches

The next morning, Ben read James' report of the burned-out ranches and scalped settlers at the officers' meeting. *With the Rodriguez family planning to return to their homestead, I'd better warn them.* He rushed through his morning tasks, and when he went off-duty at the noon Mess Call, he asked the captain for a pass.

Maybe Cadence would like to go along. Then sniffing at the unlikelihood, he saddled Althea and rode alone.

The madrone tree's red bark caught his eye, stirring memories of their near kiss. As he repositioned himself in the saddle, he groaned. *What was I thinking? Bad enough she's the captain's daughter—cultured and educated out East—but she's West's woman, and he outranks me.*

"Where's Cadence?"

Still lost in thought as he approached the camp, he flinched at Mariana's greeting. Like a slap in his face, he winced at the familiar sting of being the unwelcome intruder, but he covered his disappointment with a smile. "Hello to you, too."

"Hello, Uncle Ben." Mariana's eyes twinkled.

"*Uncle* Ben?" Her unexpected nickname boosted his spirits. "That's better."

"Isn't Cadence with you?" She looked behind him.

"She—" He hesitated before fibbing. "—had other duties."

"Oh." A shadow passed over Mariana's face, but a smile quickly replaced it. "We're going home today."

"That's what I want to talk over with your family." He dismounted and handed her the reins. "Would you water Althea?"

"*Sí.*" Her eyes twinkled.

He waited until she was out of hearing before he gathered the Rodriguez family. "An Apache war party attacked two ranches south of the fort, scalping the men." He met Lupe's gaze. "They tortured and raped the women."

The light behind her cataracted eyes faded. Shoulders slumping, she glanced in the direction her granddaughter took the horse.

"We've seen Apaches here, too." Saddling the mule, Juan tightened the cinch. "Who knows where they'll strike next?"

Nodding, his two brothers grumbled.

"We appreciate all you've done." Juan adjusted the bridle. "But after we rebuild, adobe walls will be better protection than canvas flaps."

"A cabin might shield you better from the sun but not from flaming arrows." Ben used his most persuasive argument. "For now, you're safer here, close to the fort."

"We want to go home." Lupe planted her feet in a wide stance.

"If you're hell-bent on leaving, the least I can do is escort you." Ben appraised their burdened mules. "And maybe carry some of your supplies in my saddlebags." He and the family backtracked to the fort and then headed south toward the arid plains. When the mules kicked up dust along the caliche trail, Ben tied his bandanna over his mouth and nose. Away from the creek, few trees dotted the landscape, but tall agave stalks stood as lonely sentinels reaching to the sky, the desiccated remains of the plants' solitary blooms.

Juan and his brothers lashed together several stalks, fashioning them into a crude travois. After unloading one of the mules, they strapped its burden on the makeshift sled and hitched the travois to the animal. Then, they collected more agave stems and bound them to the sled, until the mule hauled a heaping bundle to their ranch.

"Why collect these dried stalks?" Ben had often eaten the baked green stalks, but he was unfamiliar with the use of the dried stems.

"They're a good building material," said Juan. "We'll make a corral for the mules with the first batch. Then, we'll line the rafters of our adobe house with the next."

As he mopped his brow, Ben nodded, admiring his resourcefulness. Mid-afternoon, he arrived at the remote, burned-out ranch. An eerie reminder of what had been a home, the derelict adobe brick fireplace rose above the smoke-stained rubble. Little else remained.

The raspy, drawn-out hiss of a black vulture drew his attention as it swooped overhead in a dubious welcome. For an instant, neither he, nor anyone else moved or spoke.

Lupe gazed at the ruins with silent tears running down her wizened cheeks. Then, she blew her nose, wiped her eyes, and assigned chores.

Moved as much by her strength of character as her

loss, Ben respected her resolve. Then without warning, his earliest memories assaulted his senses, and he stared at the adobe shell without seeing. Instead of the wreckage before him, he envisioned Comanches setting fire to his parents' homestead and murdering his family. The imagery all too real, he smelled the smoke, heard his mother's screams amid the war whoops, and swallowed the bitter metallic taste of his fear.

Taking deep breaths to dispel his revulsion, he suppressed the images. Then he turned from the ruins, glancing instead at the sun's angle. *Should be enough daylight to help them set up the tent and fasten the agave stalks into the mules' corral.* When the afternoon's heat subsided and the sun dipped in the west, he shared a hasty taco dinner with the Rodriguez family before starting back to the fort.

"Thank you for your help." Lupe gave him a tight hug.

"Come back and visit us." Juan clapped him on the back, while his brothers shook Ben's hand.

"Goodbye, Uncle Ben." Mariana pulled him toward her as she stood on tiptoe and kissed his cheek.

"*Adios.*" He mounted Althea and was about to rein her toward the fort.

"Tell Cadence I miss her."

Her voice stilled his hand on the reins. His chest contracted as if all the air squeezed out.

"*Vaya con Dios.*" Lupe waved goodbye.

Ben turned in the saddle to wave back, when the familiar pangs of isolation gripped him. As the family settled in for the night, their campfire burning cheerfully in the gloaming, he was the drifter moving on—the outsider looking in. Never belonging, he was always alone. Then wary of the long shadows and the threat of Apaches, he spurred Althea toward the fort. *Will I ever belong?*

****

Ben was tired, sore, and sweaty as he rode into Fort Davis. Taking a shortcut through the back alleys of Chihuahua—the Mexican section of town—he spotted a familiar figure on the back stairway of the What Cheer House and Saloon. *James...*

His arm slung around a saloon girl's waist as the two descended the wooden steps, James laughed at something she said. Then he swatted her behind and lit a cigar, its tip glowing in the shadows.

Ben swallowed hard. *With his chest puffed out, West looks like a bantam rooster leaving the hen house and crowing over his conquest. How does someone like him win a woman like Cadence? What's he got?* A sniff passing for a dry laugh, he answered his question—a West Point education and family connections. Feeling sorer and wearier than before, Ben clicked to his mare, urging her on.

Though exhausted when he reached the fort, he brushed Althea's coat and picked her feet before he saw to his own needs. Crouching while he filed a chipped hoof, he stiffened as James rode up to the Captain's house, knocked on the door, and was welcomed inside. Disgusted and frustrated, Ben gave an impatient snort at the irony. He still trimmed Althea's hoof several minutes later, when from the corner of his eye, he saw Cadence approach. Her petite, gloved hand rested on James' arm. Behind them followed the captain and his wife.

Ben stifled an aggravated sigh. Though sweaty and

covered in grime, he took comfort in one thing. *I don't feel dirty*.

"When you're through grooming your horse, lieutenant"—James snickered—"you'd better take a dip in the water trough." A muffled chuckle followed.

Ben gently set down Althea's foot then he straightened his back. Coming to attention, he saluted the captain. "Good evening, captain. Ladies." He glanced at Cadence.

In the moment her gaze locked with his, she lost her grip on James' arm. Then jerking her chin, she edged closer to her escort and linked arms. "Good evening."

Her words brusque, she gave him a fleeting, tight-lipped smile. *Fine—if he's the kind of man she wants, let her have him*. His gaze shifting to West, Ben acknowledged him with a slight nod. "Lieutenant."

James' stare traveled up and down every inch of Ben's frame as he inspected Ben head to foot, eyeing the wet patches beneath his armpits and the caliche dust caked to his sky-blue trousers.

"Lieutenant, you're a disgrace to your uniform."

Cadence stiffened. Then her eyes narrowing, she tilted back her head and studied James. "Is that what you think of everyone returning from a dusty ride? Myself included?"

"Never." James smirked while the words tumbled from his lips. "You, my dear, are always as fresh as a morning glory."

Though the phrase had the ring of a compliment, Ben resented the man's glibness.

Cadence scowled. "As I recall—"

"If you'll excuse us, lieutenant." The captain's wife

flashed a taut smile. "We're meeting the Purdues to discuss the Harvest Ball. Have a good evening." With a nod, she strolled away on her husband's arm.

"Ma'am." Ben returned her nod and saluted the captain. Then he resumed filing his horse's hoof before retreat sounded for the evening. When he glanced up, he saw Cadence walk away, her arm linked with James'. Without warning, she glanced back over her shoulder, her eyes two smoldering embers.

What is she thinking?

****

His stomach growling, Ben adjusted his jacket's buttons as he hustled to the church social and bake sale auction. Just returned from a two-week patrol to Fort Quitman, he pushed his men, starting the ride back before dawn and not breaking for breakfast. He was famished.

The soldiers carried tables from the mess hall and placed them in a shady area of the parade grounds, where the ladies' guild set out lunch: fried chicken, pickles, freshly baked rolls, and sweet tea.

Picnickers lounged on blankets as they lunched and chatted with neighbors. Cadence sat with her parents and James beneath a large cottonwood, while the Purdues sat on the McShanes' right, and Ben joined the McIntyres, flanking the McShanes' left. The enlisted men sat nearby, the married ones with their families, and the single soldiers in small clusters.

Ben watched Cadence in his peripheral vision. *Wonder if she's over our falling-out?* She appeared fascinated with West's conversation, never taking her copper-flecked, amber gaze from his. Then without warning, she turned toward Ben, greeting his gaze with the same hungry-wolf look she wore at their first meeting. He caught his breath. Mesmerized, he held her gaze as he recalled the lonely nights on the trail.

As the meal wound down, the ladies cleared away the picnic food, transforming the table into a showcase of desserts.

"If I could have everyone's attention." The chaplain raised his arms over his head.

As if he were giving a benediction, he spoke in a sing-song vibrato. The chatter subsided. Ben sat up and listened.

"To raise money for the area's widows and orphans, the good ladies of our chapel have outdone themselves in creating culinary confections." He turned toward the assistant beside him. "Mrs. Ratichek, what's our first item to be auctioned?"

"Sally, isn't this frosting mocha?" Calling to one of the picnickers, she handed the chaplain a double-layer chocolate cake.

"It is." She smoothed errant wisps of hair into place. "I used coffee grounds in the cake and thinned the frosting with strong, fresh-brewed coffee."

"Who'll open the bidding on this coffee-chocolate cake?" The chaplain looked over the group.

Sally nudged her husband, Sam.

"Forty cents," he called.

Blushing, she pressed her lips together, barely containing a toothy smile.

"I'm bid forty cents." The chaplain scrutinized the assembly. "Do I hear fifty cents?"

"Fifty," called an enlisted man in the back.

"I'm bid fifty. Do I hear sixty?" The chaplain scanned the crowd. "Fifty, going once."

Sally turned to view the bidder. Then, she poked her husband in the ribs.

"Fifty, going twice. F—"

"Sixty cents," called Sam.

"I'm bid sixty cents. Do I hear seventy?" The chaplain caught the second bidder's gaze.

"Too rich for my blood." The soldier shook his head.

"Sixty cents going once." The chaplain scanned the group. "Sixty cents going twice. Sixty cents"—he glanced at the soldier one last time—"sold."

Sam paid for his cake and returned to his blushing spouse.

Cupping her fingers around her lips, the assistant whispered as she handed the chaplain the next dessert.

"I understand Miss McShane not only handmade these treats but collected and shelled the pine nuts herself." The chaplain held up the tarts for all to see. "What's my opening bid for her Honey and Pine Nut Tarts?"

"Ten silver dollars." James took the cigar from his mouth long enough to speak. Then wearing a smile, he reached into his pocket and pulled out the jangling coins.

A buzz went up from the crowd, then silence as all gazes turned toward him.

"Ten dollars…Now we're bidding!" His eyes wide, the chaplain beamed. "Ten dollars going once. Ten dollars going twice…"

As if anticipating no contest to the extravagant offer, the man's speech was rapid-fire. Ben took the bid as a challenge.

"Ten—"

"Eleven," called Ben if for no other reason than to give him a run for his money.

"Eleven dollars…Well, now…" The chaplain's eyes lit up at the counterbid. He glanced at James. "Do I hear twelve?"

All gazes followed the chaplain's.

James eyes were flinty and his face devoid of humor. "Twel—"

"Thirteen," Ben shot back, sensing the same adrenaline rush as in the heat of battle.

"I'm bid thirteen. Do I—"

"Fourteen." James chewed on his cigar.

All faces turned to watch the bidding match.

"Do I hear fif—"

"Fifty dollars." Enunciating clearly, Ben spoke in a deep, resonant voice.

The group gave a collective gasp.

"Did I hear right?" The chaplain gulped. "Did you say fifteen or fifty?"

"Fifty. Five-oh." Straightening so he stood at his full six-foot-three inches, he met the man's gaze as he calculated the sizable dint his bid would make on his savings.

"Fifty dollars going once." The chaplain peered at James. "Fifty dollars going twice…" His eyes narrowing, he hesitated.

James wore a scowl as he jutted out his chin and drew on his cigar.

"*Sold* to Lieutenant Williams for fifty dollars."

Swept up in the heat of the auction, Ben bid beyond his means. As he stepped forward to collect his tarts, he smiled, pleased with his prize. *Life's about choices.*

"On behalf of the widows and orphans, thank you for your generosity, son." The chaplain clapped him on the back as he collected the money and handed him the plate of tarts. Then he turned toward Cadence. "Your pastries have set a new fort record."

Blushing, she bobbed her head and acknowledged the chaplain with a curt smile.

Drops of perspiration forming at his temples, James puffed on his cigar as the smoke billowed about him.

Reminds me of the chimney of an open-throttled locomotive. Ben swallowed a smile as he resumed his place with the McIntyres. Then turning toward the captain's family, he offered the plate to Mrs. McShane. "I've plenty to share. Please help yourself."

"Thank you." She hesitated before choosing one. Then she cupped her hand around her lips.

He leaned forward, curious.

She spoke in a whisper. "Considering your bid's worth almost two weeks' salary, you paid a high price for my daughter's tarts."

"The money's going to a worthy cause, ma'am." He gave a cordial nod before presenting the plate to Cadence. "Would you care to sample your handiwork?"

She glanced sidelong at James. Then her eyes twinkled as her face warmed in a smile, and she selected a pastry. "Thank you."

Returning her smile, he leaned forward in a slight bow, catching the tarts' nutty, buttery aroma. Then, he offered the plate to the captain. "Can I interest you in a tart, sir?"

"No, thank you." The captain waved him off.

Ben acknowledged his gruff voice and abrupt snub

with a nod before holding out the plate to West. "Lieutenant?"

"Enjoy the fleeting taste of victory while you can, Williams."

Ben strained to hear his *sotto voce* words.

Scrambling to his feet, James turned in a formal bow to the McShanes. "If you'll excuse me, I must attend to other duties."

Ben passed the plate to the McIntyres.

"Well played." As she chose a tart, Sarah winked.

Tom gave him a thumbs-up before making his selection.

When the bake sale bidding ended, the soldiers quit the area and pitched horseshoes or played baseball.

The children wandered out of earshot, amusing themselves with marbles, jump ropes, or dolls.

Only the officers and their families remained.

"Would anyone care to hear the latest chapter of Anthony Trollope's *The Duke's Children*?" Cadence glanced at their faces.

Amid nods and assenting murmurs, the small group concurred.

Still seated beneath a shady tree, she took a magazine from her handbag and started reading aloud.

The sun backlit her hair, forming a silky, auburn halo. The speckled light filtered through the tree, highlighting her face, so she appeared to glow from within. Her cheeks—the color of cream and strawberries—rose in a smile as she glanced toward Ben from time to time, and her dancing honey-colored eyes cast a spell over him.

After she finished reading the serial chapter, she closed the periodical.

"Is that all?" Sarah turned toward the others. "I liked being lost in the Duke's world and don't feel like returning to the real world quite yet. Does anyone else agree?"

"Do you have anything else to read on this lazy Sunday afternoon?" Helen raised her brow. "Maybe a book of poetry?"

Cadence searched her handbag until she pulled out a slim volume. "How about Emily Dickinson?" At their nods, she paged through until she found a poem and read in a clear voice.

Ben recalled the first time she recited poetry at their chapel in the glen. Then as now, he listened—intrigued—and when the afternoon ended, he waited until the others left. "May I see you home?" He swallowed the sudden lump in his throat.

Her pupils dilating and her long lashes fluttering, she opened wide her gold-flecked eyes. Then her eyes narrowed to slits as a series of expressions swept across her face.

The seconds ticked slowly while the sound of children playing clapping games wafted on the breeze. "A sailor went to sea, sea, sea…"

"Whatever I said or did to upset you wasn't intentional." After three weeks of reflection, he spoke quickly, anxious to resolve their misunderstanding. "Believe me."

Facing him, she stared hard. Then, a smirk played along her lips. "What?"

Unsure how to interpret her expressions, he pushed on. "I never meant to offend you."

"I thought you…" She broke off with a laugh. "Maybe, I misinterpreted"—she gave him a slow smile—"something." Finally, her gaze met his in a smile, and she gave a crisp nod. "I'd like you to see me home."

With their disagreement apparently settled, he breathed a relieved sigh. Turning in unison, he walked in step with her, side by side, as they crossed the parade grounds. "I like listening to poetry." His mouth still dry, he swallowed. "Maybe because I'd never heard poetry until you recited that day at the glen, but I enjoyed your reading today."

"Like Sarah said, fiction—or poetry—sweeps you away to another time and place." A slight frown creased her brow. "How sad that you've never been introduced to poetry."

"Until now." Her empathy encouraged him, and on impulse, he reached for her hand.

She did not pull away.

Instead, he sensed a connection—as though they were reunited after a much longer separation than several weeks. Captivated, he stared into her fiery, amber eyes.

Only the raucous honking and cackling of ducks overhead broke the spell.

Glancing skyward, he saw the V-formation of migrating, green-winged teals, and a thought came to mind. "Poetry's like a flock of words, lifting you on its wings."

"I've never thought of words as wings to whisk you away." Her eyelids fluttering, she parted her lips in a slow smile. "If anything, I've compared them to stones, little crystals of thought."

Crystals. Her sparkling citrine eyes reminded him of two symmetrical crystals. *Where did I see twinned crystals?*

****

When Ben entered the library Saturday night, he took in the main room's festive changes. Transformed into an autumn wonderland for the Harvest Ball, the book-filled walls were trimmed with grapevine wreaths adorned with yellow-gold leaves, tiny gourds, and miniature ears of multicolored Indian corn. Pumpkins and flickering candles graced the fireplace mantel. Hay bales functioned as seating around the room's perimeter, while jack-o'-lanterns and bundled corn shocks in the corners completed the decor.

The cinnamon scent of spiced apple cider filled the air. Two groaning tables of sweet and savory tidbits lined one end of the large room, and the Tenth Infantry band played on an elevated platform at the other end. Couples waltzed around the room's center, while small groups clustered on the sidelines.

Freshly shaven and wearing his dress uniform, Ben was a blend of stress and anticipation. New territory for him, he had never attended a ball or waltzed in public, but he knew the basic dance steps. *Hope they're good enough.* Then spotting Tom, he joined him.

"Well, what do you think?" Tom gestured toward the waltzing couples.

"I've never seen the like. This Harvest Ball is impressive."

"The ladies have outdone themselves with the decorations"—he glanced at the heavy-laden tables—"and the refreshments." His eyes twinkling, Tom surveyed him. "How about you? Are you ready to enter the fray?"

"Other than dancing around your parlor or a

campfire, this kicking up my heels is all new." Ben gave a dry laugh. "Let's say I'm relatively prepared."

"Cadence looks fetching tonight in blue velvet." Tom nodded toward a group of young ladies across the floor.

Ben took in her tiny waistline and curvy silhouette despite her dress' lavish drapes, folds, and pleats. Her creamy shoulders were bare except for the auburn curls brushing seductively against them, and the midnight-blue ribbon choker at her neck contrasted against her glowing complexion. Unused to viewing a woman's exposed shoulders, arms, and neck, he caught his breath.

"And she's glancing this way." Tom nudged him. "Why don't you ask her to dance?"

"What would I say?" Crossing his arms, Ben went cold.

"Just say"—Tom's lips pursed in a suppressed smile—"may I have this dance?"

"I've faced men in battle and haven't broken out in a cold sweat, but this…" He gave a nervous laugh, expelling some of his tension.

"Welcome to 'civilization.' " Tom clapped him on the back.

Will I survive it?

Chapter 8
Harvest Ball

Cadence stood with a group of merchants' daughters—civilians she hardly knew, but young women of her own age—who enthusiastically assessed the eligible bachelors.

"Too bad he doesn't dance." Susan arched a brow when she spotted Ben. The weight of her upswept hair held in place with elaborate combs tipped back her head.

"Whyever not?" Another girl shot her a blank look, her loose curls flying as she spun toward her.

"My dear, haven't you heard?" Susan fanned herself. "He's a Comanche."

"Oh, my word. No…"

The clique turned in unison to stare.

"What a shame." Her hair piled high into a bun, a third young lady twisted one of the curly locks falling onto her shoulder. "He's so tall."

"And handsome." A girl with short, frizzed bangs smoothed the braided hair coiling around her head as she gawked.

Her jaw clenching and unclenching, Cadence prickled as the young woman with the bun tucked in an errant curl and hid a wicked smile behind her fan. *What's she smirking about?*

"But wouldn't dancing with a heathen be

exciting?"

Watching him, the girls giggled and snickered.

"He isn't Comanche. They simply raised him." An angry tingling crept up the back of Cadence's neck toward her cheeks. Gritting her teeth, she carefully controlled her tone. "He's really a gent—"

Susan hissed. "He's coming this way."

Cadence caught her breath as Ben crossed the room. Her pulse racing, she fixed her gaze with his.

"Cadydid." Emerging from nowhere, her father smiled. "If I don't ask you now, I fear I won't stand a chance competing against these young gentlemen."

His sudden appearance posed a dilemma. At his warm, paternal smile, she glanced away to gather her thoughts and saw Ben approach in her peripheral view. *Now what?*

"May I have this dance?" Her father held out his hand.

Arm's length from her, Ben pivoted ninety-degrees on the ball of his foot, turning to the nearest girl, and parroted her father's words. "May I have this dance?"

"Of course." Susan's lips parted in an O as she fanned herself, and her lashes fluttered as her eyes widened. "I'd be delighted."

What? Placed in the awkward position of choosing, Cadence made the only selection she could. Still she felt a mixture of guilt, remorse, and betrayal. She glared at him, her eye muscles tightening until she squinted through narrow slits. Then breaking eye contact, she turned toward her father with a smile and raised her voice for Ben's benefit. "I can't think of anyone I'd rather dance with than *you*."

As she waltzed, she peered over her father's

shoulder, keeping a close watch on Ben.

"You have a bee in your bonnet." He inspected his only child while he held her at arm's length. "Has your preoccupation anything to do with the rumors of James' proposal?"

His words captured her attention. Wrenching her gaze from Ben, she stared at the man who taught her to ride and encouraged—even applauded—her tomboy escapades as a child. Though she was not a male heir to carry on the family name or military tradition—or if truth be told, the son he probably would have preferred—she knew he cherished her. His love was implicit, and she had never doubted his affection. *But James' affection?* "I'm not sure." She lifted a shoulder in an indifferent shrug. As she danced, she studied Ben, who appeared to get on well with his partner. *Too well.*

"What aren't you sure about?" A crease formed between her father's eyes.

"Proposals, marriage, whether I'm ready…" She turned her head quickly, tossing her long, auburn curls over her shoulder. "Whether James is the one I want to marry"—her laugh was dry—"assuming the rumors are true."

A broad smile lifted his lips. "I happen to—"

"Would you mind if I cut in, sir?" Michael tapped her father's shoulder.

"Age steps aside for youth." Her father's smile was wide as he presented the lieutenant with Cadence's hand.

"Are you nervous?" Michael took her hand in his.

"Whatever do you mean?" Wrenching her attention from Ben and Susan, Cadence gave him a blank stare.

"Everyone on the post knows tonight's the night."

117

Michael grinned as he led her about the dance floor.

"How does 'everyone on the post' know my business?" His tongue-in-cheek tone annoyed her, and she jerked her chin, setting her curls flying.

"This fort's an outpost." His grin widened. "Everyone knows everyone's business, often before they do themselves…" He raised a brow.

His lopsided, self-satisfied smile irked her. She made small talk until the number ended. Then she gave Michael a polite, though curt, *thank you* and rejoined the group of merchants' daughters.

"He's so good looking." The girl with the short, frizzed bangs patted her hair into place as she ogled Ben.

"And such a graceful dancer." The young woman with the upswept bun sighed.

"My dear, you have no idea." Susan smiled behind her fan. "After waltzing with him, I wouldn't mind dancing the kipples…if you get my meaning." Winking, she hid behind her fan.

What a two-faced hypocrite. Cadence bristled at her whispered insinuations. Annoyed with him for asking Susan to dance and galled with her for first belittling and then gushing over him, most of all, Cadence was furious with herself for caring. Struggling between righteous indignation and green-eyed jealousy—between loyally defending him and squirreling him away for herself—Cadence lost her patience. "I'm surprised you'd give a 'heathen' a second glance, Susan…let alone fadoodle with one."

"Well…I never…" Susan leveled a frosty gaze toward her, whispering behind her fan to the others as they crowded around.

Cadence stepped away from the clique while she glimpsed Ben joining Tom and his wife. When the music began, he asked Sarah to dance, and the two whirled about the floor as easily as if they were practiced.

"My wife seems otherwise occupied." Tom approached her, wearing a wide smile. "Would you care to dance?"

"It'd be my pleasure." Despite his curious smile, she accepted his outstretched hand. Then as she put her left hand on his shoulder, she gestured toward Sarah. "Your wife dances beautifully."

"Doesn't she, though?" With a gleam in his eye, he glanced at the couple and grinned.

Once more, Tom waltzed her around the room.

Then, Ben tapped his shoulder. "Would you care to switch partners?"

"Delighted." Smiling, Tom passed Cadence to Ben as he reached for his wife's hand.

Sarah gave her a conspiratorial wink during the exchange.

Irritated, yet amused by the maneuvers, Cadence gingerly accepted Ben's hand, but the moment their fingers touched, static electricity bolted up her wrist and along her arm, making the downy hairs stand on end. Bolts of energy raced toward her shoulder, tingling and raising the hairs on the back of her neck. Then she shivered as the shock waves barreled down her spine, and butterflies tickled her stomach. She glanced at her hand in his. As if a part of her that had been lost was reconnected, the two melded into one.

Does he feel the connection, too? She gazed into his eyes and saw the same intensity. As he put his left hand on her waist, she responded with a light shudder. Dreamlike, she rested her hand on his shoulder, and off they danced as if they prepared for this moment all their lives. When the music's tempo increased, she held on tighter, dancing in perfect unison as her body pressed ever closer, instinctively responding to his subtle dips and sways. After making several rounds on the dancefloor, she turned toward him, breathless. "I didn't know you could dance."

"You mean waltz?" He chuckled. "I've joined in Comanche dances around campfires most of my life."

Laughing, she let herself be swept away in yet another dizzying round.

When the music ended, she led him to a nearby bookshelf, where she had left her purse. "I hoped to see you tonight." She took a slim volume from her handbag. "I have something for you."

His jaw dropped, his eyes opened wide, and his lips parted in an O.

"It's Emily Dickinson's poetry." She pressed the book into his hands.

"Thank you." He thumbed through the poetry, slowly turning each page. Then, his eyes dewy, he gazed into her face. "No one's ever given me a gift like this."

"High time someone did." Endeared by his appreciation, she smiled.

"By chance, I have something for you, too."

After slipping the volume into his inner vest pocket, he took out a glinting crystal.

He wore a shy smile, as though unsure if such a gift were appropriate.

"What kind of stone is this?" She held the mineral

to the light, twirling it in her fingers to better view the two glittering crystals grown into one.

"Twinned-crystal calcite." He gazed into her eyes. "Since you compared words to crystals of thought, this stone reminded me of you."

"It's beautiful, like two enormous diamonds dancing together. Thank you." She had the urge to stand on tiptoe and kiss his cheek, but, at the last moment, she remembered they were in full view of everyone. Glancing about the crowded room, she shrank from the people's watchful gazes, and the moment passed. Instead, she pressed the stone against her heart. "I love crystals. Where did you find it?"

"In the Davis Mountains, near the Rodriguez family's ranch." His Adam's apple bobbed as he swallowed. "Maybe sometime, you'd like to go rock hunting with me?"

Interested in more than military maneuvers and promotions, he's so refreshing. She looked into his dark eyes, wishing she could read his thoughts. *He isn't like anyone I've ever known. What goes on in his mind?* Still studying him, she nodded. "I'd enjoy hunting for stones."

"You don't mind, old boy, do you?" Just as the next waltz began, James appeared. Holding out his kidskin-gloved hand to Cadence, he stepped in front of Ben.

Not phrased as a question, his tone was a command—a senior officer speaking to a subordinate. Catching her breath, Cadence stiffened.

Ben's dark eyes flashed. Then his features slackened, and he stepped aside. "Of course not, sir."

She wanted to stay with Ben, but courtesy

demanded she dance with James—despite his unwelcome intrusion. "Thank you again." Clasping the stone, she caught Ben's gaze.

His lips pressing together, Ben came to attention and returned a curt bow.

"What's in your hand?" James took her in his arms.

"Nothing." She stiffened. Wrenching her hand from his, she broke away from his clutch and tucked the stone in her purse.

"So, the redskin learned to dance, has he?" James sneered at Ben as he again took her in his arms and swirled her across the dance floor.

"He isn't a Comanche." Though she kept in step, she distanced herself, turning her body at an oblique angle and holding him at arm's length. "He was just raised by them."

"Maybe that's where he learned to dance…whooping around the campfire." James snickered.

"I wish you wouldn't say those things." Breaking from propriety as much as his grasp, she stopped mid-step and shook off his hands, forcing the other dancers to swerve around them. "He's a graceful dancer and a gentleman…"

"Come now, Cadence." Again taking her in his arms, he smiled. "Let's not waste the evening disagreeing. Let's talk of pleasanter topics."

Galled by his prejudice toward Ben, she fumed as the hairs prickled at the back of her neck. *What do I do? Argue? Walk away?* To avoid making a scene, she did neither. Instead, she let James guide her steps on the dance floor, while over his shoulder, she watched Ben rejoin Tom and Sarah.

Their heads close together, the three began an animated conversation. A moment later, Ben and Sarah started dancing.

"Mind if I cut in?" Tom approached and tapped James on the shoulder.

James' eyes narrowed, but then with a wide smile, he offered her hand as he backed away. "Of course not."

She and Tom had not gone halfway around the dance floor when Ben cut in.

Cadence chuckled at Sarah's mischievous smile as the two couples again switched partners.

The moment Ben's hand touched hers, the same energy pulsed through her as the first time. Electricity raced up her arm, sending pleasant shudders down her spine, and when she felt his arms about her, pressing her against him, she caught her breath.

Around the dance floor she twirled, clasping Ben ever closer as the tempo increased, again dancing in unison while her body moved with his.

Abruptly, the music stopped, and mid-spin, she came to a teetering halt. The momentum swayed her skirt, but she paid no attention. Still enveloped in Ben's arms and gaze, she stared back, wrapped in his spell.

"Ladies and gentlemen, my apologies for interrupting this waltz, but may I have your attention? I have an important announcement."

James' voice stole into her private world. The sound was faint, like a fly buzzing at the window. Forcing herself to break Ben's gaze, she watched as James unabashedly strutted across the band's raised platform toward her father.

Amid hoots and giggles from the dancefloor,

Captain McShane put up his hands.

A hush fell over the crowd. Their faces expectant, the group seemed to hold its collective breath.

"Cadence, dear, everyone at the fort expects us to marry, and we mustn't let them down." Addressing her from the raised platform, James chuckled as he glanced at the crowd. "When do you want to set the date?"

While the assembly listened for her answer, a deeper stillness descended on the dance floor.

Someone coughed.

The nerve. Her jaw and neck stiff with suppressed rage, she turned toward Ben, embarrassed almost as much for him as for herself. Then she shifted her gaze to James, her father, her mother, the grinning faces in the crowd, and back to James. *He didn't propose marriage. He issued an order and expects me to obey.* Her eyes narrowed as she regarded the room's beaming faces. *Military tradition is the reason behind his arrogance. Everyone* expects *me to accept the dashing West Point officer's proposal.*

"If anyone presumes to know my mind, he is sadly mistaken." As she straightened her spine, she spoke in a loud voice.

"Come now, Cadence, when's the joyful day?" Blinking, James gave a short snort of a laugh. "When shall I tell the chaplain to be ready?" He flashed a wide smile.

Does he expect me to swoon after gracing me with his bright smile? Knowing her mother's matrimonial sentiments, she avoided glancing her way. Then, she paused, deliberating her next words. "Though I've heard rumors, tonight is the first you've spoken of a proposal—and in such a public setting. I need time to consider, and I'll have to consult with my father—"

"Your father's already given—"

"*I'm sure*"—she held up a hand, none too courteously silencing him—"you wouldn't want me to make any rash decision we'd both regret…"

A beat passed, and then another.

James' eyes narrowed as he spoke through gritted teeth. "I'm waiting for your answer."

The room was so quiet, everyone seemed to hold their breath.

Then, Susan dropped her fan. As it clattered to the floor, the sound echoed in the stillness.

Not appreciating his dark tone, Cadence gave him a sour smile. "I'll have my answer tomor—when I've decided."

A rash of murmurs filled the room.

The gathered people looked from him to her, their heads turning in unison as if watching a tennis match.

Eyes bulging, neck veins pulsing, and his face purpling, James looked apoplectic.

"If you please, let's resume the waltz." Holding her head and spine erect, Cadence waved to the band leader. "I haven't finished this dance."

Whispered conversations buzzed about the room.

The band leader looked at Captain McShane.

His chin resting on his chest, he gave a slight nod and stepped from the platform as the music started.

"Are you sure you want to flout convention?" Ben raised his brow.

"Surer than I've ever been of anything in my life." She tossed her chin.

He laughed, took her in his arms, and began whirling her around the empty dance floor.

James stomped over to the group of young ladies, snatched the nearest girl's hand, and joined the waltz.

Couple by couple, the dance floor filled again, but the dancers' smiles turned to pursed lips, which changed to furtive whispers.

Guilt-ridden, she felt a gnawing distress as she glanced at the others. She sighed and gazed at Ben. "The party's mood has changed. I'm afraid I'm a killjoy."

"I, for one, am proud of you." His white teeth gleaming against his tanned face, he chuckled.

"Why?" She peered through her lashes at his admiring half-smile.

"Most people would have stooped under West's pressure, no matter how they wanted to respond. Standing up to him took courage."

"I couldn't let him order me about—dominate me." She huffed a sigh. "I didn't hear anyone ask anything. All I heard were commands couched as requests." She tipped her face toward him. "I'm not a broken-spirited horse to be hobbled."

"Breaking your spirit isn't possible." He held back his head and met her gaze. "You were born a lead mare—a trail blazer—and I mean those words as a compliment." The corners of his eyes crinkled in a smile. "You think for yourself and make your own decisions. Then once you make up your mind, you pin back your ears and stand your ground."

Me a trail blazer? Shoulders back and head high, she blinked. *Is that how he sees me?*

****

After the ball, Cadence stifled a frustrated sigh as she slouched in the parlor chair. She sipped a cup of tea that had grown cold during her father's lecture.

"You made a serious mistake tonight." Her father peered through narrow, squinting eyes. "Let's hope you haven't made an enemy, as well."

She wrinkled her nose at his cool, insistent stare.

"Don't you turn up your nose, young lady." He harrumphed. "James West is an accomplished officer, who graduated at the head of his class at West Point. You couldn't ask for a finer husband, and yet, you humiliate him in front of the entire fort. What is wrong with you?"

"What's wrong with *me?*" Sitting up straight, she thumped her chest and scoffed in disbelief. "You should be asking what's wrong with him commanding me to choose a wedding date. I heard no declaration of love or romantic proposal, just an order to be obeyed...*On. His. Cue.*" As her words resonated, she stood. "I'm not about to be bullied. If this mandate is how he 'asks' me to marry him, think how his 'manners' would deteriorate after the wedding."

"I can't reason with her." Her father threw up his hands. Then rising from his chair, he turned toward his wife. "She's your daughter. You talk sense into her." With a snort, he stomped off.

Mother sat motionless by the fireplace, her gaze distant as if deep in thought.

The only sound was the clock ticking on the mantel.

After several moments, she looked at Cadence, rose, and walked toward the sideboard's crystal decanters. "Would you like a glass of sherry?"

Surprised at the offer and unsure what to expect next, Cadence opened her eyes wide.

"I'll take your gaping stare as a yes." Her mother poured as she chuckled. Then, she handed her daughter a crystal glass. "Tonight's a turning point—a defining moment."

"Why? I've disappointed everyone." Shoulders drooping, she groaned. "Father's exasperated with me. James isn't speaking to me, and I crushed everyone's expectations." She took a deep breath. "I don't know what to do."

Neither smiling nor frowning, the older woman simply watched as she sipped the sherry.

"James never asked how I felt about marrying him." Uncomfortable with the silence, she peeked at her mother, expecting a rebuttal, but none came. "Everyone considers him a good match, but I don't think he's interested in marrying me—except to become Father's son-in-law. James wants to be his protégé—not my husband."

"Don't you think he loves you?" She lifted a brow.

Her mother's tone was more receptive. Still, she hesitated, unsure how to answer. "I don't know. We've never discussed anything to do with love or marriage."

"You seem to enjoy his company."

"He helped pass the time, but..." She struggled to think of one affectionate moment between them.

"How do you feel about him?" Head tilted, Mother pressed her lips together.

"I don't dislike him. I just don't love him, and..." With a frustrated sigh, she shrugged.

"And what?" The older woman's forehead creased.

"I think..." She glanced at her mother's face, debating whether to continue. *Or have I gone too far already?*

"You think what?" A shadow of a smile lifted her lips.

"Maybe James isn't the right one." Uncomfortable with discussing love and courtship with her mother, she squirmed. "Maybe someone else would be better suited."

"Anyone I know?" Her mother arched a brow. "The new lieutenant, perhaps?"

Butterflies fluttered in her stomach. "Maybe."

"Has he ever…?" The woman paused, pursing her lips.

Is she reaching for the right words?

Then, her gaze intent, she peered at her daughter. "Has he declared any feelings for you?"

Unable to meet her gaze, she glanced at the floor as she shook her head.

"What about you? Do you have feelings for him?"

Do I? Fixing her gaze on nothing, she thought aloud. "Ben isn't like anyone I know. After learning his background, I admire him for how far he's come." She thought of James acting as if she were his broken-spirited horse, while Ben called her a lead mare and trail blazer. She compared James turning away the refugees to Ben coming to their rescue. Recalling their excursions and conversations, she smiled as Ben's "flock of words" came to mind.

"He's kindhearted and considerate, yet even Father's commended him on his bravery in action." Her pulse quickening, she glanced at her mother. "He's clever. He knows where to find wild plums, pine nuts, pecans, and twinned-crystal calcite, and he's—"

"Handsome?" The woman's lips stretched into a smile.

"And hand…" Agreeing with a deep nod, she glanced into her mother's twinkling eyes and lost her momentum. *She always could trick me.* She struggled to suppress the smile flirting at her lips.

"And you like him?"

She bobbed her head in a terse nod.

"You remind me of something I've never told anyone." She scrutinized her daughter before taking a deep breath. "This secret is between you and me. Even your father doesn't know."

Her mother spoke with a wistful voice, and her eyes glowed, as if with a distant memory. Intrigued, Cadence leaned forward.

"Before I married your father, I also loved a determined young man." Her face dimpled into a smile. "But I chose your father because he was stable and dependable. Marrying him, I knew what lay before me, while my future with the other suitor would have been an uncharted course."

She loved another man? Looking beyond the gray at her mother's temples, the creases in her forehead, and the matronly set of her mouth, Cadence did a double-take trying to visualize her as a young woman in love. If a more youthful version did not emerge, the parallels between them did. *Mother faced a situation like mine. What else do we have in common?*

"Was the man a lieutenant?"

"No, he was a railroad superintendent." Her smile drooped. "My father couldn't imagine me marrying anyone who wasn't a West Point graduate—an officer and a gentleman. 'He won't amount to a hill of beans,' were his words."

"Whatever became of your railroader?" Nodding as

she sipped her cream sherry, Cadence recalled her maternal grandfather, a stiff-backed military man that she called *Sir*, never *Grandfather*.

"After I refused his proposal, he stopped calling." Her voice caught, and she cleared her throat. "But on lonely nights, when your father's away on missions, or when I wake early on misty mornings, I think of Andrew and wonder what life would have been like with him."

The remorse in her voice concerned Cadence. "You never heard of him again?"

"I said I never heard *from* him."

Confused, she jerked back her head to stare.

"Several years later, I heard *of* him." Eyes dancing, the older woman wore a crooked smile. "He invested in the oil business and became a millionaire."

"The irony." Scoffing, she shook her head at the story's bittersweet turn of events. "Do you...did you ever regret marrying Father?"

"No, I don't. I love your father—" Her gaze distant, her mother paused. "—but sometimes I do regret not marrying Andrew."

I'm meeting her for the first time. Looking through a new lens, Cadence examined the woman she had known all her life and gave her a sympathetic smile. Though the revelation saddened her, she was flattered to be her confidante.

Mother chose the safer path but lived with disappointment. As she met her mother's gaze in mute understanding, Cadence rose from her chair and gave her an impulsive hug. *How did I not see her quiet resolve?*

****

After church the next morning, as Cadence helped her mother set the table, a sharp rap startled her, and she opened the front door.

"I'm so happy for you." The feathers on her hat bobbing in tandem with her fluttery, birdlike movements, Flossie cooed. "When's the date?"

"A date for what?" Cadence maintained a calm voice as she led the guest into the parlor. Then, she glanced at her mother for support.

"Why—" Scoffing, Flossie paused. "—The date for your wedding, of course. When do you marry Lieutenant West?"

"I haven't set a date." *This news can't come as a surprise. She heard me refuse him last night.*

"You haven't?" Flossie's jaw dropped. Looking down her nose, she glanced at Helen before turning back. "My dear, you must reconsider Lieutenant West's offer of marriage. Think of your future. I wouldn't be surprised if he became General West one day."

"Perhaps we shouldn't get ahead of ourselves…" Cocking a brow, Helen stiffened.

"I can see you now, entertaining ambassadors and senators in Washington."

As she spoke, she spread her hands wide, as if encompassing that future. Her gaze focused on an envisioned time to come, Flossie wore a faraway expression as if visualizing Cadence's prospects or glimpsing some distant horizon.

Head back, Cadence frowned as she surveyed the woman's behavior.

"Who knows? With James' leadership, you may live in the White House one day. Your sons will all graduate from West Point, and your daughters will marry—"

"My daughters will marry?" Cadence scowled. "Flossie, just listen to yourself. You're describing where I am now. To hear you talk, my life has ended before it's begun. You make my entire future sound plotted out on a chart, where I'll have no choices or options." Exasperated at hearing her life pass without living it, she struggled to define the future she envisioned. "I don't want a neatly laid-out tactical maneuver of my husband's design. I want adventures and challenges."

"My dear"—Flossie gave a deep-throated chuckle—"James will lead you on many an adventure, and just wait until you have children. Every day will bring new challenges."

Her chest heaving in a silent sigh, she glanced at her mother, standing wordless.

Flossie's gaze followed hers. "Helen, what have you to say?"

"Your advice is practical…" She peered at Cadence. "But I say follow your heart, not your head."

"Thank you, Mother." With a fervent nod, she took a deep breath.

"Oh, no." Flossie gasped and held up her hands. "Don't throw away this opportunity." Then, she waggled her index finger. "The *wise* thing is to marry James and live happily ever after."

The woman brushed her hands as if that were that.

Though Flossie's views aggravated Cadence, she suspected the woman's intentions were good—just misplaced. *Maybe those are her aspirations, but they're* not mine. *Besides, my future's none of her business.*

"If you'll excuse me, I need a breath of fresh air."

She forced a stiff smile as she strode out the door.

"Well, I never…What an ungrateful girl. James would teach her a lesson if he withdrew his offer."

Escaping the woman's shrill voice and meddling advice, she shuddered like a dog shaking itself dry. She needed a long, brisk walk to work off her frustration, but when she reached the bottom step, she spotted James.

No, I can't face him. Not now. Not yet.

"Cadence, dear."

Wearing an unperturbed smile as he approached, he appeared to hold no grudge.

"You seem in good spirits today…" She studied his face for clues.

"Why not? This is a new morning, and I'm in the company of a beautiful woman. What more could I ask?"

His eyes glittering like rhinestones, he curled his lips into a smile.

"I thought"—skeptical, she tilted her head to inspect him—"after last night—"

"Oh, that." He shrugged off the previous evening's turn of events. "It's a perfect day for a stroll. Walk with me."

His eyes surly, he gave her a winning smile.

Something isn't right. Squinting as she guessed at his intentions, she wavered. "Maybe a short stroll—"

"That's my girl." Instead of crooking his arm for her, he put his hand at the base of her skull and steered her.

The gesture made her uncomfortable. *Why?* Feeling like a ventriloquist's dummy, she shrugged off his hand.

He strode quickly, like a man with a mission, until he paused in front of the trading post.

"Why are we stopping here?"

"You'll see."

Again, he pressed his fingers into her neck, steering her none too gently up the steps, inside the store, and toward the dry goods section. Stopping at the cabinet of rolled fabrics, he handed her a bolt of ivory colored silk.

"What's this material for?" Shrugging off his hand, she ran her fingertips over the smooth fabric.

"Your wedding gown."

"What?" Shocked, she spoke so loudly, other shoppers' heads turned.

"And use this pattern for your wedding dress." After choosing a paper packet from the table, he all but threw it.

"Have you lost your mind?" Though she caught the packet by instinct, she scowled at his condescending tone, as if he were barking orders at a recruit.

"Come now, Cadence. You know you're marrying me. Why keep on with this foolish charade?"

She huffed at his patronizing words, too furious to speak. Then she saw a Chihuahua on a short leash, and everything fell into place. *He keeps his hand at my neck to manipulate me—control me.*

"You don't want a wife. You want a poor, broken-spirited creature. Marry a hobbled horse for all I care, but I wouldn't have you if you were the last man in God's creation." She started out in conversational tones, but by the time she finished, she shouted. With a frustrated, guttural roar, she threw the dress pattern and silk on the cutting table and stormed out.

People standing at the doorway, gawking, could not jump out of her way fast enough.

Once outside, she hiked her skirts and took off running, unsure where she was headed. Enraged and self-righteous, yet equally contrite, she could only imagine the repercussions for her unladylike behavior. She would have to face the consequences for her actions sooner or later. *But not now.* Too angry to stop, she ran until she was out of breath.

Then finding herself in front of the stables, she mounted one of the tethered horses. Still no destination in mind, she took off at a gallop. Her one goal was to escape the fort's prying eyes. She had to find somewhere private to think.

She paused a half-mile later, glancing at the heavens as she let her horse catch its breath. Clouds poured over the Davis Mountains, turning the Texas blue skies into a roiling gray.

The weather looks as stormy as I feel. Now what? Grimacing, she considered going back but shook her head, not yet ready to face the aftermath of her rash behavior.

*If only the Rodriguez family was still at the camp, I'd visit them, or if I could speak to the chaplain...*Looking at the sky, she voiced her thoughts into the wind. "God, I don't know what to do. Tell me." Then she remembered Emily Dickinson's poem, and Ben's outdoor "chapel" came to mind.

The long, low rumbling of an approaching storm broke through her thoughts. *At the very least, I can wait out the storm there.* Clicking her teeth, she spurred her horse through the hilly brush country toward the glen. Mesquite and prickly pear cactus dominated the chaparral, and the catclaw ripped her trailing skirt, but she ignored it in her rush to find shelter.

Her growling stomach reminded her she had not eaten since the ball, thanks to skipping breakfast and Flossie's interruption before Sunday supper. *Spring water and grass for the horse…shelter and wild plums for me.*

Finally, the rocky outcrop loomed ahead. So close, she could smell the wild plums' sweet scent, and she urged her horse faster.

Then, a deafening peal of thunder erupted overhead as a dazzling white flash crashed not ten feet away.

Spooking, the horse reared on its hind legs, throwing her off and tangling her tightly laced shoe in the stirrup. She pulled herself free before he galloped off with her shoe, but she wrenched her ankle, tumbling headfirst into the caliche dust that was quickly turning to mud.

Now what? Walk back in stocking feet? She tried to stand, but when she put weight on her foot, her ankle buckled, and she screeched in pain. *I'm miles from the fort with no horse and a twisted ankle. How will I get back?* She sank her face in her hands, letting her tears mingle with the cold rain. Then the wind picked up, whipping the downpour into driving sheets of pelting drops.

I've got to get out of this storm. Her back drenched and her dress muddied, she crawled toward the V-shaped crevasse in the rocks and took cover beneath an overhang. Besides protection from the deluge, the rocky cleft offered a steady trickle of rain, providing a fresh source of water.

But as the hours crept by, the growling in her

stomach grew louder. Worse than her throbbing ankle, hunger pangs gnawed at her stomach.

She glanced at the tree limbs high overhead, sagging beneath the ripe plums' weight. *Out of reach. If I could just climb those branches.* Using the rocks as leverage, she hoisted herself to her feet, but the moment she put weight on her foot, she screamed as she collapsed in pain. Famished and frustrated, she ignored the tears rolling down her cheeks. *Now what?*

Plop. A ripe plum fell inches from her. As she reached for it, she noticed dozens of overripe plums scattered beneath the tree. Using a stick, she swept the fruit toward her and rinsed them in the pooling rainwater. Though they gave off a yeasty scent and had an acidic aftertaste, she was so hungry, she gobbled them until she could eat no more.

Then listening to the patter of the rain, she lifted her gaze to the heavens. *How will I get back?*

Chapter 9
Crevasse

"Everyone's talking about Cadence's clash at the trading post." Tom broke the news to Ben.

News travels fast at a fort. He grimaced, beginning to understand her yearning for freedom and privacy. "Did anyone see which way she rode?"

"She just took off at a gallop, her petticoats flying."

Debating whether to interfere, Ben stifled an uneasy sigh, but when her horse strolled back to the fort, muddied and riderless several hours later, he could wait no longer. After saddling Althea, he rode to the captain's quarters and rapped at the door.

A heated discussion came from within, but the voices stopped as Mrs. McShane answered the knock.

"Good afternoon, lieutenant, won't you come in?"

Her voice was calm and polite. Only the haunted look in her eyes betrayed her panic.

"Do you know where Cadence went?" Other than removing his hat, he dispensed with formalities.

Swallowing hard, she shook her head.

"You heard what happened?" Nervously toying with his hat's rim, he pulled the brim through his fingers in a slow circle.

"Hasn't everyone?" She sniffed. Then giving him a welcoming smile, Helen opened the door wide. "Won't you come in?"

Surprised by her hospitality, Ben did a double-take. "Williams, is that you?"

The captain's voice boomed from within.

"Yes, sir." Ben entered the parlor through a haze of smoke.

West sat puffing a cigar, as unruffled as at a dinner party. His dislike for the man deepening, Ben wrinkled his nose as much at West's evident lack of concern as at his cigar's acrid stench.

"Have you any news about my daughter?"

The captain's eyes had the same haunted look as his wife's.

"No, sir, I don't, but that's the reason I've come." Ben tightened his grip on his hat, twisting the rim between his fingers. "Have you sent out a scouting par—"

"Of course. I led one immediately." West curled his lip in a sneer. "She's nowhere to be found—as if she's fallen off the face of the earth. My men and I scoured the area for over an hour."

"Did you take a tracker with you?" Clenching and unclenching his hat rim as he curled first one side and then the other, Ben struggled to keep the frustration from his voice.

"None needed."

Cigar in hand, West waved off the idea as if too absurd to consider.

Gritting his teeth at the man's incompetence, Ben crushed his hat between his fingers. "You didn't find her, yet you returned?" He wanted to add, 'with an Apache war party, roving bandits, and a cougar in the area,' but after glancing at Mrs. McShane's pinched face, he bit his tongue.

"No luck." West puffed on his cigar, calmly sending up smoke rings.

Ben's nostrils flared as much at the reek of West's cigar as his uselessness. On edge and needing an outlet for the adrenaline coursing through his body, he whacked his hat against his thigh as he turned toward the captain.

"Request permission to search for Cadence, sir."

"Searching will do no good once the sun sets." Talking over the captain, West spoke from the side of his mouth, his cigar moving in tandem with his lips. As ashes fell on his jacket's lapel, he nonchalantly brushed them aside. "Soon it'll be too dark to see anything."

"With your permission, sir?" Straightening, Ben turned his back on West and appealed to the captain as he mashed his hat's rim between his fingers.

"Take as many men as you need, lieutenant."

His voice faint, the captain gave a weary nod, apparently drained.

"The fewer, the better." Ben shook his head.

"As you wish."

The captain's voice sounded hollow and distant.

"Thank you, sir."

"After dark, you're wasting your time." West chewed his cigar.

"Don't forget, Comanches taught me to track—day or night." Ben lowered his chin to gaze at West.

"If you think you can find Cadence, while my men and I couldn't…go ahead and make a fool of yourself." Scoffing, West took his cigar from his mouth. "Then in the morning, we'll have to search for two."

No wonder Cadence bolted from this jackass. Refusing to dignify West's remark with an answer, Ben turned his back on him, saluting the captain and pausing only to speak to his wife. "Don't worry, ma'am. I'll find your daughter."

"God help you." She fervently clasped his hand between hers.

He closed the door behind him, glanced at the sun, low on the horizon, and agreed with West about one thing—little daylight remained in the mountains. Then not slowing to readjust his misshapen hat, he pulled it on, dashed down the stairs, and hopped on Althea.

If Cadence went to town, someone would've seen her. She wouldn't have gone to the Rodriguez' camp now that they've left. Eliminating routes she wouldn't have taken, he touched his vest pocket, remembering the book of poetry Cadence had given him. *The "chapel."*

The downpour washed away her horse's hoofprints, hampering his search. He saw a few broken branches—potential clues—but he was uncertain of her direction until he spotted threads from her skirt's hem dangling from the catclaw.

Despite the rain ending, temperatures plummeted as night fell in the high desert. Ben rode faster to generate heat, buttoning his jacket and turning up his collar against the biting wind. Though bundling up kept out the cold, the layers didn't prevent troubling thoughts from penetrating his mind. He recalled reports of banditos causing trouble in the saloon. *They could be hiding in the mountains.*

A coyote's howl pierced the gloom. Ben scowled, remembering puma tracks he had seen earlier, and he rode faster still to find Cadence before either man or beast.

Then, in the twilight's shadows, he spotted a woman's shoe. He dismounted to retrieve it and tied his horse with a quick-release knot. He noticed the mud's indentation where she had been thrown and begun to crawl, and the sound of faint singing beckoned him. Ears perked, he recognized the song's lyrics as he got closer.

"All around the mulberry bush, the monkey chased the weas—*hic*. The monkey stopped to pull up his sock. *Hic* goes the weasel."

Cadence? Pushing aside the plum tree's branches, Ben ducked beneath and entered their "chapel" glen. He gawked, unsure whether she had lost her mind.

Half sitting and half reclining, she wore a dazed smile as she sang the nursery rhyme. Wet tendrils hanging in tangles, her hair had come undone from her braided upsweep. Her skirt was muddy, its hem torn and unraveled, and her soaked bodice clung to her chest.

He could not resist glancing at her proud nipples. "Cadence?"

"Oh, hello." She looked up and lost her balance, giggling as she tumbled backwards. When the laughter subsided, she righted herself. "Oh, Ben, am I glad to see you."

Though concerned, he had to grin.

"Oh, here, you've *got* to try these plums." She glanced at the stash of plums in her skirt and offered him a handful. "These are the *best* plums I've ever eaten in my whole, entire life. The *best.*"

Kneeling beside her, he accepted one of her plums, slurped its contents, and swallowed a smile. "Cadence…"

"*Hic.*" Wearing a silly grin, she swayed as she lifted her gaze. "Huh?"

"You're tipsy."

"What?" She started to laugh off his assertion but hiccupped instead. "Ladies don't get tipsy. *Hic.* I'm no such thing."

"Trust me." He chuckled in his throat. "You're tipsy."

"I am not"—she shook her head—"but I *am happy.*" She leaned toward him to make her point and tipped over, starting another round of giggles.

"Can you get up?" Despite the urgency of the situation, he could not suppress a chuckle.

"Of course, I can." Still swaying, she came to attention. "First you accuse me of being tipsy, and then you ask if I can get up? Sir, are you casting aspersions?" Leaning toward him, she stared him down.

"No, indeed." He swallowed a smile. Kneeling, he put his arm around her waist. "Can you stand?"

"Of course." As she started to stand, the plums fell from her skirt, scattering underfoot. Then, when she put her weight on her twisted ankle, she screamed in pain, whimpered, and fell back. "No…"

"Let me see your ankle." Ben's smile switched to a grimace.

"You accuse me of being tipsy, and then you want to see my ankle? What sort of lady do you think I am?"

"An injured one." As she vainly slapped at his hands, he molded her skirt and petticoats around her legs, with only her foot and ankle showing—distended, red, and beginning to bruise. Then he ripped her petticoat's hem, tearing off a strip. "Your swollen ankle needs bandaging."

"Stop that." Again, she slapped at his hands. "Stop it, I say!"

"Your foot's close to double its size." He exhaled as he shook his head. "Just hope your ankle isn't broken."

She moaned once while he bandaged it, but for the most part, snored lightly as she slipped off to sleep.

After he finished, he gently shook her awake. "Think you can ride Althea tonight?"

"Of course. It's a"—she tried to snap her fingers and missed, only succeeding on the third attempt— "snap."

Half-lifting her and acting as her crutch, Ben helped her stand.

Propped up by his arms, with her weight on her good leg, she took a wobbly step and slumped against him. "I'm just so sleepy."

With a sigh, he lowered her back to a sitting position, only then realizing her teeth were chattering, and she was shivering. He shook his head at the irony. "Those fermented plums kept you from feeling any pain but will be the death of you if you catch pneumonia. You've got to get warm."

With the sun below the horizon, the only light was starlight. He considered building a fire to warm her, dry her clothes, and keep cougars or coyotes at bay, but a campfire would also attract any Apaches or banditos in the area. *On the other hand, the flames might draw a cavalry search and rescue party.* Then remembering James was on duty, he dismissed the idea as too ludicrous to consider.

After unsaddling Althea, he took his canteen, a leather bag of pemmican, and his sleeping blanket from his saddle bags. Sitting beside Cadence, he wrapped the blanket around them, tucking in her feet. Then he sliced off a piece of jerked meat, gave hurried thanks, and nudged her awake. "Here, eat this pemmican. The food will warm you."

"What's pemmican?" Weaving as she propped herself on an elbow, her head lolling, she examined the dried brown strip.

"Dried bison and chokeberries."

Nostrils distended, she made a face, but she nibbled it. As she chewed, her face relaxed into a wide-eyed smile. "Not bad."

"Here." He handed her the canteen. "Wash down the pemmican."

She took a long draught, handed back the canteen, and then noticed they shared a blanket.

"Sir." She scowled as she eyed him up and down. "Are you making advances?"

"No, ma'am, just sharing body warmth." He struggled to keep a straight face.

"See that you don't." Her expression stony, she stiffened.

"Yes, ma'am." He swallowed a smile.

Moments later, she began snoring lightly.

As he watched her drift to sleep, an overwhelming desire to protect her gripped him. He tucked his half of the covers around her. Then, pulling his rifle closer, he propped his back against the rock wall and stared into the darkness.

Even if cougars or Comanches don't find us tonight, how will we get back tomorrow?

Chapter 10
Wild Onions and Sour Grapes

The next morning dawned cold and blustery. Shivering, Cadence woke with a headache, unsure where she was or how she got there. Looking around to get her bearings, she saw the sleeping form beside her and let out a blood-curdling screech.

"Apaches?" Ben bolted upright. Grabbing his rifle, he looked about. "Bandits?"

"What do you think you're doing?" Huddling, she clutched the blanket to her chest.

"What?" He blinked.

"What's the meaning of sharing a bed with me?"

"How much do you remember?" He sighed as he wiped the sleep from his eyes.

"Oh, you *cad!*" Outraged at his impudence, she huffed as the blood rushed to her head, making her temples pound. She stifled a groan. "Are you implying you took advantage of me and then expect me to 'forget'?"

"How much do you recall, so I don't have to begin at the beginning."

"My horse threw me. Then I crawled here"—she half-smiled, starting to remember—"and found some wild plums."

"Uh-huh." He nodded. "Plums that were fermenting. You were tipsy when I found you last night."

"I was no such thing. Now you're just adding insult to injury, you, you…" Stammering, she huffed again. "Ladies do not get tipsy. It simply isn't done."

"You were tipsy and shivering from the cold—just too danged tipsy to realize the fact at the time—or remember it now." He stared. "Can you stand? Let me see your ankle."

"What?" Uncomfortable with his appraising stare, she gathered the blanket around her and tucked her legs beneath her.

"Not this tussle again." Sitting back, he massaged the bridge of his nose. "Look at your foot."

"Oh, the…the stories you're—" Frustrated, she sputtered, unable to get the words out fast enough. Then she saw her dressed ankle and stopped, confused. "What happened?"

"Your ankle was so swollen that I bandaged it."

She tried to stand and, wincing, fell back. She turned toward him, searching his eyes. "You're telling the truth?"

"Yep." He nodded. "You were feeling no pain last night. In fact, when I found you, you were singing."

"I was not…" His stare unwavering, she blinked, questioning her memory. "Was I?"

"You were." Wearing a kind smile, he leaned forward. "Now, let me see your ankle."

His calm expression and soothing tone persuaded her. She tucked her skirt and petticoats around her calves, showing him only her foot and ankle.

"Does that hurt?" He gently wobbled her ankle.

"A little."

"How about that?" He wobbled her foot the other

way.

The pain too sharp to think straight, she screeched, shut her eyes, and lightly massaged her ankle. Not until she felt his hand's consoling grip on her shoulder did she open her eyes.

"Sorry."

He winced as if sharing her pain. Then seeming to gather his thoughts, he rubbed his chin, his hand on the stubble sounding like sandpaper on wood.

Despite her throbbing head and ankle, Cadence found the rasping sound—as well as his nearness—provocative.

"All right, you ride Althea, while I walk alongside."

"Getting back to the fort will take all day." Cadence shook her head.

"Travel will be slow." Scrambling to his feet, he drew a deep breath. "But the more headway we make, the closer we'll be when a search party finds us."

Finding his proximity comforting, she sensed a loss when he stood. "Can't we both ride Althea?" She looked forward to sharing a saddle.

"The weight would hurt Althea's back." He glanced at the plum tree. Then his gaze followed its trunk to its low-hanging limbs. "But if we could…" Unsheathing his knife, he cut off two long branches and several shorter ones.

"What are you doing?" She studied him.

"Making a travois."

"A *what*?"

"A pole sled." He lashed together the boughs with leather thongs from his saddle bags and strapped his blanket to the poles and cross braces to make a crude sleigh. When he finished, he saddled Althea and harnessed the sled to her.

Then his strong arms lifted and carried her to the improvised hammock seat.

"You aren't serious?" She looked at the seat and arched her brow.

"This way, we can both ride." He set her on the makeshift cart. "Try it."

She tested it, lightly bouncing on the stretched blanket as she held onto the two long poles. Feeling the spring and give of the blanket tautly wrapped over the cross braces, she smiled. "Not bad."

"We'd better eat breakfast before starting back." After gathering fresh plums and slicing the pemmican, he set the food in front of them.

Her mouth was poised to slurp a plum when his voice stopped her.

"It's only right to say grace."

She glanced about the snug, inviting ravine and the alpine meadow of mealy blue sage and blazing stars, recalling the reason for choosing the "chapel." Nodding, she bowed her head.

"Thank You for providing food, water, and shelter—and keeping Cadence safe from cougars and coyotes."

"Amen." Sorry she suspected his motives, Cadence scrutinized him. *He's so different from anyone I've ever known.*

" 'Wild beasts honor me, jackals and ostriches, For I put water in the wilderness…' Isaiah 43:20."

As he recited, his tone changed, and his quote piqued her curiosity. "Did ostriches exist in biblical times, I mean, in the Holy Land, not Australia?"

"They still do on the Arabian Peninsula."

"You never cease to amaze me." She studied him from her pole-sled perch. "Where did you learn such an odd fact?"

"Spending time alone is the advantage to being the outsider." A ruddy tinge crept across his cheeks. "Reading's filled my mind, as well as the time."

Self-taught. What other surprises do you have in store, Ben Williams?

****

Cadence smelled James' cigar before the small search and rescue party came into view—nearly in sight of the fort.

Riding at the front and wearing long, white leather gloves, James raised his arm to halt his men. Then dismounting, he tossed his horse's reins to a private.

She wrinkled her nose. *So theatrical—as if he's the marshal leading a parade.*

"Cadence, my dear, you're safe."

"No thanks to you." Sitting tall, she pulled her indignation around her like a shawl.

With a furtive glance at his men, he stiffened and turned to Ben. "Where was she?"

'She'...when I'm right here. "I was lost, and now I'm found. Again, no thanks to you." Tossing her chin at his words and gruff tone, she raised her voice. "If you're through, lieutenant…"

West's eyes flashed as the blood drained from his face, and his ashen lips bunched in a choleric scowl.

"My father won't be pleased if you detain us…" Glaring, she left her words hanging.

"Carry on." His eyes pinched together into dark slits as his gaze flicked from her to Ben.

"Lieutenant." Ben saluted informally before clicking to Althea.

Cadence caught his muted smile before she turned to watch James become smaller and smaller in the distance.

After arriving at the captain's lodging ten minutes later, Ben lifted her from the travois and carried her upstairs.

"Cadence…" Holding open the door, her mother reached for her hand. "Are you all right?"

"I'm fine, no matter how bedraggled." She smiled, relieved to be home. "A bath and a change of clothes, and I'll be good as new."

"She's sprained her ankle." Ben shook his head. "You'd better call the doctor."

Covering her mouth, her mother gasped.

"I don't believe the bone's broken"—Ben deposited her on the settee—"but that's for him to decide."

"Private"—the captain called to a passing soldier—"fetch Doc Freeman." Then he turned to his daughter. "Now, what happened?"

"James was impudent, and I needed to get away to sort things out. Then my horse spooked, threw me, and I crawled to a rock shelter with a spring and wild plums." Omitting the part about being tipsy, Cadence glanced at Ben, silently urging his discretion.

Though his eyes twinkled, he kept still.

Within minutes, the doctor arrived and examined her. "Who bandaged this ankle?"

"I did, sir." Standing at a discreet distance, Ben spoke up.

"Fine job, son." He tested her ankle, wobbling the

joint one way and then the other. "Does that hurt? How about that?" With a smile, he turned toward her parents. "It's just sprained. Keep her foot elevated and tightly wrapped." Turning back to Cadence, he propped one of the sofa pillows beneath her ankle. "That and bed rest, and you'll be ready to dance at the next ball."

"Thank you, doctor." Cadence caught Ben's gaze.

"That's comforting news." Her mother gave a relieved sigh. "Let me see you to the door, doctor."

"Now, then." The instant his wife left the room, her father snapped his head toward them. "This matter of you two spending the night together—explain yourselves."

"We've nothing to explain." Cadence pulled herself to her full seated height. "Ben was a perfect gentleman."

He harrumphed. "What have you to say for yourself, Williams?"

"My only intention, sir, was to bring your daughter back safely."

"And that you did." The captain studied his face. Then he scrutinized his daughter's and cleared his throat. "Mrs. McShane and I were worried sick we'd never see our Cadence again. We're much obliged."

"You two must be starving." Her mother came bustling back into the room. "Lieutenant, won't you join us for breakfast?"

"I'd be right pleased, ma'am." His eyes opened wide as his face brightened in a smile.

Cadence started to rise.

"Oh, no, you don't, young lady." Her mother put a light hand on her shoulder. "You stay put. I'll bring you a tray, and we'll eat in the parlor to keep you company."

Cadence sighed, grateful to be waited and doted on. Then exhaling, she pressed her lips together. "What I did was foolish—a childish reaction to something I couldn't face. Thank God, Ben's the tracker he is, or I might still be out there."

"Or worse." Helen arched her brow as she looked from her husband to Ben. "Don't think I hadn't heard rumors of the Apache war party, puma tracks, or roving bandits." Then she looked at Cadence. "No matter how headstrong you are, you can't be reckless on the frontier. Fort Davis isn't Manhattan, you—"

A sharp rap at the door interrupted her words.

"It might as well be New York." The captain huffed. "It's as busy here as Grand Central Sta—"

An impatient hammering at the door interrupted him.

"I'll get it." Hurrying, Jenny wiped her floured hands on her apron.

James' curt voice came from the foyer. Not waiting to be ushered inside, he barged into the parlor.

"I rushed here immediately"—he gave the captain a quick salute—"that is, after assigning a detachment to construct telegraph lines." Then turning toward Cadence, he started removing his long, white leather gloves. "My dear, I'm so relieved you're safe."

"No thanks to you, lieutenant." Curling her lip, she sneered. "Now, if you don't mind, we're just sitting down to breakfast."

"I'd be delighted." He smiled as he continued removing his gloves, finger by finger, making himself at home.

"You weren't invited." Staring him down, Cadence

snickered at his assumption, as well as his crisply pressed and pleated uniform. "If you'll excuse us…lieutenant…"

Opening his mouth to speak, he looked from her to the captain.

As though he expects my father to contradict me. Cadence fumed.

His face impassive, the captain remained silent.

West then graced Helen with a wide smile, as if anticipating an invitation from an old ally.

Lips pinched shut, her mother eyed him coolly as Cadence sneered.

"I see." West turned a bright red. Then snorting through his nostrils as he peered from Cadence to Ben and back, his eyes narrowed until his pupils were tiny dark coals. "Good day then." He slapped his long, white leather gloves against his thigh and stormed out.

"Cadydid, tweaking his nose wasn't wise." Her mother's face was stern, but her eyes flickered.

"Fiddle-de-dee." Cadence tossed her chin. "I'm through bowing to his wishes." *The egotistical peacock.*

Jenny served breakfast buffet style in the parlor. An urn of freshly brewed coffee and platters of steaming pancakes with wildflower honey, hickory-smoked bacon, and buttery eggs scrambled with tangy wild onions filled the sideboard.

Her mother fixed Cadence a tray, while the rest of them balanced their plates on their laps.

Not recalling a more enjoyable or informal meal in their home, Cadence inhaled the bouquet of aromas. Then she breathed a sigh of relief to be home.

After breakfast, Ben caught Jenny's gaze as she cleared the plates. "Do you have any more onions?"

"Yes, in the warming kitchen. Follow me."

He excused himself and returned a few minutes later carrying a dish towel.

"What's in your hand?" Canting her head, Cadence gave him a puzzled smile.

"Warm, chopped onions wrapped in muslin."

"Onions?" She shared a with blank stare with her parents. "What for?"

"A home remedy for your sprain." Approaching her with the compress, he glanced at her ankle. "May I?"

"What do onions do?" Cadence peeked at her parents before delicately raising her skirt and petticoats an inch to allow him access.

"They lessen the swelling and relieve the pain." He tied the muslin ends around her ankle, positioning the juicy onions over the inflammation. "Leave the poultice in place and change it every few hours. Your ankle will heal in a week."

"You're sure?" Her eyes teared at a whiff of the onions' pungent odor, and she pulled back her head.

"Trust me." He gave her a lopsided smile. "Thank you for breakfast, Mrs. McShane. It was delicious, but I'd better return to my duties. I have a report to file." His smile fading, he saluted the captain. "Sir."

"Don't be a stranger," Cadence called as he started for the door.

"I won't." Grinning, he met her gaze.

Her stomach fluttered, and a pleasant chill slid down her spine, making her squirm. *What is this sensation?*

****

Ben returned the next day with a bouquet of

wildflowers. The day after, he brought a sack of onions, and the following day, a piece of honeycomb. Never staying more than a few minutes, he would pop in bearing a small gift and then leave.

"Ben seems shy." After one of his brief visits, her mother sat in a nearby chair, embroidering.

"I don't think he's bashful as much as afraid to overstay his welcome." Cadence mulled over her mother's words. "I think he doesn't want to impose."

"Such a gentle man…" Hesitating, her mother stared at her stitchery.

"And a gentleman." Cadence nodded.

"Is he?" She peered hard at her daughter. "More to the point, *was* he a gentleman when you spent the night together?"

"Mother…" Cadence blinked at her boldness. "He most certainly was. You have no need for concern. Ben behaved with far more consideration than many others—James included."

"What happened between you and James?" Helen met her daughter's gaze. "You've never told me."

"You must have heard the story from others." She swallowed the bitter taste in her mouth.

"Several times." Her mother sniffed. "But I'd like to hear what happened from you."

"James steered me into the trading post with his fingers pressed around my neck." Cadence wrinkled her nose at the memory. "Then after he chose a bolt of silk, he practically threw a dress pattern at me, *ordering* me to not only marry him, but sew my wedding dress."

Her mother opened her mouth as if to speak but promptly shut it.

"Then, I saw a Chihuahua on a collar and leash…"

Scowling, she peered through narrow slits. "James made me feel like his dog on a chain—not an equal and certainly not a cherished fiancée. I told him in no uncertain terms I'd never marry him."

"Your rejection at the ball must've set the blaze, and your refusal the next morning must've fanned the flames."

Her mother nodded absently as if her thoughts were elsewhere.

"What do you mean?"

"I didn't want to alarm you"—she focused on her daughter as she set down her embroidery—"but I've heard rumors…"

"What kind of rumors?" Her mother's lips quivered as though she struggled for the right words or held back tears. Cadence leaned forward, getting more concerned the longer she watched. "What's wrong?"

"You might as well hear the gossip from me first." She took a deep breath as she met her daughter's gaze. "Your honor…your reputation's in question."

"What?" Cadence bolted upright.

"James spread rumors that Ben ruined you." She sneered. "He swears he broke off your engagement because of your 'clandestine meetings with the redskin.' "

"What!" Cadence jumped to her feet and, groaning, immediately regretted it. Still seething, she returned to her perch on the settee. "How dare he spread such ridiculous lies? He's a…a…cad."

"You mean a bastard." The corners of her mouth turned down.

"Mother! You…surprise me." Shocked, Cadence stared in fascinated horror. Ever since she could remember, her mother had always been the consummate lady, who never raised her voice or used strong language. As their gaze met, she began grinning and then chuckling, which gave way to giggling.

Feeding off each other's pent-up tension, her mother joined in until they were both laughing out loud and did not hear the captain return.

"What's all this jollity about?" As he walked into the front room, her father removed his hat and began unbuttoning his jacket.

"James' rumors about me." Catching her breath, Cadence broke out in a fresh round of laughter.

"Hear, now." Planting his feet in a wide stance, he glared. "This gossip is no laughing matter. News travels fast from fort to fort, and too often perception passes for truth. As things stand, you're damaged goods. If this line of talk continues, you won't be considered marriageable material, and no officer will take you for his wife."

"Oh, fiddle-de-dee." Sobered by his sharp tone, she curled her lip in contempt. "The trading post was full of people, who heard me break off any imagined engagement with James. If people want to believe his lies, they're fools, whose opinions shouldn't matter."

"Consider your reputation." The skin bunching around his eyes, her father studied her.

"Then take James to task for spreading lies." She tossed her head, her upswept curls flying. "I've done nothing wrong, and neither has Ben. Anyone with an ounce of common sense will see James' dishonesty is nothing but sour grapes."

"Common sense is a flower that doesn't grow in every garden." Her mother's brows knitted in a frown.

"But it is odd that no one's come calling these past few days…except Ben."

A polite knock caught them off guard.

"Speak of the devil." Her mother rushed to open the door. Then her voice wafted from the foyer. "Come in, Sarah. Tom, it's good to see you both."

"Maybe this sponge cake will make you feel better." After she was ushered inside, Sarah presented a towering cake to Cadence.

"A slice of Sarah's angel-food cake is a slice of heaven." Tom wore a wide smile.

"We wanted an excuse to drop by and see you how your ankle's doing." Sarah squeezed her shoulder.

"How thoughtful." Cadence smiled, genuinely glad to see her. "Thank you, Sarah."

"Please have a seat." Her mother bustled into action. "Let me get coffee and plates, so we can try Sarah's angelic cake."

"Tom, can I interest you in a brandy?"

Her father's broad smile reflected his delight at the visit.

"Thought you'd never ask." Tom joined him at the other side of the room.

Her hand cupped around her mouth, Sarah pulled a footstool near Cadence and leaned close. "Just want you to know that Tom and I support you. James is nothing but a blowhard." She scowled. "And the way he's behaving is shameful."

"Thank you, Sarah. Your words—and your friendship—mean a lot." Cadence reached for her hand.

Her mother brought plates, forks, a cake knife, and a small, earthen crock. Then she held the jar for all to see. "The last of the strawberry preserves from June.

Let's make this visit a festive occasion."

Cadence glanced from the airy sponge cake to the smiling faces. *What makes a celebration? Food or friends?*

****

Sunday, her ankle was strong enough to walk to church. Her first outing in a week, Cadence breathed in the fresh morning air. Her spirits revived, she wore a ready smile and walked with a spring in her step. All traces of a limp were gone. Reprieved from the doctor's prescribed "house arrest," she was eager to leave her confines and hear the good news.

Direction was what I needed last Sunday.

Ben joined them at the chapel door, but before they entered the sanctuary, a mustachioed, florid-cheeked man intercepted her father. Cadence recognized him as one of the town's merchants.

"Captain McShane, a word with you, sir."

"Yes, Mr…?" The captain paused.

"Jack Kelly"—the man removed his bowler hat—"proprietor of the What Cheer House and Saloon. One of your men created a disturbance—"

"Causing"—interrupted his buxom companion—"a week's lost wages—"

"Causing me and the missus a loss of income," continued the red-nosed man. "A word with you if I might."

"Church is neither the time nor the place to discuss business, Mr. Kelly." He glanced at his wife and daughter. "Meet me at my office first thing in the morning, and I'll be happy to discuss your complaint then." Tipping his hat, he gave the man's wife a cordial nod. "Good day, Mrs. Kelly."

"What did he want?" her mother whispered as they walked into the chapel.

"Probably one of the enlisted men broke a chair or neglected to pay a tab." He led his family and Ben to the front pew, removed his hat, and sat. "Nothing to concern yourself with, my dear."

"Today's sermon"—the chaplain leaned forward as his shoulders hunched and his hands gripped the pulpit—"is about Jesus' encounter with the fallen woman."

As if fixated, his penetrating stare never strayed from Cadence's face.

Sitting front and center, with her parents on her right and Ben on her left, she gazed into the man's stern, narrowed eyes. *Is he looking down his nose at me?* Cadence glanced from him to several congregants across the way, who turned their heads to glare. *Are they staring, or am I imagining it?* Swallowing, she straightened her spine.

"As Jesus traveled through Samaria, he stopped at a well in the shadow of Mount Gerizim. As I picture the scene, a Samaritan woman approached Him with a penitent humility—just as we're each forced to consider our past actions when we encounter Jesus through His word." The chaplain paused, peering now from her to Ben and squinting.

Is he assessing my reactions? Uncomfortable, she glanced at Ben, trying to determine if he also sensed the scrutiny.

His gaze was glued to the pulpit above.

"At first, the woman questioned Him. Was He greater than Jacob? Was He a prophet? Was He the Messiah? Jesus told her He was the living water.

Whoever drank from Him would never have to drink again." Again, the chaplain homed in on Cadence, his gaze never leaving her face.

"Jesus told her to return with her husband. When she told him she was not married, He reminded her she'd had five husbands and was living with a man, who was not her husband."

"Tart…"

"Jezebel…"

"Strumpet…"

Sibilant whispers behind Cadence made her turn her head.

People nearby swiveled in their pews to leer with narrowed eyes and disapproving frowns. Then a rash of murmurs broke out in the congregation.

Responding to the whispers behind her, she glanced over her shoulder. Except for Tom and Sarah's sympathetic smiles, only steely eyes and judgmental scowls met her.

I'm not *imagining their stares*. A tingling began at the nape of her neck and swept toward her cheeks and ears. Her self-esteem plummeting as she struggled to make sense of their hostility, she felt humiliation's hot sting coursing through her body. *Do they compare me to the fallen woman?*

Her palms sweating, she wiped her hands against her thighs. Breathing in shallow gasps, she peeked at the accusing faces across the aisle and then sat back, cringing from view.

This can't be real. Like in a nightmare where she was naked, she felt exposed and vulnerable. She pinched herself, hoping to wake. Instead, she saw she was trapped in the front pew.

Escape. Glancing from the door to her parents to Ben and back to the door, she gathered her skirts to make a dash for the exit.

Ben brushed his hand against hers. With a sidelong glimpse, he subtly shook his head and moved his arm, so it pressed against her shoulder, offering reassurance. Then, his back ramrod straight, he sat at attention.

Brave it out he seemed to say. Swallowing her disgrace, she drew her shawl closer. As she crossed her arms over her chest, she dug her fingers into her biceps and sat back against the pew, bracing herself for the sermon's conclusion.

"Jesus forced the woman to confront her past just as He urges each of us to admit our fallen ways." His eyes narrow slits, the chaplain scrutinized Cadence. Then his gaze swept the congregation. "We all have sins for which we're ashamed. How will we deal with these regrets?"

Hands out, he raised his arms high as his robe's sleeves slipped to his elbows. "Ignore them?" Then elbows akimbo, he gripped the podium's sides while he surveyed his congregation. "Admit we erred, but not change our ways?" Leaning forward, he fixed his gaze on Cadence. "Or will we confess our sins and sin no more? Those obedient to God will spend eternity with the Father, but…"

Shaking his bony index finger at heaven, he surveyed his congregants. "*Woe* onto those who lead promiscuous, lascivious lives." Pointedly staring at Cadence, he snapped shut the Bible.

"The gospel"—he squinted at Ben—"according to John."

Subdued, Cadence, her parents, and Ben filed out

silently after the closing hymn.

Several churchgoers gave stiff smiles or restrained bows but said nothing. Others openly snubbed her, sneering or turning away, their noses in the air.

"Good morning, Captain." Flossie nodded to his wife. "Helen." Then raising her chin, she looked down her nose at Cadence, about-faced, and strode away.

"Join us for supper," Cadence murmured to Ben.

Walking across the parade grounds to their house was a quiet affair. Numb with mortification, Cadence gripped her elbows.

The others were silent, seemingly absorbed in their own thoughts.

"This gossip is more serious than I'd imagined." Once behind closed doors, her mother faced them, her lip curling and her expression dark.

"James turned the community against me." Blinking, still unable to comprehend the hostility, Cadence shook her head.

"He should be horsewhipped." Her father's jaw rigid, he balled his hands into tight fists. "His slander is malicious. It's defamation of character."

"They're treating me like the 'fallen woman.' " Her chest aching as if her ribs were being squeezed, she curled her shoulders over her upper body and took shallow, constricted breaths.

"He's destroyed your reputation." His nostrils flaring, her father's face flushed an angry red.

"I've been charged, convicted, and condemned—"

"Without a hearing or trial." Ben grit his teeth as a vein twitched at his temple. "Because of me."

"*Because* you were the one person skilled enough…concerned enough to find me." Indignant at the injustice, she uttered a guttural roar. "Spreading rumors about me isn't bad enough. James slandered you for rescuing me." *Sour grapes.* Scowling, she turned toward her father. "Where was James last Sunday evening?"

"West led a search party." His white lips pinched thin. "But an hour later, he reported back, saying you were 'nowhere to be found.' " Her father stomped toward his humidor, bit off the top of a cigar, and spit out the tip.

"Ben and I have nothing to hide, so what's James basing his accusations on—circumstantial evidence?" As the initial shock and sting of humiliation passed, she began to think more clearly. "Did he say he saw us in some compromising situation, or is he simply casting aspersions?"

"Good questions." His eyes narrowing, Ben gazed into the distance. The veins of his neck stood out as he clenched his teeth.

"And where was James the night I was shivering in the cold, unable to get back?"

Chapter 11
Puffed Up Roosters and Henhouses

After Sunday supper, Ben called on Tom and Sarah. "What rumor is West spreading about Cadence and me?"

"I can tell you." Her nostrils wide, Sarah turned down the corners of her mouth as though she smelled sulfur. "It's the talk of the fort. Flossie Purdue said James told her husband Michael and everyone else who'd listen that he saw you and Cadence in a 'compromising position.' " She swallowed hard.

"And when was this event supposed to have happened?" Ben's chest heaved.

"The night she ran off, and you…" Blushing, she faltered. "*As he tells it*, you met her at your usual trysting place, which is why you found her when he couldn't."

"He's telling everyone this rendezvous happened Sunday night?"

Sarah nodded. "He says the proof is the two of you returning together the next morning."

"West was just starting out Monday morning as we approached the fort." Ben shook his head at the man's lack of character. "He was as surprised as the rest of the troop to see us."

"The man's nothing but a blowhard." Sarah rolled her eyes.

"No one with any sense listens," added Tom.

"But apparently quite a few *are* listening." Ben grimaced. "I couldn't care less about my reputation, but Cadence…" His shoulders sagging, he sighed.

"West's nothing but a bag of wind. His hearsay will all blow over."

Though Tom offered a sympathetic smile, he spoke without conviction. Ben clenched his teeth.

"But at what cost to Cadence?"

"You know how small forts are, full of petty people looking for fresh gossip." Sarah gave a reassuring nod. "Another month or so, and they'll find someone else to talk about."

"I'm not so sure the damage can be undone." His arm muscles tensing, he flexed his fingers. "Gossip's like a pillow's feathers scattered to the winds. Cadence's reputation will never be intact. People will always wonder."

What can I do?

****

After dark, Ben followed a hunch, tracking West to the What Cheer House and Saloon. Then, he waited in the shadows several minutes before entering.

"Buy me a drink?" A brassy, red-haired woman in a low-cut dress approached him. Her eyes flashed as she smiled through rouged lips.

Guess I didn't pass unnoticed. "Sure. What're you drinking?"

"Whiskey."

"Whiskey for the lady and a beer for me." He recognized the bartender as the man he had seen earlier at the chapel, Jack Kelly.

"Lady?" She smiled coquettishly. "You must be

new to these parts."

"Just new to this establishment." He shrugged as he glanced around the mirrored bar and sawdust floor.

"Could I"—her smile was practiced—"help you with anything?" She leaned into his arm.

"Actually, you can." He smiled back.

"Tell me how, soldier." Hanging on his biceps, she pressed her substantial bosom against him.

"Did you see a cavalry officer come in here a few minutes ago?"

"You mean Jimmy?" Letting go her grip, she stood back to view him, her smile morphing into a sneer.

"Did you see where he went?"

"Yeah, upstairs." Wrinkling her nose, she nodded toward the stairway.

"You know him?"

"You might say that." Her lip curling, she gave a dry laugh.

"What do you mean?" He studied her, trying to interpret her actions.

She inhaled while she looked into his eyes, seeming to debate whether to confide in him. Apparently, she trusted what she saw.

"Yeah, Jimmy and me are 'old friends.' " Her mouth twisted in a sneer.

"You don't sound fond of him." His interest piquing, Ben leaned forward.

"He was here last Sunday in a foul mood. Stormed in like he owned the place. Grabbed my arm, hauled me upstairs, and…" She broke off, scowling and inhaling.

"And what?"

"And tried to strangle me." Brushing back her hair, she pulled down the shoulder of her dress, exposing a series of bruises ranging in color from black and blue to yellow and green.

"You're in a hard line of work, ma'am." Ben grimaced at the welts and discolorations. Then he sucked in his breath at the fingermarks on her neck. *She could be Cadence.*

Lips pressed together, she shrugged and covered up.

He sipped his beer while he gathered his thoughts. "You wouldn't remember what time he came into the What Cheer, would you?"

"Five o'clock." She nodded. "I'd just come on shift."

"After I went looking for Cadence," he mumbled.

"What?"

"Just thinking out loud." He gave her a quick smile. "Would you be willing to tell others what you told me?"

Her back to the mirror, she smiled as she rested her elbows on the bar. Then, arching her back to show off her ample bosom, she lightly trailed her fingertips along the wood's polished surface.

"Depends on the price."

With no idea of the going price, he pulled out several silver dollars.

"That ain't what I'm thinking." She covered his hand with hers.

Her leering smile left no question as to her intentions. Shaking his head, he pulled his hand away. "Ma'am, I—"

"All the good ones are taken." She gave a throaty laugh before downing her drink with an adept flick of her wrist. "Whoever she is, she's lucky."

Accustomed to rejection, he disliked being its source, and he gave her a friendly smile to make amends. "What's your name?"

"Belle. I'm the belle of the ball."

Her sneer was self-effacing. "Belle, would you mind repeating what you told me about—"

"Jimmy?" She smirked. "Gladly."

He pushed the silver dollars toward her.

"Buy me another drink, and we'll call it even." She shook her head.

"Will you be here in an hour?" Ben ordered her a whiskey.

"Just came on duty."

"Thanks." He tipped his hat before turning to leave. *But if it's her word against West's, will a "soiled dove's" testimony carry weight?*

****

A scant half hour later, Ben returned with Captain McShane. He bought another round of drinks and then turned to Belle. "Would you mind telling the captain what you told me?"

She repeated her story and showed them her neck and shoulder.

"Thank you, Belle." The captain hung his head, mumbling into his chest.

Jack spoke from behind the bar, his cluster diamond pin sparkling in the mirror's reflected light. Wearing a crisp white shirt, black bowtie, and black satin vest over a white apron, the man personified a prosperous saloonkeeper. "This is what I wanted to discuss with you, captain. Belle ain't worked in a week, which is lost wages for her and lost business for the What Cheer."

His shoulders slumping, the captain stifled an unsettled sigh. "And to think Cadence could have married—"

Shrill laughter rang through the saloon, and Ben turned toward the stairway.

West was returning to the bar with a saloon girl, his arm familiarly slung around her waist.

Halfway down the steps, he caught Ben's gaze, and his smile dissolved. Looking from him to the captain to Belle, West let go the girl.

"Lieutenant," called Captain McShane. "Come join us in a friendly drink."

West lit a cigar, puffing slowly, as if buying time or thinking through his options.

He worked his mouth, his cigar waggling as his gaze shifted left and right. Then he glanced at the door.

Setting down his beer, Ben tensed, ready to give chase.

After several moments, West swaggered down the stairs and joined them. His gaze dark and intense, he glowered at Belle.

"What'll you have?" The bartender hiked his sleeves with his garters.

"Brandy." Tiny beads of sweat broke out above West's upper lip as he puffed vigorously on his cigar.

As though he's gasping for breath. Ben wrinkled his nose as much at the man's evident fear as at the cigar's fetid stench.

The bartender poured West a glass.

"To honor." The captain lifted his drink in a toast.

"To honor." Swallowing the words, West raised his glass just high enough to reach his lips and drained it. "Thank you, gentlemen, but I must be get—"

"We're not through." His lips taut and white, the captain wore an asymmetrical smile. "Jack, another round for our"—he ground his teeth—"friend."

Shaking his head, West held up his palm, refusing.

"Oh, but I insist." The captain gestured to the bartender to refill their glasses. Then, he raised his drink as his jaw tightened in a hard smile. "To my daughter's honor."

The brandy was halfway to West's lips before the words registered. He paused, his eyes darting left and right. Then he slapped his shot glass on the bar and sneered at Ben before turning toward the captain.

"I refuse to drink with the man who ruined your daughter."

"Strong words, lieutenant." The captain jeered, the corners of his mouth turning down. "Can you support them with evidence?" He crossed his arms.

"You saw Williams return with your daughter the next morning. You know they spent the night together."

"Spending the night does not constitute defiled honor." The captain's eyes narrowed in a harsh squint. "Do you have evidence for your assertion?"

"I…I saw them myself."

"You did?" Jerking back his head, the captain raised his eyebrows. "After looking an hour for Cadence, you reported she was 'nowhere to be found.' Williams did not leave to search for her until after you returned." He flashed a cold smile. "When did you see them together?"

"The next morn—"

"I repeat. Spending the night together does not equate defiling my daughter's honor." His eyes flinty, his pupils narrowed to pinholes. "When did you see them?"

"I…" West glanced at Belle and the bartender as he licked his lips. "I followed him. I saw them…together…in a compromising position."

"What time would you say that occurred, lieutenant?" Unfolding his arms, the captain leaned aggressively into West's space.

Ben stood poised to spring into action.

Belle remained poker-faced as she sipped her whiskey.

Seemingly disinterested in the conversation, Jack hovered behind the bar as he meticulously polished a glass.

West wiped off the beads of sweat from his lip.

"We're waiting, lieutenant." The captain scrutinized him. "You've made serious claims against a fellow officer. Unless you want this matter brought before a military court, you'll answer us now."

"I followed Williams"—gulping, West spoke in halting phrases—"to their trysting place…and…and saw the whole sordid affair."

"And where, pray tell"—the captain curled his lip—"did you see this 'affair?' "

"Why…uhm…" His eyes shifting left to right as he blinked, West seemed to struggle to think clearly. "I saw them near the fishing hole by…by…" He licked his lips.

"Limpia Creek?" offered the captain.

"Yes." His feverish eyes lit up. "Yes, that's where."

"Sunday night?"

"Yes." West downed his brandy.

"And at what time did you see them?" The captain

eyed him.

Taking sidelong glances, West neither met his gaze nor answered.

"Four o'clock?" The captain prompted him. "Five? Six?"

"Five, thereabouts." Leaning away, West shrugged. Then he slowly turned without making eye contact. "Well, I must be go—"

"Try to leave once more"—Ben's hand on his knife, he grabbed West's arm—"and I'll cut out your lying tongue."

His Adam's apple bobbing, West gulped.

"The captain asked you a question. Don't make me repeat it."

"Five o'clock." West pulled away his arm, dropping his cigar on the sawdust floor.

"You're sure?" His hand still on his knife, Ben scrutinized him.

"Yes." West nodded as he stubbed out the lit cigar with his boot.

"You're *absolutely* certain?"

"Yes." His tone sharp, West rolled his eyes. "Five o'clock."

"Louder." Ben called over a sergeant sitting at the bar and several enlisted men lounging at a nearby table. "These witnesses didn't hear you. When and where did you see Miss McShane and me?"

"Sunday"—West's voice was a whisper—"at five o'clock by Limpia Creek."

The men heckled and jeered among themselves.

The sergeant spat in the nearest spittoon.

Ben turned to Belle. "I understand you met with Lieutenant West at that hour?"

"I did." She sneered.

"You saw Belle after Lieutenant West finished with her last Sunday didn't you, boys?" Jack spoke to the sergeant and enlisted men from behind the bar.

The men all agreed, nodding and speaking over each other.

"Five o'clock is when Jimmy took out his frustrations on me." Belle pulled down her sleeve, revealing her bruised shoulder and battered back, and swept back her hair from her neck, exposing the choke marks. Then letting go her hair, she jerked her dress back up, covering the marks he had left on her body.

"Sergeant, men." Ben turned toward the soldiers. "Would you swear in a military court you saw Lieutenant West here at that time?"

"Glad to." The sergeant spat again, just missing West's shined shoes. "One thing I can't abide is a woman beater."

"You've made grave allegations against a fellow officer." His jaw clenching and his lips white, the captain gritted his teeth as he turned toward West.

The lieutenant gazed at his polished shoes.

"Look at me when I address you."

His eyes glassy, West met his gaze.

"And you've made serious accusations against my daughter." The captain's voice shook. "What have you to say for yourself?"

Sullen, West mumbled.

"Speak up." Standing at his full height, Ben stepped into his space. "These witnesses didn't hear you, and neither did I. What do you have to say for yourself?"

"Sorry," he muttered.

"You'll have to do better"—the captain pounded his fist on the bar—"and in front of my daughter, my wife, the community, and the chaplain, or your slander against my daughter and Lieutenant Williams goes on your permanent record."

"I did nothing—told a fib." West's eyes opened wide. "Not even that, a joke."

"A 'joke'?" Ben gestured to Belle's bruises. "Like this 'joke'?"

"She's a saloon girl—a hustler." Sneering, West turned up his nose. "What's a whore matter?"

"Apologize to the lady." Ben had seen enough brutalization on the frontier. Seeing its effects in "civilized" society rubbed him the wrong way.

West gave a short, disgusted snort. "What lady—"

"Apologize." In a single motion, Ben pulled his knife from its sheath and held its blade against West's neck.

"I apologize." Trapped, his back to the bar, West spoke through gritted teeth as he strained away from the knife.

"Now show the lady how sorry you are for your actions." Ben pressed the blade into his neck.

"*All right.*" As West glared, a thin line of red appeared at his collar. "What do you want from me?"

"Give her your wallet."

"What?" West's eyes flashed.

Ben pressed the blade harder.

West groaned and slid his bulging wallet across the bar.

"Ma'am, take whatever lost wages he caused you and then some for putting you through this pain and suffering." Ben glanced at her without letting up his knife's pressure. "If I were you, I'd take his last dollar."

With a grateful smile, she nodded, almost shyly. Then tossing her chin at West, she took out every bill before shoving the empty wallet across the bar.

Ben withdrew his knife.

"Are we done?" West pocketed the wallet.

"We're just beginning. You have another lady's pardon to ask—actually two." The captain turned to the men. "Sergeant, I know you and your men are off duty, but will you escort this"—he sneered—"*officer* to the chapel?"

"With pleasure, sir." The brawny Irish sergeant spat again, this time missing the spittoon and hitting West's shoes. He wore a self-satisfied smile. "This way, lieutenant…if you please…"

"Williams, assemble the officers and their wives in the chapel."

"Yes, sir."

"And Williams." The captain's voice cracked. He dipped his chin and cleared his throat. "Thank you for coming to my daughter's rescue…again."

"Glad to help, sir." The image of the ripped feather pillow came to mind. *But is West's confession too little, too late?*

****

Less than an hour later, Ben assembled the chaplain, officers, and their wives at the fort's chapel.

"What's the meaning of this disturbance?" The chaplain fiddled with his spectacles.

"Jesus at the well." Ben answered his demanding tone with an ironic half-smile.

His face bruised and bleeding, West walked in looking the worse for wear.

"The lieutenant took an unfortunate spill dismounting his horse." The sergeant abruptly turned toward him. "Ain't that so, sir?"

West's eyes blazed, but he gave a terse nod.

The enlisted men smothered chuckles.

Cadence walked in with Mrs. McShane as the McIntyres and Purdues arrived with the others.

"What's going on?" Cadence stared at James' cut and bruised face before turning to Ben.

"Gathering feathers…" Ben grimaced. "The chaplain gave a sermon this morning about the woman at the well." He turned toward the pastor. "What were your words? 'We all have sins for which we're ashamed. How will we deal with these regrets?' Am I right?"

The man summarized his sermon, ending, "Admit we erred, but not change our ways? Or will we confess our sins, and sin no more?"

"Lieutenant West." His eyes steely, the captain turned toward him. "You've made quite a few accusations this past week. Now make amends." He glanced about the room. "Tell these good people what you told us earlier."

"I apologize for any inconvenience I've caused." West licked his lips as he looked from face to face, his gaze resting briefly on Cadence.

"Not good enough." The captain shook his head. "You've caused a lot more damage than 'inconvenience.' Apologize."

"Sorry," West mumbled.

"Sorry for *what?*" The captain sneered.

"Sorry for everything."

"Not good enough." His gaze unwavering, the

captain scrutinized him. "Tell these people again how you 'saw' my daughter and Lieutenant Williams in a morally compromised position."

Pausing, West peered at his scuffed shoes. He swallowed. He took a deep breath. "I didn't."

Murmurs broke out among the gathered people.

"You didn't *what*?" When the man did not answer, the captain raised his voice. "Look at me when I address you."

His chest heaving, West raised his eyes, narrow red slits in his apoplectic face.

"You didn't see them in any dishonorable position because...where were you?"

"At the saloon..."

"As witnessed by the owner of the What Cheer House and Saloon, Jack Kelly, his employee, the sergeant, and these enlisted men." The captain turned toward the group. "Lieutenant West slandered the good name of my daughter. In addition to believing his lies, *worse*, many of you repeated them and shunned her. A lot of folks need to apologize to Cadence, starting with you, chaplain."

"No harm intended, Miss McShane." Removing his spectacles, the chaplain busied himself polishing them with his handkerchief.

Several others murmured *sorry*.

She acknowledged them with distracted nods and turned toward her father. "With the truth out, what will become of James?"

"Lieutenant West has requested a transfer, *effective immediately*." The captain's expression was grim. A deep V between his eyes, he turned toward the man. "Isn't that so?"

West's jaw fell open. Then he pursed his lips and gave a quick nod before staring at his shoes.

"Sergeant, escort Lieutenant West to his quarters to pack only the necessities. Have the rest of his gear shipped to Fort Clark. Then bring him to my quarters for his transfer papers."

"Yes, sir." The sergeant stepped into West's space, forcing him to move. "After you, lieutenant."

As they left, the captain turned to the officers and their wives. "I trust Lieutenant West's confession and departure will bring a halt to this gossip." Satisfied by their nods, he harrumphed. "Then good evening to you."

"Glad this is over." Sarah hugged Cadence on her way out.

Flossie followed with a whispered, "Sorry, Cadence."

The group departed amid a chorus of good nights, leaving just the McShanes and Ben in the chapel.

"How did you ever get James to confess?" Cadence studied her father.

"Cady"—he glanced at Ben—"why don't you ask Lieutenant Williams?"

Chapter 12
Schoolmarm

With James' departure, life at the fort returned to normal, and socializing resumed, but Cadence quickly tired of the rounds of teas and dinner parties.

"I need something more to do than just fill my time. Something worthwhile," she told Ben on one of their walks. "You're so lucky. You have a career—a job—while I fritter away my time, entertaining or being entertained."

"Isn't that what officers' wives and daughters do?" He chuckled. "Socialize?"

"To some extent, but they also have duties. Sarah and Flossie stay busy managing their households and making clothes for their family. As the captain's wife, my mother hosts visitors and lends a sympathetic ear to young recruits, but I have no responsibilities."

"You mean you're tired of playing parcheesi and pinochle?"

"Drinking tea and reading periodicals aren't enough." She rolled her eyes at his tongue-in-cheek inquiry. "I want to *do* something—accomplish something."

"Like what?"

"I don't know. Fort life doesn't have duties for women. Well, milking cows or washing laundry, but the enlisted men's wives and the women on suds row do those chores. I have nothing to do."

He rubbed his chin. "Maybe you could start a business?"

"Doing what?"

"Dressmaking?" He shrugged.

Though she had considered becoming a seamstress and sewing ladies' riding outfits, the idea reminded her of James forcing the wedding-dress pattern on her. Scowling at the memory, she shook her head.

"All right, if dressmaking doesn't suit you, maybe start a hat-making shop?"

Raising her brows, she gave him a sour smile. "Good idea if the town had enough women to support a millinery store."

"Then what about writing?"

"Maybe I could start keeping a journal?"

****

"Have you heard?" Flossie let out a great sigh over tea the following week.

The ladies' ears perked.

"The schoolmaster's leaving to go back East."

"No." Her hand flying to her chest, Sarah jerked back in her seat. "Now, who'll teach the children?"

"I will." Her teacup poised at her lips, Cadence spoke before she thought.

"Not if your father has anything to say about the subject." Her mother raised her brow. "You know how he feels about women working."

"Fiddle-de-dee. I wouldn't earn money or be employed. I'd just volunteer my time for a worthy cause." As Cadence sipped her tea, she swallowed a grin. *That logic should satisfy him…shouldn't it?*

****

"You'll do *what?*" His face red, his eyes opening wide and then squinting as he set down his cigar, her father shook his head. "No daughter of mine is earning a living, not while I have a breath of life in me."

"But I wouldn't accept a dime." Palms upturned, Cadence shrugged. "I'll just volunteer my services until the schoolmaster's position is filled."

"Though I oppose women working—adamantly, I might add—filling that position *would* resolve the education issue." He grumbled as he gave her a stern look. Then seeming to reconsider, he waggled his finger. "But just until a new schoolmaster is found—not a minute more."

Throwing her arms around him in a bear hug, she winked at her mother. *Who'd have thought?*

****

Cadence wore her mother's cameo on her high collar as she joined Mr. Haberdasher and the children in the chapel, which doubled during the week as the school. Her on-the-job training began with observing how the schoolmaster taught all eight grades by himself.

Four children were in the first grade and two in the second. Two were in the fourth grade. Two were in the sixth grade, and one each in the seventh and eighth grades.

"It's the largest enrollment the school has ever had." His face devoid of humor, Mr. Haberdasher eyed her dubiously.

He gave Cadence the impression he doubted her capability, and she straightened her spine as she squared her shoulders.

"This profession demands a firm hand. The

classroom's no place for feminine oversentimentality. You must lead the classroom in the same manner your father leads this post."

She nodded as she sat beside him in a semi-circle at the front of the room. Two first graders sat on her left, sharing one McGuffey Reader, and the other two sat on his right, sharing another.

The children took turns reading aloud as Mr. Haberdasher corrected their pronunciation or defined words. The rest of the school's children sat writing on their slates or reading books while the teacher worked with the first graders.

After forty minutes, Mr. Haberdasher instructed the children in the semi-circle to sit at their desks, and he called the second graders. Bringing their slates with them, one sat next to the schoolmaster, and one sat next to Cadence.

"Four plus four equals what?"

The children scribbled the math problems on the slates and showed him their work.

"Sandra, your handwriting is illegible. Good penmanship indicates tidiness and accuracy." His stern mouth pursed, he frowned. "Erase the slate and write four plus five plus two. What's the answer?"

After forty minutes, he sent them back to their desks and called the two fourth-graders to the front for a spelling bee. When they could not correctly spell a word, he opened the floor to the rest of the students. "Anyone?"

The seventh grader raised his hand. Mr. Haberdasher called on him, and he not only gave the correct spelling, but demonstrated for Cadence how the open-classroom method worked.

It teaches all the students, not just those in the grade being instructed.

During the next period, the sixth graders ran through their elocution exercises.

"Practice the vowel sounds." Mr. Haberdasher enunciated clearly. "Using B, for example, place a consonant before each vowel thusly: bay, bee, bah, boh, and boo. Now repeat them, starting with the consonant C, then D, and so on."

The children intoned their exercises, working through the alphabet.

"Now for the plosives." Mr. Haberdasher pursed his lips. "Practice saying these letters, three times in quick succession: P-B-T-D-K-G."

As the children repeated by rote, their monotone voices droning, Cadence stifled a sigh. "Why don't we make this drill more fun? How about a tongue twister, like 'I saw a kitten eating chicken in the kitchen?' "

The children chuckled as they stumbled over the words.

"Or try saying this sentence fast three times." Cadence swallowed a smile. "If a dog chews shoes, whose shoes does he choose?"

Other students mumbled the tongue twisters at their desks.

"Say 'stupid superstition' five times fast."

The classroom exploded with muttered sibilants and laughter, not quieting down until Mr. Haberdasher rapped on his desk, calling for order.

His dark expression caught Cadence off guard.

"We'll take a fifteen-minute recess, children, after which the seventh and eighth graders will come to the front for their geography lesson."

As the students filed outside, one girl hung back. "Will you be our new teacher, Miss McShane?"

"Yes, Emily, starting tomorrow morning." Cadence smiled, recognizing Tom and Sarah's daughter from her fair-haired braids. *She has her father's thick, blond hair.*

"I'm glad," the girl whispered.

"Me, too," Cadence whispered back, meaning it.

When the room emptied, Mr. Haberdasher gave her a constipated frown.

She took a deep breath, steeling herself.

"Miss McShane, children must be controlled with a firm hand. Strict discipline must be maintained at all times."

She bristled, remembering James' heavy-handed manipulation. She still felt his fingers pressing into the back of her neck.

"*Controlled* is a strong word, Mr. Haberdasher. I prefer a less rigid approach. Changing the pace by combining educational games with dull drills not only breaks the monotony of memorization, but the exercises build verbal skills and challenge the students."

"Stern supervision is necessary from the outset, Miss McShane, and I fear you cannot manage this group."

"I disagree, Mr. Haberdasher, but since you're leaving in the morning—and until the position is filled—I'll be the substitute teacher." Lifting her chin, she sat erect. "Now, would you care to share your lesson plans or not?"

****

The following Saturday, Cadence went rock hunting with Ben to celebrate surviving her first week of school.

"How did your classes go?"

"I love the students. They're a smart group, and I enjoy their company." She flashed him a bright smile. Then looking inward, she paused. "More importantly, I'm accomplishing something—doing something worthwhile."

"I know what you mean." He nodded. "Doing a good day's work is its own reward but sharing your knowledge with someone is especially satisfying."

"You've taught children?"

"Not children, but I've trained young men to hunt and track." He gave her a lopsided grin. "Not quite the same as teaching school, but similar—sharing knowledge and passing the torch."

Talking with him is so easy. Not polite chitchat, just a quiet meeting of the minds. Studying him, she returned his smile.

"What are you thinking?"

"Since you enjoy educating so much, teach me what to look for—that is, if you expect me to find anything unique." Rather than admit her attraction, she changed the subject.

"Unearthing stones shouldn't be difficult. This area's teeming with fossils and agates." Kicking at the dusty caliche with his boot, he uncovered what looked like a clamshell and handed Cadence the fossil.

"It feels like a rock." After weighing the stone in her hand, she fingered the ridges. "Yet it looks like a shellfish."

"The Gulf of Mexico used to cover this entire area." He gestured to the hardscrabble.

"This desert?" She glanced at the surrounding

chaparral and bare rock. "You're not serious."

"I am." He nodded. "What you're holding in your hand is a piece of the distant past."

"Amazing." She studied the relic from all angles.

"Fossils are everywhere in this area but especially common in arroyos or wherever rain has washed gullies, exposing them."

She dropped the petrified clam into a bag tied on her belt. Then she noticed something on the ground. The rock looked like quartz but was a pale, translucent blue. Retrieving the stone, she examined its color before showing him. "Is this one anything special?"

"You have a good eye." Nodding slowly, he arched his brow. "This is chalcedony—usually a pale blue color or white—but this mineral can also come in a semitransparent red or orange."

"I'd love to find one of each color." As he handed back the rock, she added it to her collection.

They searched for several hours, picking and digging near the surface. When the sack grew too heavy for her belt, Cadence transferred the rocks to her saddle bag.

"Think you have enough stones and fossils for one day?"

"More than enough." She chuckled.

"Then, how would you like to have lunch on that cliff?"

Pointing, he spoke almost too casually, as if being careful not to let on a secret.

Is he hiding something? After scrutinizing him, she shrugged off her suspicions. "Sure."

When their horses reached the crest, Cadence sat tall in her saddle, peering over the bluff's edge. "This setting's beautiful—perfect for a picnic." She turned toward him. "How did you ever find this outlook?"

"My Comanche father used to take me here hunting wild hogs. I loved this view."

"I can see why." Gazing at the rugged landscape's successive ranges of mountains and craggy peaks, she nodded.

"No matter where I traveled, I always compared those lands to these and said I'd come back"—he swallowed—"when the time was right."

"And now you have." She turned toward him with a congratulatory nod.

"This property's the only land I've ever wanted." He licked his lips and swallowed. "I've saved for it since I joined the cavalry."

"You must have quite a nest egg by now." She grinned. "Despite the dent from your bake sale bid."

"Despite the bid." He gave a wry laugh. Then his smile fading, he grew serious. "I still had enough money to put a down payment on this property."

"You own this land?" Surprised, she studied him.

"The bank does, but as long as I make the payments, the land's mine. Just signed the papers yesterday."

His smile was tentative—almost bashful.

"Good for you." Glad for his success, she smiled her congratulations.

Raising his brow in a questioning gaze, he worked his jaw as though he had something more to say.

"Yes?" She leaned toward him, listening.

The seconds ticked by. Two mockingbirds perched on branches overhead, vocalizing with whistles and trills. A rock squirrel chittered, its tail swishing back and forth while it scolded them.

Despite the bucolic surroundings, the tension became palpable. "What will you do with the property?"

"Ranch the pastures." His gaze searched her face. "Once I build a few corrals, I plan—"

"You're leaving the cavalry?" As his words sank in, her shoulders drooped. Used to career officers, she could not envision him leaving the Army before retirement.

He nodded.

"When?"

"The end of the year."

"Oh…" Her voice dropped, ending in a disappointed sigh.

"Is anything wrong?"

"No. Well…every man I know is a soldier or officer. I haven't spent any time with civilians— ranchers." Fidgeting, she frowned. "Besides, I've gotten used to seeing you at the fort, and I'll mi—" Nearly blurting out her feelings, she made a feeble attempt at a smile. "Guess the next time I want to go rock hunting, I'll have to come calling."

"The land's not far from the fort, only a mile or so from the Rodriguez ranch."

"What?" As though a thunderhead passed overhead, her sundrenched day lost its luster. "Your ranch is *that* close to the Apache raid? I had no idea we were so far from the fort."

"Only an hour and a half's ride."

Chewing the inside of her cheek, she peered over the cliff's edge, searching for signs of Indians. Then bracing herself against the pommel, she sat tall in the saddle, looking in all directions and checking the bluff behind them, making sure their exit route was clear. Finally, she turned back. "Maybe we should have a quick lunch and…" She bit back the words, *Return to the fort*.

"Sure." Ben's shoulders slumped. His smile wilted. "We can eat on the bluff. The ground's level there." Dismounting, he carried the basket containing the tablecloth, tin cups, bread, cheese, and wine to a shady spot beneath a mountain mahogany tree.

Uneasy, Cadence kept a watchful eye for Apaches as she spread out the tablecloth.

Ben sliced the cheese with his hunting knife, while she poured the wine.

Then struggling to be sociable, she clinked her tin cup against his. "Congratulations again on buying this gorgeous property."

"Thanks." His eyes dull and distant, he curled his lips into an unconvincing smile.

The sun was shining. The sky was Texas blue, not a cloud in it, but the day's mood had changed. Instead of Ben's easy banter, his exchanges seemed stilted and forced.

What did I say?

"Anything wrong?" She trained her gaze on him as she sipped her wine and mentally replayed their recent conversation. "Have I said something to upset you?"

"No, I was just thinking."

"About what?" His chest moved as if suppressing a soundless sigh.

"Maybe you'd like to visit the Rodriguez family after lunch?"

"Yes, I'd love to see how they're doing." Seeing

Mariana and Lupe again outweighed any threat of Apaches.

After a quiet lunch, she and Ben repacked the picnic basket, remounted, and left the Davis Mountains behind. They reined their horses south toward the Chisos Mountains and the Rodriguez ranch, riding through a wide, grassy valley with tufts of black grama grass, spiny canes of ocotillo, and spiky spirals of sotol.

"Aunt Cadence, Uncle Ben." Mariana was the first to spot them, calling as she ran to meet them.

"Hello," Cadence called back, startled at Mariana's use of English.

The girl chattered in an excited patois while she led them to the Rodriguez' adobe cabin.

Cadence chuckled at her enthusiasm but had trouble following her patter.

Ben interpreted the mixture of English and Spanish, telling her the gist of the girl's conversation every few sentences.

"How are you learning to speak English?" Cadence spoke slowly, enunciating each word. "Is someone teaching you?"

"*Si*." Mariana nodded. "Neighbor *movido en las inmediaciones*."

Cadence looked to Ben for the translation.

"A neighbor moved into the ranch nearby." He smiled.

Lupe joined them, wiping her hands on her apron. Then welcoming them with warm hugs and rapid Spanish, she invited them into the rebuilt cabin.

Ben congratulated Lupe on the progress they had made, showing Cadence what they had accomplished in just a few weeks.

"The cabin's roof had burned and collapsed inside the cabin's burnt shell. Not only have they removed the rubble, they've restored the roof."

Kicking aside a rag rug, Lupe showed them the *"trampilla."*

"A trapdoor?" Cadence turned toward Ben for confirmation.

"It's a root cellar, good for storing vegetables and canned goods." He nodded as Lupe lifted the hatch and pointed to the narrow steps descending. Then he grimaced as he translated. "But the cellar's also a safe place should the Apaches ever return."

Safe place? Cadence caught her breath. Hearing about refugees' narrow escape while safe inside the fort was one thing but standing where these people had been attacked once and seeing how they prepared for another raid put teeth in the risk. Suddenly Cadence was afraid for Lupe and Mariana. Then she looked at Ben. *Soon he'll be in the same danger.*

"What's wrong?"

"Apaches." She swallowed.

His face darkened in a scowl.

Lupe's happy chatter broke off in a subdued hush. Then, with a forced smile, she asked if they were hungry. Could she make them lunch?

"Thanks, we've already eaten." Ben shook his head. "We just wanted to say hello."

Wish I'd known we'd visit. I'd have brought a gift. Then Cadence remembered the rocks and fossils they had found, and she motioned them to follow.

Before they left the cabin, Lupe lowered the trapdoor, carefully covering its outline with the large rag rug.

As Cadence watched, a cold chill raced down her spine, and she rushed outside into the sunlight. Taking deep breaths to stave off the sudden panic attack, she spread the contents of her saddlebag on a makeshift table—an upturned barrel.

"Help yourselves."

"*¿De verdad?*" Her dark eyes widening, Mariana looked to Cadence.

"Yes, choose as many as you like."

The girl fingered through the colorful rocks as if they were priceless gems.

"This." Finally choosing a piece of translucent white chalcedony, she spoke in English.

"Take more." Her palm spread open, Cadence gestured toward the stones.

"This." Mariana shook her head as she held the stone against her heart.

"You'll have to visit us at the fort." Cadence gathered the rest of the stones.

"*¿Cuando?*" Mariana's eyes sparkled.

"*Pronto.*" With a wry chuckle, Lupe put her hands on the girl's shoulders.

Cadence smiled while she untied her horse.

"No go." Mariana threw her arms around her. "No go, Aunt Cadence."

"I'll see you again soon." She hugged the girl. "*Pronto.*"

"*¿Promesa?*"

****

"How safe is the Rodriguez family?" Cadence studied Ben as he led the way back to Fort Davis.

He lifted his brow as he inhaled and then sighed.

"I see." His silence told her more than she wanted

195

to know. "Is frontier life that dangerous away from the fort?"

"The times are changing. Most Apaches have moved to reservations in Arizona, *but* renegade war parties still roam the area." His eyes as hard and dark as lava rocks, he caught her gaze. "Believe me, I'd like to put your fears to rest, but the danger is real."

Looking away, she grimaced. "I'm worried for Lupe and Mariana." She glanced sideways. "And you."

"Me?" His brow lifted.

"Once you move out of the fort and live on your ranch, I'll worry about you, too."

Mute, Ben bit his lip, leaving Cadence to interpret his silence.

Has he no words to console me, or is he afraid of saying too much?

****

The days passed as quickly as the autumn winds sweeping through the mountains. Up at six to ready the classroom and prepare her lessons, Cadence spent the days teaching and the evenings grading papers.

One night as Cadence edited English compositions, her mother brought her a cup of sassafras tea.

"Thank you." Inhaling the brisk, root-beer aroma, she breathed a contented sigh. "Tea is just what I needed."

"Nothing like a hot drink to chase away the chill." Her mother rested her hand on Cadence's shoulder as she scanned the paperwork. "How do you like your new routine?"

"My days are full." She stopped mid-sip, gathering her thoughts. Then she smiled. "Teaching is challenging but rewarding. It gives my days meaning."

She set down her cup and lightly squeezed her mother's hand.

"Then I'm glad you took this position." The older woman leaned over to hug her.

"Me, too. Besides, working makes the time go by faster when…" She turned toward her mother with an embarrassed laugh.

"When Ben's away?" Wearing a sympathetic smile, she nodded. "When is he coming back?"

"Not for another week, but staying busy keeps me from worrying." She made a face. "Helps, anyway."

With James gone, the fort was an officer short, so the remaining officers had heavier rosters escorting mail coaches and the occasional wagon train. Ben was gone every two of three weeks, leading patrols to and from Fort Quitman.

The separation was painful because each round trip took twelve to fourteen days, but her fear for his safety was worse than their time apart. Thanks to marauding Apaches and banditos, every time they parted, she knew it could be their last. This was war—whether declared or not—and each time they said goodbye, she worried. *Will I see him again?*

****

October slipped into November almost unnoticed. With Ben gone so much, she spent most of her time at school, teaching and developing warm relationships with her students. Although she maintained a teacher / student gulf between them, she referred to her pupils as "my little friends."

Tom and Sarah's eighth-grade daughter, Emily, quickly became her assistant, helping the younger students with questions and homework, while Cadence taught the classes.

"Miss McShane."

"Yes." She glanced from grading the sixth-grade history tests.

As the girl erased the chalkboard one day after school, she abruptly turned toward her. "I'm glad you didn't marry Lieutenant West."

"What prompted that remark?"

"Lieutenant Williams is so much handsomer." Emily blushed.

James had not come to mind for weeks, but she had thought of Ben—and often. He was her last thought before drifting to sleep and her first thought on waking, like taking off and putting on glasses. She smiled at the analogy. *He's become the spectacles I use to view life.* Then she sat erect. *What about when I'm sleeping? Is he the man of my dreams?*

Chapter 13
Trapdoors

After safely escorting the stagecoach to Fort Quitman, Ben learned a rogue band of Mescalero Apaches had been spotted heading southeast. He caught his breath. *How close to the Rodriguez ranch and my property?*

He led his patrol home along a more southerly route than usual and approached the Rodriguez ranch from the Chihuahuan Desert, hoping to surprise any covert Apaches and channel them north. But the view through his field glasses alarmed him. No men worked the fields, and the mule pens were empty.

His heart sinking, he advanced cautiously. The corral posts had been torn down. The mules either had escaped or, more likely, been stolen. Worse, he heard no welcoming cry from Mariana. Then, as he smelled smoke, he noticed turkey vultures circling overhead, and he said a silent prayer, hoping his instincts were wrong.

He found Juan and his two brothers just outside the cabin door, their bloated bodies shot with so many arrows, they looked like pin cushions.

Ben's worst suspicions confirmed, he held up his right hand, halting the men, and turned to the sergeant. "Assemble a burial detail."

"Dismount." The burly sergeant chose six

cavalrymen for the task.

Walking behind the smoldering adobe cabin, Ben found the naked, raped body of Lupe, her breasts cut off and her throat slit. Taking deep breaths to dispel his revulsion, he said another silent prayer as he called two men to cover her with a blanket and bury her near her sons.

Remembering her determination to rebuild, he stared at the adobe shell without seeing. Once again, he envisioned Comanches setting fire to his parents' cabin and killing his family. He heard his mother's screams above the war whoops, and he swallowed the bitter metallic taste of his fear.

He looked for Mariana, unsure which would be crueler—finding her tortured body or finding no trace. The cabin was burned to its foundation, causing the roof to collapse. Only ashes, warm embers, and rubble remained. He scoured the surrounding fields but found nothing. *She's likely been captured and sold into slavery.*

"The men finished burying the bodies, sir." The sergeant grimaced. "Would you care to say a few words over their graves?"

Already? How long have we been here? He checked his pocket watch and turned toward the hastily dug graves. Then a nagging thought stopped him in his tracks. *What am I forgetting? What have I overlooked? The root cellar!*

"Have a detail of men haul away the collapsed roof's refuse."

The sergeant's eyes narrowed to doubtful slits.

Though he held little hope the cellar had gone undetected, Ben stared him down.

"Yes, sir." After a beat, the sergeant saluted. Then he turned to the men. "You three, cleanup detail. Remove the fallen crossbeams. Clear out the cabin."

Though he also suspected the task was a waste of time, he owed it to Lupe to be sure. Even if the Apaches had not discovered Mariana, he doubted the girl could have survived in the cellar's tiny airspace after they set fire to the cabin.

After the men carried off the scorched timbers and scooped out the worst of the cabin's debris, they called him.

To his surprise, charred remnants of the rag rug remained. Taking a deep breath to bolster his resolve, he reached for the trapdoor and lifted. Expecting silence, he all but dropped the door when muffled crying came from within.

"Mariana, is that you?"

A pitiful sob escaped from the dark space.

Then a small voice called, "Uncle Ben?"

"Yes, Mariana, come out. You're safe. The Apaches are gone. These men are soldiers." He shouted to the sergeant. "Get my canteen and some rations."

Out crept a bedraggled, soot-covered girl. Blinking at the sunlight and sobbing, she struggled to focus her bloodshot eyes as if trying to make sense of the burned-out scene.

"Uncle Ben, is my family…?"

"It's over." Unable to look at Mariana's bewildered gaze, he brought her to his chest and held her close. "You're safe now."

"But my family?" She pulled her head back, watching him. "¿Abuela?"

Grimacing, he shook his head. "They didn't

survive."

"I heard screaming." Her red-rimmed eyes filled with tears. "I wanted to come out, but grandmother made me promise not to make a sound…not to come out until…until she told me. I was so afraid."

What do I say? Unsure how to ease the girl's pain, Ben motioned to the sergeant for his canteen. After removing its cap, he held the canteen against her lips. "Drink this water. You'll feel better."

She took a long draught and then took a deep breath.

"Are you hungry?"

"Grandmother stored food in the root cellar." She shook her head.

At a loss for how else to help, he rubbed his hand across his chin. Finally, he looked Mariana in the eyes. "We're holding a burial service for your family. Would you like to join me?"

Still sobbing as tears ran down her face, creating grimy streaks, she nodded.

"Take my hand." He slowly led her to the shallow graves, mounded over with heavy rocks.

The soldiers made crude crosses from sticks, and the moment Mariana saw them, a new round of tears spilled down her cheeks.

"Are you sure?" Seeing her raw grief rekindled memories of his own orphaned childhood.

She nodded.

"Heavenly Father." Ben removed his hat.

The men followed suit.

"We're gathered…" Glancing at the girl, he choked. Then, after clearing his throat, he started over. "We're gathered here to remember the brave men and women who died defending their family and their land. We ask You to take their souls to dwell with You in eternity. Amen."

"Amen," the men mumbled, putting on their hats.

"Which one is *Abuela's*?" She stared at the rock-covered graves.

After Ben translated, the sergeant glanced at the nearest mound.

Mariana fell to her knees. Face down, she lay on Lupe's grave, her tears splattering the stones.

"Sergeant, have the men mount up." *Give her what privacy we can.*

"Yes, sir."

After the soldiers withdrew, Ben waited several minutes. Then he tugged Mariana's hand. "We need to leave now—before it gets dark."

Silent, she shook her head as she remained prone on the grave.

Out of ideas, he tried one last tactic. "Don't you want to see Cadence?"

She looked from her stone bed, sniffling. Then taking a jagged breath, she nodded, placed her small hand in his, and stood.

She can't stay here, but where can she stay?

****

With the wisp of a girl riding in front of him, asleep in the saddle, Ben had time to think. Children weren't allowed in the unmarried officers' quarters. Tom and Sarah might take her in temporarily—but their quarters were already cramped. Possibly the chaplain would know of someone willing to take in another mouth to feed, but locating a family could take time.

As they approached the fort, Ben reined his horse

toward the captain's quarters. Dismounting, he helped Mariana down and then handed his reins to the corporal.

Cadence was on the veranda, waiting for them when they reached the top of the stairs.

"What happened?" As Mariana ran to her arms, she took one look at the muddied girl and lifted her gaze to Ben.

"Apaches attacked the Rodriguez ranch, and she has nowhere to stay tonight." Mentally exhausted from the scenes he had witnessed—as well as the memories they called to mind—he struggled to stay detached and composed.

Whether the captain's wife heard the fatigue in his voice or sensed his anguish, she stepped forward, speaking to the girl as he translated. "How about a bath, dinner, and then we'll make you a bed on the settee tonight?"

Not letting go of Cadence, the girl shook her head, pulling back.

"This is my mother." Nodding toward her, Cadence sank to her knees and held the girl close. "She'll help you with your bath. Then after you eat dinner"—her shoulders drooped—"you'll sleep with me tonight, all right?"

The girl nodded, let go of Cadence, and accepted the older woman's outstretched hand.

"What's your name?" Her chin trembling, Mrs. McShane forced a bright smile.

"Mariana." She stared behind her, watching Cadence.

"I'll be inside in a minute." She held up her index finger. As soon as they were alone, she turned toward him. "What happened?"

How do I describe the scene? Vivid images of the Rodriguez family's tortured, disfigured bodies surfaced in his mind like the bile rising in his throat. Pushing aside the flashbacks, he swallowed his anger and revulsion, only to find the visions replaced with fears for Mariana's future. She was vulnerable now as an orphan, and her helplessness stirred recollections of his own stolen childhood. All he could trust himself to say was "Apaches…"

"Lupe?"

He shook his head.

"Juan? His brothers?" Her voice cracked.

"They're all"—he spared her the particulars—"gone…"

Still kneeling, she swayed.

He caught her in his arms, steadying her. Again an overwhelming urge to protect her gripped him, and he helped her to her feet.

"I hope you don't mind my bringing Mariana here." He drew a deep breath as he loosened his grip. "But she has nowhere to stay, and I couldn't think of anywhere else to take her."

"Of course, Mariana can stay with us…at least until we find her relatives."

"I wouldn't know where to begin looking…" He shook his head at the plan's futility.

"I see." Blinking, she seemed to digest his words. "You did the only thing you could. She's already been through so much. After her mother died last summer, giving birth, how can she deal so soon with losing the rest of her family?" She met his gaze. "And how did she survive when no one else did?"

"The root cellar." He shared the details.

"That poor girl's lost so much…"

"Everything." Her bittersweet smile tugged at his heart. Sorry he had entangled her in Mariana's dilemma, he wished he could untie the knots.

"Something will work out. It has to, but in the meantime, she's welcome to stay here, and…*I know*." Catching her breath, she gave a deep nod. "I'll take her to school. Somehow, this tragedy will work itself out."

"For her sake, I hope so." Grateful, he clasped her hand. "Thank you for taking her in tonight. I don't know what I'd have done if you hadn't."

"After all she's been through, I'm glad we can help, but a bed and meal seem so…inadequate." As her shoulders sagged, Cadence faltered, stumbling.

He caught her in his arms and drew her close, comforting her as much as finding comfort. Through his wool jacket, he felt the rise and fall of her chest against his, and the intimacy roused him. Her nearness, the clean scent of her hair, and the feathery tickle of her breath on his neck stirred him, and he bent his head to kiss her. As he lifted her chin, bringing her lips to his, he became aware of the irregularity of his actions, and he froze.

What am I doing? Clearing his throat, he held her out at arm's length. "I'll, uhm"—he swallowed—"I'll see if Sarah can spare another dress for Mariana." Slowly letting go her arms, he grasped her warm hands in a parting squeeze. *What was I thinking?*

Chapter 14
Families

Cadence teetered on her feet as she clung to his hands, steadying herself.

Seeing Mariana in her bedraggled state and hearing of her horrors had stunned her. Then Ben's arms around her, crushing her as they consoled, triggered a tumbling sensation, and her lips still tingled from the warm brush of his breath.

Now his sudden retreat left her frustrated and baffled—emotionally sapped. Too drained to move, she stood immobile while he let go her fingertips, one by one, as if reluctantly.

He gradually edged toward the stairs until he left with a final, parting tug.

A static spectator, she watched him walk into the night. Several moments passed before she regained her composure. Then the weight of her new responsibilities sank in. Taking a deep, fortifying breath, she opened the door and ventured inside.

Mariana sat in the warming kitchen, where Cadence's mother heated water for a sitz bath. Her father had carried in the galvanized tin tub and set it close to the hand pump and stove.

"Would you like some warm milk?" Cadence showed Mariana the milk bottle and pointed to the stove.

The girl nodded. "*Si.*" She paused, then added, "Thank you" in English.

Cadence gave her a half-smile, impressed she could remember her manners at such a sorrowful time. While the milk and water heated, she found a shrunken flannel nightgown close to Mariana's size.

When Cadence returned, her mother was ladling out the warm milk as she spoke to the girl in English.

Her dark eyes wide, Mariana looked on as though trying to follow the conversation.

By the time the bath water was ready, Mariana had finished her milk. Cadence and her mother helped her undress, and they found the chalcedony stone, cameo, and scarf tucked in the pleats of her bodice.

Of all her possessions, these are the ones she kept. Recalling the circumstances, Cadence stiffened.

"What's this rock?"

"I gave her this stone the day Ben and I went rock hunting."

"She's attached to you." Her mother's eyes dewy, she smiled.

"With all she's lost, I think she's clinging to whatever she can."

An hour later, Mariana had bathed, eaten a light supper, and was ready for bed.

Cadence tucked her in and added a heated brick wrapped in flannel to warm her feet. Then she changed into her nightgown and slipped between the sheets.

"*Buenas noches*, Aunt Cadence."

"Good night, Mariana." Exhausted, she fell asleep until thunder woke them. She rolled over and was drifting off when Mariana's sobbing revived her. "What's wrong?"

"*Abuela*," was all she said before tears choked her.

"It's all right." Motigoning her closer, Cadence stretched out her arm, while she held up the covers. "I'm here."

As Mariana rested her head on her shoulder, she whispered, "You're safe," over and over until the girl fell asleep. *But what if I can't always be here for her?* Her eyes wide open, Cadence stared into the dark. *What will become of her?*

****

The next morning, Cadence answered a knock at the front door.

"Lieutenant Williams stopped by last night and told us what happened." Emily held out a neatly folded bundle of pressed clothes. "Mother asked me to deliver this skirt and top I outgrew."

Dark eyes wide, Mariana peeked from the hall.

"Hi." When Emily spotted her, she grinned from ear to ear.

"Come in. I'd like you to meet Mariana." Cadence waved the girl over. "This is Emily."

"Emily."

The corners of Mariana's eyes crinkled into a shy smile.

"Emily, maybe you can help Mariana get dressed while I make coffee." Cadence got an idea. "Would you like to stay for breakfast?"

"Yes." Her eyes lighting up, Emily nodded, and the two girls retreated to the bedroom.

"Emily hasn't any other playmates her age." Cadence caught her mother's gaze. "Something tells me these two will become close friends."

"I hope so." Her smile wavered. "If they can

overcome the language barrier."

If it's not one thing, it's another. Cadence stifled a sigh. "Communication will be a challenge."

"Isn't that what you wanted?" Eyes twinkling, her mother watched her. "Challenges?"

****

After breakfast, Cadence, Mariana, and Emily crossed the parade grounds on their way to school.

Emily rang the hand bell, calling the other students to class, and then shared her desk and books with Mariana. From their smiles and muffled giggles, both girls seemed to enjoy the arrangement.

After the children took their seats, Cadence called Mariana to the front. "This is our newest student, Mariana Rodriguez. I'd like you to welcome her to our school."

Despite the stares and whispers, all the students said hello, waved, or smiled except the seventh grader, Billy Nichols.

The moment Cadence turned her back, he whispered, "Bean-eater."

"Billy Nichols, I'll have none of that language in this school, do you hear?"

"Yes'm."

"And that goes for the rest of you children." Gritting her teeth, Cadence counted to five. "Mariana needs to feel welcome here, and I intend to see she does."

Other than a few dirty looks from Billy, the rest of the morning passed without incident.

After lunch, Mariana accompanied Emily and Billy when they met for social studies. All went well until Mariana answered a question with "*Sí*" and immediately corrected herself with "Jes."

"Jes?" Mocking Mariana's accent, Billy sneered. "What's the matter? Can't you say yes? Stupid—"

"That will do, Billy." Cadence silently seethed. "You may return to your seat. From now on, you'll join the sixth graders." When he left their semi-circle, scowling, Cadence took a deep breath. *Now what do I do?*

****

The next day, Cadence, Emily, and Mariana arranged a small table at the back of the room and moved the rest of the desks closer to the front.

"This setup will keep you from disturbing the other students, and you'll have a little privacy."

"Privacy?" Emily's eyes glistened. "Is this a secret?"

"In a way." Cadence swallowed a smile. "Emily, I'm giving you a big responsibility. I want you to be Mariana's tutor. When you study, help her learn along with you."

"But Mariana doesn't speak English, Miss McShane." A small V appearing between her eyes, Emily cocked her head to one side. "At least, not much, not yet."

"I know." Cadence empathized with Emily but relied on her help. "And another thing."

"Yes?" The girl's eyes opened wide.

"For the rest of the semester, don't worry about answering the other students' questions. I'll help them. Just concentrate on teaching Mariana English."

A slow smile grew on Emily's face.

Mariana blinked, looking from one speaker to the other, as though struggling to follow their conversation.

"I'm asking a lot." Cadence studied Emily. "But will you accept this challenge?"

****

During the first few days, Emily gathered items from around the room, teaching Mariana how to pronounce their English names. After she exhausted the articles at school, she brought a different bag of objects from home every day, teaching Mariana those words.

When two weeks passed without a hitch, Cadence tentatively congratulated herself on the arrangement.

At home each night, Cadence coached Mariana, not just reinforcing her vocabulary and grammar, but schooling her in the rudiments of reading and writing.

Then, their striker began lingering after he brought the firewood, seeming to eavesdrop.

One evening in the warming kitchen, as Cadence helped Mariana study in the oil lamp's glow, a creaking board on their back porch startled her. Cadence held her finger to her lips and motioned to Mariana to continue conjugating the verb *go*, while she crept to the door.

"I go. I went. I will go." Nodding, the girl continued. "I am going. I was going. I will be going."

Her back stiffening, Cadence put her ear to the back door and heard a man's mumbling voice repeat the exercise after Mariana. She wrenched open the door, and Private Smith tumbled into the room.

"Explain yourself, private."

"I…I…I was mem'rizing, ma'am."

"Memorizing what?"

"The Rs, ma'am."

Puzzled, she studied him as she repeated his words. "What do you mean?"

"Readin' n' writin', ma'am."

"Why?"

"They says I be a free man, but I's not free."

"What do you mean?" She squinted.

"I's not free to look for jobs if'n I can't read."

"You've never learned?"

"No, ma'am." He shook his curly head. "Fiel' han's wasn't allowed to go to no school, not 'til after the war."

Cadence let his words sink in. "And when the war ended, you joined the cavalry?"

"Yes, ma'am, I took the onliest job I could find." He looked her in the eye. "They ain't many jobs for ex-slaves. Room, board, clothing, reg'ler meals, n' thirteen dollars a month sounded right good at the time."

"Yet you earn extra pay as our striker." She arched her brow. "It mustn't have sounded that good to you."

"Ma'am, I wanna buy me a piece of lan'." He took a deep breath. "I figure, if'n I can learn to read n' write n' cipher, I might could be hired on as the comp'ny clerk n' earn more money."

She looked from him to Mariana and back. "You already have two jobs. When would you find time to study?"

"I be thinkin' o' that, ma'am. I's good at mem'rizing. I mem'riz the lessons at night n' then runs 'em over in my head the next day while I be doin' my chores."

"I see." She debated between his logic and the military's division of rank. Tutoring Private Smith while she taught Mariana after hours made sense. *Teaching two wouldn't be much more work than teaching one.*

But Father and the army would view it as crossing

the lines of rank and discipline.

On the other hand, Smith's ability to read could help him advance to company clerk, which would benefit the fort. Playing devil's advocate, she considered the dilemma from her father's perspective. *If Smith were literate, he could fill an essential role.*

She peered at the man, gauging him. "If I teach you, would you promise to keep up with your studies, or would you lose interest after a week or two?"

"No, ma'am. I'd stick with my studies. You has my word on that."

But would he neglect his duties?

As she assessed the soldier, he seemed to sense her question.

"And learnin' won't interfere none with my chores, neither."

Convinced, she nodded. "Very well, I'll speak with the captain. If he agrees, you can join Mariana's after-hours class."

"Yes, ma'am." His dark eyes lit up.

"And it's *won't interfere with my chores, either,* not 'won't interfere none with my chores, neither.' " She smiled. "Triple negatives aren't needed."

"'Scuse me, ma'am?" His brow wrinkling, he tilted his head.

"Using three negatives—*won't, none,* and *neither*—isn't necessary. Just say, 'Learning won't interfere with my chores, either.' "

"Yes, ma'am." After carefully repeating the words, he grinned. "When can we start?"

****

When Mariana went to bed, Cadence joined her father in the parlor, pulling a footstool near the fire to warm her hands. Then, she faced him at an oblique angle as he read in his chair.

"Any word on getting reinforcements from Fort Clark?"

"Unfortunately, no." He set aside his paper with a sigh. "We're an officer short, as well as in need of a schoolteacher and a skilled workforce."

"I knew of the officer shortage, and for the time being, I'm substituting for the teacher"—she saw her opening—"but what kind of skilled labor does the fort need?"

"Mostly masons and carpenters but also literate men—company clerks and supply clerks to track and order the provisions."

"Doesn't the army have plenty of soldiers to fill those positions?" She tried to sound uninterested as if only making conversation.

"Out East, yes, but on the frontier, recruitment's low, and the men we have, though fine soldiers, are generally illiterate. The Tenth Cavalry consists mostly of unschooled former slaves. We need men who can read and write"—he drew a weary breath—"add and subtract."

"The three Rs," she mumbled.

"What did you say?"

"The three Rs"—she spoke up—"reading, writing, and arithmetic." She crooked her head as she studied him. "Why can't the soldiers attend basic classes here?"

"That's exactly what Washington recommends." He gave a dry laugh. "Congress ordered permanent garrisons like ours to open schools for the men, but we don't have the resources. We're not only underfunded; we're understaffed. We don't have an instructor."

"What about me?" She turned toward him.

"You're volunteering your time with the children until a replacement arrives—against my better judgment, I might add—but I will not allow my *unmarried* daughter to instruct a frontier garrison."

"Not a garrison"—she brushed imaginary lint from her skirt—"but what if I taught one soldier?" She met his gaze.

"What do you suggest?" He scrutinized her.

"What if I found a way to teach Mariana to read along with Private Smith?"

"Our striker?" He shook his head. "He's already working a double shift, and I won't tolerate dereliction of duty."

"He wants to learn to read, so he can apply for the company clerk position."

"Does he now?" His eyes dancing, the captain scrutinized her. Then he scowled. "Fraternizing across ranks is frowned upon."

"By whom? The army?" As she raised the question, she lifted her brow. "Why couldn't the regulations be relaxed if his ambition benefits the regiment?"

"Perception passes for truth, and your conduct—however well intentioned—would raise more eyebrows at the fort." He shook his head.

"Bridges." Her mother stood poised at the door, listening. "One of the biggest lessons in life is deciding which ones to cross and which ones to burn. Don't be afraid to do what's right because of what people will say. People will talk no matter what." She winked at her daughter. "Although you *do* seem to attract controversy."

Hearing the truth, Cadence swallowed a smile. "How can I make changes if I don't make waves?"

****

The next evening, she and Mariana sat studying at the kitchen table when Private Smith delivered the firewood. Detached as he filled the wood bins, he seemed indifferent as he opened the door to leave.

"Would you care to join us?" She glanced at the striker.

"Did I hear right, ma'am?" His eyes flashed. Then squinting, he studied her.

"You did, private." She swallowed a smile. "If you're still interested in learning to read, take a seat beside Mariana."

"Yes'm."

As he ventured a cautious smile, she placed a copy of McGuffey's Spelling Book, *The Pictorial Alphabet,* in front of her two students. Pointing out the letters and pictures as they sang the ABCs, she and Mariana taught the grown man the alphabet song. Then she placed a copy of McGuffey's *Eclectic First Reader* in front of her two students, opening the book to Lesson I.

"Repeat after me. Here is John."

"Here is John," echoed Mariana and Private Smith.

She pointed to the book's picture of three children, tapping the boy's image on the left. Then pointing out each word as she read, she repeated, "Here is John."

At the end of the hour, she pressed a paper into Private Smith's hands. "These are the ABC's, the building blocks of all the words in the English language. Mariana already knows hers, but you need to catch up."

"Yes'm."

She stared into his eyes, trying to determine his resolve. "Can you memorize them by tomorrow?"

****

Though Cadence coached Mariana in the rudiments of reading and writing, she focused on the girl's conversational English, and when Ben returned from patrol, Mariana answered his questions with simple sentences.

"Your progress calls for a reward." He reached into his pocket and pulled out a jump rope.

"Thank you, Uncle Ben." The girl grinned from ear to ear and threw her arms around him. Then, she turned to Cadence. "I show Emily?"

"*May* I show Emily?" She nodded with a smile.

"May I show Emily," echoed Mariana under her breath as she ran out of the house.

"I can't get over the change." Ben turned toward her, his eyes shining. "You're working wonders."

"Most of the progress is thanks to Emily." With a shy smile, she shrugged off his compliment.

"Emily McIntyre? Tom and Sarah's girl?" His eyes opening wide, he chuckled. "I have a confession to make. Emily and Sarah taught me how to dance."

"No." Tickled at the image, she laughed out loud.

"If not for them, you and I might never—"

The front door slammed.

"Mariana just ran past us on her way to Emily's," called her mother. Her husband on her heels, she stopped abruptly when she saw Ben. "Oh, I didn't know you had company."

"Just got back from patrol this evening, ma'am." Ben scrambled to his feet and gave the captain an informal salute. "I wanted to check on Mariana."

"She's doing well, isn't she?" Her mother's eyes glowed.

"Yes, ma'am." Nodding, Ben chewed his lip. Then, he gave Cadence a wide smile. "Your daughter's doing a mighty fine job with the girl. I don't know how she's accomplished so much in so little time."

"Don't forget Emily. She's the real miracle worker."

"Did my daughter tell you about her adult student?" Her father wore a smile.

"No, sir, she didn't." A baffled V between his eyebrows, he turned toward her.

"Private Smith has shown an interest—and an aptitude—in learning how to read and write."

"You're generous to teach him." The corners of Ben's eyes crinkled in a private smile.

"Might as well fill two needs with one deed." Uncomfortable with his praise, she shrugged.

"Lieutenant Williams"—her mother removed her gloves—"will you join us in a cup of mulled wine?"

"I'd be right pleased, ma'am." He wore a lopsided grin.

"Couldn't we dispense with the formalities?" Cadence recalled the first time he had joined them. *That dinner seems so long ago now.*

The three eyed each other. Then Ben and her parents turned toward her.

"Why not call each other by your Christian names?" She smiled. "Mother, I'd like to introduce you to Ben. Ben, please meet my mother Helen."

"It's about time"—Helen chuckled—"Ben."

"Helen." His smile was shy as he stooped in a slight bow.

"Captain will do." Her father harrumphed. Then biting off the tip of a cigar, he entertained a smile at his lips. "But I shall refer to you as Ben when we're off duty."

"I'm glad you're on a first-name basis." She gave Ben a winning smile as she left him in her father's company and joined her mother in the kitchen.

When she returned with the mulled wine several minutes later, she breathed a sigh of relief to see them chatting.

"Let's sit at the table." Her mother set a platter of cookies in the center. "It's easier than balancing our food on our laps."

Cadence glanced from face to face. "What about a game of pinochle?"

****

The next day at recess, she glanced out the window at Mariana and Emily taking turns at jumping rope. Watching Mariana transition into fort life warmed her heart.

Then, Billy Nichols came from behind and shoved, tripping her.

Cadence rushed to the door but too late.

Mariana picked herself up and faced off with the bully. Though he was an inch taller, she clenched her fingers into a fist, drew back her arm, and punched him in the chin.

As his head snapped back, Billy went down backward, landing on his keister.

"No do." Mariana stood over him, glaring. Her nostrils flaring and the whites of her eyes blazing, she raised her fist again. "No."

After checking in both directions that no one had

seen her, Cadence backed away from the doorway and returned to the window. Peeking out, she chuckled. *Mariana's holding her own.* Then she took a sharp breath. *But what about the larger problems she can't handle?*

Chapter 15
Retribution

The incessant pounding at his door woke him.

"Yes?" Still half asleep, Ben stumbled from bed.

"The captain wants to see you on the double," boomed the gruff voice. "In his office, sir."

Before reveille? "Thank you, sergeant." Ben yawned as he pulled up his suspenders and pulled on his boots. Then hustling to the office, he tapped at the captain's half-open door. "You wanted to see me, sir?"

"Come in, Williams. Close the door and take a seat."

Stiffening at the need for secrecy, Ben followed orders.

"A settler just reported another Apache raid near the Rodriguez ranch."

"Is the rider here? Questioning him might help."

"He's in the infirmary. Scalped and left for dead, he somehow escaped, but he's in no condition to answer questions."

Another raid near my property. Ben recalled Cadence's fear of living outside the fort. "No wonder settlers won't homestead the area."

"You can't blame them." His face drawn and pale, the captain held up a telegram. "Just received a wire from the District of New Mexico's commander. As you know, a renegade band of Apaches is making forays

222

into Texas."

"They've been raiding ranches for months, sir—"

"Yes, but they're getting bolder." The captain scowled. "In the past, they stole livestock and anything of value before retreating to Mexico or the Arizona / New Mexico Territories. Now, they torture and murder anyone in their path"—the edges of his mouth turned down—"as you're aware."

Familiar with the Mescaleros' history, Ben nodded in recognition. After the Department of the Interior relocated them from their tribal grounds, the Apaches resisted reservation life and repeatedly returned to their ancestral homelands.

At first, he sympathized with them—believing the Department's treatment unfair—but the renegades' recent raids into Texas had turned brutal, destroying any compassion he once held. The image of Lupe's mutilated body flashed before him, and his anger rose along with the bile in his throat.

"Over a hundred Mimbreño, Mescalero, and Chiricahua Apaches are in the war party."

"Victorio's band?" Surmising the answer, Ben glanced at the captain for confirmation.

"What's left of them since the Mexicans killed him at *Tres Castillos*." The older man nodded. "The remaining renegades use their reservation as a supply depot, then make incursions into Texas."

Ben recalled a packer's summary of the situation. "While their squaws camp in the reservation, drawing rations, the bucks come and go at will. War parties could be gone a month, but the federal agent wouldn't be the wiser."

"What are my orders, sir?"

"For once, the War Department and the Department of the Interior agree." The captain drew a deep breath. "Crush the renegade band."

Ben's eyebrows shot up.

"This is a war party, not a camp or a community. These mavericks are the remnants of Victorio's band." His back stiff, the captain met his gaze. "The telegram made the mission clear. Take no prisoners."

Ben nodded as he digested his orders.

"You're to leave at once—and another thing." The captain's expression was grim. "Don't share these orders with your men until you're several miles out. I don't want to alarm anyone…"

"Yes, sir." Anyone *meaning Helen, Cadence, or Mariana*.

"After getting to know Mariana and seeing firsthand what these Apaches have done, I want to eradicate these Mescalero and Chiricahua renegades and make sure west Texas is safe for settlers." The captain's eyes hardened as they homed in on Ben. "Don't stop at a cursory pursuit. Take Lieutenant Purdue and two companies of men. Put an end to these raids."

"Yes, sir." The image of Mariana sobbing face down on Lupe's grave came to mind.

"One more thing, Williams." The captain gave him a bleak smile. "Be careful."

"Yes, sir." With a clear understanding of his directives, Ben saluted as he stood. "Will that be all, sir?"

****

Ben organized the men, telling them their orders were to rendezvous with a wagon train and escort the settlers to Fort Quitman. When they were two miles out, he told them their actual mission.

As they crossed through the Rodriguez property, Ben said a silent prayer for the buried family members. Then they rode on to the next ranch, where the adobe cabin still smoldered. *Was this the neighbor who taught Mariana a few words of English?*

Approaching the ruins, he smelled the acrid stench of burned hair. Then he saw why.

Bound to a tree was the body of a man tied upside down, his head and face still roasting over the hot coals beneath him.

Poor bastard. Ben winced, imagining the man's agonizing death.

One of the soldiers vomited at the sight and smell.

Halting his men, Ben turned to his sergeant. "Assemble a detail. Cut down that man and dig a grave. The least we can do is give him a Christian burial."

"Yes, sir." Turning toward the troop, the burly sergeant chose three men. "Dismount."

Ben scoured the grounds for other casualties. At the back door, he found the scalped, charred remains of another man and surmised the circumstances. *The renegades set fire to the roof, waited, and then ambushed him when he tried to escape.*

"Bury him by his kin." Ben picked three men. Then he brushed aside some of the smoking rubble, poking through the ashes for warm embers. Judging from the heat, he figured the war party had a five- to six-hour lead on them.

He assigned a small guard at the spring behind the ranch, creating a subpost to prevent the renegades from accessing water on any future forays. Then he scouted the area for clues as to which direction they had taken. Broken branches, sheep hoofprints, trampled undergrowth, and bits of tangled wool stuck to the greenbrier indicated Apaches were driving the stolen herd east.

With his men standing at attention, Ben said a few words over the fresh graves. Then he ordered them to mount, and he began tracking the livestock. By mid-afternoon, he spotted the sheep in the distance with only three Apaches herding them.

"Our orders are to take no prisoners." He instructed his troop to circle around front. Then he led two sharpshooters to a bluff overlooking the renegades, where they routed the Mescaleros toward his waiting men.

Ben sent a detail to bury the dead and drive the sheep back to Fort Davis. Then he pushed his troops to close the distance between them and the war party.

The mountainous terrain offered a hundred possible escape routes, and without the sheep's clear trail, tracking became all but indecipherable. The hardscrabble showed few signs of the retreating Apaches. Since hooves left negligible imprints in the thin, arid soil, horse scat and crushed underbrush were the only indicators.

Then Ben spotted something out of place, and he halted his men.

"You see something?"

His tone skeptical, Lieutenant Purdue frowned.

"Horseshoe tracks." Ben dismounted to inspect.

"Nothing odd about horseshoe tracks."

Purdue scoffed, his disdain thinly veiled behind a dismissive wave.

"Indian ponies don't wear shoes." Ben eyed the caliche, carefully checking the stony soil for more clues. "Looks like the Mescaleros are running the stolen horses with their own, figuring their ponies' hoofprints would hide the horseshoe tracks." *And their plan's worked until now.*

Remounting, he followed the sparse signs. A half-mile later, he discovered more tracks leading up the side of a steep, rock-strewn cliff.

That route doesn't make sense. Climbing the butte would leave them no escape. Scratching his head, Ben again dismounted to inspect on foot. The tracks doubled and suddenly ended. Though he searched in all directions, the tracks vanished.

Then, as it clicked, Ben nodded. *Clever Apaches.*

"Which way?" Lieutenant Purdue removed his hat and wiped his brow.

"West."

"West? They were headed east."

His tone argumentative, the man pulled on his hat before turning to look.

"The Apaches doubled back here." Ben showed him the tracks. "This point is where they forced their horses to retrace their steps, making their hoofprints appear to continue east."

"No, their trail goes to the butte." Gesturing to the cliff, Purdue narrowed his eyes to slits. "Besides, if they'd doubled back, we'd have seen their tracks where they turned around."

"Not if they'd covered them." Ben mounted and signaled his men to follow. Several yards later, he pointed to where the Apaches had used a long branch to whisk away their horses' tracks in the sandy gravel. A few feet farther, he found the discarded catclaw branch—its end blunt-cut with a sharp knife, not broken—near several westbound horse tracks. Now certain of the direction, he led his men in hot pursuit, not stopping to eat.

As the afternoon wore on, Ben recognized the terrain from the times his Comanche father had taken him hunting, and he called his sergeant. "If memory serves me, we'll find a small spring hidden behind the hardpan ridge. We can rest and water the horses, but no campfires. Hardtack and salt pork for dinner."

After an hour's respite, they broke camp, but Ben left two guards at the spring, creating another subpost to prevent the Apaches from accessing the water.

"Why station men here? The fort's already shorthanded."

His stance wide and confrontational, Purdue balked.

"No water means no renegades." Ben resisted the urge to roll his eyes at the officer's inability to grasp the significance. "The Tenth Cavalry and District of the Pecos blocked Apache access at most strategic trail crossings and springs—but not all. I'm finishing what they started. No one can pass through the Chihuahuan Desert without water—not even Apaches. Without waterholes, they'll be forced to retreat."

Ben continued tracking the renegades until the last glimmer of sunlight faded, and the Indian campfires glowed in the distance. At his signal, his men surrounded the camp and opened fire, dispatching several Apaches and routing the rest. The one injury the cavalry sustained was to Lieutenant Purdue, struck by a soldier's ricocheted bullet.

"Post sentries," Ben told his sergeant. "Keep an eye out for Mescaleros hiding nearby or in case the war party regroups and retaliates."

He spent a watchful night, but no Apaches appeared. In the morning, he assigned details to bury the dead, destroy the Apaches' camp with its stash of mescal seeds, and recover the stolen goods: eight horses, four rifles, two cavalry pistols, and three cavalry saddles. Then, he assigned a guard at the waterhole, creating a third subpost, before leading the soldiers back to Fort Davis.

During the six-hour ride to the fort, he mentally outlined his report.

In the two days my men and I were gone, we rode forty-five miles, destroyed two Apache encampments, recaptured stolen goods and over two hundred head of livestock, inflicted heavy enemy casualties, and drove off the remnants of Victorio's war party. With troops now stationed at the Chihuahuan Desert's last three unfortified waterholes, the Apaches have no choice but to withdraw from west Texas.

Satisfied he had routed the renegades, his thoughts turned to Cadence. *Maybe now she'll consider living outside the fort.*

As her image came to mind, he characterized her—strong yet compassionate—unlike anyone he had ever known. *But how?* As he rode, he realized her strength stemmed from her independent spirit. He smiled, thinking of her stubborn streak—how she stood up to West's intimidating tactics and then braved his gossip. How unconventional she was taking over a "man's job" to teach school and how openminded to take in a Spanish-speaking orphan and tutor a buffalo soldier.

Cadence thinks for herself. She makes up her own mind. Maybe she'd even take a shine to a loner like me...?

Chapter 16
Thanksgiving

Despite her father's attempt to keep the latest Apache attack secret, news of the scalped survivor blazed across the fort. With Ben and half the soldiers gone on patrol, Cadence surmised their mission and prayed for their safe return.

When the squadron returned with the recaptured sheep, more details leaked out, and news of the man who had been roasted alive became the outraged talk of the fort.

At tea, she waited until Mariana went outside to play. Then she turned toward her mother. "Why do settlers risk their lives for a plot of land?"

"I'm not the one to ask. Being married to a military career man, I've always had housing provided, but for many, homesteading is the only way to afford a home of their own. Some emigrate from Europe because of famines or land shortages. Some seek religious or political freedom; others pursue fortunes, but all seem willing to invest their time and talent to realize their dreams."

"But to risk your life for a few acres…" Cadence's thoughts drifted to the recent horror stories, and she shook her head. "I can't understand gambling with your safety."

"Maybe you can't imagine taking a risk of that

proportion because you've always had a home and a family." Her mother suppressed a sigh. "Not everyone does."

You call living here a cage. I call it belonging, whether to a fort, tribe, clan, or family. What you call free, I call friendless. As Ben's words came to mind, she thought of Mariana. Orphaned by the Apaches, she had no real family or home. *Neither has Ben.*

Then she recalled the picnic on his property. *He'd seemed so proud to show me his land and share his achievement…Was he…?*

"Cadence. Cady."

"Sorry." As she resurfaced from her thoughts, she caught her mother staring. "I just remembered something Ben said."

"What?"

"He told me about—showed me—the land he'd just bought."

"He owns land?" Her mother's eyes opened wide.

She nodded. "When his tour ends, he plans to leave the cavalry and start ranching."

"Anytime soon?"

"At the end of the year, but what he *didn't say* has me wondering."

"About what?" The woman raised her brow.

"After he showed me the land and talked of building corrals, all I questioned him about was leaving the cavalry." While relaying the story, she reconsidered Ben's response.

"That's understandable." Her mother shrugged.

"Then, when he mentioned how close his property was to Mariana's family, all I could think about was the danger of living so far from the fort." She winced as she recalled more details.

"The danger's real. Your fears are well founded."

"Yes, but that's when Ben's mood changed. I seemed to put a damper on his plans...*Plans!*" As a thought took hold, she caught her mother's gaze. "You don't suppose he tried to propose, do you?"

****

The evening passed at a snail's pace. Every few minutes, she looked up from tutoring Mariana and Private Smith, thinking she heard horses outside. After the striker left, she sat on the porch, shivering beneath a shawl, waiting for Ben's return until too dark to see.

Then after they turned in for the night, she lay awake listening to Mariana's steady breathing. *Wish I could fall asleep as fast.* Rolling on her back, she replayed Ben's conversation the day at his property, guessing at his intentions and worrying about his safety.

Where is he? Why hasn't he returned yet? Was he wounded? Killed? Sighing, she turned over to look at the clock—midnight.

A sound from outside startled her. *Horses?* Careful not to wake Mariana, she crept from bed, peering out the window as tumbleweed glided past the officers' quarters. *Just the wind.* She went into the parlor and read by the fire until she fell asleep, book in hand.

When she woke at four, she was chilled and stiff. A cursory glance out the window showed no signs of the soldiers. Again, she climbed into bed, tossing and turning until she fell into a troubled sleep.

Everything dim and dusky, she found herself on the bluff overlooking Ben's property, the scenery shadowy—gray and twilit. Then startled by a noise behind her, she spun around. *Ben?* Instead, an Apache rushed from the underbrush and grabbed her. She struggled, screaming, screaming—

"Aunt Cadence." Mariana leaned over her, shaking her. "Aunt Cadence."

"What?" She gave the girl a blank stare.

"Bad dream."

"Who's the adult here? You or me?" Getting out of bed, she tucked the covers around Mariana. "Sorry I woke you. Now go back to sleep." Dressing in the dark, she shuffled into the kitchen and added firewood to the stove.

She recalled Mariana's first nights, when the girl had sobbed herself to sleep on her shoulder. Then the tears had dwindled. *Now, she's comforting me.* She chuckled despite her angst over Ben.

Her hands cupped against the parlor window, she saw nothing except her breath condensing on the icy pane. Then she stirred the last of the fireplace embers and added more logs, busying herself.

Where is he? The possibility of his death lurked like the suffocating smoke from the chimney's cold flue. The lump in her throat palpable, her fear choked her. *What if he never comes back? What would I do without him?*

Reeling at the depth of her sentiments, she sank into a chair. *Could this be…love?*

What a foreign concept. With neither personal nor secondhand experience from friends her age, she was naïve. A schoolgirl crush, James had never triggered these emotions. His courtship had been like attending a planned social function. Nothing had been spontaneous or genuine. *What is this feeling?*

She caught her breath, feeling light-headed and

unfocused. Only one thing would clear her mind.

Coffee. While the drink brewed, she inhaled its rich aroma as she listened to the percolator's soothing gurgle. Then she poured a cup and, elbows resting on the table, sipped her coffee as she examined her feelings.

Even if this sensation were love, Ben would leave the cavalry to ranch in Indian territory. She had no death wish to die at the hands of renegade Apaches. *Love may be blind, but I'm not that short-sighted.*

A sound like sandpaper on wood drew her attention as her father's slippers scuffled across the floorboards.

"You're up early." He glanced at the stove. "Good, you made coffee." Pouring a cup, he joined her as he reached for the sugar and canned evaporated milk.

She studied the man on whose lap she had learned to drink coffee. As a child, she dunked her cookies in his sweetened café au lait to soften them. Her mother always took her coffee black, which was still too strong for Cadence's taste. She smiled, glad for her father's company.

"What're you doing awake at this hour?" He blew on his coffee to cool it.

"Couldn't sleep." Uncomfortable about sharing her feelings before she sorted them out, she shrugged.

"Is that so?" The corners of his eyes crinkled in a smile as his gaze met hers. "You're not worried about a certain lieutenant, are you?"

She stared, stunned by his insight.

"Cady, I've known you all your life. Do you honestly think you're inscrutable?" Wearing a gentle smile, he shook his head. "Don't ever play poker."

"A nightmare woke me."

"Was the same lieutenant in your dream?" His eyes twinkled, and as he sipped his coffee, his cup almost hid his grin.

"In a way." She straightened and then nodded with a begrudging smile.

"He's a capable officer."

"That's high praise coming from you." She studied him.

"Because he's earned my respect"—he dropped his smile—"which is why I commissioned him to lead this task force."

Swallowing hard, she understood it was her father's orders that had sent Ben on this mission. Both men were only doing their duties, but that knowledge did not make Ben's absence any easier to accept. Head bent to hide her panic, she nodded.

"He's the ablest lieutenant in my command. If anyone can rid the area of these renegades, he can."

As his tone softened, she looked up, grateful for his reassurance but still sick with worry. *No matter Ben's capability, will this area ever be rid of these renegades?*

****

When she left for school with Mariana, she put on a bright smile.

"Uncle Ben fight Apaches, yes?" Mariana's face looked pinched as they crossed the parade grounds. Whether from worry or the frosty morning, Cadence was not sure.

"If anyone can rid the area of these renegades, Ben can." She parroted her father's words, hoping they sounded as convincing to Mariana.

The girl chewed her lip.

With most of their fathers away on patrol, the children were distracted. The students' attention scattered, their ears seemed perked for the sound of returning horses, so after recess, she devised an activity to hold the children's attention.

"With Thanksgiving only two days away, let's make a thankful tree." She gave the older children newspapers, scissors, an ice pick, and string. "Cut out paper leaves. Then poke a tiny hole in each and thread the string through, knotting the ends."

After demonstrating, she helped the younger children gather tree branches, tie them together into a "tree," and stand it in a galvanized bucket, weighted down with pebbles. "Next, take two paper leaves. On each, write one thing for which you're thankful. Then we'll hang them on the thankful tree. Mariana and Emily, help the younger children."

When Mariana handed in her two leaves, she could not help peeking as she hung them on the tree. *Uncle Ben* was printed on one and *Aunt Cadence* on the other.

"What about you, Miss McShane?" Emily turned toward her after all the leaves were hung.

"I'd need thirteen"—she gave a bashful smile as the warmth rushed to her cheeks—"a leaf for each of you." *And another for Ben.* "Let's go around the room and share what we're thankful for this year. You start, Emily."

"I'm thankful for new friends." After she smiled at Mariana, she glanced out the windows, and her face lit up. "They're back."

One by one, the students flew to the windows, pressing their noses against the panes.

"Let's give the men time to dismount and tend to

their horses." Her heart thumping and her fingers trembling, Cadence wanted to race outside to greet Ben, but she gathered her composure. "After a few minutes, we'll break for—"

A knock sounded at the door, and she gasped.

"Got room for another student?" Cracking the door, Ben stuck his head inside.

"Recess," she called as the children scrambled outside.

She was not sure if she ran into his arms or he took her in his, but she found herself entwined in a kiss that left her breathless. "Hi," she finally said, catching her breath and opening her eyes.

"Hello." A sigh sounded deep in his throat. "Pleased to meet you…finally."

"Why did we take so long?"

Clearing her throat, Mariana stood patiently, holding a leaf.

Cadence gave an embarrassed chuckle as she dropped her arms from his neck. "It appears Mariana has something for you."

"Welcome back, Uncle Ben." Wearing a shy smile, she handed him her paper leaf.

"She's thankful for you." Still basking in the afterglow of his kiss, Cadence pointed to their tree.

"This gift's the best homecoming I ever got." As he lifted the girl to hug her, he winked at Cadence. *Second best*, he mouthed.

Over dinner later, Ben emphasized the safety of the area now that their troops had routed the Apaches, but he changed the topic whenever anyone brought up the dangers his patrol encountered.

Sitting beside him, Cadence glanced around the

table. Three pairs of eyes focused on him as her parents and Mariana listened in rapt attention. She stifled a sigh as she said a silent prayer. *Thank You, God. I need another leaf for his safe return.*

Then she went cold. *He's driven off the Apaches, but for how long?*

****

On Thanksgiving, Cadence, Helen, and Jenny spent all morning in the kitchen. They pared and sliced vegetables; basted the turkey Ben had shot earlier that morning; and made soup, side dishes, bread, and pies.

Mariana busied herself with decorations. She fashioned candleholders by tying trimmed corn husks around votive candles, holding them in place with raffia, and adorning each with a guineafowl feather. She filled a glass hurricane lamp with miniature white pumpkins, arranging fresh rosemary sprigs and bittersweet berries at its base. Then she dressed the windowsills by tucking bittersweet stems into gold, green, and clear apothecary bottles, interspersing tiny green and orange gourds between them.

"You're so creative, Mariana." Cadence gave her a side hug as she admired the handiwork. "You have an artist's eye."

Blushing pink, Mariana grinned as she glanced about the home.

Chrysanthemums bloomed in the sunny parlor, bringing the room to life. The dinner table gleamed with the good china, crystal glasses, and silver flatware. Tapered candles lit the dining room with a soft, mellow glow, and the hearth blazed with a cozy fire.

"This so pretty." Hunching her shoulders and clasping her hands, Mariana squirmed. "I add."

"You wanted to add your own touch." Smiling, Cadence nodded her approval.

"Yes." Mariana's response sounded like a sigh.

"Dinner's almost ready." Her cheeks rosy from the warm kitchen, her mother's smile was wider than usual as her gaze rested on Mariana and Ben. Then she put her arm around the girl as they returned to the kitchen together.

Is it my imagination, or does she look younger? What's different about Mother? Cadence gave her a second look. Then glancing at the surroundings, she answered her own question—*Mariana and Ben. She likes having a "family" to entertain, not just Father and me.*

She smiled at their retreating figures, beginning to recognize her mother as a friend. Then, she noticed Ben staring after them. "Mariana seems to be adjusting, doesn't she?"

"I think of what she's been through—*come* through—and I'm so proud of her. She's a survivor, but you're the one who's made the difference in her life."

"Mariana's enriched a lot of lives, not just mine, but my mother's and Emily's." She gestured toward her father with her chin. "I think even his."

"From things the captain's said, I know she has." The corners of Ben's eyes crinkled in a warm smile.

"Like what?"

"Mariana's presence made him more aware of the danger to settlers." His smile faded. "If not for her influence, he might not have taken such a hard line against the renegades."

"I'm sure you minimized the hardships the night you returned." She hesitated. "Other than that, you've never mentioned the raid."

Sighing, he shook his head. "I'll never forget that strike, but I'd rather not discuss it—especially not on Thanksgiving."

He gazed into the distance, seeming to gather his thoughts. When he glanced back, his eyes had a hollow, haunted look.

She bit her lip, guessing at what he had witnessed.

"Cady, can you help?"

Her mother's soft drawl crept into her thoughts. "Coming."

Before leaving for the kitchen, she leaned over and kissed his cheek. "If you ever need someone to listen, will you come to me?"

Chapter 17
Precious Time

She cares. Her words moving him, Ben stared after Cadence.

"I hear you're leaving the service at the end of your tour." The captain's voice broke into his thoughts.

"Yes, sir." Flinching, he covered with a quick smile. "After fifteen years—between enlistment and commission—I'm resigning my command."

"We'll miss you." The captain's shoulders drooped. "You're a good soldier and a fine officer. In fact, I've put you in for a medal of merit. Ridding west Texas of those renegades has made the area safe for travel and settlement."

"Thank you, sir." He nodded his appreciation, but the words conjured unwelcome images of Lupe and the others.

"What are your plans when you leave?"

Though the language was plain enough, he did a doubletake at the captain's tone. "Are you asking me my intentions toward your daughter?"

"You are direct, aren't you, lieutenant?" He cleared his throat.

"Yes, sir. Life's taught me not to waste time." Flashbacks of the tortured settlers' bodies resurfaced in his mind, along with regrets for Mariana's and his stolen childhoods. He met the older man's eyes. "Life's too precious to squander."

"In that case"—the captain stiffened—"what *are* your intentions toward Cadence."

"I'd like her for my wife if she'll have me. I believe I could provide for her. I've bought property near here with good pasture for cattle."

"Is your land far from the fort?" He met Ben's gaze.

"It's about an hour and a half's ride due south—adjacent to the Rodriguez ranch."

"So routing the renegades was more than mere duty." The captain's eyes opened wide.

"Yes, sir. Mariana's family made the assignment personal." Then taking a deep breath, he studied the man's face. "Which leads us back to my intentions toward Cadence. I also wanted to make the area safe for my family."

"I see."

The worried V between his eyes and his wrinkled brow reflected the older man's reservations. The emotions swept across his face as his eyes glazed over.

"I know I don't have the background or education you'd like in a son-in-law. I don't have any family connections back East. I didn't go to West Point. An enlisted man, I was promoted on the battlefield."

"Yet you're an able officer." Making strong eye contact, the captain smiled. "With your record and the fort being shorthanded since Lieutenant West's transfer and Lieutenant Purdue's injury, I'm considering promoting you to First Lieutenant."

"You're generous, sir, and I appreciate your confidence in me." Ben met his gaze. "But this offer won't change my mind. I'd planned to submit my letter of resignation to you in the morning. I'm resigning my commission on December thirty-first and entering 1880 as a civilian."

The captain's shoulders slumped. His disappointment evident in the grim set of his face, he clenched his jaw. Then a melancholy smile flickered briefly at his lips.

"I see."

"Of course, you can call on me as a guide to lead expeditions, should you ever need my services. I'll only be an hour and a half away." He studied his commanding officer as he took a deep breath. "I've laid down my cards, sir. Now, I'd appreciate your showing me your hand."

The captain grunted as he ran his fingers over his chin. With a sigh, he met Ben's gaze. "You're a good man, Williams. If my daughter will have you, you have my blessing."

"Dinner's ready." Resting her hand on her husband's arm, Helen joined them. "Didn't you hear me call?"

"Sorry, my dear." He patted her hand. "We were deep in conversation."

"You two certainly had your heads together." She looked from one to the other. "What are you plotting?"

"The future." The captain met Ben's gaze.

Ben sat next to Cadence as they gathered at the table. The captain sat at the head; his wife faced him at the other end; and Mariana sat between them, across from Cadence.

"Let's bow our heads." The captain clasped his hands. "Heavenly Father, bless this food…and bless our family. Amen."

"Amen." Her eyes snapping open, Cadence glanced at her father.

"You seem happy today." Helen turned toward Mariana.

"First." Her eyes twinkling, Mariana beamed.

Helen squinted, struggling to understand the girl's abbreviated English.

"*Esta es mi primera Acción de Gracias.*" Mariana turned to him.

"This is her first Thanksgiving dinner."

"I happy."

Helen reached for her hand. "We're happy you're here, too."

Cadence caught his eye and squeezed his hand under the table.

"The oysters are canned, not fresh, but at least we have oyster stew for Thanksgiving." Helen started ladling the steaming soup from the tureen. She passed each bowl to Ben on her right, who passed on the dish to Cadence, the captain, and then Mariana. Wearing a distant smile, Helen seemed to gaze into the past. "Reminds me of our holidays back East."

Mariana inhaled the creamy stew's sea scent and wrinkled her nose, but after sampling a spoonful, her face lit up.

"Do you like oyster stew?" Helen laughed.

"Yes. Good." Barely stopping to breathe, she gobbled the soup.

After Jenny cleared the bowls, she brought out tureens of buttery mashed potatoes, sweet potatoes baked with a crusty brown sugar and nutmeg topping, and roasted, buttered acorn squash, dusted with cinnamon. Then, she brought the *pièce de résistance* on an oversized platter—the oven-browned turkey with sage dressing.

His mouth watering at the sight and scent of home cooking, Ben inhaled the spices' pungent aromas and the turkey's savory bouquet.

The captain carved the bird, handing the plates first to Mariana on his right, who passed them on.

"This is a beautiful turkey." The captain gave him a wide smile as he carved into the plump breast's white meat. "Did you shoot it near here?"

"About an hour and a half from here." Sensing a new-found ally, he caught the older man's gaze and returned the smile.

"Good hunting on your land?"

"It's rich bottomland"—he glanced at Cadence— "with good cover for wildlife in the higher elevations."

"Do you intend to raise cattle?" Helen passed the gravy.

"Yes, ma'am"—he nodded—"longhorns."

"So then you know your plans…"

From her tone, Helen's comment was phrased as a question.

"Some of them." He almost reminded them how safe west Texas was now that he had routed the renegades, but after glancing at Mariana, he bit his tongue rather than stir memories. Then, he caught Cadence's gaze. "I've also hired a construction crew to build a cabin."

She raised her brow, then turned abruptly toward her mother. "Would you pass the sweet potatoes, please? They're delicious."

"Thank you, dear." She held the tureen for her daughter.

They chatted about the food and weather, but eventually, the conversation turned to fort matters.

"I've wired Fort Clark for reinforcements. We've been shorthanded since Lieutenant West's transfer—especially so since Lieutenant Purdue's injury." The captain turned toward him. "Additional officers will take the burden off you and Tom."

He nodded, keenly aware of the officer shortage.

"What with Ben resigning in a little over a month, that leaves just Lieutenant McIntyre and me." The corners of his mouth downturned, the captain stifled a sigh. "The fort needs two more officers, even after Lieutenant Purdue returns to duty."

"We can't entice you to stay, Ben?" Helen chewed her lip.

"I offered him a promotion to First Lieutenant, but even that incentive doesn't persuade him."

His eyes dull, the captain spoke in a listless monotone.

"Can't we do anything to make you stay?" Her smile sagging, Helen leaned toward him and rested her hand on his arm.

"I appreciate your concern, ma'am." He returned a sympathetic smile. "I do, but my mind is made up."

"Cadydid, can't you convince Ben?"

"He's a grown man, Mother, and he knows what he wants." Inhaling as she straightened her back, she gave Ben a sidelong glance. "He's determined to resign his commission…no matter what." Then she turned toward him, their faces only inches apart.

"I've enjoyed my stint as a soldier and officer, but I grew up on the land." Speaking softly, he maintained his reserve. "The Davis Mountains are part of me, and I belong to them. My roots are here in west Texas."

"I see." She turned away from him, her jaw set and her eyes dark.

The tension between them palpable, the only sound was Mariana munching on pine nuts.

"Who's ready for dessert?" Helen rose from her chair and turned toward her daughter. "Cadence, can you help me clear the table?"

Chapter 18
Propositions

Cadence gathered the plates, bracing herself for their whispered kitchen conversation to follow.

Not until after they had scraped and stacked the dishes in soapy water did her mother turn toward her.

"You seem rather distracted for a holiday dinner."

"Today isn't the issue." She stifled a sigh. "I can't stop thinking about the future."

"Do your prospects involve Lieutenant Williams?"

"Am I that obvious?" She lifted her lips in a half smile.

"Maybe not to Mariana, but you are to the rest of us." Her mother wore a sympathetic smile. "What's on your mind?"

"I *would* like to spend my life with him..." She sighed uneasily.

"But...?"

"I can't live in a roughhewn cabin, worrying day and night when Apaches will attack." She shook her head. "Putting my life at risk is asking too much."

"I agree with you about the danger, but Ben's *rid* the area of those renegades." Pausing, her mother smiled. "Besides, aren't you the same young lady, who complained about not having adventures?"

As her words returned to haunt her, she gave her mother a sheepish grin.

"And something you may not have considered since you've grown up in garrisons. Did you know my parents tried to talk me out of following your father from fort to fort?"

"They did?" She frowned at the news. "Why?"

"Because they said the same thing you just did. Life on the frontier is too dangerous for a woman. They said I was used to the finer things in life. They were sure I couldn't adapt to fort life—living out of trunks or moving from post to post." Her eyes searching left and right, she watched her daughter's face.

"You're right." Stunned by her mother's mettle, she caught and held her gaze. "I never thought of our way of life from your perspective…or theirs."

"Of course you didn't. As an army brat, you were born into the military life of disruption and relocation from one assignment to the next."

"And it's always seemed perfectly normal." Suddenly she saw her mother in a new light. "You're more of an adventuress than I'd realized."

"Perspective." She spoke in a quiet voice, barely above a whisper. "So much of life is simply putting things into perspective."

"So are you telling me I should throw caution aside and live in a crude cabin, out in the middle of nowhere, waiting for the next roving band of Apaches to attack?"

"I'm saying nothing of the kind." Inhaling, her mother stared into the distance as she seemed to search for the right words. "Weigh the pluses and the minuses. Sometimes, what appears to be the *end* of the road is nothing but a *bend* in the road. Pray for guidance. Think through your options, but…"

"Yes…?" Cadence tilted her head, listening.

"Do as I say, not as I do." Her mother's smile was wistful. "Follow your heart, and you'll find the right path."

Hearing the unspoken regrets in her mother's voice, Cadence nodded.

"Now"—her mother's smile trembled—"let's serve the pie before they come looking."

"Thank you." She gripped her mother in a warm hug.

"I help?" Mariana brought her plate into the kitchen.

"Yes." She handed her a stack of dessert dishes. "Set the table with these, please."

The girl nodded and carefully carried the porcelain plates in her small hands.

Using thick potholders, Cadence took the mincemeat pie from the warming oven. Cloves, cinnamon, nutmeg, ginger, apples, currants, and dried apricots bubbled together in a buttery lattice pastry. As she carried it into the dining room, its spicy aromas wafted back, and she breathed them in along with memories of earlier Thanksgivings with her parents.

"What were you two doing?" Her father wore a mischievous smile. "Making the pie from scratch?"

"Women talk." Cadence winked at her mother.

After dinner, they sat in the parlor sipping freshly brewed coffee and liqueurs, when Emily stopped by. The two girls started a game of checkers in front of the fire while the adults chatted.

"What kind of cabin are you building, Ben?" Her mother caught his gaze.

"I'm thinking of double-pen architecture with a roofed breezeway between the two units to start,

251

ma'am." He glanced at her. "I reckon as a family comes along, I can add a second story."

"A dogtrot, you mean." Her mother nodded in recognition.

"Yes, ma'am." Again, he glanced at her. "Of course, at this stage, I'm open to suggestions."

"Are you planning to use hewn logs?" Her father lit a cigar.

"No, sir, I'm thinking of box and strip construction, then finishing the interior with center-match siding."

"Sounds like a fine home." Her mother glanced at her.

"I hope so." Ben smiled. "I figure to start small but use quality material and then add to the house as needed."

"So you're *not* thinking of a one-room adobe cabin then?" Cadence turned toward him.

"No, ma'am." A deep chuckle escaped. "I'm building a home for the future, not just a temporary structure."

She made a dubious, humming noise in her throat.

"Why?" Ben studied her.

"I thought you said *cabin*"—she shuddered— "which conjured images of dirt floors and adobe walls without windows."

"No, ma'am, a hut's not what I have in mind." Smiling, he shook his head. Then his smile fading, he became thoughtful. "What kind of home do you want…someday?"

"A dogtrot with a breezeway would be good in the summer weather, but the house would need windows for cross drafts." She gazed into the distance, trying to imagine the ideal home. "Lots of windows, so the rooms would be light and airy, and I'd like sturdy, hardwood floors." Glancing toward him, she raised her index finger, emphasizing the next item's importance. "And a wide veranda that, over time, could expand into a wraparound porch."

"Seems you've given some thought to the home you want." The corners of his eyes creased in a smile.

"Some." Unable to pull off a shrug, she gave him a sheepish smile.

For what seemed minutes, Ben stared into her eyes as if trying to decipher something.

With a deep breath, he rose to his feet and offered her his hand. "Care to walk off dinner?"

Wary of agreeing to more than just a helping hand, she paused, searching his face for clues. Not until she saw the tenderness in his gaze did she accept his outstretched hand. "Let me get my wrap."

"I put your shawl away." Her mother jumped to her feet. "Let me show you where."

Finding the wrap where she had left it, Cadence turned toward her, squinting in confusion.

"Tread where your mind meanders." Her mother's brow arched. "It's where you'll find your heart."

Cadence hugged her, melting into her arms. This woman was her first love, even before she was born. During the past months, she had become friend, confidant, and ally. Now, she sensed she was saying goodbye.

Her mother wrapped her in a warm embrace, her grip tight. Then with a sigh and a trembling smile, she let go.

A lump in her throat, Cadence met Ben at the door and called "Goodbye" before walking into the crisp, autumn evening. The brisk breeze galvanized her, and she breathed in the scents of freshly fallen leaves, pine needles, and smoke from hickory firewood.

She side glanced at the tall lieutenant beside her and trembled. *From what?*

"Cold?" He reached for her hand.

With a shiver of anticipation, she accepted his strong, calloused hand. At his touch, a tingle shot up her arm, and she pressed against his arm, sharing body warmth.

As they crossed the gusty parade grounds, the damp wind picked up, turning into a wintry blast.

"Want to duck into the stable and visit Althea?"

Glad to escape the cold, she nodded. "Definitely."

The mare raised her head, greeting them with a whinny, and her breath steamed in the frosty air.

"Hello, girl." Cadence scratched beneath her forelock.

The horse recognized her, nuzzling her hand.

"Althea likes you." Ben smiled.

Cadence reached over to rub its neck, but the horse shifted its weight, and her hand brushed Ben's chest.

He came to attention, and his gaze locked onto hers.

She caught her breath as he leaned into her space, bending as if to kiss her. Instinctively inclining her body toward him, she closed her eyes and lifted her lips. As they met, she answered his kiss with a passion she did not know she possessed.

He pulled her toward him, pressing her against his taut body.

Cadence flung her arms around his neck. Dizzy and breathless in his clinch, she clung to his chest. When their lips parted, she was still entwined in his arms, staring into his eyes. "Hello again," she breathed.

A moan sounded deep in his throat as Ben pulled her toward him once more.

This time, their passion fed off each other, rising higher, until they were wrapped in each other's arms. Her back wedged against the stable's wall, and his body insistent against hers, she lost sense of time.

Distant voices slowly woke her from her longings. Lifting her head to listen, Cadence gasped as their mouths drew apart. She did not want to break the moment or their connection of mingling arms and lips, but the voices were distinct and coming close.

She pulled apart just as two figures appeared at the stable door. Then turning, she pretended to visit Althea's stall.

Seeming to conspire, the mare nickered while its velvet nose nuzzled her hand.

One of the two soldiers called out. "Sorry, sir. Didn't see you and Miss McShane. Just stopping by for my horse's halter. With the weather turning, I want to soften the leather with lanolin."

"Fine idea, soldier."

Ben's no-nonsense voice sounded calm and composed. His tone contrasted against her racing pulse, and she stole a quick glance at his face. Then she ducked her chin as a mischievous smile tickled her lips.

"Goodnight, sir—ma'am," the soldiers called a moment later.

"Have you noticed how little privacy a fort has?" Ben's eyes glowed in the scant moonlight filtering through the windows.

"All my life." She rolled her eyes. "Which is why

I've envied you your freedom to come and go."

His eyes lost their shimmer. "Would you ever consider living away from a fort?"

This is it. What do I do? What do I say? Her body became still as the seconds ticked by. She gulped.

"Would you?"

"I've always wanted to escape the fort's narrow-mindedness." Horse blinkers hanging on the wall caught her gaze, and she ran her fingers over their firm leather squares. "Not just horses wear these blinders. People do, too. Like looking down a long tunnel, they see just a sliver of the whole picture, a narrow perspective of life." She stared at his face. "I told you once before. Living on a post is like living in a cage."

"And I said, 'You call living here a cage, but I call it belonging. What you call free, I call friendless.' " He gave her a half-smile.

"In a fort, I feel confined, like I'm in a tightly laced corset and can't take a deep breath, or restrained, like I'm wearing a bit and halter." She ran her hand over the row of dangling horse harnesses before she turned toward him. "But to be honest, I'm also afraid to live away from the fort's protection."

"You're afraid of Apache attacks," he stated more than asked.

Then he drew a deep breath and chewed his lip as if he were prepared for the conversation.

"Yes, and my concern's legitimate—not just a child's fear of the dark or a boogeyman."

"I agree." He placed his arms on her shoulders. "But the war party was made of remnants of Victorio's renegades, and they're gone now."

"How can you be so sure?" His touch invited her to

take a step closer. Despite the importance of their discussion, she had difficulty resisting the urge to lift her lips to his and mold her body against his.

"Because if any more renegades raid west Texas, I'll lead an attack against them." He put his arms around her. "I'll never let anyone hurt you."

Despite the layers of clothes between them, his nearness brought a deep sigh of relief. Then she winced as another thought took hold. "And something else…"

"What?"

"I feel more than an attachment to Mariana. I feel a responsibility." She struggled to express her thoughts. She held back her head to better view his expression. "I want to adopt her."

"How can you raise a child? You're not even married."

Pursing her lips, she swallowed a smile.

Though Ben spoke in his deep bass voice, rousing her, his tone was tongue-in-cheek.

"What would people say?"

"I can't imagine." Her lips curled at the corners. "Can you help me find a solution?"

"I was adopted—twice." His gaze serious, Ben peered into her face. "To repay the Comanche and Anglo families that took me in, I *need* to adopt." Straightening his spine, he pulled himself to his full height. "Miss McShane, would you do me the honor of making an honest man of me? Become my wife, so we can adopt Mariana?"

"Lieutenant Williams." Tickled by his choice of words, she used her Sunday-best voice. "Making an honest man of you would be my utmost pleasure." Standing on tiptoe, she threw her arms around his neck.

As their lips touched, he crushed her against him, and Cadence lost herself in his embrace.

When they finally drew apart, he whispered hoarsely, "When would you like to set the date?"

A dank chill washed over her as his words echoed James' demand—"We mustn't let everyone down. Cadence, dear, when do you want to set the date?"

Shuddering at the memories, she let her arms slip from his neck, and her hands hung at her sides.

"What's wrong?" His smile drooped.

"Your words reminded me of James' ultimatum." She sneered. "I won't dignify his 'orders' by calling them a proposal."

"I'm sorry. Upsetting you was *not* my intent." The corners of his mouth turning down, he grimaced. "Let me word this another way. First, would you like to get married?"

"Absolutely." She nodded.

"All right, *when* would you like to get married?"

"As soon as possible." Again, she lifted her arms around his neck and clung to him in a kiss that left her breathless.

The negative memories dispelled, she gave a contented sigh. Then stiffening, she remembered the fort's inadequate housing. "But the married officers' quarters are full." She wrinkled her nose, wincing. "I hate to suggest this, but maybe we should wait until after the house is built. When will the builder finish?"

"About the same time I resign"—his eyes twinkling, he smiled—"the end of December."

She grinned back, blatantly in love. "Then, shall we say the day after Christmas and hope the construction crew finishes ahead of schedule?"

"Marrying you is the perfect Christmas present." Sealing the deal with a kiss, he reached into his coat pocket and pulled out a carved, wooden case.

"What's this?" Tipping back her head, she peered through her lashes.

"An early Christmas gift."

Inside the box, she found a white chalcedony cabochon brooch. "This pin is stunning. Thank you." After lightly running her finger over the polished stone, she reached up to kiss him. "Where did you find it?"

"On my—*our* land." He smiled as he corrected himself. "I found it the day we went rock hunting—the day I *almost* proposed to you on the ridge."

"I knew it." Memories stirring, Cadence groaned. "The day I worried about renegade attacks. The day we visited the Rodriguez family. The last time we saw Lupe—"

"Alive," he whispered, swallowing hard.

"It wasn't supposed to happen then." She winced at her choice of words. "Your proposal, I mean. All things in God's time. Maybe He meant us to be a family: you, Mariana, and me."

"Could be."

A gust of wind blew open the stable door. As it banged against the wall, Cadence snapped her head to look. The driving sleet whooshed into the stable along with a soldier leading three horses.

"Our cue to share the good news with my family." Shuddering from the wind's icy tendrils, she turned to Ben.

He put his arm around her shoulders, shielding her from the worst gusts, and they started back to her quarters.

When she saw Emily walking into her house, she called, "Good night."

The girl turned and waved, but the wind drowned out her response.

Her head down, ducking from the sleet, Cadence hurried up the stairs, still huddled against Ben.

Elated with their new status, she laughed at the wintry weather as she bolted the door behind them. Shutting out the cold, she barricaded them from the world and its troubles. Sealed inside, they were safe and warm. Nothing could disrupt her happiness.

Then men's voices drifted from the parlor.

"Who's here?" Cadence gave Ben a perplexed look. As she listened, one of the voices sounded familiar. "*James?*"

Suddenly colder inside the house than out, she shivered. Trespassing on her betrothal, James violated her sense of security, and she walked into the parlor dragging her feet.

James and another officer stood by the hearth talking with her father.

"Come in," he called. "Lieutenants West and Monroe were transferred here from Fort Clark. My daughter, Cadence."

"Welcome to Fort Davis, Lieutenant Monroe." Ignoring James, Cadence addressed his companion.

"Thank you, ma'am." His head bobbed in a formal bow.

"I'm Ben Williams." He held out his hand to the new lieutenant. "Welcome."

"And I'm Charles. Pleased to meet you." Shaking Ben's hand, he glanced at James as he turned back to the couple. "I believe you know Lieutenant West."

"We've met." Her posture stiff, Cadence was unable to keep the sneer from her voice.

Charles blinked, glancing from one to the other.

"Lieutenant West." Her father cleared his throat. "You know your way. Take your old quarters and show Lieutenant Monroe to the room next to yours."

"Yes, sir." James lingered, looking from the captain to Cadence.

What? Is he expecting an invitation?

"Dismissed."

The captain's tone unmistakable, the officers saluted and turned toward the door.

On his way out, James wore an impudent smirk as he looked Cadence up and down.

Her gaze flicked upward, where she kept it until the front-door latch clicked shut. "What's *he* doing here?"

"When I called for reinforcements, he volunteered. Tonight was the first I'd learned of his transfer." Her father inhaled sharply, then let out an irritated sigh. "If I had any other options, I'd send him packing—*again*. What possible reasons could he have for coming back?"

"They can't be good." Her mother shook her head as she entered the room. "After alienating half the fort, he must realize he isn't welcome." Then squinting, she cocked her head as she peered hard at Cadence and Ben. "What's different?"

Even James' unwelcome intrusion could not dim her delight for long. Taking Ben's hand in hers, she grinned as she met her parents' gaze. "Ben's proposed, and I've accepted."

Her mother kissed her cheek as her father shook Ben's hand. Then Cadence hugged her father, while

Ben embraced her mother.

"Your engagement calls for a toast." Helen wore a warm smile. "I've saved a bottle of sparkling Catawba for just such a special occasion."

"For *what*?" Rounding the corner, Mariana walked into the parlor.

Cadence glanced at Ben as she crouched before the girl and took her hands. "How would you like to come live with Ben and me?"

"You mean…family?" Mariana blinked, looking from one to the other.

"What do you think?" Unsure how the girl would accept another change, she watched her response.

"I pray for this." The girl clasped her arms around her neck, hugging her.

"Then you agree?" A gentle smile played at Ben's lips.

"Yes." Grinning from ear to ear, Mariana nodded.

A loud pop erupted from the warming kitchen, followed by the splash and burble of fizzling wine.

A moment later, her mother returned to the parlor, carrying a tray of slim crystal flutes.

Cadence and Ben both took one, smiling into each other's eyes.

After her father took a glass, her mother set down the tray, gave a scant half-glass to Mariana, and lifted her glass in a toast. "To the new couple."

As Mariana clinked glasses and sipped, she giggled. "Tickles nose."

Sharing a warm smile, Cadence sat next to Ben on the settee as the group gathered around the crackling fire.

"When are you getting married?" Cocking her head

to one side, her mother studied them.

"The day after Christmas." With the intruders gone, Cadence smiled, relaxing.

"The house should be finished by then"—Ben caught her gaze—"just a few days before my resignation."

"This way"—she sighed—"we won't have to worry about finding married officers' quarters at the fort—*or being ranked out*."

"No 'falling bricks'?" Her mother wore a wry smile.

Cadence wrinkled her nose at the practice of higher-ranking or more senior officers confiscating junior officers' quarters. In theory, if they were forced to vacate, Ben could evict a junior officer's family, but since Ben would be the lowest ranking married officer, the point was moot.

"We hope to avoid that ordeal." She shook her head.

"What about Mariana's property?" Her father lit a cigar.

"I reckon we can manage the land for her until she's of age and then turn it over to her." Ben glanced at Mariana. "Once the property's fenced, the cattle will graze the pastures. Otherwise, it shouldn't require much upkeep since the land's adjacent to mine—*ours*." Catching Cadence's gaze, he shared a smile.

"Which reminds me." She reached into her pocket. "In the excitement, I almost forgot. Look what Ben gave me." She opened the box, displaying the brooch for all to see.

"It's beautiful." Her mother leaned forward to see. "Where did you get the pin?"

"I found the stone on our property, but a jeweler in San Antonio made it into this brooch."

"*Es tan lindo.* Pretty. *Es como mi piedra.*" Mariana turned toward him for the English.

"It's like her stone," he said, translating.

She nodded, repeating the words in English. Then her smile faded. "Like my *calcedonia rosario.*"

"Chalcedony rosary."

"What do you mean?" Cadence studied her.

"*Lo dejé en el raiz sótano.*"

"She left her rosary in the root cellar."

Cadence remembered the night he had brought Mariana home. Besides the clothes on her back, the only items she had brought with her were the chalcedony stone, cameo, and scarf, tucked in the pleats of her bodice. She turned toward the girl.

"Why did you leave your rosary?"

"I pray and pray. Then drop." Her face clouded over before glancing at Ben. "*Se me cayó cuando oí voces de los hombres.*"

"She dropped it when she heard men's voices." Then he turned toward her. "The voices frightened you?"

"I think Apaches." She nodded.

Cadence tucked the brooch in her pocket and leaned over to hug the girl. "You're safe now, and don't worry. We'll get you another rosary."

"My mother rosary. She give me"—Mariana glanced at Ben—"*día de mi santo.*"

"For Mariana's saint's day."

"When is your saint's day?"

"*Segundo de diciembre.*"

"December second."

Silently repeating the date, Cadence got an idea. *Wouldn't finding Mariana's rosary be a lovely surprise for her saint's day?*

Chapter 19
Blood Money

After inspection the next morning, James stopped Ben. "Let's let bygones be bygones." He flashed a cold smile. "Especially now that we're neighbors."

"What do you mean?" Ben did a double-take.

"Just what I said." James' smile morphed into a sneer.

"No land's available near mine." Ben stared, shaking his head. "The only adjacent property is the Rodriguez ranch, and that land's not for sale."

"No, it isn't…" Smirking, James turned on his heel and strode away.

"Do you know what he's talking about?" Ben glanced at Tom.

"He's been bragging all morning—says he owns the land bordering yours." Tom sniffed.

"He's up to something." Ben scowled at James' retreating figure. "Just wish I knew what."

After his duties, he rode into town, visiting the district clerk's office. "I understand Lieutenant West just purchased land south of here. Could you tell me which property?"

The clerk referred to his ledger and gave him the land description.

"The ranch belongs to the Rodriguez family." He shook his head. "It's not for sale."

"The records indicate the land belonged to the county. A Lieutenant James West was just issued a Homestead Grant."

"It can't be. The Rodriguez family owns the property."

Shrugging, the clerk turned the ledger to show him.

"Where's the deed?" Ben scowled.

"I see no record of any previous owner." The clerk showed him the ledger. "The land was just surveyed three weeks ago."

"The property is a burned-out ranch. I know the owner. This land had no business being surveyed or put up for sale."

"Do you have its certificate?" The clerk arched his brow.

"Apaches set fire to the house." Ben shook his head. "I doubt any papers survived."

"I'm sorry." The clerk closed the ledger. "You can contest the sale, but unless you prove previous ownership, legally, the property belongs to Lieutenant West."

"A family cemetery and burned-out shell of the house still remain." Flashbacks of the tortured bodies and hastily dug graves came to mind.

"Without paperwork, in the eyes of the law, those people were nothing but squatters." The clerk gave him a sympathetic smile but shook his head.

"Any good lawyers in town?" At a loss, he rubbed his forehead.

"Greg Barlow." Again, the clerk shrugged. "But without producing a land grant, headright certificate, or some proof of prior ownership, the courts can do nothing."

Ben thanked the man for the information and rode back to the fort. Still considering the options, he met Cadence as school let out.

Her eyes lit up when she saw him and then dimmed at his expression. "What's wrong?"

He relayed the district clerk's words as he walked her home. "Mariana's not only lost her family. She's lost her inheritance."

"This time, because of white renegades. We know James is devious, but do you think…?" She squinted as her brow creased. "You said the land was surveyed just three weeks ago?"

"Yes." He nodded. "Why? What are you thinking?"

"It's all too convenient the way he had the land surveyed *just after* the renegades killed the Rodriguez family." Pursing her lips, Cadence took a deep breath. "Do you think Mariana might know where her family kept a deed?"

"We could ask"—he shrugged—"but even if she knows, nothing's left of the house."

"Still, she might have a clue." She called Mariana as they entered the house.

"Yes?" The girl came running with Emily at her side, each toting a rag doll.

"Do you know where your family might have kept their important papers?"

Mariana looked off into space, squinting and blinking.

How much does she remember?

"*Abuela* and my father say 'buried treasure' and '*joyas de la familia*.' "

"Family jewels."

"What do you mean?" Cadence shook her head.

Mariana turned toward him. "*Dijeron que cuando grabaron su muerte en la Biblia.*"

"They said those words when they recorded her mother's death in the Bible." He winced as he relayed the message. *Poor kid.*

"Know no more." Chin on her chest, the girl lifted her gaze to them.

"Thanks, Mariana." She gave her a sympathetic smile as the girls returned to their dolls.

He pinched his bottom lip, thinking. Then he turned toward her. "I'd just told you nothing was left of the Rodriguez house."

She nodded.

"Nothing, except for the root cellar."

"Let's ride out and look. Even if we don't find any paperwork, maybe we'll find Mariana's rosary." A smile crept across her face. "Wouldn't she be surprised if we found it?"

****

Saturday, as he and Cadence rode to the old Rodriguez ranch, he prepared her for the changes since her previous visit. "The house is gone—burned to the ground. Instead of Lupe, Juan, and his brothers, a family cemetery holds their remains."

"They died defending this land." She looked at the crude graves, whispered a prayer, and then turned toward Ben. "We owe it to them to recover Mariana's property."

"I agree." He took two kerosene lamps from his saddlebags and led the way to the root cellar. "Any profit from this land is blood money. We can't let West or any crooked surveyor cheat Mariana of what's rightfully hers."

He inspected the collapsed structure. Though the clean-up detail had removed the fallen crossbeams and scooped the worst of the debris, the cabin was a dismal testament to the misery inflicted beneath its roof. He swallowed hard, remembering the mutilated bodies of Lupe, Juan, and his brothers.

After lifting the trapdoor, he lit their lamps and led her down the roughhewn wooden ladder.

"How could Mariana breathe in here after the renegades set fire to the cabin?" She looked about the tiny space, staring at the framed underpinnings of the adobe brick house.

"I don't know." He shook his head. "She must have a guardian angel."

"I don't know how she didn't suffocate." She took a deep breath.

Ben lifted his lamp to better see inside the nooks and crannies.

Dried bundles of herbs and ropes of chili peppers and garlic bulbs hung from the wooden rafters overhead. A few canned goods, as well as baskets, gardening tools, and kitchen utensils lined the wooden shelves.

They began moving things aside, looking for what might be hidden in the back.

The floor was compacted earth, but the soil was soft to walk on. Then, something crunched underfoot. Setting down his lamp, he brushed away the whitish-gray caliche.

There lay the rosary, its pale blue, off-white chalcedony beads half buried in the loose soil.

"You found it." She broke into a wide grin. "The

'hunt' is a success."

"I wouldn't call our search successful unless we find a deed, land grant, homestead grant, or headright certificate." He handed over the rosary.

"I've heard of the others, but what's a headright certificate?" Tilting her head to the side, she squinted.

"Just another name for a land grant." Pursing his lips, he stifled a sigh. "The realtor explained the naming convention when I bought the property. To encourage families to immigrate, Texas issued documents to the heads of households, entitling them to parcels of land. The state had four classes of headright certificates ranging between 320 and 4,605 acres."

"So the best class was entitled to 4,605 acres?"

"The *first* class was entitled to 'a league and a labor.' "

"Which is?" She gave him a blank look.

"The 4,605 acres. Fourth class headrights received 320 acres, and homestead grants were awarded 160 acres."

"So finding any of these certificates would establish Mariana as the legal owner." Nodding, she continued rifling through the shelves.

He searched the spaces overhead between the rafters, his gloved hand reaching where he could not see. *Maybe they built a secret compartment between the joists—*

Her blood-curdling screech broke the stillness, making his hair stand on end.

"What?" One hand at his holster, he lifted the lantern with his other.

"A scorpion fell on me." Shrieking, she slapped her head, brushing off her hair. "Eeuw. *Get it off.*"

"Hold still." Relieved her scream wasn't in response to Apaches or bandits, he took a deep breath as he brushed the scorpion from her hair and stepped on it.

"*Eeuw.*" Staring at the dead scorpion, she shuddered. "I hate those things."

"Maybe we should call it quits." He chewed his lip, debating whether to waste any more time in the search. "We've raked over every inch of these shelves, and I've looked between the rafters."

Her gaze glued to the trampled scorpion on the dirt floor, she mumbled, "True, but…"

"But?" As the pause lengthened, he tugged her hand. "What are you thinking?"

"We've checked everything in sight." She glanced about the tiny crawl space. "And I'm *not* anxious to stay in this scorpion-infested cellar a minute longer than necessary…but what about what's out of sight?"

"What do you mean?" Squinting, he studied her.

"Most of this dirt floor is tamped down but look how loose the soil is in the corners." She tapped the compacted soil with her foot.

"They just haven't been walked on as often." He shrugged. "They're off the beaten path."

"You're probably right." She studied the floor's unevenly compacted soil, then searched his eyes. "But what if something's hidden in one of the corners? Mariana did mention 'buried treasure.' "

"Good point." He found an old garden trowel and began turning up the loose soil in the nearest corner, but after ten minutes of digging, all he had to show was a mound of soil. He tried the opposite corner, but from his kneeling position several minutes later, he shook his head. "Nothing."

"Maybe digging wasn't such a clever idea…"

"Might as well finish what we started." Though Ben also questioned the search's feasibility, he tried the third corner, which also proved empty.

The wooden ladder blocked the last corner. To access it, he had to dislodge the ladder, which required tight maneuvering to squeeze past each other in the cramped quarters. Finally, he unhinged the ladder, set it aside, and began digging. After five minutes of tilling, his trowel squawked as it grazed a metallic surface.

Sharing a gleeful smile, he dug with renewed interest, tossing aside scoops of caliche soil. A few more minutes of tilling, and the outline of a flat metal box emerged. "This could be it…"

"Hope so." Crossing her fingers, she held the lamp closer.

He dug around the container, loosening the soil until he could pry the box from the ground. Then he opened its latch. Inside was a worn family Bible and a creased, ink-stained paper embossed with the state seal of Texas. Unfolding the document, he read the contents. "Board of Land Commissioners, Rodriguez, Juan— Unconditional Certificate #128 for Fourth Class Headright #166."

"You found it!" She laughed out loud.

"And this Bible must be the 'family jewels.' " He paged to the back. "Here's the family's record of births, deaths, and marriages."

"Which proves Mariana's heritage." She wrinkled her nose. "Now, neither James nor any court of law can dispute her legal claim to this ranch."

He replaced the ladder, and they climbed out of the

root cellar.

"This coverup won't stop meddlers"—she scattered debris over the trapdoor, concealing the entrance—"but it should hide the stairway from any casual passerby."

He sighed deep in his throat.

"What are you grinning about?"

"You." Taking her in his arms, he nuzzled her neck. "You're not only beautiful. You're smart. How did I get so lucky?"

"I'm the lucky one." She curled against him.

You? He pulled back his head, studying her face. "Why would you say such a thing?"

"If you hadn't come along when you did, I might've married James." She shuddered.

"You'd have found him out, sooner or later."

"Just glad it was sooner and not too late." Her scowl morphed into a snicker. "What'll he do when he learns Mariana owns this land?"

****

On the way back to the fort, Ben reined in his horse as they approached their property. "Would you like to have our picnic lunch on top of this bluff?"

"Isn't this cliff where you took me the last time?" She glanced at the commanding view.

"You caught me red-handed." His affable smile turned serious as he studied her face. "I wondered if you'd like this location for our house."

"The view's gorgeous." She stared at the vista's cascading tiers of craggy mountain ranges. Then sighing, she turned toward him. "I can't imagine waking up to a prettier sight each morning."

"Me, either—other than you." He slid his arm around her back and breathed in the fresh, mountain air as they gazed at the panorama. "But the builders start Monday." He began gathering and stacking stones into four piles. "I'll tell them to use these rocks as rough markers for the cornerstones."

"Perfect—just make sure the front windows face this view." She gestured to the panorama. Then wearing an impish smile, she spread out the picnic blanket in the center of the four stacks. "How about celebrating with our first dinner in the 'dining room'?"

Chapter 20
Retaliation

Monday afternoon, she and Ben stopped by the district clerk's office.

"I was here last week about the Rodriguez land." Ben removed his hat.

"You questioned Lieutenant West's title to the land south of here." Nodding in recognition, the clerk opened his ledger to the land description.

"The land belongs to the Rodriguez family." Ben tapped the paragraph with his finger.

"Can you prove their ownership?" The clerk stifled a weary sigh.

"The land belongs to this child." She handed him the headright certificate and opened the family Bible to the page showing Mariana's birth.

Exhaling, the clerk stared at the certificate without seeing, as if thinking.

Then he frowned as he looked from the documents to Cadence and Ben. "These documents change everything. If the surveyor and Lieutenant West committed fraud, I need to inform the sheriff."

"And we'll take this matter to the military authorities." She nodded in tacit agreement.

When they returned to the fort, she made sure Mariana was out of the house. Then as she and Ben told her parents the story, they showed them the paperwork.

"What?" Her father shook his head. Pressing together his lips, he made a growling sound deep in his throat. "The man should be court-martialed. I'll wire military chief Reynolds about the proceedings, but in the meantime, throw West in the guardhouse on charges of attempted fraud."

"With pleasure, sir." The corners of Ben's mouth turned down. "Though to be safe, we should still see a lawyer for a writ of possession for Mariana."

"The district clerk told us not to worry." Catching her mother's eye, she managed a wry smile. "He said the evidence will stand on its own merit in any court of law, but a writ of possession would be a wise precaution."

"Enough talk about James." Her mother's lip lifted in a sneer. Then she took a deep breath and expelled it quickly. "Let's discuss a pleasanter topic—like Mariana's saint's day."

"All right. How do we celebrate?" After looking at the blank faces, Cadence shrugged. "Guess we'll have to ask her when she comes in, but I imagine a saint's day celebration is something like a birthday party—cake and gifts."

"If that's the case, I'll let her choose whatever she wants for dinner and bake a cake." Her mother nodded.

"We can return her rosary, but I'd like to give her something, too." A brooding V settled between Ben's eyes. "Any ideas?"

She swallowed a smile. "What if…?"

****

December second, Cadence set the table with the finest linen and porcelain china.

As the five sat down to dinner, Jenny brought out a

sizzling platter of thinly sliced steak, onions, and red, yellow, and green peppers.

"You remembered the fajitas." Mariana's eyes sparkled.

"How could we forget?" Cadence teased. "You've reminded us every day this week."

After they said grace, Mariana helped herself to a toasted flour tortilla, still steaming from the griddle. Then she scooped the sliced flank steak, red and green peppers, and onions onto the tortilla, topping the fajita with shredded cheese and chunky salsa.

Cadence breathed in the sweet aromas of the caramelized onions and sautéed bell peppers mingling with the smoky scent of the chargrilled steak. Then she bit into the colorful Mexican entrée and found it delicious.

As they discussed the day's events, the group passed bowls of *guacamole*, *pico de gallo*, refried beans, and diced tomatoes. Then after dinner, Jenny brought out dessert—a three-tiered birthday cake made from unsweetened chocolate baking squares and frosted with chocolate icing.

"This best saint's day *always*." Mariana's eyes opened almost as wide as her smile.

"Would you like anything else?" Cadence studied her.

"Oh, no." Mariana shook her head emphatically. "This everything I want."

She glanced at Ben before taking a tiny package from her pocket and placing it in front of Mariana. "Not even this?"

"What is?" The girl cocked her head, looking from her to the gift to Ben and back.

"Open the box and see." His eyes crinkling at the corners, he smiled.

Nodding, she lifted off the cover, and her eyes welled up. As the tears began spilling down her cheeks, she pressed the rosary against her chest.

"You find my mother rosary. Thank you."

She remembered all the nights Mariana had sobbed herself to sleep. These were tears of joy. Still, Cadence struggled to keep from sniffling along, and she forced a bright smile instead.

"And I made something for you." She reached beneath the table and handed the girl another box.

"You make? For me?" Her eyelashes still wet, Mariana smiled through her tears. As she unwrapped the box, she gasped when she found a convertible riding skirt. Standing, she held the skirt against her waist, admiring its panels, and then hugged Cadence. "Beautiful. My dress like yours. Thank you, Aunt Cadence."

"Why don't you see if the skirt fits?"

"Yes." Her eyes looked as big as the chocolate birthday cake. "Be right back."

After Mariana left the room, Ben stood. "I have something for her, too."

When Mariana returned, she modeled the split skirt, first twirling to show off its flared legs and modesty panels, and then taking a wide stance, demonstrating the divided skirt's trousers.

Cadence noticed the waist was a bit loose. "I'll take in the waistband tomorrow."

"*Es precioso sólo la forma en que lo es.*"

"It's beautiful just the way it is." He translated from the doorway. His eyes twinkling, he turned toward

Mariana. "You have one more present waiting in the warming kitchen. Would you like to see?"

"Oh, yes." Mariana clasped her hands as her face brightened into an even wider grin.

They followed him, watching as he brought out a wooden crate from behind the stove. Inside the box was a crumpled blanket. Then the blanket moved and whimpered.

Her eyes glowing, Mariana approached cautiously—eager yet unsure. When she pulled back the coverlet, a Catahoula puppy woofed. Laughing while her eyes filled with tears, she lifted the spotted dog and gazed into his face. "Oh, Uncle Ben, thank you. *Thank you.*"

"What will you name him?" His eyes misted.

Giggling as the puppy's tongue licked her ears, she wriggled in delight. "Tickles."

Cadence bit her lip as Ben's dewy eyes homed in on the girl. Then his jawline hardened. He cleared his voice and spoke in his no-nonsense voice.

"Tickles is a fine name, but he's yours now, which means he's your responsibility, *tu responsabilidad.* You understand?"

"Yes, oh, yes." She nodded earnestly.

When he was ready to leave, Cadence walked Ben to the front porch. "I think the puppy was her favorite gift."

"I think the whole evening was her favorite gift." Chuckling, he put his arm around her shoulders as they gazed at the crescent moon. "My guess is Mariana doesn't expect much from life—not after all she's lost. Maybe celebrating her saint's day will help restore her trust that she's safe and what she has won't be taken away."

"Once she lives with us and falls into a routine, I think she'll outgrow her fear of the future. Hope so, anyway." She nodded, remembering the girl's earlier, nighttime tears. Then glancing at the waning moon, she turned toward him. "Today's December second. Do you realize in less than four weeks, we'll be married?"

"Can't wait." Tightening his grip, he swung her toward him.

"Me, neither." Her cheek to his chest, Cadence snuggled, molding her body to his as she lifted her lips.

At the captain's cough, she flinched, and they broke apart.

"Didn't hear you come outside, sir." Ben lowered his arm from her shoulders.

"So it seems." The captain cleared his throat. "I didn't want to mention this news at Mariana's party, but military chief Reynolds wired me about West's Show Cause Board of Inquiry."

"Yes, sir."

"In addition to attempted fraud, West's charges are willful dereliction of duty for ordering a subordinate to falsify civilian records, as well as conduct unbecoming to an officer."

"Couldn't happen to a nicer person." She spat out the words like taking aim at an annoying gnat.

"His preliminary inquiry is Monday," said her father. "This isn't his trial, but West requested a judge and declined a panel of three officers to sit in jury."

"Sounds like he's throwing himself on the mercy of the court." She sniffed. "Evidently, he doesn't trust his fellow officers' opinions."

"According to Chief Reynolds, West's entire

defense is based on his prior record. He requests his recent actions be overlooked." As he surveyed his daughter, he shook his head. "To think you might have married him…"

"No love lost there. Heaven had someone else in mind." Then taking Ben's hand, she smiled. "Do you realize, in less than four weeks, I'll be Mrs. Williams?"

"Four weeks." Her father shook his head again. "Seems like yesterday you were Mariana's age. Now, you're to be married." Stifling a sigh, he turned toward Ben. "How's the house coming?"

"I plan to ride out tomorrow, but the builders tell me it's framed and roughed-in."

"Want company?" Her pulse quickening, she imagined its progress. "I'd like to see our house, too."

"Don't you have to teach tomorrow?"

"Oh, you're right." She frowned. "How could I forget?"

"I have to meet with the construction crew tomorrow"—he tugged her hand—"but maybe you'd like to ride with me Saturday?"

****

The next evening, she watched through the window as Ben took the porch steps two at a time. Opening the front door, she gasped the moment he lifted his face.

"What's wrong?"

"Our house is gone—"

"What? How?"

"Burned."

"No…" She stepped back to let him in, and the acrid smell of smoke wafted from his clothing. "Can anything be saved?"

"Very little…if any." His shoulders slumped. His

cheeks and forehead were black with soot, and his hands and sleeves were as dark as his expression. "The frame is nothing but charred wood now."

"What happened?" A dozen questions on her mind and at her lips, she looked to him for the answers. "Lightning? Wildfire?"

"Kerosene." Rimmed in red, his eyes looked feverish. "I found the cans nearby. Someone's set fire to our house."

"No…" Dazed, she slumped into the nearest chair. "Apaches?"

"They wouldn't use kerosene." He scowled.

"Then who'd do such a thing?" Though stunned by the news, she could not envision anyone being so malicious.

"Who do you think?" He arched his brow. "Even locked in the guardhouse, West finds partners in crime." Grunting, he pressed his fist to his lips. "But that's just a hunch. I have no proof."

"Who else would be so spiteful?" Their plans in tatters, all she could think of was the brief time until their wedding. Everything hinged on completing the house. *Now this setback.* She groaned. "What'll we do?"

"Start over." His chin tilting down, he slowly shook his head. Then he lifted his bloodshot eyes. "What else can we do? But this time, I'll post a guard."

"When we ride to the ranch Saturday, let's look for clues." She forced a smile, struggling not to show her disappointment. "The way you noticed kerosene cans and knew Apaches didn't set the fire. Maybe you can find something to tell us who *did?*"

****

Though the air was crisp and dry Saturday, snow flurries swirled about, collecting on the horses' backs, as well as Cadence's hat and shoulders.

An enormous stand of prickly-pear cactus covered with hoarfrost drew her attention. Morning dew had collected on the razor-sharp spines, coating every thorn with a feathery crystal sheath. As the sun brought the fragile shells to light, she marveled at the desert's winter wonderland.

But when they reached the property, the sight disheartened her. Only charred wood remained. Though the builders salvaged what they could of the singed and smoke-damaged timbers, reusing them where possible, they needed to replace the burned rafters with fresh beams.

"We might as well use the scraps to build a campfire." Ben pointed to a stack of charred lumber behind the framed house with mounds of sawdust and wood shavings nearby. "The wood's not good for anything but kindling."

His jaw jutted out defiantly, giving him a stubborn, bulldog frown. The fire had taken a personal toll on him. Dark circles underscored his glazed, bloodshot eyes. Wrinkles had etched their way into his brow, and he spoke softly as if exhausted.

"At least, the builders are making progress." Her heart aching for him, she put on a cheerful smile.

"But will they finish by Christmas? Whoever set this fire cost us not only money, but time." His chest heaved in a silent sigh. "Maybe we should consider postponing the wedding."

"No." Adamant, she shook her head. "We've made the commitment. No matter what happens, I don't want to wait. Let's marry when we planned—the day after Christmas."

"If the house isn't finished in time, where would we live?"

He wore the wry smile she was beginning to recognize, the one he used when trying to reason.

"Too bad we couldn't share the room you have now, but I know." She held up her palm, ending his argument before he made it. "We wouldn't be allowed to stay in the unmarried officers' quarters." She searched her mind for other options. "Well...we could live with my parents for a few days...weeks, however long construction takes." She shrugged. "That scenario's not ideal, but it *is* an option in case the builders aren't finished in time."

"Only as a last resort." He wore a hangdog smile. "Let me start a pot of coffee. At least, we can warm ourselves."

While he gathered charred lumber for the campfire, Cadence scoured the area for clues. She kicked through tufts of scorched grass and outlying mounds of wood chips, sawdust, and ashes, hoping to turn up clues, but all she found were scattered nails and scraps of wood.

Then something shiny beneath a singed pile of wood shavings caught her attention. Her pulse raced as she drew closer, trying to keep sight of the object's glimmer in the tall weeds and wood shavings.

The sun ducked behind a cloud, and the reflection disappeared.

Impatient to catch another tantalizing glimpse, she struggled to hold still, afraid to lose sight of potential evidence.

Finally, the clouds parted, and the sun peeked

through, lighting the item like a dazzling beacon. She reached into the shavings, pulling out what appeared to be a polished brass pocket watch.

"Ben." She raced toward him. "Look what I found."

"Smells like kerosene." He sniffed the metal case. Then he raised what looked like a latch with a string running through its center.

"What is that contraption?"

"It's a hinged sight." He lifted a lid with a hole cut in its center. Inside was a compass, its glass cover cracked where kerosene had seeped in. "This is a surveyor's compass."

"Surveyor…" She flipped over the case and saw the initials CWS. "Do you think it belongs to the surveyor that helped James?" Her eyes narrowing, she studied him. "Could he have set the fire?"

"Even if he did, this compass wouldn't be enough evidence to convict him."

"Maybe not, but if these are his initials, it proves he was here—"

"Trespassing."

"He's attempted fraud once with James. Maybe they collaborated again…"

Apparently lost in thought, he did not respond.

"Do you know the surveyor's name?" Cadence asked.

"No, but the district clerk might. Let's stop by his office on the way back." He poured a steaming cup of coffee and handed it to Cadence.

Warming her hands on the tin cup, she breathed in the brew's fortifying aroma. Despite no milk or sugar, she gladly drank it black to stave off the day's chill.

"Morning." The crew's foreman stomped toward them.

Ben offered him a cup as he introduced Cadence.

"No, thanks." Shaking his head, the foreman waved it off. Then, he held his hands toward the campfire, warming them.

"Will the house be ready by Christmas?" She studied the man's posture and facial expressions as much as listened to his words.

"If I were a betting man"—he raised his brow and gave a faint nod—"maybe, but then I'm not a betting man."

Reading more into his mannerisms than his comments indicated, Cadence smiled, and after he left, she shared her hunch with Ben. "I think the crew will finish by Christmas. He just didn't want to raise our expectations."

"Don't set yourself up for disappointment." He made a dubious humming sound in his throat.

Ben's reaction did little to raise her hopes. *What will we do if the house isn't finished?*

****

She and Ben stopped at the district clerk's office on their ride back.

"Sorry to hear about your house catching fire." The clerk glanced from his ledger. "Sure was a bad piece of luck. Was it lightning?"

She shook her head.

"Kerosene." Ben wore an inscrutable expression.

"Arson?" The man's eyes opened wide behind his spectacles.

"In my opinion." His jawline rigid, Ben nodded. "You wouldn't know the name of the surveyor who worked for Lieutenant West, would you?"

"Yeah, Chuck Stevens."

"Does he have a middle initial?" She fingered the compass in her pocket, tracing the inscription.

"Why?" The clerk studied her.

"We found something with a monogram." She glanced at Ben. At his nod, she showed the clerk. "We wondered if this tool belongs to Mr. Stevens."

"Seems to me…" Chewing his lip, the clerk paged through his ledger. "Yes, here's his full name—Charles Woodrow Stevens."

Was he James' henchman?

Chapter 21
Board of Inquiry

The morning of the Show Cause Board of Inquiry, the captain asked Ben to accompany him.

"I thought West didn't want a jury of peers present." Surprised, he raised his brow.

"Keep in mind, this investigation isn't his trial," said the captain. "It's just an inquiry to 'show cause' why he shouldn't be discharged from the cavalry, but you have evidence that may shed light on the proceedings. Bring that compass along with the paperwork—just in case."

School was let out for the day, so the military could conduct the inquiry in a makeshift courtroom.

Cadence stayed home, baking gingerbread men with Helen, Mariana, and Jenny in an oven-warmed kitchen fragrant with the holiday aromas of molasses, cinnamon, and ginger. As he left, she followed him out the front door and pulled him back in a furtive goodbye kiss. "For luck."

"I'll be glad when you're Mrs. Williams, and we don't have to sneak kisses." He grinned.

Giving him a tight squeeze, she gazed into his eyes. "Won't married life be grand?"

****

"The inquiry into the dismissal of Lieutenant West is now in session."

Ben eyed West, sitting at the table in front of the improvised bench to the judge's left.

The senior officer struck the gavel. "Lieutenant, do you have representation present?"

"I do." West rose from his seat and gestured to the man beside him. "Mr. Toomey is a civilian military defense attorney."

"The charges against Lieutenant West are attempted fraud, willful dereliction of duty for ordering a subordinate to falsify civilian records, and conduct unbecoming to an officer." The senior officer removed his glasses to peer at West. "Be aware, at any time during these proceedings, you have the right to submit a resignation in lieu of court-martial and dishonorable discharge."

"Yes, sir." West remained expressionless.

"You may take your seat." The senior officer turned toward the attorney. "Counsel, what have you to say for the accused?"

"I call Mr. Charles Woodrow Stevens as a witness." The attorney caught the gaze of a lanky, small-boned man as he sauntered to the front.

The clerk asked, "Do you solemnly swear to tell the truth, the whole truth, and nothing but the truth, so help you God?"

Stevens' gaze darted left and right, never once glancing at the clerk as he read the oath. At the end, he mumbled, "I do."

"Please be seated," said the attorney. "Would you tell this Board of Inquiry how you happened to survey the parcel of land in question?"

"James…I mean, Lieutenant West hired me."

"Were you aware this land was not for sale and you

trespassed on private property?" Captain McShane, one of the inquiry's three senior officers, surveyed the man.

"The county records indicated no certificate of ownership." Stevens shrugged. "Besides, the land was vacant when I surveyed it."

"Didn't you find fresh graves and a burned-out cabin on the property?" His jaw rigid and his eyes flinty, Captain McShane persisted in his questioning.

"Squatters." Stevens sneered.

"Lieutenant Williams has discovered a headright certificate establishing prior ownership of the land." McShane nodded toward Ben.

"Were you aware of this preexisting claim?" Another of the three senior officers continued the line of reasoning.

Stevens shrugged.

"Address the hearing with a *yes* or *no*, Mr. Stevens." The senior officer crossed his arms.

"Nope." He shook his head.

"Didn't you and Lieutenant West conspire to defraud the rightful owner of the property in question?" The third senior officer addressed him.

"This is the first I've heard of any previous owner." The chinless man smoothed his sparse mustache with his small hand.

"The county had no record of prior ownership when Mr. Stevens was hired to survey the property." The defense attorney rose. "If a certificate was found after the fact, no fraud was committed. Having the land surveyed was merely an oversight, not dereliction of duty or conduct unbecoming to an officer."

"Lieutenant Williams"—the presiding officer turned toward him—"please present the headright certificate to the court as evidence."

"Yes, sir." Ben approached the bench with the certificate.

"Even *if* this document were to establish prior ownership, I understand Apaches dispatched the previous tenants. Since no titleholder survived the raid, legally, the property reverted to the county." Addressing the three officers, the defense attorney dismissed the case with a wave of his hand. "In either situation, surveying unoccupied land—which belongs to the county—is no violation of the law."

Danged fast talker. Ben sat at attention, struggling to hold his peace.

"One family member did survive the attack, Mariana Rodriguez." The captain's jaw line hard and his backbone rigid, he gestured toward Ben with a nod. "Additionally, Lieutenant Williams discovered a family Bible, establishing a bloodline and proving Miss Rodriguez to be the rightful beneficiary and proprietor."

"Lieutenant Williams"—the presiding officer again turned toward him—"please present the Bible as evidence."

"Yes, sir." Ben once again approached the bench and opened the Bible to the family's records of births, marriages, and deaths.

"Call the interpreter to the stand to translate the documents." The presiding officer gestured to the court clerk.

Moments later, a uniformed officer approached the bench.

The clerk swore him in and handed him the document. "Please be seated."

"Yes, sir." The man read aloud, translating as he

went. "All here as stated, sir. According to the family Bible, Miss Rodriguez is the legitimate heir."

"Thank you. You may step down." The presiding officer turned to the gathering. "The background of Texas law is Spanish, where only legitimate descendants can be forced heirs, but since 1856, Texas has used a community property system. Either way, this hearing accepts this evidence, establishing Mariana Rodriguez as the lawful landowner." He turned to the lawyer. "Does the defense have anything to say?"

"My client labored under the assumption the land belonged to the county. Having the land surveyed did not constitute fraud." Toomey slowly shook his head. "No, indeed. West has committed no wrong in the eyes of the law."

Taking his seat, Ben stifled a frustrated sigh, resenting what looked like collusion between the lawyer, West, and the surveyor.

"From the evidence submitted, Miss Rodriguez clearly is the rightful owner. The title of the property in question reverts to Miss Rodriguez," said the presiding officer. "However, what has yet to be established is whether Lieutenant West knowingly hired Mr. Stevens to survey land belonging to Miss Rodriguez."

Ben took a deep breath and sat back in his chair, relieved the law supported Mariana's claim. But then the presiding officer's words registered—*knowingly hired Mr. Stevens. Can West weasel out of the charges?* He caught the captain's gaze.

Seeming to read his mind, Captain McShane turned to the surveyor. "Please tell the court your full name."

"Charles Woodrow Stevens."

"And what are your initials?"

"CWS." Stifling a sigh, the man rolled his eyes.

"Mr. Stevens"—Captain McShane held up the compass—"can you identify this item?"

"Where did you get that?" His jaw gaping and his eyes bulging, Stevens came to attention.

"Please identify the item for the court, Mr. Stevens."

"Surveyor's compass." Mumbling, he wiped his perspiring lip and smoothed his scanty mustache.

"Have you seen this item before?" asked Captain McShane.

"Where did you find it?" He stared at the tool as if in a daze.

"Does your response constitute a yes, Mr. Stevens?" His jaw unyielding, Captain McShane pressed his lips together.

Swallowing, the man shrugged.

"Address the hearing with a *yes* or *no*, Mr. Stevens," said the senior officer.

"I'm not sure."

"Does this compass belong to you?"

"I can't say." The man looked from West to the lawyer.

"Can't say"—Captain McShane glared—"or won't?"

"I don't know." Stevens shrugged.

"The case has your initials on it—CWS." Captain McShane eyed the witness as he handed the evidence to the court clerk. "How many surveyors have the initials CWS engraved on a compass? Is this compass yours or not?"

"Where did you get it?"

"Address the hearing with a *yes* or *no*, Mr.

Stevens." His posture rigid and the cords twanging in his neck, the senior officer raised his voice. "Is this compass yours?"

"I need to check." The man sat on the edge of his chair, squinting to see.

The court clerk approached him with the tool.

Stevens barely glanced at it. Instead, he eyed the defense attorney and lifted his brow as if looking for direction. Then he stared at West. When neither met his gaze, he licked his lips. "It might be mine"—he shrugged—"or not. I'm not sure."

"Have you ever been hired to perform other tasks for Lieutenant Williams besides surveying?" Captain McShane's gaze never left the man's face.

The man shrugged.

"*Yes* or *no*, Mr. Stevens." The senior officer pressed his fist against his lips.

"Yes."

"What kind of tasks?"

The man's gaze shifted left and right. Again, he glanced at West and then at the defense attorney as if searching for guidance.

"Address the question, Mr. Stevens." The senior officer came to attention. "What kind of tasks?"

"Odd jobs." He shrugged.

"Please elucidate."

Scowling, the man cocked his head as if confused.

"Describe for the hearing what you did in these odd jobs." The senior officer tried again.

Looking from West to the defense attorney, the man chewed his lip.

"Let me assist your memory Mr. Stevens." His hands behind his back, Captain McShane paced. "Were you ever on Lieutenant Williams' property?"

"No." The man's eyes opened wide as he glanced at West and then shifted back to the captain.

"Never?" McShane's gaze drilled into him.

"No."

"Can you explain how your surveyor's compass was found on Lieutenant Williams' property?"

"I might have ridden through the property when I surveyed the adjoining ranch." Stevens jerked back his head, leaving his chin high.

"So you admit this surveyor's compass, found on Lieutenant Williams' property, is yours?"

"What if I do?" He rolled his eyes as he stifled an irritated sigh.

"Address the question, Mr. Stevens." The senior officer's eyes bulged.

"I s'pose so." He shrugged.

"*Yes* or *no*?"

"Yes." Speaking in a weak voice, he pressed his elbows into his sides, making his body as small as possible.

"Note its smell." The veins protruded on Captain McShane's neck. "Kerosene was used to set fire to Lieutenant Williams' house. Can you explain how your surveyor's compass was found on his property, steeped in kerosene?"

"Oh, no…" Shaking his head, he pulled back in his seat. "Oh, no, you don't. I'm not the one on trial at this hearing." The little man smirked, showing uneven, yellow teeth. "You can't pin the blame on me. I'm a civilian."

"Don't think you can't be tried under civil law." The senior officer sat erect. "This Board of Inquiry will notify the sheriff, district clerk, and justice of the peace of the proceedings and submit the evidence to the courthouse in San Antonio. Keep in mind, this evidence can and *will be* used against you."

Flinching, the man grew pale.

"Mr. Stevens, did you intentionally, deliberately, and maliciously set fire to Lieutenant Williams' property?" Captain McShane scrutinized the witness.

"That's a lie!" The man sprang to his feet.

"No, Mr. Stevens, that's a question." The senior officer unclasped his hands and pointed. "Take your seat and keep in mind you're under oath. Did you, or did you not commit arson? *Yes* or *no?*"

"You're badgering the witness." The defense attorney rose from his chair.

"Did you, or did you not commit arson?" repeated Captain McShane. "*Yes* or *no?*"

"I object." The defense attorney shot him a dirty look. "That's a leading question."

"Mr. Stevens, the evidence proves you trespassed on Lieutenant Williams' property." The captain rephrased his question. "Can you explain how your surveyor's compass was found there, saturated with kerosene?"

His gaze shifting left to right—from the senior officer to the defense attorney to Captain McShane to West and back again—the surveyor did not respond.

"Did you, or did you not commit arson?" The senior officer persisted. "*Yes* or *no*, Mr. Stevens?"

"I'm not the one on trial here. West is." Then chewing his lip as he rubbed his jaw, he took his hand from his chin and pointed at West. "He made me do it. He said if I didn't help him, he'd—"

"I wish to resign my commission." West jumped to his feet.

The defense attorney's jaw dropped as he looked at West. "My client would like a short recess—"

"You wish to submit a resignation in lieu of court-martial and dishonorable discharge?" His eyes disapproving slits, the senior officer appraised the lieutenant.

"I…I wish to resign…*now*." West gulped, then ran his hand through his hair. "That is…on condition the board concede an honorable discharge."

"Sign this paper." The senior officer gave the court clerk a document and pen.

The clerk presented them to West, who scribbled his name and handed them back.

"This Board of Inquiry accepts Lieutenant West's resignation and recommends he be removed from active duty, effective immediately." Eyes narrowing, the officer turned toward the surveyor. "I wouldn't travel far if I were you, Mr. Stevens. Remember, this Board of Inquiry will submit the evidence of these proceedings to the sheriff, district clerk, and justice of the peace, as well as the courthouse in San Antonio." Then he banged the gavel. "Inquiry adjourned."

Wearing a hangdog expression, West hunched his shoulders.

Ben pinched his mouth tight. *He's beaten now, but how will he retaliate?*

****

After dinner, Ben and the captain shared the hearing's findings with Cadence and Helen.

"West was disciplined under military law, but civil law in this area isn't quite as responsive." The captain grimaced. "No criminal act's been punished in two years."

"Why's that?" Squinting, Ben tilted his head.

"Largely because of the four-hundred miles between here and the courthouse in San Antonio." The captain raised his hands, palms up. "Despite the evidence and his virtual confession, odds are, the surveyor will go free."

"We've already accepted the possibility." Ben glanced at Cadence, and she gave him a begrudging nod.

"We just want to be sure Mariana inherits the property her family fought so hard to protect." She bit her lip.

"Which reminds me. When I got the writ of possession to remove West from Mariana's property, I asked the lawyer about her rights. He said the evidence 'conclusively proves' she's the legal heir." Ben stifled a sigh. *But with West no longer under military jurisdiction, what will he try next...?*

Chapter 22
Christmas

A week before Christmas, Cadence and Ben rode south toward their property. The sun glowed honeycomb gold in the cloudless Texas blue sky, and the temperature was so mild, she unbuttoned her jacket. When they reached the bluff's crest, she sat tall in her saddle, straining to see the builders' progress.

"They finished!" Squealing with joy, she saw the wooden shingle roof of their freshly painted house rise above the scrub oaks, nearly to the tops of the pines.

"At least, the exterior's done." His half-smile was lopsided. "Let's see the inside before we celebrate."

They dismounted and climbed the plank-board stairs to the front porch and breezeway.

Without warning, Ben swept her off her feet and carried her across the threshold into the living room.

"But we're not married yet." Laughing and shrieking with delight, Cadence pulled open the screen door. Then nuzzling against Ben's chest, she remembered the first time he had whisked her into his arms—when she had let go her skirts, scattering the pecans.

The sound of hammering from the warming kitchen was deafening, and the fresh varnish fumes drifting from the dining room reeked, but Cadence beamed. *The sounds and scents of progress*.

"Anyone here?" Ben set her on her feet.

She snuck a quick kiss before smoothing her dress and composing herself into a semblance of modesty.

"Howdy." Rounding the corner, the foreman entered the living room.

"You've made good headway." Assessing the room's progress, Ben shook the man's hand.

"We've added another carpenter to the crew hoping to make up for lost time."

"Think the house will be finished in time to move in next Sunday?" Cadence studied the foreman's mannerisms.

Avoiding their gaze, he faced them at an oblique angle, as if anxious to sidestep their questions.

"Maybe." Edging toward the kitchen, he half turned his back toward them. "The living room and main bedroom are finished, but the carpenter's still working on the kitchen cabinets, and the varnished floors in the dining room still need to cure. Plus, we need to lay the linoleum in the kitchen."

The report was not what she wanted to hear. "What do you think?" Frowning, she turned to Ben.

"I hear we can move in—just not into the whole house."

Though the foreman nodded, he crossed his arms. "You can move your furniture into the living room and main bedroom—this side of the dogtrot—but I can't guarantee the other rooms will be ready."

If only the fire hadn't delayed us. Cadence bit her lip, trying to swallow her disappointment.

"How long will the varnish take to cure?" After glancing at the foreman, Ben caught her gaze.

"Depending on the humidity—with any luck, the

floors should be ready to walk on by Sunday." As the foreman shrugged, his arms went slack and dropped to his sides.

She ventured a half smile at the man's gestures. "Then only the kitchen's left, right?"

"True, but both the floors and cabinets need finishing." The man's lips pressed together. "Keep in mind, the workmen would be underfoot…"

She turned toward Ben.

"Think you can manage without using the warming kitchen a day or two?" Ben glanced her way.

"Until it's ready, we can just eat pemmican." Relieved they had a place to move into, she laughed.

"We'll do our best to finish before Christmas." The foreman shook Ben's hand. "In the meantime, enjoy the holidays and congratulations on your upcoming wedding." Then with a wave, he left the room, responding to a laborer's question.

"Without a kitchen, eating meals will be like our first 'dinner' here." She winked.

"You mean, like our second 'dinner?' " He answered with a wry smile. "Don't forget the picnic the first time I brought you here, when I tried to propose."

"Why didn't I accept *then*?" She cringed, annoyed with herself.

"Because the timing wasn't right." Reaching for her hand, he smiled as he paraphrased her words in the stable. "All things in God's time…finishing the house…and even getting married."

"True, but we could be an old married couple by now." She heaved a sigh. "Why did I waste time?"

****

Christmas Eve morning, the living room was

turned upside down with holiday decorations and last-minute wedding preparations.

Cadence sat near the sunny front window with its southern exposure. While Ben set up the ponderosa pine, she breathed in its fresh, Christmassy fragrance as she put the finishing touches on her white tulle veil.

Her father and Mariana sat by the crackling hickory fire, the burning wood giving off a homey scent like freshly smoked ham. After popping corn over the hot coals, they threaded the kernels into long garlands, while the puppy teethed on a piece of rawhide at Mariana's feet.

The mingled aromas of baking and cooking wafted in from the kitchen as her mother and Jenny prepared holiday treats. Along with the spicy fragrances of molasses, cinnamon, star anise, and ginger, the women's cheerful banter floated through the house, while they chopped vegetables on the old butcher block, rhythmically whisked meringue in a copper bowl, or rattled cast-iron pots and pans. An air of expectancy seemed to grip the household.

Christmas magic. As Cadence gazed at the extended family, she sensed the anticipation. *Maybe because a child's in the house, the old is new again. We're seeing Christmas through her eyes*. Then she looked at Ben. *Or maybe because of our wedding, we're excited by the future*.

"Cadydid."

Her father roused her from her musings. "Yes?"

"Why don't you read *'Twas the Night Before Christmas*?"

"Good idea." Tying the last stitch with a French knot, she nodded as she put aside her veil. "Mariana, have you ever heard *'Twas the Night Before Christmas*?"

"What is?" The girl's dark eyes sparkled.

"What is *it*?" She smiled as she pulled the book from the shelf, remembering the first time her father had read the story. "It's a Christmas poem by Clement Moore." She sat on the divan, opened the slim book, and began reading. "'Twas the night before Christmas, when all thro' the house, Not a creature was stirring, not even a mouse…"

"For children, yes?" When the story ended, Mariana scratched her head.

"Children of all ages." Cadence caught Ben's gaze and grinned.

"Not make sense." Frowning, Mariana pointed at the fireplace. "Fat man not fit."

"You just have to believe." She gave her a warm smile. "It's part of the Christmas charm."

"Why stockings by chimney?"

"So they could dry, but you heard the poem—so Saint Nicholas could fill them."

"With what?"

"You'll see." Cadence had to chuckle. "How did you celebrate other Christmases?"

"With *piñatas.*" Mariana turned toward Ben. "*Llenaríamos un recipiente de papel maché con forma de animal con golosinas…*"

"They'd fill a papier-mâché container shaped like an animal with treats," Ben translated. "Then they'd hang it from a sturdy bough, and blindfolded, they'd take turns poking the *piñata* with sticks until its toys and candies spilled out."

"Did I hear someone say candy?" Her mother

walked into the front room, her eyes glistening. "Anyone up for a taffy pull?"

A chorus of yeses and the sound of chairs scraping against the wood floor answered her.

"Wash your hands and join me in the dining room."

Five minutes later, they reassembled at the table. A buttered plate containing a brown, tennis-ball-sized lump of sticky goo sat in front of each person.

"First grease your hands." Her mother passed the butter dish. Then she demonstrated for Mariana. "Pull the taffy until it's double in length. Then fold it in half. Keep pulling and folding until the taffy turns a golden bronze color, and it's too stiff to pull anymore. Then roll it into thin ropes, cut those into bite-sized pieces, and wrap each candy in wax paper." She smiled at Mariana. "Sound good?"

"*Si.*" Her dark eyes sparkling, Mariana shook her head as she corrected herself. "I mean, yes." Then flinching and giggling at the gooey taffy's texture, she began stretching it between her small hands. "Tonight Saint Nicholas comes, yes?"

****

As they joined the children's party in the library, Cadence took in the main room's changes. Grapevine wreathes decorated with juniper greens, red holly berries, and star anise seeds gave off peppery licorice scents as they trimmed the room's book-filled walls. Polished red apples, green pine boughs, deer antlers, red-and-white striped candy canes, and flickering white candles graced the fireplace mantel. Mounds of clove-and-orange pomander balls released their citrusy and spicy scents, while aromatic pinecones strung from red ribbons completed the decorations.

"Remember the Harvest Ball?" She recalled the library's autumnal splendor with a sigh.

"Was that dance only two months ago?" Wearing a mischievous smile, he stole a kiss.

A fragrant pine tree stood near the front, decked with handmade red-and-green paper chains and a garland of stars crafted from pinecones and twine. One table overflowed with gifts for the children and a second held Christmas sugar cookies, hard candies, frosted cakes, and fruit punch.

She opened the party by leading them in a Christmas-carol sing-along.

Then dressed as Santa Claus, the captain passed out gifts to the children. When Mariana's turn came, he gave her hand-knitted red mittens.

Her eyes twinkled in recognition, but she kept his secret with a wink.

After the party, they crossed the parade grounds to the chapel, where several members of the infantry band softly played *It Came Upon a Midnight Clear*.

She gazed at the familiar room that doubled during the week as the school. *How much I've enjoyed teaching here—enjoyed life since Ben transferred here. All the challenges and choices...*Then the hairs tickling the back of her neck, she sensed his gaze on her, and she turned toward him. "The day after tomorrow we'll be here again..."

"But as man and wife." He squeezed her hand.

During the chaplain's sermon, she recalled Emily Dickinson's poem. *Yes, life is heavenly—now that Ben's in it."* She stifled a sigh.

As they walked back to the captain's quarters after

church, Private Smith caught up with them. He saluted the captain and Ben, then turned toward Cadence. "I wanna' thank you ag'in for he'ping me with my Rs."

"Glad to help." She nodded, meaning her words.

"And a new schoolmaster's arriving after the holidays," added the captain, "a chaplain, who'll combine his Sunday duties with teaching the fort's children *and* organizing classes for the men."

"I 'preciate it, sir." Private Smith nodded his thanks.

"I'm glad you can keep up with your studies." Cadence gave the soldier a warm smile.

"Thank you, ma'am." His white teeth flashed in a wide smile. "But I sure will miss you teaching Miz Mariana n' me."

"Me, too." As the consequences of her choices unfolded, she sighed. *I'll miss all my students. Thank God, I'll have Mariana to tutor.*

"So, soldier, do you still think 'painted dolls' have no business at forts?"

Ben's tone was no-nonsense, but his eyes twinkled.

"You ain't gonna hold that against me none, is you, sir?" Private Smith's eyes opened wide, the whites showing around his dark irises.

Shaking his head, Ben smiled.

"No, sir, you's right. A woman sure can make a man's life more tol'ble. Miz McShane done proved that, and to wish y'all a Merry Christmas"—he turned toward the girl, pressing a toy horse into her hands—"I done whittled a li'l somethin' fo' Miz Mariana."

After meeting Ben's gaze in a private smile, Cadence turned to Mariana. "What do you say to Private Smith?"

"Thank you." Mariana's dark eyes lit up as she studied the carving's clean lines. Then she crushed the toy against her chest. "I love horses."

****

Following a light supper of clam chowder and brown bread, Cadence and her family gathered in front of the fireplace. The Christmas tree took center stage, decorated in popcorn garlands, hand-crocheted snowflakes, miniature cardboard cutouts, apples, wrapped taffy candies, gingerbread men, and tiny wax candles in clip-on holders—so many candles, the tree seemed ablaze.

" 'Santa' here, too?" Mariana peeked beneath the boughs at the wrapped gifts.

Her father chuckled as he chose one and read the tag. "To Mariana."

Her eyes opened wide before crinkling in a smile. Then, she giggled as she accepted the gift.

"Unwrap it." Her mother smiled and then glanced at her husband. "It's from us."

"For Tickles," read Mariana. "Thank you." Her face beaming, she took the dog collar and leash from the box, hugged them both, and fastened the new collar on her puppy.

"To Ben." Her father took another present from under the tree and read its gift tag.

"For me?" His eyes opening wide, Ben accepted the gift with a shy smile and carefully unwrapped the paper. Inside were three pairs of hand-knitted socks.

"Made them myself." Cadence squeezed his hand.

"Then, I'll treasure them even more." He kissed her cheek. "Thank you."

"Knitting them was a labor of love." Pleased at his

response, she smiled.

"Speaking of a labor of love…" He stood. "I designed something for you that was too large to fit under the tree. Be right back." He returned from the warming kitchen, wheeling in what appeared to be a low cabinet.

Cadence cocked her head while she stared at the furniture. Then she stood and ran her fingertips over the varnished wood and smooth stone top.

"I reckoned you might like a reminder of your schoolmarm days, so I commissioned a sideboard, using the back of a slate chalkboard for the countertop." He grinned.

"Our first piece of furniture." Hugging him, she kissed his cheek. "It's so original—and meaningful. I love it. Thank you."

"Be right back." Her father returned a moment later, carrying a brass rail headboard decorated with an oversized red ribbon. "Your second piece of furniture." He glanced at his wife before turning toward her. "Your mother's idea."

"We had a horsehair mattress and bedframe delivered to your house this morning," her mother added.

"The headboard's beautiful. Thank you." She slid her fingers over its polished brass bars before hugging her parents.

Her father reached under the tree and, with a smile, handed her a large box.

Inside was an eiderdown quilt and two sets of embroidered sheets and pillowcases.

"Did you make these?" She turned toward her mother.

"We ordered them through a catalogue"—she smiled—"*but* I embroidered them."

"They're beautiful." Again, she hugged her parents. "Thank you so much."

After they opened the rest of the gifts, Ben turned toward Mariana. "Was Santa Claus good to you?"

"Yes, Uncle Ben." Her eyes flashing, she gave him a wide grin.

"I understand Santa had another gift too large to bring in the house." His eyes twinkled. "Want to see what he brought?"

"Oh, yes." Hunching her shoulders, she brought her hands to her lips in a prayerful pose.

"Then meet me on the front porch in ten minutes."

After donning shawls and jackets, they stepped onto the veranda, watching as Ben led an Appaloosa Indian pony toward them.

"For me?" Eyes bulging, the girl gasped.

"Your very own." Cadence nodded.

Mariana hugged her, and then ran down the steps, two at a time, the puppy barking and chasing after her heels. Thanking Ben with a bear hug, she approached the pony from the front.

"Horses' eyes are on the sides of their head, so they can't see straight ahead." He took her hand. "Come around to the side, where it can see what you're doing. Then pet its neck, not its face."

Following instructions, she gave the pony a gentle greeting, and it nickered in response.

"Now introduce yourself the way Comanches do. Breathe into its nostrils."

"Why?" She cocked her head as she studied him.

"Your breath is the fastest way for a horse to

recognize you."

Seeming to recall a fond memory, Ben briefly gazed away as he lifted his lips in a half-smile.

"Your horse will know you anywhere, anytime, even years from now." Putting his face close to the pony's head, he exhaled into the air it breathed. "Like that."

The girl followed his example, gently blowing, not in, but near the pony's nostrils, so it could smell her breath. The horse's ears lifted, and it nickered again.

"He likes you." Ben gave her an approving nod. "What'll you name him?"

Mariana looked at the clear skies. Millions of stars shone back, reflecting off the pony's glossy, white coat. Beaming, she turned toward Ben. "Starlight."

As a private returned Starlight to the stable, Ben and Mariana rejoined the family on the porch.

A quartet of caroling soldiers stopped by on their rounds of the fort, singing *God Rest Ye Merry Gentlemen* in four-part harmony and regaled them from below. Following with *The Twelve Days of Christmas,* they finished with *We Wish You a Merry Christmas*.

Then calling "Merry Christmas" as the soldiers left, the family went inside the house.

But Cadence hung back, tugging Ben's hand. When his gaze questioned her, she peered at the mistletoe suspended above the front door.

"Merry Christmas, soon-to-be Mrs. Williams." Wrapping his arms around her, he drew her close in a kiss.

All things right with the world, she sighed. Melting into his arms, she molded her body against his, enjoying the warmth of his embrace.

Then a strong gust of arctic wind howled through the mountains. Sounding like a great moaning beast, the airstream whipped at her petticoats and wrenched her shawl from her shoulders.

Gasping and shivering from the cold shock, she reached for her shawl, breaking away from the embrace.

"Texas Norther." Ben buttoned his jacket. "The temperature's dropping already."

"Ill blows the wind…" She shuddered not only from the wind's icy fingers, but from the sudden pins-and-needles numbness in her exposed hands and face. Then an inexplicable sense of calamity gripped her, and crossing her arms, she wrapped her shawl around her shoulders. "Think this wind will last into tomorrow?"

****

The next day, the troops' cooks prepared a special feast of venison, wild turkey with sage dressing, buttermilk fried chicken, barbecued pulled pork, side vegetables, and apple streusel pie for dessert. The mingling aromas from the mess hall's groaning tables announced Christmas as much as the troops' wide smiles.

Following tradition, the officers and their families inspected and sampled the fare before returning to their own quarters to celebrate the holiday.

The McShanes invited the McIntyres to join them for dinner. Mariana, Emily, and Travis shared a smaller children's table, while Cadence, her parents, Ben, Tom, and Sarah sat at the dining room table.

Dinner did not begin until after they said grace and her father carved the prime rib. Then everyone began chattering and passing dishes all at once.

"You must be excited"—Sarah passed her the mashed potatoes—"what with the wedding only hours away."

"Tomorrow can't come soon enough." Her cheeks burned as she spooned potatoes onto her plate. Then passing the bowl to Ben, she turned toward him with a subtle wink.

"Christmas dinner, followed by the troops' party tonight—it'll be a long day and a longer night of festivities." Wearing a wistful smile, her mother passed the peas and pearl onions as her gaze rested on Cadence. "Then in the morning, our girl's getting married. How fast time flies."

"Yesterday, I thought how different the library looked from the Harvest Ball—all reds and greens and Christmas wreaths instead of orange pumpkins and corn shocks." She drew a deep breath as if inhaling the memory.

"Hard to believe the dance was just two months ago." He shared a private smile.

"Did you know Sarah and Emily taught Ben to dance?" Tom grinned as he passed the creamed corn.

"No…" Her mother sat up straight.

"Isn't that right, Emily?" Sarah called to her daughter.

"And my brother played his harmonica." Nodding, the girl smiled at Travis.

"Wish I could've seen that." Cadence chuckled.

"He did it for you, Miss McShane," called Emily from the children's table, her eyes sparkling.

"I did it for love." Ben's laugh was dry. "Nothing else could've convinced me to make such a fool of myself."

"I think you cut a dashing figure on the dancefloor." She turned toward him with a private smile, and her gaze locked with his. *Will we always be so in love?*

****

Wearing their Sunday best and dress uniform, Cadence and Ben, along with the other officers and their families joined the B Troop, Tenth Cavalry's Christmas party.

Beds and gun racks pushed aside, the infantry band played on an elevated platform at one end of the barracks, while its opposite end boasted three groaning tables filled with food. Two fruit-decorated Christmas trees graced the long room, one at each end.

Though the strict military system was relaxed for the evening, the fort still observed protocol. The band opened with a waltz, and couple by couple, the officers and their wives began dancing, followed by the enlisted married men and their wives.

Then just as the band struck up a quadrille, the wind blew open the barracks' doors with such force, they slammed and banged against the wall.

His arm in a sling, James West walked in, accompanied by a young Tejano woman and a boy in obvious pain, his shirtsleeve bloodied and torn.

One after another, the musicians stopped playing to stare at the intruders. From a barracks ringing with music and laughter, the sound level dwindled to near silence.

"*Persona non grata,*" Lieutenant Purdue muttered.

James' boots echoed on the plank floor while he led the two Tejanos toward the commanding officer.

"You're not welcome here." Captain McShane

314

stepped in front of his wife, shielding her from West. "What do you want?" His eyes narrowing to suspicious slits, the captain studied the man's face.

"I came on the boy's behalf, sir." James gestured toward the youth's arm with its protruding bone. "If the doctor could set his bone, we'll be on our way."

Swallowing hard at the sight, Cadence looked away as the captain called for the doctor.

"Yes, sir," called Doctor Freeman, making his way through the crowded dancefloor.

"Take this boy to the infirmary. Set his arm and make him comfortable." The captain turned toward Ben and Tom. "Williams, McIntyre, escort West and his companions. They're in your charge. Dismissed." Then he turned toward the band leader, signaling for the quadrille to resume.

The music started up, and the doctor led James and his friends toward the infirmary as Ben and Tom brought up the rear.

Cadence retired to the refreshments table, where she ladled punch for Sarah and herself.

"I can't imagine James helping anyone other than himself." Scoffing, Sarah arched her brow. "Can you?"

"No, but who are those people with him?" Cadence glanced at the retreating figures, irritated James chose to return on the eve of her wedding. *The timing can't be a coincidence.* Then she recalled the Tejano's exposed bone, and concern overtook her dark thoughts. "Just hope the boy will be all right."

"I'm sure Doc Freeman can set his arm, so don't let that—" Her smile sympathetic, Sarah paused. "—or James' appearance ruin your evening. Let's talk of happier things—like your bridal gown. What color is

315

it?"

"I'll wear my mother's silk wedding dress, which time has turned an antique, creamy-white." Though upset over James, she composed her face into a smile for Sarah's sake. "But why ask about the color?"

"You know what they say. Married in white, you've chosen aright..." Sarah winked.

"And what do 'they' say about other colors?"

"Married in gray, you'll go far away. Married in black, you'll wish yourself back. Married in blue, he'll always be true. Married in pink, your heart will sink, and married in brown, you'll live out of town."

Despite the evening's unexpected downturn of events, she had to chuckle at Sarah's sing-song recitation. Then James reinvaded her thoughts. *He wouldn't make trouble at the wedding, would he?*

Chapter 23
New Leaf

Ben kept his eye on West and his companions as the doctor examined the boy's arm.

The Tejano girl divided her time between comforting the boy and attempting communication with James.

West spoke little Spanish, yet he and the girl seemed to have a rudimentary understanding of each other's words.

Despite his distaste for the man, Ben could not stand idly by, watching them struggle. Taking a deep breath, he turned to her, translating as the doctor administered morphine to the boy.

Apparently relieved someone could understand Spanish, she answered rapidly, her words overrunning one another.

From her hurried narrative, he pieced together the story. The boy was her fourteen-year-old brother. They were orphans raised by their grandmother, trying to homestead their deceased parents' ranch. Her brother had fallen from his horse while trying to pull a stump from the field.

"Isn't he young for such work?" He glanced at the youth's slim frame.

"*Ramón es el hombre de la casa.*" Her eyes were serious.

Fourteen and already the "man" of the house. He shook his head. Then not wanting West to speculate about their discussion, he gestured toward him rather than use his name. "How do you know this man?"

"Ramon found him wandering and delirious from a gunshot wound."

"He appears to be all right now except for the arm sling." Ben's eyelids narrowed.

"His shoulder's mending." She squared her shoulders. "Our grandmother knows herbs. She's a *curandera.*"

"A healer?"

She nodded.

"If your grandmother's a medicine woman, why did he bring your brother here?" He glanced at West, assisting the doctor. Then he turned back to the girl.

"Grandmother tried everything she knew, but Ramon's pain was too great for her to set his arm. When she only made the wound worse, James kept saying 'fort,' but we were afraid." Her eyes hardening, her frown deepened into a scowl. "The soldiers had turned us away in the past."

Recalling West's indifferent treatment of the Rodriguez family, he raised his brow. *Was West behind other refugees' rejections?* He glanced from the man to the young woman, shaking his head at the irony. *Why's he helping them now?*

Then he saw the tender smile she gave West. To his surprise, West's face softened. No sneer or smirk, his expression showed concern and genuine affection. *What in tarnation happened to cause this change?* He calculated the time since the inquiry—less than three weeks.

"Tell them the morphine will ease the boy's pain."

Doctor Freeman's words cut into his thoughts.

"When the boy's—"

"Ramon," he corrected. "His name's Ramon."

"When Ramon's comfortable, I'll examine and clean the wound—and then set the bone."

Again, he translated, and the girl encouraged her brother.

"West"—he stepped away—"a word with you."

James touched the girl's shoulder, gesturing he would return.

"No." Her eyes opened wide.

"I just have a few questions." He intervened, assuring her they were in no danger.

Apparently trusting him over her instincts, she gave a curt nod.

He moved a few steps away, far enough so Tom and the doctor could not overhear, yet near enough to relieve the girl's misgivings.

"What kind of game are you playing now?"

"Based on my past actions, I can't blame you for asking, but I swear I just want to help the boy." West sucked in his breath. "When Maya couldn't set Ramon's arm, my only thought was to bring him to the post's doctor."

"Why help these people?" Not persuaded, he narrowed his eyes. Staring him down, he crossed his arms over his chest. "What's in it for you?"

"I owe them my life." West swallowed hard. "I…I want to repay them."

"Coming from you, the idea's too far-fetched to even consider." He snickered.

"I understand your skepticism, but…" West stifled

a sigh before beginning again. "After the hearing, I hit bottom. Drunk and reckless, I left Fort Davis at sunset." He tapped his arm sling. "Out of nowhere, a band of Apaches ambushed—"

"Apaches?" His arms unfolding, he came to attention. "You're sure? I thought we'd rid the area of Victorio's renegades."

"It was too dark to see. I just assumed—"

"What kind of bullet did they dig out of your arm?"

"A Colt .45 cartridge."

"Apaches use flint muskets, fusees, or arrows." Doubtful, Ben squinted at the man. "If the bullet came from a Colt .45, Apaches didn't wing you."

"Whoever they were, they stole my horse and saddlebags and left me for dead. After I woke, I wandered half delirious, until Ramon found me and brought me to his house. Maya and Camilla cleaned my wounds and nursed me back to health." His Adam's apple bobbed as he swallowed. "I owe them my life." Then, West straightened his spine. "I don't care what you think of me or do to me. I just want to help the boy."

"Williams," called the doctor. "Hold Ramon while I set his arm. Despite the morphine, it'll hurt."

As he held down the boy, he considered James' words. *How much should I believe?*

****

An hour later, Ben, Tom, and the doctor reported back to Captain McShane.

"Where are they now?"

"In the infirmary." The doctor shrugged. "No one else was using the room, and the boy couldn't travel tonight."

"Good thinking, Freeman. Appreciate your help." The captain nodded his assent. As the doctor left, he turned to Ben. "Did West say why he brought them here?"

He relayed the story as Cadence and Helen joined them.

"Do you believe James?" Cadence asked later, when they were dancing.

"The odd thing is I do." Ben's smile wavered.

"You're not serious?" Holding her head back, she surveyed him. "After all his lies and the misery he's caused?"

"I know he doesn't deserve—hasn't earned—our trust, but…"

"What?" Her eyes shifted left and right as she studied his face.

"Maybe he's had a change of heart." *Maybe I'm sentimental because it's Christmas or the eve of our wedding, but I can't help thinking…* He shrugged. "Who knows the roles we play?"

"What do you mean?"

"Who knows the real reasons we do things?" His mind honed the idea as they waltzed across the makeshift dancefloor. "We think we're the ones skipping stones across the water, but after we see the ripples of our actions, we realize we were just the stones…not the skippers."

"I don't follow." Squinting, she watched him. "Give me an example."

"For instance"—he recalled their first outings—"we thought we were helping the Rodriguez family when we brought them supplies. But if we hadn't lent them a hand, we might never have gotten to know each other."

"So actually, we helped ourselves." She nodded. "And if James hadn't been so insufferable that day in the trading post, I might not have ridden off in a huff, and you and I might never have gotten together."

"Exactly. We may *think* we're doing things for our own reasons, but I bet we're all just part of a larger divine plan. We're not the skippers. We're the stones being skipped." As the music ended, he drew a deep breath. "We don't know the parts we play in people's lives until after we see the ripples of our actions."

"So what does your theory have to do with James?" She slowly let go his shoulder as they waited for the next dance.

"His 'ripples' affected us just as much as ours affected him. If we're all just stones making waves that move each other"—he lifted his brow—"maybe we shouldn't be too quick to judge."

"I suppose everything has a purpose—even if it isn't obvious—but since James made his own choices, he's responsible for the consequences." She shrugged.

The band began playing *Home, Sweet Home*, signaling the party's end.

"Midnight." As their ears perked, he glanced at his pocket watch and then gazed into her amber eyes, dancing and flickering like candleflames. "Just a few more hours until we're Mr. and Mrs. Williams."

"I can't wait," she murmured. "Can you?"

Chapter 24
Wedding Day

After a restless night, Cadence grabbed a shawl and slipped out on the front porch. Too excited to sleep, she watched the sun scale the mountains, bathing the valley in a luminous glow, while it transformed the dusky sky into a clear, cerulean blue. *A perfect day—not a cloud in sight.*

Daybreak was her favorite time. Before reveille, the morning belonged to her alone. *And today's our wedding day.* In love with Ben, she was in love with life. As she inhaled the fresh air, she breathed in the moment, letting the new morning's promises fill her senses.

Then she spotted James. *No...* Like a thick fog obscuring the sun, the golden day lost its shimmer. She turned to go inside.

"Please stay."

Her hand on the doorknob, she froze, teetering between fight and flight. Then summoning all her willpower, she about-faced to confront him. "What do you want?"

"Can I...do you mind if I come upstairs to talk to you?"

She drew in her breath, debating. "I have to get ready…"

"I'll just be a minute." He hesitated. "I promise."

Though wary, she relented at his meek, unassuming tone and gave a stilted nod. "Be quick."

His steps heavy, he climbed the stairs. Then shoulders stooping, he took off his hat with his good hand and stood before her, head bowed. "I owe you an apology…several, actually."

What's this? Her head snapped back.

"My behavior was unconscionable. I can't make amends for the trouble I've caused you, but I can repay you and Williams for the damages to your house."

Her hand still grasping the doorknob, ready to make a quick exit, she neither trusted nor believed him. Her muscles taut, she studied him.

"I hear you're marrying Williams."

She gave a curt nod.

"Congratulations."

She acknowledged his strained smile with a tight-lipped wince.

"I'm…" He cleared his throat. "I've decided to wed Camilla, the girl you saw with me last night."

Will he bully her, *too?* She rolled her eyes.

"Since we're already at the fort, I thought today would be as good a time as any to get married."

"What?" Her lips stiff with rage, her voice shook. "Are you trying to ruin Ben's and my wedding, too?"

"No." The whites of his eyes flashed. "No, nothing of the kind. I didn't mean any offense by it. We'll…we'll wait until after your wedding's over to speak to the chaplain."

She studied him, trying to read his thoughts.

"It's true. I swear."

"I can't believe you're not plotting something…scheming something." She shook her head.

"What do you want?"

"All I *want* is to make amends." He sighed. "The day of the hearing, when I resigned—"

"You mean the day you dodged a court-martial." She snickered.

"I won't deny I'd hit rock bottom." He glanced at his shoes. "I had nothing to show for my years in the military." His gaze penitent, he looked into her eyes. "I'd lost you, my career, and my self-respect. Still, I blamed you, Williams, your father—"

"Everyone but yourself." Repulsed by his sight, she couldn't forgive the man who had slandered her, tried to swindle Mariana, and then set fire to their home. She curled her lip as she fought the urge to spit in his eye.

"You're right." He nodded. "I did blame everyone but myself. Shot and left for dead, I should've died, but for whatever reason, I didn't. I wandered, out of my head with fever, until the boy you saw found me. He took me home, where Camilla and their grandmother nursed me back to health." He stood straight. "I owe them my life…in more ways than one. While I recovered, I had time to think."

Cadence eyed him through narrow, disbelieving slits. If he were anyone else, she would give him the benefit of the doubt. *But I can't forget the gossip and misery he caused me.*

Her chest rose and fell in pent-up anger as her mother's words echoed in her mind. "Your reputation's in question…James spread rumors, saying Ben…ruined you…and he 'broke off your engagement because of your clandestine meetings with the redskin.' "

"You've made your choices. Now live with the consequences." Fuming, she shook her head. "After all you've done to Ben and me, I'll never forgive you."

"Then please just believe me—"

"Believe you? You expect me to believe you've had a change of heart in *what*"—she snickered as she tallied the time—"less than three weeks?"

"Then please suspend your disbelief until I can reimburse you for your property…and your lost time in building your home." His eyes pleaded. "All I *ask* is to let me make amends. *Please*."

"If this story is just another of your lies…" While she watched his expressions and assessed his response, her resolve weakened. She groaned, expelling her disgust. "The best I can do is reserve judgment."

"Thank you." As reveille sounded, he nodded humbly. Hat in hand, he turned to leave. Then reaching the steps, he turned back. "Congratulations again on your marriage to Williams. I truly hope he makes you happy." Wearing a melancholy smile, he pulled on his hat and left.

"Huh." Surprised, Cadence watched his back as he descended the steps and walked away. *After all he's done to harm us, can I believe anything he says*?

****

Cadence found her mother in the warming kitchen, sifting flour for the wedding breakfast's pastries.

"Need any help?" She washed her hands, rolled up her sleeves, and pulled on an apron.

"This morning is the last you'll help me as my daughter." Her mother's fingers covered with flour, she kept her hands out to the side as she kissed Cadence's cheek.

"At least, as your unmarried daughter." She hugged her mother's shoulders. "I'll just be a short ride away.

We'll visit each other and bake together for many mornings to come."

"Hard to believe my little girl's getting married."

"Hard for me to believe, too." Her mother's wistful expression made her reflect. As they mixed the ingredients, she told her about James' visit.

"Think he meant what he said?" Her mother stopped kneading the dough to glance her way.

"Maybe I'm getting soft, but I think he did. At least, when James told me, I think *he* believed it."

"What will you do?"

"Nothing." She shrugged and then glanced at her mother. "Why?"

"If he's made an overture of this scale, maybe he deserves a similar response."

"What do you mean?" Frowning, she cocked her head.

"Inviting him to the wedding breakfast would be a nice gesture."

"His words were hollow, Mother. He hasn't proved himself yet." Her frown deepened into a scowl as she recalled James' past injustices.

"I'm paraphrasing, but what does the Bible say? Something about not just being kind to your friends, but to your enemies, too. Don't judge, and you won't be judged. Forgive, and you'll be forgiven."

"Easier said than done." She rolled her eyes.

"Of course." Her mother nodded. "Actions speak louder than words, which is why forgiving James is the right thing to do."

"I'll think about it." She silently groaned. *As if I don't have enough on my mind this morning.* Then she pictured Ben, and her resentment faded. *How lucky—*

no, blessed—*I am.* Blinking, she recalled the series of events leading to their wedding. *In a way, James was the reason behind our engagement—his 'ripples' propelled us toward our wedding.*

Musing, she remembered Ben's ideas about their roles in life. "Who knows the real reasons we do things? We may think we're the ones skipping stones across the water, but after we see the ripples of our actions, we realize we were just the stones…" *We're the pawns—the* means *of the actions—not the actors.*

Waxing philosophical, she sighed. *What do I do?*

****

"This gown carries tradition in its folds. Wearing your wedding dress means so much more than ordering one through the catalogue or even making one." After they fastened all the buttons, Cadence smiled at her mother through the mirror. Then she gazed at her reflection. Her antique-white, grosgrain silk dress was trimmed with Brussels lace. A yellow satin sash at her waist and Ben's chalcedony brooch at her neck completed her ensemble.

Her face beaming, her mother surveyed her. "It isn't every day your daughter gets married in *your* wedding gown. Now sit, while I fasten your veil."

Her hair pinned up in a soft French twist, Cadence watched her reflection as her mother arranged the tulle. Then standing and turning to the side, she saw the veil cascade down her back in a waterfall of white lace and netting.

"Something old for stability"—her mother lovingly trailed her fingers over the silk gown—"and something new for an optimistic future." She wore a fond smile as she straightened the veil. Then she took a pair of blue sapphire earrings from her pocket. "Something borrowed to borrow happiness, *and* something blue for fidelity."

Pressing her mother's hand to her cheek, she studied the woman who had become her recent friend. "Thank you…for everything."

They shared a smile as her mother gave Cadence's hand an affectionate squeeze. "I'd better get dressed— wouldn't want to be late for my only daughter's wedding. Meet you in the parlor in a few minutes."

"Looks like you'll have this room all to yourself a few nights." When her mother left the bedroom, Cadence turned toward Mariana. "Will you be all right?"

"I fine, Aunt Cadence."

"Is that what you want to keep calling me?" Hearing Mariana's name for her made her smile. "Maybe you'd like to call me Cadence?"

"Maybe I call you Nina?"

"Why Nina?" Tilting her head, she studied the girl.

"It short for *madrina*, godmother." Mariana's bright eyes watched her. "You not but are mother. I call you Nina, yes?"

"I think Nina's a fine name." Touched by her words, she nodded as she held out her arms to the girl. "I like it."

Mariana clasped her, throwing her arms around her slim waist and clinging tightly. Then the girl's shoulders began shaking.

"Are you crying?" She held her at arm's length to see what was wrong.

"Everyone leave me." Tears spilled down her face. "Mother, grandmother, now you."

"Mariana, no, I'm not leaving you. Ben and I will never leave you." Again drawing the girl close, she hugged her. "We're going to our new home for a few days." She motioned back and forth between Mariana and her. "*Our* new home: *yours*, Ben's, and mine. You're just staying with my parents for a short while. Then we're coming back to take you home with us."

"Yes?" The girl's eyes glistened through her wet eyelashes.

"Yes. I promise." Cadence wiped away her tears. "You'll never be alone again."

They left the bedroom, arm-in-arm as nostalgia washed over her. Viewing the home she had known for the last time before moving was like seeing it for the first, and she memorized details she'd taken for granted. Her gaze lingered on the dining-room table, where she had shared so many meals and family celebrations with her parents. She glanced at her mother's crystal stemware proudly displayed in her grandmother's hand-carved china cabinet, her father's portrait over the fireplace, and his humidor beside his favorite chair.

But except for the familiar furnishings, she hardly recognized the front rooms between the Christmas trimmings and wedding decorations. Yellow wildflowers filled every table and niche. The sideboard was equipped with the good china and the gleaming silver tea service. A bleached linen tablecloth graced the dining-room table, festooned with white paper chains.

The end of an era. She took a deep breath.

Jenny smiled back as she set out serving platters for the post-wedding buffet-tea.

Her parents stood by the door—her mother,

wearing a trembling smile and an elegant black silk gown, and her father in his dress uniform with tears glistening in his eyes.

"You look fetching"—he kissed her cheek as she joined them—"just like your mother the day we married." Blinking back tears, he smiled as he swallowed hard.

She collected her bouquet of bright yellow, Thimblehead wildflowers—the only blooms she could find in late December. Then gathering her dress as she descended the steps, she climbed into the waiting ambulance, the one carriage at the fort.

A soldier drove them to the chapel, where her father helped her out and escorted her inside.

Ben waited at the altar, and Tom, his best man, stood beside him. Both looked handsome in their dress uniforms.

She peered around the familiar room. The fort's entire personnel and many of the town's residents filled the chapel, with people standing two-deep at the back. She smiled at the receptive faces: black, white, and brown, all smiling back.

Then she saw James, looking pale and ill at ease.

Camilla clung to his good arm, while her brother shadowed her, his arm hanging in a sling.

From somewhere—nowhere—she got an idea. Immediately plagued by second thoughts, she bit her lip, debating. *Should I spring this on my family at the last moment?* She took a deep breath. *Now or never.* She whispered in her father's ear.

"What?" He turned to stare.

She whispered again, trying to explain.

"You're serious?" Sighing, he pressed his fingers

into the bridge of his nose. At her nod, he summoned a soldier. "Bring Lieut…bring West here."

She watched James' reaction as the soldier addressed him. His jaw dropping, he stared at her and her father. Then he motioned to Camilla to wait and, wearing a hangdog expression, he followed the soldier.

"Yes, sir." James addressed the captain without glancing at her.

"My daughter has something to say."

James' eyes opened wide, the whites flashing. Then coming to attention, he stood at his full height, seeming to brace himself for what he was about to hear.

She swallowed, losing her resolve. *What will Ben think…do?* Then taking a deep breath, she gestured toward Camilla. "Were you serious about marrying this woman?"

"I was and am serious"—he glanced from her to Camilla—"but we'll wait until after you've—"

"Nonsense." She shook her head, her veil fluttering. "I insist we make this a double wedding."

"I must have heard wrong." His eyes flew open. After a stunned moment, he gave her a puzzled smile. "I thought—"

"You heard right." A smile played along her lips. "Invite your fiancée to join me." She winked at her mother, standing nearby.

Swallowing a smile, the woman nodded her approval.

"Would you mind if the girl"—he glanced at Mariana—"asks Ramon to be my best man?"

She blinked, processing, not having thought through the details. "You don't speak Spanish, do you?"

"I'm learning, but no, I don't." He gave a rueful smile.

"Mariana"—she placed her hands on the girl's shoulders—"would you tell Camilla and Ramon what's happening and then bring them here?"

"Yes, Nina." Her eyes shining, she glowed when the wedding party turned toward her, their ears perking at the new name.

"Thank you for being our clever translator."

Her face beaming, Mariana hurried toward Camilla and her brother. Then, she began an animated conversation, first pointing toward Cadence and then toward the altar.

As Camilla listened, her eyes widened along with her smile.

The boy stood mute but never took his gaze from Mariana.

"I'm proud of you, Cadydid." Her mother hugged her. "You did the right thing."

After Mariana led Camilla and Ramon to her, she studied the woman. "Does Camilla understand what we're doing?"

Mariana questioned the woman in Spanish and nodded.

Camilla followed her lead, her face glowing as she smiled at James.

She loves him. Surprised, she watched as James smiled back, his expression gentle and tender. *And he loves her. Huh...*

She turned back to Mariana. "Does Ramon know what to do?"

Mariana questioned him, and both nodded. "He know, Nina."

"Are we ready?" Using a stage whisper, the guitarist they hired for the wedding march approached them.

Cadence gasped as she reviewed the adjusted sequence of events. *Ben and the chaplain don't know*.

"Almost." She hiked her skirts and ran down the aisle to the altar. Then catching her breath between words, she summarized the change of plans.

"Only you would have a last-minute, double wedding with your ex-beau." Shaking his head, Ben snickered.

She winked before turning toward the chaplain.

"This is *highly* irregular."

"But not impossible…" She questioned her idea's practicality. "Is it?"

"Do they have a marriage license certificate from the district clerk?" Lips pursed, the chaplain gave an irritated sigh.

"I don't know." Her shoulders slumped. "If they don't, can you still marry them?"

"I can go through the motions"—he made a face—"but their marriage won't be legal until they present a certificate."

"Fair enough." With a nod, she thanked him, hiked her dress, and trying not to giggle at the congregation's stunned expressions, rushed to the back of the chapel. When she reached the double wedding party, she repeated the chaplain's words, smoothed her dress, straightened her veil, and caught her breath.

"Ready?" The guitarist's eyes crinkled in a smile.

"Ready." Standing tall, she took a deep breath. Then as the music began, she turned toward her mother. "Would you like James to escort you to your seat?"

"Bet you never imagined this turn of events at your daughter's wedding." He held out his good arm.

"Never." Smiling, her mother took his arm and held out her other hand for Ramon.

"Mariana, as the junior bridesmaid, you're next." Then she got another idea. "Why don't you ask James' best man to escort you?"

Mariana translated while Ramon's sensitive dark eyes studied her face. Then with a shy smile, he offered her his good arm, imitating James.

Resting her hand on his elbow, Mariana straightened her shoulders with all the dignity of a princess. Dressed in white muslin, she wore a short white veil, falling from a wildflower wreath to just below her waist. A bright-yellow satin sash around her waist matched her garland.

She looks like a miniature bride. Proud of the girl's composure, Cadence smiled, watching as the two couples walked toward the altar: Helen and James followed by Mariana and Ramon.

Her father crooked his elbow.

With a smile, she hooked arms with him.

Then he crooked his other elbow.

Camilla faltered but placed tentative fingertips on it.

Arms linked, the three marched down the aisle.

As Cadence approached the altar and saw both Ben and James waiting, she panicked.

But James had eyes only for Camilla.

Ben did not take his gaze from her, and the awkward moment passed.

"Dearly beloved," the chaplain began, "we are gathered here today…"

Her mind wandering, the ceremony flew by as she relived the events leading to this moment. Too soon, they were exchanging vows. "I, Cadence, take you, Ben, for my lawful husband, to have and to hold from this day forward, for better, for worse, for richer, for poorer, in sickness and health, until death do us part."

Ben's gaze never faltered as he pledged his love.

Then with Mariana's help, James and Camilla exchanged their promises.

After Ben slipped the white gold wedding band on her finger, the rest of the ceremony was a blur. Before she knew it, she was walking down the aisle on a cloud, her husband at her side.

Happy with the world and overflowing with good will toward all, she asked James, Camilla, and Ramon to join them at her parents' home.

"We need a certificate from the district clerk." James glanced at his bride as he shook his head. "Then we need to get back home. *Abuela* is waiting, and I'm sure she's worried. Besides, I'm not welcome at the fort." Grimacing, he glanced at his shoes. Then he met her gaze with a grateful smile. "But we both thank you for"—he swallowed—"your generosity."

"The men are holding a celebration in the barracks." Ben gestured toward the garrison. "Everyone's invited."

"I don't think my presence would be appreciated there, either, but thank you for inviting us. I appreciate it." He gave a dry laugh. Then, he swallowed hard. "I'll repay you for the damages to your home. You have my word." He shook Ben's hand as the fort's ambulance arrived.

Turning her back to the wedding guests, Cadence

tossed her bouquet over her shoulder. About-facing, she laughed as Mariana leapt high to catch the wildflowers. Then she and Ben stepped inside their commandeered carriage and snuggled.

"Do you have what you wanted, Lieutenant Williams?" She leaned against his shoulder, her lips inches from his.

"I have you, Mrs. Williams." He tilted his head to study her. "You're all I want."

"Me, but also Mariana and my parents—a readymade family—as well as friends at the fort." She squirmed, liking the sound of her new name. "Isn't being part of a family what you've always wanted?"

"You're right. Belonging is what I've craved all my life. It's what I've missed." He nodded slowly, as if the realization were sinking in. Then his lips grazed hers. "Thanks to you, I belong to a family now, but what about you? As I recall, *you* wanted adventures, challenges, and most of all, freedom."

"Ever since you rode into Fort Davis, my life's been turned upside down." She laughed. "I went from being naïve—thinking just because everyone else believed James was the perfect husband for me, I should marry him—to thinking for myself and marrying the man I love."

"You mean, you chose me over the most eligible officer at the fort?" His eyes danced with a mischievous gleam.

"*You're* the most eligible officer at the fort. At least, you were until five minutes ago." She leaned closer to kiss him.

"But what about the adventures and challenges you wanted?"

"Since I met you, I've flouted convention by riding horses astride, riding alone with you, unescor—"

"You mean, racing me through the fort."

"True." She snickered, recalling the ladies' disapproving stares and cool receptions. "Thanks to your encouragement, I've taught school and held a job."

"And started classes for the soldiers," he added. "You've helped the Rodriguez family, adopted Mariana…and even forgiven James."

"I wouldn't say I've forgiven him. I don't think I can, not after…" Stiffening, she took a deep breath to dispel the dark thoughts. "Let's just say, because of the happiness you've given me, I can treat him with kindness."

This time, he leaned over to kiss her. Then he sat back to watch. "What about the freedom you wanted…especially now that you're married?"

"Freedom?" She arched her eyebrow. "We're leaving the fort, which is what seemed a cage more than a haven. Here, I was confined and criticized for the slightest infraction of etiquette or military protocol." She ventured a half smile. "Besides, you compared freedom to loneliness. Now we'll each be free— *together*—and never be lonely."

He leaned toward her in another kiss as the ambulance rolled to a stop.

With the officers and their families close behind, Cadence and Ben stepped out of the carriage and welcomed them upstairs for their wedding breakfast.

Jenny had set out heaping platters of food on the dining-room table: sliced beef served with eye-watering horseradish sauce, smoked and honey-glazed ham, steaming Swedish meatballs in cream sauce, crispy buttermilk-fried chicken, and aromatic cinnamon rolls still warm from the oven and gooey with cream-cheese icing. Spicy chorizo slices and cheddar cheese cubes were served on a recent invention—toothpicks. Chilled bottles of sparkling wine and a punchbowl of fragrant apple-cider filled one sideboard, while the sterling silver tea set occupied the other, perfuming the air with the Earl Grey tea's orangey bergamot scent.

As the callers entered the house, she, Ben, and her parents greeted them, inviting them to help themselves at the dining room buffet.

Mariana and Emily served tea and punch as the guests set their gifts on a table in the parlor.

The officers and their wives stood in small clusters, chatting and nibbling, in the overcrowded quarters.

As brunch ended, Jenny cleared the plates and brought out the wedding cake, a spice sheet cake made with red and green candied fruit, currants, and sliced almonds.

Then Helen offered the adults slim flutes of sparkling wine.

"Join me in a toast to my daughter and the man she's chosen as her life's companion." Her father lifted his glass with a wistful chuckle. "Sometimes, I doubted this day would ever come, and sometimes, I feared it. Though she's a grown woman, my daughter will always be my little girl. May happiness and joy be her and Ben's companions."

Blinking back tears, Cadence kissed her father's cheek.

"I'd like to thank Captain and Mrs. McShane for their daughter's hand." Smiling as he raised his glass, Ben swallowed hard. "I'm not sure they realize how much joining their family means to me."

"Hear, hear." Tom raised his glass high.

When everyone had toasted the newlyweds, Ben turned toward them. "The enlisted men also want to wish us well, and they've invited us all to a breakfast buffet and dance. They've left up the band's platform and again pushed aside their beds and gun racks. Please join us in the barracks."

Twenty minutes later, the officers and their families reconvened, but instead of observing Christmas as they had the night before, this morning, the Tenth Cavalry celebrated Ben and Cadence's wedding.

The hall's two groaning tables boasted assorted breakfast tortillas, roasted tomatillo and garlic salsa, scrambled eggs, pan-fried potatoes, hickory-smoked bacon, refried beans, rice, fresh coffee, and a chocolate wedding cake.

As they walked into the gathering, Cadence smiled back at the friendly faces. Nodding, she acknowledged the congratulations on everyone's lips. Then she turned toward Ben.

Apparently overwhelmed by the soldiers' obvious good will toward him, he swallowed. "Since I rose through the ranks, the men consider me one of their own."

"It's not that simple." She shook her head. "You've had to earn their respect just as much as you've had to earn the officers' respect"—she kissed his cheek—"which you've done admirably."

"Congratulations, ma'am." Private Smith approached them, nodding to Cadence. "I wanna thank you 'gain for teachin' me how to read n' write." Then he turned toward Ben. "Congratulations, lieutenant. Bein' as how you the man o' the hour, the ban' be waiting on you to begin. Should I give 'em a sign, sir?"

"Have at it, soldier." Ben smiled his approval.

Smith waved his hat high over his head as he let out a Texas whoop, and the band struck up.

Flashing a wide smile, he turned to his wife. "May I have this dance, Mrs. Williams?"

"I'd be delighted, Lieutenant Williams." She gave a demure curtsy.

Then he put his arms around her, drawing her close, and off they waltzed, circling the room twice, swirling together on the makeshift dancefloor.

He whispered, "Doesn't this dance remind you of the first time we held each other?"

"At the Harvest Ball…how can I ever forget?" Nodding, she recalled the energy—how the electricity had surged up her arm, sending pleasant tingles down her spine.

Before she caught her breath, he whirled her around the room a third time. Dancing in unison as the tempo increased, she tightened her grip on him and lay her head against his shoulder, content in his arms.

"You know I'd do anything for you"—his eyes creased in a smile—"even learn to waltz."

"And I'd follow your lead anywhere."

Chapter 25
Recipes

Mesquite Cornbread

Ingredients
>3/4 cup cornmeal
>3/4 cup white flour
>1/2 cup mesquite meal
>2 teaspoons baking powder
>1/2 teaspoon baking soda
>1/2 teaspoon salt, or to taste
>2 large eggs, beaten
>1-1/2 cups milk
>3 tablespoons honey (or agave syrup)
>6 tablespoons melted butter or corn oil

Directions

Preheat the oven to 425 degrees F. Grease an eight-inch baking pan.

In a large bowl, whisk the cornmeal, flour, mesquite meal, baking powder, baking soda, and salt together.

In another bowl, mix together the eggs, milk, honey, and butter or oil. Fold the egg mixture into the cornmeal mixture and stir for one minute. Note—the batter will be lumpy. Pour the mixture into the greased baking pan.

Bake for twenty to twenty-five minutes or until a toothpick inserted in the middle comes out clean.

Remove from the oven and let cool to room temperature before serving. Serves eight to twelve.

~*~

Gingerbread

Ingredients

2-1/2 cups white flour

2-1/2 teaspoons yeast powder (or 1 packet instant yeast)

2-1/2 teaspoons ground cloves

1 teaspoon ground cinnamon

1 teaspoon ground ginger

4 egg yolks, beaten

1/2 cup butter, melted

1 cup brown sugar

1/2 cup agave syrup (or maple syrup)

Directions

Preheat the oven to 350 degrees F. Butter one oblong baking pan. Combine the dry ingredients. Mix the egg yolks with the butter, sugar, and syrup. Combine the dry mixture with the egg mixture. Turn into the buttered pan. Bake for thirty-five minutes, or until center springs back when touched. Serve warm with canned peaches, if desired. Serves twelve to sixteen.

Honey and Pine Nut Tarts

Ingredients
> Pie crust, prepared
> 2/3 cup honey
> 1/2 cup granulated sugar
> 1 teaspoon salt, or to taste
> 1 cup butter, softened
> 1/2 cup heavy cream
> 2 large eggs
> 1-1/4 cups pine nuts, shelled

Directions

Preheat the oven to 325 degrees F. Roll the prepared pie crust until it's one-eighth-inch thick and eleven inches wide. Arrange in a ten-inch tart pan with fluted sides (and if possible, a removable bottom). Press the pie crust into the bottom first, and then up the sides.

Combine the honey, sugar, and salt in a medium saucepan. Add the butter and stir over medium-high heat until it comes to a boil. Transfer to a large mixing bowl and let cool twenty minutes. Whisk in the heavy cream and eggs.

Sprinkle the pine nuts over the bottom of the tart and ladle the custard mixture into the crust until it reaches the top. Place the tart on a baking sheet to catch any overflow. Bake for thirty-five to forty minutes, or until golden brown and the custard sets but still wobbles. Let cool before removing from pan. Serve at room temperature. Serves eight.

Turkey Giblet Soup

Ingredients

    1 turnip, pared and sliced

    1 carrot, pared and sliced

    1 medium onion, peeled and sliced

    2 tablespoons butter, divided

    1-1/2 cups turkey giblets, minced

    1/4 cup flour, sifted

    4 cups chicken bouillon or water

    1/4 teaspoon ground pepper, or to taste

    1/2 teaspoon salt, or to taste

Directions

Sauté the vegetables with a tablespoon of butter in a Dutch oven over medium-high heat for eight minutes or until tender. Remove with a slotted spoon. Dredge the minced giblets in the flour and sauté in the remaining butter for eight minutes or until brown.

Stir in the bouillon or water. Return the vegetables to the Dutch oven, add the seasonings, and simmer for 4 to 5 hours. Serves four.

Old-fashioned Molasses Taffy

Ingredients

    6 tablespoons butter, softened, divided

    2 cups molasses

    1 cup sugar

    1/4 cup water

    2 teaspoons white vinegar

    1/2 teaspoon baking soda

Directions

Grease a baking sheet with 2 tablespoons butter. Bring the sugar, molasses, water, and vinegar to a boil in a saucepan over medium heat. Stir until the sugar reaches the hard ball stage, 250 to 260 degrees F, or until a small amount of syrup dropped into icy water forms a brittle string.

Remove from heat. Stir in 2 tablespoons butter and the baking soda. Stir until it stops foaming. Then pour the mixture onto the prepared baking sheet, and let stand until cool enough to handle, 10 to 15 minutes.

The more helpers, the merrier! Butter your fingers, using the remaining 2 tablespoons butter. Working in small batches, fold and pull the taffy for 15 to 20 minutes, or until firm but pliable. Shape into 1/2-inch-wide ropes. Then slice into bite-sized pieces. Repeat with the rest of the taffy, wrapping each candy in waxed paper. Yields about 12 dozen candies.

Thank you for purchasing
this publication of The Wild Rose Press, Inc.

For questions or more information
contact us at
info@thewildrosepress.com.

The Wild Rose Press, Inc.
www.thewildrosepress.com